and

In Secret Sin

Rose Doyle graduated in English from Trinity College, Dublin, and went on to become a successful journalist. She is the author of three bestselling children's books, written following the broadcast of her first radio play. Her first adult novel, *Images,* was published in Ireland in 1993, followed by the UK publication of *Kimbay, Alva, Perfectly Natural* and, most recently, *The Shadow Player.* Rose lives in Dublin with her two sons.

Also by Rose Doyle

Perfectly Natural
Alva
Kimbay

ROSE DOYLE

The Shadow Player

and

In Secret Sin

PAN BOOKS

In Secret Sin first published 2000 by Pan Books
The Shadow Player first published 1999 by Pan Books

This omnibus edition published 2002 by Pan Books
an imprint of Pan Macmillan Ltd
Pan Macmillan, 20 New Wharf Road, London N1 9RR
Basingstoke and Oxford
Associated companies throughout the world
www.panmacmillan.com

ISBN 0 330 41506 9

1 3 5 7 9 8 6 4 2

A CIP catalogue record for this book is available from
the British Library.

Typeset by SetSystems Ltd, Saffron Walden, Essex
Printed and bound in Great Britain by
Mackays of Chatham plc, Chatham, Kent

The Shadow Player

To Clodagh and Eamonn –
there for two pages a day

Acknowledgements

In Seattle I was given the guided tour, and a sense of life in that wonderful city, by Ellen and Gerry Coyle and by Eileen West and Adrian. Many, many thanks to all of you.

'Keep up appearances; there lies the test;
The world will give thee credit for the rest.
Outward be fair, however foul within;
Sin if thou wilt, but then in secret sin.'

from 'Night' by Charles Churchill

Chapter One

Sunday, 2 January

January is not a month I've ever cared for. The days are too short, the nights too long and nothing grows. Nothing much anyway. It's a monochrome, brooding time of year.

And still I wasn't prepared when January did its worst to me, pulled the plug on life as I'd known it. I had no premonition, none at all, the Sunday it all began. It was a day like any other, the pall of a Christmas past lying over it.

I awoke that morning to a frost covering the square I lived in. The entire city of Dublin could have been under a ten foot ice-cap for all I cared. My corner of the world was all right and I'd a lazy day ahead of me. I got up, made tea and retreated to my warm, solitary bed with a book. Simple pleasures, but then mine, at that time, was a simple life.

When the doorbell rang I ignored it. Whoever it was could take what they were selling down to my landlady in the basement. If it was heavenly salvation they were dealing in then Delia needed it every bit as much as I did. When it rang again I swore before turning a page. On the third ring I gave up and rolled out of bed. It rang twice more as I went down the stairs and shivered my way across the hallway. Number 9

Makulla Square, in which I rented two floors, had changed very little since its Victorian heyday and the lack of central heating gave the place a tomblike chilliness. I was thinking fond thoughts about the bed I'd just left as I yanked open the front door and saw the woman and children standing there.

Even allowing for the cold and miserable time of year, they were a sad trio. The woman was pale, wafer-thin and pretty in an underfed kind of way. Her eyes, green with dark lashes, would have done something for her pinched face if they hadn't been so red-rimmed. The girl, who could have been anywhere between seven and ten, was an angular, straggly little thing with freckles and her mother's dark hair. The boy was no more than a toddler and quite beautiful.

It was as the boy stared up at me out of grey, gold-flecked eyes that I felt a first faint warning jingle of things to come. I ignored it.

'Are you Norah Hopkins?' The woman had a wan, girlish voice.

'Yes,' I said, 'that's me.'

I hugged myself and tightened my dressing-gown and waited for her to say what they were doing on my doorstep. All three were blue-faced with the cold, three sets of prints on the frosty footpath to the house indicating they'd arrived on foot. There had to be a good reason for them being here.

I smiled encouragingly at the woman, who stared at me but said nothing. The little girl prodded her mother and the woman took a deep breath. She was on the point of saying something when the boy plonked his bottom on the glacial granite of the step and began to bawl.

2

'Oh, Justin, don't sit in the cold, baby. Come on now, get up . . .'

The woman bent down but it was the girl who swept him into her arms, stood him briskly on his feet and jollied him until he stopped crying. This lasted for as long as it took for him to turn and look at me, a sight which set him howling again, loud enough this time to drown the bells from the Three Patrons in Rathgar, ringing for ten o'clock mass. It was 9.45 a.m.

'Please, come in,' I said. 'It's far too cold to talk out here.' I'd spent more than my store of cheer and charity over Christmas but, given the frozen state of the four of us, asking them in seemed the logical thing to do.

They filed past me into the hallway, the woman first, then the children. I closed the door and they stood silently looking up at me. I am tall and I am not graceful. I have good bones and skin and for these assets I am usually grateful. But that morning, towering over them in my hallway, I just felt like a colossus.

'We'll be warmer in the kitchen,' I said. I kept a storage heater there.

'My mam wants to talk to you.' The girl looked around. 'Do you have a television for me and my brother to look at?'

Envious of such assurance, I looked questioningly at the mother. Her face had grown bleaker standing there.

'I'm Alison McCann,' she said and my stomach gave a dull, sickening flop. I made a small, protesting sound too, before my mouth went dry and all I could do was stare.

Of course she was Alison McCann. And the boy with

the gold-flecked eyes was Darragh McCann's son. I should have known when he first looked at me, I should have heeded the warning jingle. Maybe then I mightn't have invited them in.

Not that it would have made any difference. Events were well on their remorseless way by then anyway.

In any event, having invited the wife and children of my ex-lover into my home, I could hardly throw them back out into the cold. Dublin being Dublin, we were bound to meet one day though I'd always hoped we wouldn't. I cleared my throat and ignored the heavy thumping of my heart and held out my hand.

'Pleased to meet you,' I said, knowing it was totally the wrong thing to say but just as totally at a loss about what the right thing might be. Alison McCann gave me an unfriendly stare.

'You're not the sort I thought you'd be,' she said.

She had a Donegal accent and her pale face was full of righteousness and dislike. But she was also clearly distraught, looking as if she might at any minute collapse. Breathing quickly, she began to string sentences together.

'I didn't see you at the funeral. But I didn't know about you then anyway. I didn't know about you until a couple of days ago.' She stopped and I prayed that she wouldn't go on, would just shut up, be quiet. But she went on, relentlessly. 'I didn't know about the child either, about your daughter. Not until Austin Finn told me . . .'

'What funeral?'

Alison McCann went quiet. In the silence she and her children stood very still and I heard the cat scratch at the back door. I hadn't fed him yet that morning.

'What funeral?' I asked again.

'Our Dad's funeral.' It was the little girl who answered. 'He's dead. His car went into the river. He drowned.'

The boy began to howl again, clinging to his mother's legs.

'You didn't know?' Alison McCann clutched him to her. 'He's been dead a week now. Dead and buried.'

'No. I didn't know . . .'

Their three figures blurred and began to weave in front of me. I closed my eyes and leaned against the wall to stop the dizziness. I prayed I wasn't going to vomit, or faint. Most of all I prayed this was a nightmare and that I would waken in my warm bed and all would be well. Alison McCann's voice came at me again. She was quite precise.

'It was the way Mollie said. He went into the river in the car. Into the Liffey, down near where it goes into the sea at Sir John Rogerson's Quay. On the day after Christmas.'

Such detail. It must be true then. Who would make up a thing like that . . .?

Something withered in me and quietly died. I was twenty-six years old and the man who'd taught me about love and passion and made a woman of me was dead and had been buried. My daughter's father would never again come laughing to meet us. Never, ever again.

'It's warmer in the kitchen,' I repeated, 'and I must feed the cat.'

Chapter Two

I was eighteen when I met Darragh McCann. By the time I was twenty I'd given birth to our child. In the year and a half between the one event and the other I grew up.

Darragh was twenty-three when we met. He was tall and dark with a practised, lazily sexy smile and a slightly out-of-kilter nose which saved him from being merely pretty. He was like nothing I'd ever known and like everything I'd ever craved.

I'd let Darragh go long before his wife and children appeared on my doorstep, but never completely. He'd meant too much to me for that. Over the years he came to see his daughter and me every month and, though I'd long stopped loving him, I never stopped remembering how we'd been as lovers. Memories would surface at the oddest times. They always seemed apart from me and, like sequences in a faded movie, curiously irresistible.

In one of the more regular of these I see Darragh on one knee, a blood-red rose in his hand as he tells me that the flower's colour signifies his willingness to die for me. I'd known him two weeks at the time and dying was the last thing I wanted him to do.

In another image it is high summer and he is

standing with me on a low hill overlooking the farm-house which had been my childhood home. This was as close as I could bring him, he being my lover and my father and grandmother being the most righteous of people. That midland part of the country is fertile and prosperous, which is not the same as saying it was socially, or even culturally, enlightened, for it wasn't, then. Darragh, in slow motion, gently leads me by the hand to where, with wonderful madness, we make love in the long grass and I finally cast away from me the million stifling reasons I'd left home.

In an image that comes to me less often he is standing by an open car door in a dark street calling in low desolation after my retreating figure. I am walking quickly away, for ever I think, because he has just told me he has a wife.

All of these are performance pieces because that's what Darragh was – a performer. I didn't know why then and now I never will. It wouldn't surprise me if his performing was, in the end, the death of him.

That first meeting happened on an early summer's evening, at a book launch in Buswell's Hotel.

'And who have we here then?' He reached out a hand as our eyes met and lifted a curl of my hair. 'A milkmaid come to town?'

'Don't do that.' I shook his hand away, splashing my beer on to his stone-coloured linen jacket – second-hand, though I didn't know that at the time. The milkmaid tag was far too close to the bone, since the buxom lass image was one I was trying to shake. Darragh dabbed at the beer spill and kept his eyes on my face, smiling.

'Salt might help the stain,' I muttered.

'Don't worry about it,' he said. 'I was out of line. My name's Darragh McCann.' He stopped dabbing and caught my hand. He held it far too long.

'I'm Norah Hopkins.' I searched, desperately, for a clever follow-up line. Nothing came.

'It was the colour of your hair did it.' He rescued the silence with a laugh. 'It's like pouring cream . . .' He was looking as if he might touch my hair again so I stepped out of range.

'Tell me what you're doing here . . .'

This was a reasonable enough question, given that the launch of a slim volume by a young poet is not something reception junkies bother with much.

'I work for Razorbill.' I nodded in the direction of my boss, Harry Gibson, small-time publisher, man of letters and, most of the time, fond friend. He was lording it at the bar. 'I'm an editor there.'

Three months before I'd been a general factotum at Razorbill Publications. That was until Harry had shoved an unedited manuscript my way and we'd discovered there was something I could do, well. Books on hobbies and educational manuals were. Razorbill's mainstays, with slim volumes of poetry an occasional indulgence on Harry's part. None of the poetry made money but he loved the brush with culture.

Harry, unseasonal in corduroy and his inevitable bow-tie, turned from the bar and caught my eye. Clutching the evening's poet by the arm, he headed my way.

'Looks as if we've got someone in common,' Darragh McCann said. 'Your poet, Conal Bergin, is a friend. I'm here because of him.'

I knew Conal Bergin, though not well. To look at he fell into the tall and bony category, with untidy red hair and specs. He was a teacher who wrote plays as well as poetry and I'd never been able to decide whether he was shy or laconic. He seemed an odd sort of friend for someone as flamboyantly sociable as Darragh McCann.

Harry arrived and did the introductions. 'Are you given to poetic scribblings too, young man?' Somewhere around sixty, Harry acts ninety and, when not doing his benign thing, can be a drill sergeant.

'I'm a backroom boy myself.' Darragh looked mildly amused; not a good idea. Harry became the drill sergeant.

'That means, I suppose, that you've bought and read your friend's book,' he snapped. 'What's your considered opinion?'

'I'm saving it for bedtime reading,' Darragh's eyes, for a second, met mine. He turned to Conal. 'I've got a signed copy from the author.'

'Writers don't make money giving books away.' Harry glared at Conal and then at the room in general. 'Small enough turnout,' he grunted.

As always, he'd invited the city's literati and was peeved that only a token few, with hangers-on, had turned up. Even they were preparing to leave.

'Party's over, by the look of things.' Conal seemed relieved. So did Darragh. He smiled and said goodbye and drifted away.

It was two days before he rang and I agreed, too eagerly, to a swim at Seapoint.

So began the summer of my nineteenth year; lazy,

crazy months during which I leaped, unprepared and needy, from girl to woman, taking on love and sex and, in the end, far more than I'd bargained for.

We made love on our second date, in the narrow bed in my basement flat in Ranelagh. It was dark down there, with a barred window on to the yard that held the rubbish bins for the other tenants. It was also damp. The up side was that these flaws kept the rent low. I filled the place with ferns and kept the lights on all the time and enjoyed the sheer joy of having a place of my own.

I'd come to Dublin six months before and losing my virginity was high on my agenda of 'must dos'. On that second date I was set on love, and on loving Darragh McCann. I polished off three glasses of a full-bodied Rioja before I served the spaghetti bolognese.

'Where'd you learn to cook like that?' Darragh finished a second helping and lit a cigar.

'Cookery book.' I didn't want to talk about cooking, or anything much else either. I wanted to throw myself at him.

'Tell me about how you grew up.' Smelling of sea and the cigar, he leaned across the table. We'd been for another swim earlier.

'On a farm, outside Duncolla, with my grandmother, father and two brothers.' I was brisk. 'My mother died soon after I was born. My grandmother's dead now too.' I tried the coquettish smile I'd been working on. 'You're an unlikely accountant,' I said, and that was all it took. He wasn't keen either on personal questions.

'Figures are what I'm good at . . .' He was curt as he opened the wine he'd brought with him. 'Let's relax.'

Easier said than done. We sat on the couch, Darragh's arm along the back and me with my legs curled under me while I sipped wine at the far end. It was a warm night and the room was all at once too small for the both of us, the couch too hard, the hour too late, the silence deafening. I uncurled my legs.

'Would you like me to do your feet?' Darragh asked.

'Do my feet?' I stared at him. He didn't look like your average foot fetishist.

'Give you a foot massage.' He was patient. 'It'll relax you, make you feel good.'

I lifted a foot on to the couch. He picked it up and gently held it by the ankle.

'I'll need some cream, or an oil. Whatever you've got,' he said.

In the bathroom, getting the baby oil, the thought occurred that he'd done this sort of thing before. I was glad that at least one of us knew what they were doing.

'Lie back,' Darragh grinned. 'Go with the flow.'

I lay back. He covered his fingers in oil and began with the ball of my foot. 'Relax,' he said.

'I am relaxed.'

I kept my eyes closed. His thumbs worked the sole of my foot in small arcs which grew to warming circles and hot feelings which crept upwards between my legs. I sighed.

'That's more like it.' His voice was soft as he lifted my other foot. 'Go with it . . .' I felt his tongue flicker along my toes before he took one into his mouth, bit gently and began to suck. The damp between my legs was making my thighs slippy.

'Don't.' I opened my eyes and looked at him and barely got the word out. 'Don't . . . please . . .' He

11

stopped and I groaned. 'Don't stop.' He ran a lazy hand up the inside of my thigh.

'You're beautiful,' he said.

I closed my eyes again and enjoyed what he was doing with his fingers.

'Would you like me to do your back?' He was conversational.

'Yes, please,' faintly.

'You're going to have to take your shirt off then.'

There were four buttons on the shirt and they took forever. I looked away from him while I unhooked my bra and when my breasts fell free I felt huge, and hugely naked. I crossed my arms and gathered them to me.

'I can't . . . do this . . .'

He turned me towards him. 'You're lovely,' he said. 'The loveliest woman I've seen, ever . . .'

I wasn't so daft as to believe him but it was the right thing to say.

'Hold me then,' I said, and squashed my nakedness against him. He held me, tightly and without any more words, one hand between my shoulder-blades, the other under my hair, at the base of my neck.

I was leaning against his shoulder when he took my hair in his hand and gently pulled my head back to put his mouth on mine. He pressed open my teeth and it was the easiest thing in the world to give him my tongue while his caressing fingers moved across my breasts and down to my belly. When he stopped, quite suddenly, it was like a glorious free-fall hitting ice.

'Why don't we go to the bedroom . . .?' he said. The conversational note was gone.

I clutched my shirt against me and staggered ahead

12

of him. In my dusty-rose bedroom, on the nylon bed-spread I'd brought from home, he took off the rest of my clothes. When I was altogether naked he spread my hair over the pillow and stood to take his own clothes off, quickly. Naked he was far finer than anything my fevered imaginings of the past days had come up with. When he came to me my spine melted into the mattress and my legs parted with a will of their own. As he lay with me, and we were body to body, I said, 'It's my first time . . .'

'I know,' he said.

I'd abandoned myself to him entirely by the time he slid between my legs. The world as I'd known it ended when he asked, his mouth on mine, 'Do you want me?'

I don't remember the words I used but they meant yes, yes please. For all that, when he lowered himself on to me and I felt the hard, demanding maleness of him, some self-preserving instinct surfaced. 'You'll have to put on something,' I said.

'It's all right,' he promised. 'I won't come inside you.'

He didn't either, not that night anyway. When he did, a long time afterwards, it was because I'd become careless, given myself altogether to the wonder of loving him and to the cocooned world we'd created for ourselves. Emma wasn't so much an accident as a consequence of too much lusty loving.

My affair with Darragh McCann lasted nine months. He was, for most of that time, the reason for every breath I took and every thing I did. Though it didn't seem that way to me at the time, I had simply exchanged a stifling life of one kind for another.

On a Friday night, when we'd known each other

13

five months, we had our first real row. Darragh, having promised to collect me from work, didn't turn up. Not for the first time either.

Harry growled and grunted about the place and finally kicked me out when it came time for him to go himself.

'It's not safe for you to be here alone.' He locked up while I hovered, hopeful still. Razorbill was in a laneway off Harcourt Street and Harry had a policy about not leaving me alone there. 'I'll drive you home,' he said. He didn't like Darragh. He didn't say so but he never, ever mentioned him, which was how I knew.

I was uneasily asleep when Darragh phoned.

'I'm sorry about tonight.' He was full of a desperate urgency I'd heard too often. 'Look, can I come over?'

'No.' The flower arrangement on the dressing-table, his apology the last time he'd stood me up, hadn't even begun to wither. 'I'm tired.'

'Don't do this to me, Norah, I can't stand it . . .'

'That makes two of us. I can't standing hanging around, being made to look a fool . . .'

'Is that all you're worried about? Being made to look a fool?' he sounded incredulous. 'Do you think I *want* to be here, away from you? Something happened, Norah. I just couldn't make it . . .'

'There *are* telephone lines into Razorbill.'

'Let me come over, Norah, please. It'll be easier to explain when I'm with you.'

Things never got explained when he was with me. 'No. Goodnight.'

I hung up, disconnected the phone and cried myself

into a nightmarish sleep in which Darragh performed impossible sexual acts with a red-haired siren who never once said no.

When I rang his office next day a secretary said he was away. I didn't believe her. He lived, he'd told me, with an eccentric aunt who refused to have a telephone, so there was nowhere else to call him. I'd never questioned his living arrangements.

It was nine days before he made contact again. By then, and though I all but poured myself down the line in whimpering eagerness when I heard his voice, the end had begun. Where before there had been a blind trust there was now doubt.

'I'd like to meet your aunt,' I said to him a week later. We'd been to the cinema, snogged our way through two hours of Italian family life, and were in the car going home.

'She's not well,' his profile frowned.

'What's wrong with her?'

'Doctor can't say.'

'Who's looking after her tonight?'

'A neighbour.'

We stopped at a traffic signal. The red light mocked dangerously and I knew I might be destroying something but went on anyway.

'Don't take me for a complete fool,' I said.

'All right then,' he said, defeat in every word. I panicked, too late put a finger to his lips.

'No, no, don't . . . don't tell me . . . I don't want to know . . .'

'I'm married,' he said, and not even the roaring in my ears could drown the words.

15

I'd known anyway. I'd known and not wanted to know and put the knowledge away from me. Now I'd forced it out of him there was no more denying it.

And still all I could think of was flight, of getting away so that, maybe, I could pretend the last few minutes hadn't happened. Only they had. So I sat there and after a while said, 'I thought you might be.'

'Well, that makes things easier.' Darragh sounded relieved.

'Why?' I asked. Why would he think my suspecting he'd been lying made things easier?

'Well, because then you understand.'

'Understand what?'

'That I love you and want to be with you. That I'm caught in a hopeless situation.'

This was the first time he'd told me he loved me. I hadn't mentioned it myself because it wasn't a word I'd had much practice using. I'd taken for granted that the churning emotion and need I felt for him was love, presumed that he must know and that all would be spoken between us when the time was right.

'Stop the car,' I said.

'Norah . . .'

'Stop the car.'

'For God's sake . . .'

'If you don't stop the car I'm going to pull this door open and throw myself into the traffic.' I wasn't bluffing.

'Don't do this to me, Norah, please . . .'

I opened the door. We were going reasonably fast.

'Jesus Christ, Norah, stop. Close the fucking door. I'm pulling over . . .' He moved into an inside lane. When a narrow side street appeared he turned into it.

16

'Christ, Norah, you frightened me. Don't ever try a stunt like that again.' He switched off the engine and turned to me. His face under the street lights was ashen. 'I'm sorry,' he said.

I stared at him. 'Sorry's no good.' Salt tears curled into my mouth. 'Sorry's useless. No, don't touch me . . .'

This time when I opened the door I got out. I walked away quickly, not looking back once as his voice called to me along that empty street off the South Circular Road, wanting to howl my pain and desolation aloud but just walking, walking on and away.

Darragh didn't come after me and he didn't phone for several days. By that time I'd armoured myself and refused to talk to him. This was easy enough, that first week. I was angry at him but I despised myself. I'd allowed him to lie to me, allowed myself to be taken in because he'd offered excitement and sex and I'd been so hungry for all of it. And because I'd loved him . . .

That first week I admitted too what I'd always known instinctively; our affair never had had a future, something which had given it a seize-the-day immediacy and upped the passion stakes. Like one of those wartime affairs in which the trenches and death were forever beckoning an end.

That was the first week. After that loss and loneliness set in and it became much harder to keep him away. The old needs consumed everything around me. I sat in cinemas and wept when lovers beside me embraced, cried in the butcher's when a woman asked for minced beef for two. When I slept I dreamed of him, in vivid

17

sight and sound and all night long. I stopped living and existed, lost in a vacuum of remembered feelings.

And then there was the night I jumped into the canal, up to my calves in mud, and a prostitute pulled me out. It had seemed the only way to end the aching misery. Plus I was drunk. It was December and I'd been to a very bad party. It was icy cold in the canal and I was weeping and flailing about when the prostitute, abandoning her Herbert Place beat, came yelling down the bank. She grabbed the collar of my coat and yanked me back to shore.

'Stupid fucking cow!' She shook me as I sat shivering on the bank. 'Are you trying to bring every bloody guard in the city down on top of us? If you want to do yourself in, you stupid bitch, then go and do it in your own patch, somewhere you won't mess things up for other people.'

She left and I got to my feet. The canal, when I looked back into it, was still as before and sneering. Within a week, with Christmas hysteria everywhere and the annual meltdown of rational behaviour well under way, I'd allowed Darragh back into my bed.

It began, again, at one of Harry's parties. I was placating the writer of a manual on chemical and biochemical processes when Darragh walked in with Conal Bergin. The author was very put out when Darragh stepped between us.

'How're you doing, Norah?' he was smiling, relaxed.

'I'm doing fine.' I took a deep breath and let it out slowly.

'I was hoping you'd be here,' Darragh said. 'I missed you.'

18

The manual writer frowned, cleared his throat noisily and left us alone.

'I don't remember sending you an invitation,' I said to Darragh.

'I missed you,' he said again, and moved too close. He reached out and touched my hair. I pulled back.

'The old bullshit won't work any more, Darragh, don't even try it.'

Only it *was* working. My body, with a gravity of its own, leaned towards him.

'I love you,' he said. 'I'm going mad without you.'

He certainly looked crazed. He'd lost weight and his eyes, riveted on mine, were wild. I felt the room close in round me. His pain was so much more important than my own, so much more terrible.

'Touch me again,' I said, and he leaned to kiss me lightly on the lips. He was shaking, his heart beating as madly as my own. 'Take me away from here,' I said. 'I want to be with you. I want to feel better.'

It probably happened that night, but it was the end of January before I discovered I was pregnant. The confirmation, when it came, filled me with a sort of calm. It was make or break time. Now Darragh would have to choose: me or the woman he was married to. I knew they had no children, it was the one direct question I'd insisted he answer.

'I'm pregnant.'

I told him late at night as we came out of a Chinese takeaway. There was never going to be a right time anyway. He didn't seem to hear so I waited until we got to the car and said it to him again.

'I heard you the first time.' He shoved the bag with

19

the food into my hand and got into the car. I stood and watched in dazed disbelief as the battered Peugeot sped away into the traffic.

A week later I came out of Razorbill to find him waiting. I climbed into the Peugeot.

'I'm sorry, Norah. I couldn't deal with it . . .' he followed this simple statement with another. 'My wife's pregnant.'

'How pregnant is she?' I wanted to weep.

He hesitated and I knew then that she was more pregnant than I was – and that he'd known for a while.

'About six months,' he said at last. 'She's not strong. I can't leave her.'

He said very little else. I don't recall saying anything myself. I could have demanded he help but pride held me back. Pride and the fact that I knew his accountancy business was doing hopelessly badly. I didn't reckon my chances of getting financial support. He drove me home and we said goodbye like strangers. That was the last I saw of him until Emma was two months old.

In that eight months I grew up, and I learned to live without Darragh. It wasn't his fault I was pregnant. It wasn't mine either. I found I was happy about becoming a mother and lived for the baby growing inside me. I always knew she would be a girl.

When I began to show I told Harry.

'Good God, Norah, women are supposed to have babies when they want them these days.'

'I want this baby, Harry. I'm going to keep her.'

'Are you indeed.' He gave me a hard look. 'In that case I suppose you'll want to make maternity leave arrangements?' His voice sharpened. 'You weren't thinking of leaving, were you?'

I shook my head and he relaxed. So did I. I'd had a small but real fear that Harry would replace me. We agreed an arrangement that would allow me to take work home, and time off.

'Is it that theatrical-looking young fellow?' Harry asked then. 'The shifty one?'

'What exactly are you asking me, Harry?'

'Is he the father or isn't he?'

'If you're describing Darragh McCann then yes, he's the father. And he's not shifty . . .'

'He's shifty.'

A reluctant bit of me agreed. The wonder of his charm and looks and fun apart, Darragh was somehow shadowy, with a definite shifting quality to him. He was never quite *there*, somehow.

Certainly not when I wanted him.

I found the flat in Makulla Square when I was eight months pregnant. Delia Brophy saw my imminent motherhood as a bonus.

'You can have the place,' she said. 'You look settled.'

I felt settled, or at least secure, from the day I moved in.

Emma arrived a week early and that was fine, even considerate of her. The rush of it all left me no time to miss or long for her father. She was also the most beautiful child ever born to woman and became the love of my life in the seconds between her initial yell and first greedy suckle at my breast.

It was some time near the end of October, as I was trundling peacefully along the early afternoon square with Emma in a sling, that the door of a parked car flew open, missing me by inches.

'Sorry.' Darragh got out.

'For what?' I snapped. Emma had been jolted awake and was squirming.

'For . . . the car door. Almost knocking you. Sorry.' He looked at the top of Emma's head and I put a protective hand over it. 'Can we talk?' he asked. He looked spruce, not to say a bit flash. Things in the accountancy business were clearly looking up.

'There's a bench in the park,' I said.

We sat under the dappled light of a maple tree.

'You're looking good.' He touched my hand.

He was looking good himself, the light through the tree making the most of his gorgeous face. I felt sadness, some loss still, but I didn't want him. He had nothing to do with me any longer.

'You look good yourself.' I smiled at him. It was easy. 'Did you and your wife have a boy or girl?'

'A girl. Mollie. She's six months old now.'

'Meet her sister, Emma.' I turned our daughter's head slightly his way. 'She's two months old.'

'I'm sorry, Norah, about everything.' He touched my cheek. All I felt was a couple of cool fingers. 'I thought about you all the time. But there was nothing I could do.'

I considered his newly prosperous look. 'You could have helped, financially,' I kept my voice even, 'and you could have come to see your daughter before now.'

'You're right . . .' He hesitated. 'I knew you were doing all right though. Conal kept me up to date on things . . .'

22

Apart from a brief hospital visit when he'd come bearing a stuffed penguin, I hadn't seen the poet myself. 'Why're you here now, then?'

'Because now I can help, I want to pay you maintenance and I want to see something of Emma as she grows up . . .' He had his most beguiling smile in place. '. . . I don't want to lose you, Norah. I'm hoping we can be friends.'

No, he wasn't. He was hoping he could get back into my bed.

'Apart from sex we've nothing in common,' I said as Emma, with an instinct for the moment that she would never lose, began to wail. 'And our daughter, of course, we've got our daughter in common.' I stood and paced in a small circle, making soothing noises.

'You're still working,' Darragh said.

'Of course I'm working.' How did he think I was living, paying for accommodation and food? I'd managed so far because Delia charged a reasonable rent and winter heating bills hadn't yet become a factor. Darragh had never seemed so unreal, so remote to me as in that moment.

'I want to help,' Darragh said. The sun had gone and his face was in shadow. 'You can't deny me that.'

'What sort of maintenance were you thinking about?'

'God, Norah, you've become hard.'

'Practical. I've become practical. I'm a mother. On her own.'

'When can I come to see her? Saturdays?'

'How much?'

'A hundred and fifty pounds a month . . .'

'Two hundred. At least.'

'I can't . . .' he looked at me, then at Emma. 'Two hundred,' he shrugged.

'By direct debit?'

'Cash. I'll deliver – say the last Saturday of each month?'

He had been, for the most part, as good as his word. There were occasional blips but his record over seven years hadn't been a bad one. When Emma was three he raised the money to £300. On her birthdays and at Christmas he'd been lavish with presents. He'd tried to get into my bed, of course, sporadically and as a matter of pride. Until, that was, I became briefly involved with someone else. Then he became irrationally jealous.

'I love you,' he yelled at me then, standing in the hallway, refusing to go. 'You've never understood that. You're the only woman I've ever bloody loved . . .'

'Go home to your wife, Darragh.' I kept my voice low because of the sleeping Emma. 'And don't ever talk to me of love again.'

He went. After that he came close to being a real friend, someone who made me laugh and who sometimes remembered things I told him. We never spoke of his wife and we never discussed the future and I always looked forward to his coming.

And he did love Emma. That was never a doubt. Nor was her love for him.

He'd last visited on 18 December. Seasonally tipsy, he'd stored presents under the tree, almost knocking it over. Afterwards we shared a couple of glasses of mulled wine and played cards, the three of us. Before leaving we stood together in the front door, listening to a tuneless straggle of carol singers across

24

the square. He left with a hug for Emma and a brief kiss for me.

I hadn't even waited for him to reach the bottom of the steps before closing the door on the cold.

And now he was dead. And oh, how I would miss him.

Chapter Three

Sunday, 2 January

Darragh's wife and children followed me along the hallway and down the steps to the kitchen. The cat, six years old and set in his ways, took baleful refuge in the window over the sink. He'd been a present from Darragh to Emma, who was that morning in their basement apartment with my landlady Delia and her husband Patsy. They loved having her and the arrangement usually gave me the chance to grab a morning in bed.

'Mac's not very friendly.' I put milk in the cat's bowl and the four of us watched as he picked a disdainful way down to it. The boy, Justin, knelt and stroked him as he lapped.

'He'll scratch you,' said his sister. 'Leave him alone.'

'He likes me.' Justin's lashes, as he looked down at the cat, were the same dark sweeps I'd admired as his father had slept beside me.

'Please sit down.' I indicated the kitchen's two stools. Darragh's wife took one, his daughter standing beside her like a small watchdog in a green anorak.

Only she wasn't his wife. She was his widow and the child had no father. In the awful silence I stood looking at them, willing this woman and her children to go away and leave me alone to weep. Yet I knew I couldn't weep either: all I really felt was a numbing cold and horrific sense of dread.

'I'll make coffee,' I said.

The act of filling the kettle eased the paralysis and released an anger with which I silently cursed Alison McCann for bringing her children. She should have come alone. Whatever she had to say was between her and me.

'The kettle's boiling.' Mollie, just four months older than Emma, was reproachful.

I made the coffee and got orange juice for the children. Life, as a French poet once said, is a day-to-day business. The boy went on fondling the cat and Mollie sipped and carefully watched both her mother and me. Their mother, righteous and bereft-looking, was definitely the human wreckage in the kitchen. She took the coffee shakily, juggling it with the cigarette she was smoking. Now that she'd thawed a bit her face had a delicate prettiness, a touch of the waif-like madonna about it. She was wearing a tightly belted black leather coat which couldn't have been a lot of use against the January cold.

'I'll take you two up to the television.' I reached a hand each to the children. Justin lifted the cat. Mollie stepped round me.

'We'll follow you,' she said.

In the sitting-room I found a Simpsons rerun on the TV, switched on the Christmas tree lights and lit the fire, laid since the night before. Darragh's children seemed happy enough as I was leaving but I don't suppose they were happy at all.

Their mother was prepared for me. 'Finding out he'd had another woman was the worst thing of all.'

She was dully accusing as I came into the kitchen. 'Losing him in the river like that was one thing. Knowing I'd lost him anyway, that you'd stolen him from me, was something else . . .'

She'd left the stool and was leaning against the draining-board. I stood, feeling guilty as a trapped criminal, while she dropped her cigarette into the coffee mug and lit another. Her voice had a high-velocity whine and I tried not to dislike her too much.

'I didn't steal him,' I said. 'I didn't know he was married when I met him . . .' It sounded, I knew, like the excuse made by every woman who'd ever loved a married man.

'Like fuck you didn't.'

The viciousness of Alison's response was a shock. I looked away from her pinched, accusing face, out over the silvery, arching branches and red-berried hollies of Delia's rear winter garden. There was no comfort there at all. Anger, guilt, confusion were followed by utter desolation until, dizziness and nausea getting the better of me, I just about made it to the sink before throwing up.

Afterwards, though cold to my very bones, I was more in charge of myself. Alison, who had wisely moved out of range, was sitting again on the stool, pale and accusing. All I really wanted now was to know exactly how Darragh had died, how he could possibly have driven into the river. His widow didn't look as if she was going to oblige with direct answers, so I began with a question I hoped would lead up to it.

'Do the children know they've got a half-sister?'

'I told them you'd had a baby for their father.' Alison shrugged. 'They had to be told some time.'

She took a long, soaking drag on the cigarette and I stifled an urge to shake her. They didn't have to know in the same week that their father died.

'Mollie's old for her age,' Alison said. 'She can handle it.'

She was going to have to. She hadn't been given a choice.

'Does she want to meet her sister?' I couldn't even begin to think how Emma was going to take all this.

'Oh, yes, she'd like that.' Alison was offhand.

'What about your little boy, Justin?'

'I told him too. He'll be four in April. I don't know what he's going to do without a father.'

Darragh hadn't told me he had a son. He'd been very thorough about compartmentalizing his life. He'd have hated the way death was unravelling his secrets. I started to ask how he'd died but Alison cut across me.

'I came because I wanted to know what you were like, what sort of woman Darragh wanted along with me . . .' She twisted her wedding ring around her finger. 'Did he love you? Did he tell you he loved you?'

'Once, a long time ago.' I wasn't sure how much of the truth she could take. I wasn't sure how much I wanted to tell her.

'Did he talk about me?'

'He liked to keep things separate. We didn't talk about his work, or about his friends either. You know how he was . . .' Only maybe he was different with her. He'd married her, after all. Married her and stayed with her. Guilt, from being a small pain, was becoming a vast, emptying ache.

'I know how he was.' She lit and dragged on another cigarette. In her leather coat and with her cheeks sucked in she looked like a drugged doll. 'Did he come to see you and the child often?'

'My daughter's name is Emma. He called every month.' I hesitated, then, firmly, I said, 'He and I stopped being lovers when I became pregnant.'

'He gave you money.' She gave a raspy cough. 'We had to do without, because of you. Did you know that?'

'No,' I said. 'I didn't know that.' I found it hard to believe. Darragh had been a lot of things but mean wasn't one of them. I couldn't imagine him leaving his wife and children short.

Alison, without warning, left the stool and lurched at me, clutching my arm. Her fingers were hard and bony through my dressing-gown.

'Are you sure he didn't talk about me? He must have said something over the years . . . surely to God he said *something* . . .'

'He spoke about you a few times . . .'

'What did he say? Did he say he loved me?'

'Yes. He said he loved you.'

We both knew I was lying.

'What else did he say? Did he say anything else?'

'He said that he would never leave you. Not ever, not for anyone.'

This, at least, was more or less true. What Darragh had said was that he *couldn't* leave her.

'And he never did leave me.' Alison let my arm go and began to pace. 'Not until now.' She began to weep then, ceaseless tears streaming unheeded down her face. She had all the helpless despair of the abandoned and it was easy to see why Darragh hadn't been able to leave her. She was flotsam, a derelict in life without him. I mopped her face with paper tissues, almost drowning in guilt myself. She sat back on the stool.

'I'd no idea death was so still . . .' she began and I seized the moment.

'You had to identify the body?'

'He was himself but not himself. It wasn't only what the river had done to him. It was that he had gone away. There was nothing of him in that terrible stillness . . .'

She stopped and I nodded encouragingly. I needed to hear this. How else could I believe he was dead?

'He'd have hated anyone to see him with his skin all wrinkled like that, and white.' Alison put a hand over her face. The nails were so bitten her fingertips looked as if they'd been dipped in red ink. 'It was the way he went on lying there, not doing anything about how he looked, that made me realize he was dead, gone . . .'

I still didn't know how he'd come to die in the river but was beginning to think I didn't want to. Not yet. 'Where's he buried?' I asked. I would have to visit his grave. Emma would have to visit his grave.

'The funeral, oh God, the funeral . . . I don't know how I got through it . . . oh, God, oh, God . . .'

Alison began to rock on the stool, back and forth and faster and faster until, afraid she might fall off, I steadied her and took her hands from her face. Holding them in mine again I asked, 'Was it big? Were there many there?'

The answer to this question, where I come from, is

31

considered to accurately measure the success, or otherwise, of the life lived by the corpse. Small numbers indicate the passing of a life truly to be pitied.

'It was a funeral,' Alison said. 'There were enough there to bury him.'

A small funeral then. And still I couldn't let it go.

'Who was there?' I asked.

'His partner in the business, Austin Finn, and his wife, Sheila. His sister came up from Cork. She was the only relative he had and if that's the last I see of her it'll be too soon. There were a few men there too. I don't know who they were.'

'Did . . . anyone say anything about him? At the graveside?'

I prayed he'd been buried with words of some sort, he who'd been so full of words. Surely Conal Bergin, at least, had said something . . .

'The priest said prayers.'

My heart constricted. 'Conal Bergin wasn't there?'

'No. He's away. Usually he came to us at Christmas. He didn't come this year.'

I'd heard he had a play in production; maybe he'd fled the pressure of rehearsals. 'So he doesn't know either, about Darragh being dead?' I asked.

'Not unless he saw the piece in the *Evening Herald*.' Alison shrugged. 'It was only a few words. There's nothing unusual, the guards said, about a car going into the Liffey like that.'

I hadn't seen the report myself. 'How did it happen?' I asked the question at last.

'He died on Stephen's Day and he was found the next day, a Monday. The post-mortem was on the Wednesday and he was buried on the Friday.'

Alison delivered all of this as if it was a recitation. When she paused I waited, not pushing. I poured us both another coffee and she sipped and after a while began to talk about Darragh's partner, Austin Finn. I stifled an anguished protest and listened.

'Austin came to talk to me about money. He told me about the three hundred pounds a month Darragh was paying to you.' She looked at me with fresh dislike. 'That's when it all came out. Darragh always said we were just managing, that there was no money for extras. He was always working, always out...' She shrugged. 'I suppose that was why. For the extra money.'

Where Darragh got the money to pay me, and how I was going to manage without it, was tomorrow's problem.

'I'm surprised Austin hasn't been in touch, that he didn't tell me...' I said, Darragh's partner, the few times I'd met him, had been sympathetic and kindly. It was hard to accept that he hadn't thought to tell me my child's father was dead. That the task had been left to his widow.

'You know the type he is.' Alison's voice was developing a hard edge. 'He wouldn't have wanted a wife and a mistress together by the graveside.'

'I was not Darragh's mistress.'

'What were you then? You certainly weren't his wife.'

'No.'

'And he went on seeing you...'

'As a friend, as Emma's father. Nothing more. My daughter doesn't have his name. She's Emma Hopkins...'

'. . . She's of an age, almost, with Mollie.' Alison cut me short. 'We were carrying babies for him at the same time, I suppose you knew that? God, but I was so filled with happiness when I fell pregnant. The last thing in the world I thought was that another woman in Dublin was . . .'

I'd had enough guilt thrown at me, for now. I cut her short. 'The girls are healthy and they're . . .' I was going to say beautiful but it wouldn't have been true in Mollie's case. '. . . Bright. We need to decide on a way to deal with . . . things. Emma doesn't know she has a brother and sister . . .'

'Half-brother and sister. And you're the one with the problem. My children know how things are.' As if seeing it for the first time, Alison looked around my kitchen. 'You're not married to anyone,' she said. 'You know how to live on your own. I don't.'

'You'll learn . . .'

'I don't want to.' Again, and all at once, she looked as if she was about to disintegrate. 'I want Darragh back. I want him alive. I don't care if he wants you too. I just want him with me . . .'

The front doorbell rang for the second time that morning.

'That'll be Emma.' I checked Alison's face for some give, some understanding of my dilemma. There was none. There was no place either that I could conveniently hide her. 'I'll have to let her in,' I said.

Delia stood on the step with Emma.

'You've got company.' Accusingly, she bundled herself and Emma into the hall. 'We saw them coming up the steps. We've been sitting below waiting for an invitation to meet your guests . . .'

34

Emma, pulling off her coat and demanding to know who my visitors were, would have gone on down to the kitchen if I hadn't grabbed her for a hug. Delia, watching me closely, started to say something but was stopped by whatever she saw in my face. I let go of Emma and told her, firmly, to take her things on up to her room. She surprised me by doing just that, and without an argument. Delia moved closer, whispering.

'What is it, Norah? What's going on here?'

Delia Brophy was somewhere between seventy and eighty. Pugnacious and interfering, she'd been mother, grandmother and friend to me in the years since I'd moved into her house. I told her everything, quickly and crudely, worried that Emma would come back down or Alison appear from the kitchen before I finished. She crossed herself and closed her eyes and muttered a prayer as I spoke.

'You poor child.' She put a hand on my arm when I finished. 'I know how fond you were of that man. Poor creature; what a terrible way for him to meet his end . . .' She paused, frowning. A woman of fierce loyalties she was, I knew, deciding her priorities. 'Even allowing for the tragic situation, his widow had no right coming here, unannounced, with her children. What'll we tell Emma? That woman didn't give a thought to that before arriving on your doorstep, did she?'

Guilt made me defend Alison, 'She's in shock and she's grief-stricken.' I paused. 'Look, Delia, I'd like you to go down to the kitchen and talk to her while I go up to her room and explain what I can to Emma.'

Delia, muttering, obliged. And that might have been that if it had been the kind of morning when things

35

went to plan. But the world as I'd known it had turned on its head and wouldn't be on its feet for a long time.

The sitting-room door was open as I passed to go upstairs. Inside, in front of the fire and the very picture of girlish, confidential huddling, sat Emma and Mollie. Emma's agreeableness had clearly been a ploy to cover her intentions to sneak back downstairs. She and her half-sister looked up when I went into the room, two small girls with serious, secretive faces.

'Looks as if I don't need to introduce you two.' I was casual as I relaxed into an armchair. They looked at me silently, slightly tilted noses betraying their shared parenthood and with expressions which were identical. Emma's slim, dark prettiness made Mollie look pale and plain but there was no avoiding their identical, accusing stares.

'Has Mollie told you about your Dad, about Darragh?' I asked the question gently, leaning forward to touch Emma's hair. She shook my hand away and moved closer to Mollie. Heart-sick, I decided that divide and conquer was the only possible move.

'Mollie, there's someone in the kitchen I'd like you to go and say hello to.' I was firm and unsmiling.

'She means Delia, our landlady.' Emma, volunteering this information, was sulky.

'I'll go when I've finished talking to Emma.' Mollie was as firm as I'd been myself.

'Go NOW, Mollie, please. And take Justin with you.'

She stared at me, wondering how outright defiance would go down. I eyeballed her back. This stand-off lasted a long minute or two before Mollie stood and looked down at Emma.

'I won't be long.' She grabbed her brother by the hand and left.

Alone with a daughter who'd become a stony-faced, distant stranger, I threw a couple of briquettes on to the fire and got down on the floor beside her.

'I know you're upset, my love, and I wish I'd been the one to tell you . . .' She squirmed as I tried to gather her into my arms.

'Why didn't you, then?' Her hair fell forward and covered her face. I didn't dare touch it. 'Why didn't you tell me I had a sister, and a brother? And why didn't you tell me you were a mistress?'

Mollie had been busy. Alison had been unstinting too in the account of things she'd given her daughter. I swore under my breath.

'I didn't tell you for all sorts of reasons,' I said. 'And what exactly do you think a mistress is, Emma?'

'A woman who steals another woman's husband and has babies with him. That's what you did.'

It was only weeks since I'd heard her tell a friend that babies were bought in hospitals. God knows what sort of understanding she had of the situation. I ached to hold her against me but her stiff little body was unrelenting.

'What did Mollie tell you?'

'She said that Darragh was their father first and that he's only my father because you stole him from their mother . . .'

She began to shiver and when I slowly pulled her against me she allowed it. 'And did Mollie tell you where your Dad is now?' I held her tight against me.

'She said he drowned in the river because he

37

couldn't get out of his car . . .' Her arms tightened around me. '. . . Is it true? Is he really drowned?'

'He really is . . .'

She broke and I rocked with her, stroking her hair, while she sobbed. I tried for words that would put a shape on things for her.

'Your father died in an accident, as Mollie said, when his car went into the Liffey. I don't know much more about it, but when I find out I promise I'll tell you. He was a good dad to you, and he loved you very much and those are the things you must think about.' I turned her wet face up to mine. I would cry myself, later. Oh, how I would cry.

'Listen to me, my darling, because what I'm going to tell you now is how things really happened.' I took a deep breath. 'I met your father eight years ago and fell in love with him very quickly. But he was married already and it wasn't right for us to be such close friends, so we parted. The wonderful thing about it all was that you happened, you were born. And even though your father lived with his wife and Justin and Mollie, he loved you just the same as them . . .'

'Why didn't he live with us then?'

'Because he loved his wife before he loved you, or me, and when he married her he made promises to her. He couldn't break a promise.'

My child's hair, as I held and looked at her, was his hair, her mouth, his mouth. I traced it with a finger as I went on. 'Your dad and I agreed to be friends forever and that he would come and see you as often as he could. And that's what he did . . . for as long as he could . . .' I stopped. I'd given her enough to be going on with. 'Do you understand all that I'm telling you, Emma?'

'Yes,' my daughter said. 'I'm not a baby.'

'No, you're not,' I agreed. Not any longer.

'I like Mollie,' she said. 'I like having a sister. Justin's all right too, but Mollie's deadly.'

Mollie was deadly all right. In the kitchen, when we went down there, she stood glowering at Delia.

'I can't go on . . .' Alison's whisper was barely audible.

'Take Justin back to the TV, girls,' I said, 'and get yourselves some chocolates from under the tree.'

Justin went with them happily. Alison's face was awash with tears. 'Everything's falling apart . . .' She pulled on a cigarette and blew smoke and pulled again and gasped and coughed up smoke. I was unimpressed. This was the woman who'd told her children I was their dead father's mistress.

'Tell me,' I leaned against the dresser and faced her with folded arms, 'about how Darragh died. Did the car skid? Was there another car involved?'

She looked from me to the silent Delia and sniffed loudly. She began to speak in a low voice. 'I only know what the guards told me. I didn't see the place, or the car . . .' Her lips tightened. '. . . No way was I going down the docks to see it. No way in this world. They wanted me to but I told them to fuck off with themselves. They said his car went off the quays and into the Liffey. They said he was dead when they hauled the car out. It had been in the river the best part of the night, they said, with him strapped inside.'

'Was there anyone with him?' I asked.

'He was alone.'

Alone. Never without company in life, dying so godforsaken and solitary in the slimy, cold depths of the Liffey with its sludgy fish population and creeping filth . . .

'What was he doing? Where was he going?' I asked.

'How do I know?' Alison said. 'He didn't tell me things. He gave me money and he looked after us and he came and went and sometimes he loved me. That was it. That was all. That was how we lived.' She was still now, grey and still as stone.

'There's to be an inquest,' she said, 'on Wednesday of this week. It's not usually so soon but there's a gap or something . . .' She paused. 'They think he might have killed himself.'

'They're obliged to think these things.' Delia was brisk. 'It's the garda mind. Put a man in uniform and he'll think the worst of the world.'

Alison ignored her and turned to me. 'Will you come with me to the inquest? I need someone and you owe me that much at least.' She paused and coughed and nibbled a finger. 'I've no one else.'

'I'll come with you,' I said. I would have gone anyway.

Chapter Four

Sunday, 2 January. Evening.

'The way I see it,' said Delia, 'you've got two choices.'

We were standing on the steps as a taxi carrying Alison and her children spun out of the square.

'You can choose to let that woman into your life and live to regret it – or you can decide to have nothing to do with her. She's trouble.'

The taxi was bound for Ballinteer. It would be snowing out there, at the foot of the Dublin mountains.

'I didn't have a choice.' I took deep breaths of the sharp air. 'I want to go for myself.'

Delia sniffed. 'Coffee and sympathy was more than enough payment for whatever guilt you're feeling. And grief . . .' She paused. '. . . Guilt and grief, Norah, are misguiding emotions. You'd do well not to allow them to lead you into a situation you could regret . . .'

'I know what I'm doing.' I scanned the sky for clouds. There were plenty of them gathering.

'I hope you do.' Delia's frown was darker than anything overhead. 'I'm going down now to that old man of mine. I'll make a bite of lunch for yourself and Emma. You look as if you could do with it. Come down about midday.'

I wasn't hungry. I hadn't the energy either to do battle over a refusal.

'We'll be there,' I said.

Emma, when I went back in, said she wanted to go across the square to her friend Jack. Bundling her into her hat and coat, I couldn't see anything in her face but her usual earnest concentration on the thing to hand.

'Are you all right?' I asked gently.

'Are you?' she asked.

'I'm feeling sad,' I hugged her, 'but I'm fine. Now answer my question. Are *you* all right?'

'I feel sad too.' She squirmed out of my arms. 'But Jack wants me to help him with his stupid Lego. You know Jack.'

I knew Jack. Five years old and totally indulged and without a friend in the world. Emma had taken him under her wing.

'Don't stay longer than an hour,' I said. 'I'll be in Delia's. She's giving us lunch.'

I roamed the house after she'd gone. It had none of its usual peace, not even in the bedroom I'd made into a sort of retreat for myself, all terracotta and muslin. I lay on the unmade bed, large enough for two though it had been a while since I'd shared it, and was immediately swamped with memories of the Darragh I'd met when I was eighteen, of the sexual excitement he'd brought to my life. The Darragh of three weeks before hovered too, laughing and fun and only thirty-one years old. All gone now.

The telephone shrilled in the hallway.

'I'll be driving by your place this evening.' My

brother Liam's voice was businesslike. 'Thought I'd drop in and see how you and the child are getting on.'

'Emma,' I said. 'Emma is your niece's name.'

Decoded, what my elder brother was saying was that he wanted to be fed. He'd assigned himself an overprotective, interfering role in my life and was the last person in the world I wanted to see just then. He was also probably the first person I should tell about Darragh. Liam was a policeman.

'I'll be there about seven.' He gave his hearty, big brother laugh. 'I'll be fit to eat a horse by that time. You could throw an auld chop on the pan for me . . .'

'Fine,' I said. 'See you then.'

No point getting into things on the phone.

After I hung up I studied my face in the coatstand mirror. Even allowing for the mirror's age (circa 1930s and a lugubrious piece of furniture), I was pale and shattered-looking. My eyes, staring back at me, were a feverish blue and my skin looked muddy as the bottom of a river. Conversations with Liam tended to return me to childhood insecurities and never helped the way I saw myself anyway. He was seven years older than me but had always behaved as if there were a couple of generations between us. He was kind and dull and, eight years after joining the Garda Siochana, was still a rank-and-file member. He was my brother and I loved him, in spite of everything and even if his Neanderthal attitudes and interfering had led me at times to contemplate fratricide. Also, I had reason too to be wary of the guards, which didn't help my relationship with him. His reactions to the news of Darragh's death didn't bear thinking about.

My other brother, Gerry, wouldn't be a problem. He was the one of the three of us who'd stayed to work the family farm and was a lot more clued in to the vagaries of life than the city-dwelling Liam would ever be. Maisie Hyland, the woman he'd married, had a lot to do with this. I'd gone to school with Maisie and for earthy pragmatism she had few equals. Four sons under six years of age were another factor keeping Gerry in touch with reality.

When I dialled the farmhouse in Duncolla, Maisie answered. She'd liked Darragh but bluntly was the only way I could manage to tell her he was dead. She gave a strangled yelp, whispered, 'Oh, sweet Jesus Christ,' and left me hanging on to a silent phone line.

'Terrible start to the year.' She spoke eventually. 'What a desperate, desperate thing . . .' Words failed her again and another silence stretched. It felt like fully five minutes before she asked, 'Was it an accident?'

'Oh, Maisie, of course it was an accident.' I wanted to cry so badly my throat all but closed. I squeezed words out. 'You knew Darragh. How can you imagine it being anything else?'

'I suppose not,' she said, 'except that it's such a melancholy time of year, Christmas. You just never know what's going on in people's heads.' She sighed. 'Don't mind me, Norah. I hardly knew the man . . .' Another pause . . . 'God, but he was lovely . . .'

'Yes,' I said, 'he was.'

I told her, eventually and slowly, about Alison's visit and about the children and the upcoming inquest. True to form she turned quickly practical.

'You and Emma need to get away from things for a bit,' she said. 'I'll expect you here for the weekend . . .'

'We've just left there, Maisie,' I protested – we'd spent Christmas on the farm. A happy one too. 'But I'll see how things go.'

When I rang Delia's doorbell just after midday the territorial Woodie, her mongrel dog, began a lunatic barking. Delia, answering the door, toed him into submission as I followed her into her sitting-room. The unbeautiful Woodie, with his short legs, long tail, going-grey black coat and one nearly blind eye, stretched exhausted by the fire and ignored me. Patsy Brophy, beside him in an armchair, ignored me too.

'Has that young woman paid her rent, Delia?' He kept his eyes on the book in his lap. Long, so angular he resembled a piece of scaffolding, Patsy made your average misanthrope look like Mother Teresa.

'Why don't you take yourself out for a turn around the square, old man?' Delia asked. 'It's brightening up nicely out there.'

'Don't be ridiculous.' Patsy turned his implacable black glare on me. 'Were you invited here?' he asked.

'Give me a break, Patsy, it's not the best of days . . .' I tried a half smile. A waste of both our times.

'I heard about your troubles.' Patsy was testy. 'So you can spare me the further details. I haven't the time to be listening to them.'

Time was what Patsy had plenty of. He closed his book and unwound himself out of the armchair. The book was a racing manual: Patsy was an armchair bookie. There wasn't a lot he didn't know about horses, or about the ancient civilizations. 'I'll be in the bedroom.' He took himself stiff-legged from the room. The dog followed.

'Sit down.' Delia plumped the cushions he'd vacated. 'Relax yourself. I'll get the port.'

Delia served port, and nothing but, at all times of the year. Her basement home had a bedroom to the front and a large sitting-room and cupboard-like kitchen to the back. The garden, when in seasonal splendour, had white bench seats beneath deep bowers of creeping plants and an ivy-draped timber pergola. Delia tended it lovingly and had once told me its glories had been created by Patsy in the first flush of their marriage. This, hard as it was to imagine, gave clues to an earlier Patsy and helped explain how she'd come to marry him. I'd once asked her about children and she'd replied curtly that she was a 'barren woman'.

Delia's sitting-room was mausoleum, den, library and womb. It held everything she owned, including the supply of port. She kept a log fire going winter and summer.

'Emma's gone across the square, I see.' Delia handed me the port. She was quintessential old Dublin and had all the generosity, sense of place and fierce protectiveness of the breed. She missed nothing that went on in her corner of the world.

'She'll be here soon,' I assured. A long gulp of her very sweet port hit the spot. 'I don't believe it was suicide.'

'No more do I.' Delia poked at the fire. The logs crumbled and collapsed and she piled on a couple more. They were damp and spat at us. 'He had great life in him, that man of yours.'

That did it. I wept with the unbearable sadness and

misery of it for fully fifteen minutes, the heat from the fire drying the tears on my cheeks as they fell. Through it all Delia sat, silent and wise enough to know there was nothing to be said or done.

'What was he doing, down the quays on the day after Christmas?' she asked when I'd stopped and she'd refilled my glass.

'I don't know. His wife . . . widow doesn't know either.'

'Strange place to spend Stephen's Day.' Delia paused before adding, gently, 'He had lovely things about him. It's a great pity when young people don't get their lives right.'

So. Even Delia hadn't been immune to Darragh's charm. You'd never have known from her brusque way of dealing with him. God, but he'd worked hard for her approval in life. A gust of unbearable loneliness swept through me. There is a great draughtiness in the space left by death.

'You'll have to keep yourself busy.' Delia gave me a hard look. 'It's a sad, sad business but you've the child to think about . . .'

'Darragh never wore a seat belt and he loved that car,' I said. 'I can't believe he would deliberately destroy it . . .'

Delia got up as Emma's voice came calling through the front door letter-box. 'You're creating a drama where there's none,' she said. 'It's likely he saw a garda coming and slipped the belt on. There's lots of guards around the quays, looking to give people tickets. Put it out of your mind.'

We sat at the table in her sitting-room and she put plates of potatoes and ham and brussels sprouts in front of us. I'd drifted into my own thoughts when a

47

nudge from Delia brought me back to what Emma was saying.

'Mollie said Dad left the house at dinner time on Christmas Day.' Emma sidelined the sprouts. 'She said there was a big row and that he didn't come back.'

'Didn't come back at all or just that night?' I poured her a glass of water.

'Didn't come back, ever. Mollie said she was lonely all Christmas night, waiting for him, and all the next day as well.' She buried her head in the glass. 'And then the guards came and said he was dead in the river . . .'

'Eat your sprouts,' Delia ordered.

'Mollie must be making a mistake,' I said carefully. 'Her mom said he left the day after Christmas . . .'

'Mollie's not stupid.' Her tone implied that Alison was. 'She said his mobile phone rang and her mother began shouting at him when he said he had to go.'

'Maybe he came back very late and Mollie didn't hear him . . .'

'No, he didn't.' Emma's eyes were too bright. 'She stayed awake all night. She heard her mom walking all around the house too . . .'

'Oh, well,' I said lightly, 'people often get things mixed up. Why don't you feed Woodie while Delia and I organize pudding?'

She gave me a glittering look but she headed for the patio, calling to the dog as she went.

'Whatever happened between Darragh and that woman on Christmas Day is none of your business.' Delia dolloped far too much cream into three bowls of trifle. 'They were husband and wife and as such what went on between them was sacrosanct.'

'But not inviolate . . .' I began.

'Let it be,' Delia was sharp. 'There's no good to be served by raking over what's done. There's another thing I want to say to you.' She narrowed her eyes. 'You are not to worry about the rent. We'll sort something out when your ship comes in.'

When I began to protest she cut roughly across me.

'Just for the next while,' she said. 'I'll be looking for it again soon enough. Now listen to me too on that other matter. The wife will recover. She's a widow, and that gives her a status. She'll get whatever her husband has left by way of an estate. You only have yourself to look out for yourself and your child. What I'm saying to you, Norah, is to leave it alone, let it be. You don't need to go to the inquest for Alison McCann's sake, nor for your own either.'

She was wrong, dead wrong. The need to know about Darragh's last hours was a growing, malignant thing in me. But things would have worked out a lot differently if I'd listened to her.

In the late afternoon I went out and bought a large amount of frozen sirloin steak. I was hoping that this, done to a nice medium rare and served with spuds, would make Liam agreeable to doing a little private police work for me. I wanted to know the official police line on Darragh and whether his death was being treated as suicide or an accident. Liam arrived late and irritable. His car had been broken into and the radio stolen. He arrived so late that Emma was in bed.

I told him about Darragh as he was enjoying the steak. For someone who'd been openly contemptuous of him while alive Liam was genuinely disturbed when

49

I told him of Darragh's death. He put his cutlery down and pushed back from the table and stared at me.

'This happened when, did you say?'

'Eight days ago,' I said. Liam slowly repositioned himself at the table and resumed eating while he worked this out.

'Stephen's Day then,' he said. 'I'm sorry to hear this, Norah. Sorry for your sake, and for the child's.'

I was about to broach the subject of Liam making private police inquiries for me when he dropped his bombshell.

'I'm sorry too to have to tell you that this might not be as simple a matter as you think, Norah.' His tone was measured. I squashed a rush of impatience. 'I'd been keeping a bit of an eye on our friend during the weeks coming up to Christmas . . .'

'Are you talking about Darragh, Liam?' I'd some difficulty believing what I was hearing. 'Are you telling me that you were spying on him? Is that what you mean by keeping an eye? Or were you following him?' I stopped to take a steadying breath. 'Just what *were* you doing, Liam?'

'I was keeping an eye on him,' Liam's voice stayed on course, 'for your sake. For his own too. He was headed for trouble Norah, if he wasn't already in it. That's what I wanted to ascertain and that's why I was watching him . . .'

'Watching him! You were spying on him! Jesus, Liam, what've you done?' I stared at his virtuous face and saw him following Darragh, saw too how he could never have gone unnoticed.

'I had reason to be concerned about the company he was keeping . . .' he began.

'I was some of the company he kept,' I said. 'Your niece was someone else he kept company with . . .'

'Let me say my bit, Norah, before you start flying off the handle. Your friend was meeting with criminal types. People the gardai are very interested in. I came across him by accident five or six weeks ago and decided to . . .'

'Keep an eye on him,' I interrupted bitterly.

'That's right,' Liam said. 'I don't have to tell you about the crime situation in this city, Norah. We're fighting a war and these people have to be watched, night and day . . .'

'Are you telling me Darragh was dealing drugs or something? Because if that's what you think then you're way off beam. Drugs were never his scene. He hated them, everything about them. He said so, often . . .'

Liam, doggedly insistent, cut me short. 'It was my duty as a member of the force to follow up on suspicious behaviour.' He carefully separated the last of the meat from the bone. 'And it's my duty as your brother to look out for you and your child.'

I could have reminded him that he hadn't been there for me when I'd needed him, years before, when I was newly pregnant. But I didn't. I don't have a killer instinct.

'You following Darragh around could be the reason he's dead,' I said. 'You're large and you're noticeable. You've no detective training. Odds are that you were seen. A garda hanging around was bound to . . .'

'Your friend was the architect of his own fate, Norah, and you're upset. Rightly so.' Liam got up and moved to the fire. He stood there, rocking on his heels with his back to the blaze. 'You're not yourself. I was doing what I thought was for the best.' He looked like our father, standing there, dark-haired, pale-skinned and righteous, with a long face and nose. Lonely too, though not in the way our father had been lonely. Liam needed a Maisie to rescue him but the chances of that happening were looking slimmer as the years went on.

'I know you were.' I was all at once without the heart for a fight, if fight this was. 'Look, Liam, it would help if I knew what the garda theory is about his death. Will you find out for me?'

'I'll see what I can do.' He opened a chink in the curtains and looked out. 'Frost's coming down again. I'd best be going.' He turned. 'I'll talk to the boys in Pearse Street. They'll be the ones looking after a drowning in that part of the river.' Our father's rare, sad smile flickered across his face. 'That was a nice piece of meat you did for me.'

'Any time,' I said, and meant it.

Chapter Five

Monday, 3 January

The river was high, the tide on the turn. I stood for a long time looking into the water without seeing a thing. I don't know what I'd expected to see.

I'd come to where Darragh had drowned because I hadn't been to his funeral. I needed to see at least one of the graves he'd inhabited after death. It would make letting him go easier.

Liam, not altogether willingly, had got me the details of where the car had gone into the water. It was a lonely spot, made lonelier by the wind whipping the waters and the gulls screaming in circles above the quayside ships. Even allowing for the single, docklands pub further back, it was hard to imagine why anyone would want to drive down there.

A nearby bollard listed drunkenly, a lump torn from the base showing where it had been knocked over before being placed upright again. It didn't take much to figure this was where Darragh's car had gone in. I sat on the bollard and said a sort of prayer by way of farewell. The choppy river threw spray across my feet and I stood again, looking out across the bay to Howth. We'd gone to Howth for a day once, Darragh and me, in the summertime. We'd spent a lot of the time looking for a quiet spot in which to make love but had been thwarted by children and dogs at every turn.

I walked back to where I'd parked the car by the pub. To warm up, and because I wasn't yet ready to leave, I decided to have a drink. From a stool by the bar I ordered a glass of draught beer.

'Sad about that car going into the river over Christmas,' I said to the barman.

'Sad all right.' He pushed the beer along the counter without looking at me. 'But sure if a man doesn't want to live, then he doesn't want to live. We see it all the time down here. Will that be all?'

'Yes. Thanks.'

The chill at the centre of me since Alison's visit was still there. I'd felt chills like it before in my life and they'd left me, in time. This one would too, in time, though probably not while I was in that pub.

It was dark in there. Vaguely musical sounds came from an old Bush wireless behind the bar, next to which there was a noticeboard pinned with withered photographs. The walls were smoky brown, the wooden floor stained, no effort spared to keep the place as it had always been. It wasn't Darragh's style but, in a city where pubs were falling over themselves to be 'themed', such unique indifference was relaxing.

We'd had a Bush wireless in the kitchen when I was very young. Until I was at least ten years old I'd thought its sole purpose was to broadcast football matches and weather forecasts. My father and brothers listened to nothing else and my grandmother listened to nothing at all. I wasn't allowed to touch the set myself.

I'd no idea how my mother felt about the radio

because she died within days of my birth. This led to her mother moving in to look after her son-in-law and grandchildren. From photographs it had been clear that I looked a little like my mother, but only a little. She'd always seemed to me beguilingly beautiful.

My grandmother was deeply religious and deeply righteous. She ruled the house by default, my father's failure to recover from my mother's death leaving him without the heart or will to oppose her. His family had farmed the same fifty acres for three generations and when he married my mother her family's adjoining hundred acres were added to this. Once, when I was about eight or nine, I heard my grandmother bitterly call my father 'an animal' who should have been content with two sons, 'kept himself to himself' and left my mother 'at peace in her bed at night' after they were born. He didn't defend himself.

Our house was six miles from the nearest town and two from the nearest neighbour and, in the years until I went to school, my playmates were a variety of fowl and one peacock in particular. That peacock taught me a lot of things I should have remembered. I called him Jake and to this day I can't see electric blue without recalling his feathers. He slept in the rafters of the hen shed and on good days would sit on the roof of the house or sleep in the high branches of the old lime tree. He had more personality than all of the other birds and animals on the farm and I was devoted to him. I thought he was devoted to me too.

When he was a year old Jake abandoned me for a peahen. They went everywhere together and I felt utterly forsaken. Then, one day, the peahen flew away, leaving Jake forsaken. She was spotted in a neighbour's place once, then no more. She probably went off to nest but I prayed, fervently, that a fox had got her.

I had Jake to myself again after that but he had taught me my first, invaluable, lesson about male fidelity. I may have ignored it, but I've never forgotten it.

By the time I was thirteen the brunt of my grandmother's fanatical energies had zoned in on my sprouting, adolescent body. I was fifteen when my father reluctantly intervened and I was allowed to attend a disco in the town. I was to be collected at eleven o'clock by Liam. Liam delivered me too, waiting while I teamed up with my friend Kate inside the community hall. He wasn't to know that Kate, who knew a thing or two about men and sex, was immediately appropriated by a hot-handed garage mechanic.

'You're not to say a word,' she warned as she skipped the hall, 'and you're not to go home without me.'

As a first-timer I found myself in reasonable demand and was flushed with the small successes of the night when Liam arrived outside at eleven o'clock to find a drunken, half-dressed Kate in the garage hand's car. I was seventeen before I went to my second disco, but that was because my grandmother had had a stroke two weeks before. When she failed to recover and died I went every week, albeit collected each time by Liam.

When I was eighteen escape arrived by way of a small bequest from my mother's estate. She'd made the will while carrying me, a child she'd been advised not to conceive, and I like to think it was her way of looking after me in the event of anything happening to her.

'I'm going to live in Dublin,' I told my father and, within a week, in spite of bitter argument, reproach and even a threat or two, I was ready to go.

On the morning I left, my father put on his hat and walked silently with me to the doorway. We hadn't spoken for two days and I was hoping he would come to the bus stop so that we might talk on the way. But he came only as far as the door and stood there while I went on alone. He was wearing a striped jersey I'd knitted for him. He'd had it six years and never worn it before.

All the way down the path to the bus stop those stripes burned holes in my back, searing the edges of my resolve. My father, after all, had been dutiful, done the best he could for me. He was a lonely man, and I was young. Maybe it wouldn't really be so terrible to spend a few more years at home. Didn't what I was doing amount to forsaking him in his old age and need? These, my father's arguments, screamed in my head as I lugged my bags slowly.

I went as far as the gate before turning. My father was standing where I'd left him. I waved and thought I saw him nod, though I couldn't be sure. By the time the bus came, five minutes later, he'd gone inside and closed the door.

I did more than leave home that day. I also shattered for ever the delicate balance which had kept my brothers and father together. Within a year my brothers' lives had changed as much as mine and my father was dead.

And now Darragh was dead too.

A sleeting rain was whistling up the quays when I

came out of the pub. I drove half-heartedly to work but in the early afternoon told Harry I was leaving and went home. Time, I told myself, time was all I needed.

I was right, in that time did in fact return me to a sort of functioning norm. But events played a part too.

Chapter Six

Wednesday, 5 January

January pulled out all its weather stops on the day of the inquest, producing a dark, teeming wet day and bitter east wind. I left Razorbill at 12.45 p.m. and walked across town to meet Alison at Busarus, opposite the Coroner's Court. I could have got a bus, or taken the car, but those are not real options on a rainy day in Dublin. I felt like walking anyway.

I got there early. Busarus is no better, and no worse, than bus stations anywhere. With buses going and coming from the four corners of the island, it invariably steams with exhaust fumes, expectations and goodbyes. I'd developed an intimate acquaintance with the place during my first six months in Dublin, before I met Darragh. After that I didn't go home much.

I made my way through the usual bedlam to the basement ladies' room where a hand drier did a reasonable job on my hair and the liberal use of a new, plum-coloured lipstick brought my face back to life. I emerged damp as opposed to dripping and badly in need of a strong, hot coffee.

I'd barely stained the cup with my plum lips when Alison arrived, all hunched anxiety as she made her way across the coffee bar. She'd scraped her hair back but otherwise looked exactly as she had the Sunday before. She was biting her lips as she sat down.

'I nearly didn't come.' She sat on her hands. 'I thought all morning that I wouldn't be able to bear it. But then the guards rang. They said it looked like Darragh's would be the first of the day's inquests . . .' She got off her hands and fumbled with a packet of cigarettes. '. . . I took that as a sign that I should be here.'

I ordered another coffee and added toasted cheese sandwiches for both of us. Liam, despite a good deal of prodding on my part, had told me only that the gardai were 'keeping an open mind on all aspects' of Darragh's death.

'Emma and Mollie seem to have got on well,' I said as we waited for the sandwiches.

'Yes.'

'Mollie's very chatty . . .'

'She's not shy.'

'She told Emma about a Christmas Day row in your place. She said Darragh left after a phone call and didn't come back . . .'

'She's mixed up. Darragh left on Stephen's Day.' Alison gave a tired look around the coffee bar.

'She seemed very clear about it happening at the Christmas dinner table,' I persisted. 'She gave Emma a lot of detail about you not wanting him to leave . . .'

'Why are going on about all of this?' Alison's face had a childishly hurt look.

'Because I need to know what happened. I want to be clear in my head about things before we go into the court.' I paused. 'You told me that Darragh went out on Stephen's Day and that that was the last time you saw him. Mollie says he left the day before and that she never saw him again . . .'

'Mollie's not yet eight years old. Children make mistakes.' Alison's lip trembled as she stubbed out her cigarette. I felt like a schoolyard bully.

'She seemed quite certain . . .' I stopped when Alison looked up at me, eyes swimming in a face about to collapse.

'Mollie's certain about everything,' she said.

'So he left on Stephen's Day?'

Alison didn't answer, just looked at me as if I were a relic from the Inquisition while she lit a second cigarette. The sandwiches came. Mine was burnt and I abandoned my interrogation while I scraped it with a knife.

'Where are you from?' Alison asked, suddenly, in a not very subtle diversionary tactic.

'A place called Duncolla, the other side of Portlaoise. Where are you from yourself?' I was polite.

'Donegal.' She turned as the tannoy announced another list of departing buses. 'I never go back there now. My family are all scattered.' She paused. 'I hate this place.'

'I don't like it much myself,' I said.

'This is where I arrived the first time I ever came to Dublin. I was sixteen.' She shrugged and bent to examine the sandwich. 'I've never been back here since then.'

I waited for her to go on, but she sat quietly nibbling. It was still teeming outside and we'd fifteen minutes to kill before crossing to the Coroner's Court. Direct questions about the Christmas Day row weren't going to get me straight answers, that was obvious. To

61

pass the time, and because I hate silences, I rambled into the story of my last visit home before my father's death. Part of me slavishly wanted Alison to understand how things had been for me when I'd become pregnant with her husband's baby.

'I was four months pregnant when I went down to tell my father and brothers the news.' I stopped to see if I had her attention but since this was hard to tell I went on. 'I went on a Friday evening bus. We were crossing the Curragh when I had an attack of nausea and the driver had to stop to let me off. I barely made it to the grass verge. A neighbour on the bus put two-and-two together. I could see it in the way she looked at me when I got back on to the bus. It was like sending a messenger ahead of me and it meant I would have to tell my father that night, before the gossip got to him . . .'

'My father died when I was eight,' Alison, interrupting, spoke quickly. 'I was the youngest of the seven children my mother had. The others had all gone by the time I was a teenager and my mother was wired to the moon most of the time.' She stopped as suddenly as she'd begun.

'Is your mother still alive?' I asked, gently. Alison shook her head and went on in the same quick, panicky way.

'No. I was seventeen when she died. Ten years ago.' She stopped again, pushing aside the half-eaten sandwich and lighting another cigarette. I waited. She looked at me blankly. I'd got as much as I was going to get of her story. There were still ten minutes before the Court opened its doors.

'My father was watching television when I got home.' I continued my own story. 'I was surprised at how thin he looked, not that he'd ever been fat. He asked me if I was hungry and went ahead of me into the kitchen. My brothers were there. The younger one said I wasn't looking well so I told them why . . .' The scene in the kitchen was clear in my head as a landscape after rain. 'None of them said anything. It was as if I hadn't spoken, as if I wasn't there even. After a while, thinking they hadn't properly heard me, I told them again and that I'd be having my baby in the spring. My father got up. He said it was of no consequence to him when I had my child. I'd shamed myself and the family and should go back to Dublin. He'd done as much as he could or would for me and wanted no part of my life from then on. He said my brothers would want nothing to do with me either.'

'What did your brothers do?' Alison leaned across and took a sip of my coffee. Ash from her cigarette had fallen into her own.

'Nothing,' I said. 'Nothing at all.' The station clock crept towards 2 p.m. and I stood up. 'My father said I could stay the night but that he wanted me gone in the morning. I went to my room and left the house at dawn and that was the last I time I saw my father.'

Alison came with me while I paid for the food. We walked, quickly, out of the building and towards the Coroner's Court.

'There's no good relying on men for anything,' Alison said. 'Darragh was the only man I ever met that I could rely on and he went and drove into the bloody river.'

63

Crossing the road to the Court I wondered why she was so intent on believing Darragh's death a suicide. I didn't believe it at all myself, but didn't know why I was so sure of that either.

Chapter Seven

Wednesday, 5 January

The building which houses Dublin's Coroner's Court has, from the outside, an unprepossessing dignity. Red-bricked Victorian, it retains a sedate composure in an area of constant roadworks and never-completed building sites. Alison and I skirted mud generated by the latest roadworks and climbed the steps.

'Are you for the Court, ladies?' a navy-suited official separated himself from a group in the hallway.

'We're for the Court,' I said, and he pushed open a pair of long polished wood doors to our right.

'No smoking in the Court.' He reached for Alison's cigarette. She took a long drag before grinding it under her heel.

The Courtroom was a dazzling example of what a good polish and several coats of varnish can do. Everything shone: the high bench seats in raised rows to the back, the panelled walls, the black of the painted floorboards, the long central table for the Press, the Coroner's throne itself. The vaulted ceiling had beams and frosted glass. As we found ourselves seats, the sky overhead got darker and more and heavier rain battered that glass.

The large number of people there surprised me. A handful of them were gawpers, sheltering from the rain. Others, two huddled groups of them, looked, like ourselves, as if they had to be there. I counted at least a half dozen garda.

A ginger-haired guard with freckled hands stood talking to Austin Finn and another man. I was relieved to see Austin Finn there, so reassuringly himself, your everyday accountant in Crombie overcoat and grey scarf, a specimen of solid continuity in a tilted world. The company's facts and figures man, Darragh had called him. When the guard with him spotted Alison he moved our way. Austin, looking strained and stiff, followed. So did the other man, a bristling, thespian type with black-grey pony-tail.

'Afternoon, Mrs McCann.' The guard was mournfully kind. 'I hope this won't be too trying for you. It might be better if you and your friend . . .' he included me with a nod '. . . took a seat closer to the Coroner . . .' He kept his gaze solemnly on Alison but I wasn't fooled. This was a country man and that one look had taken in everything about me.

'We'll stay here,' Alison said.

The man with the pony-tail stood back a little, the picture of dignified grief as he observed things. Austin Finn gave me an apologetic look and put a consoling arm about Alison's shoulders.

'I tried ringing you,' he said, 'but couldn't get through . . .'

'I gave up answering the phone.' Alison leaned against him. 'I didn't feel up to talking to people. Except for Norah. I went to see her after you told me about . . .'

'I'm sorry . . .' Austin, with agonized formality,

66

extended a hand to me. 'Alison had to be told . . . this is a terrible thing . . . a bloody awful mess . . .'

He floundered into silence and I took his hand and nodded. 'Of course Alison had to be told,' I said, 'and I'm glad it was by you.' At least Austin's version would have been pared of the frills and gore of gossip.

The garda was still standing beside us, patiently waiting to know who I was.

'I'm Norah Hopkins,' I said. 'I was a friend of Mr McCann.'

'Neil Redmond, Sergeant,' he said. 'I was the investigating officer at the scene. Mrs McCann,' he turned to Alison, 'your statement will have to be read to the court, the one you made after identifying your husband.' Alison didn't respond and he went on, quite gently, 'You can do it yourself or we can ask the Court Clerk to do it for you.'

'I'd like that.' Alison seemed to come back from some lost place. 'Someone must read it.'

'I'll see to it,' said the Sergeant.

'Just one thing, Sergeant, before you go . . .' The pony-tailed man, with a nifty shuffle which brought him to Alison's side, made himself part of the group. 'How long is this business expected to take?' His glorious baritone carried around the room. Not a man to be ignored.

'Unless there are problems arising it shouldn't take very long,' said Sergeant Redmond.

'Cannot you be more precise?' Pony-tail was indignant. 'Are we to anticipate an hour in Court? Ten minutes? This is quite distressing enough as it is . . .'

A door at the top of the room opened and silence

fell as a man in a dark suit quietly took his place in the Coroner's seat. The Court Clerk followed into a pew below him. After a deal of shuffling and conferring Sergeant Redmond moved off to stand by the wall with the other guards.

'This is Malachy Woulfe.' Austin introduced Pony-tail in low tones. 'A friend of Darragh's . . .'

The name struck a chord and I rattled it round my head for a few moments, trying to remember where I'd heard it before. Nothing came to mind.

'More than a friend.' Malachy Woulfe took Alison's hand in a hairy clasp and held it tenderly. 'We also had a business relationship. Darragh didn't mention me to you?' Even his whisper carried around the court.

'No.' Alison's expression was dazed.

'How unfortunate.' Malachy Woulfe's sigh had a weight of unhappy resignation about it. 'I'm so terribly sorry to meet you under these tragic circumstances, Mrs McCann. What an unbearably tragic thing to have happened . . .'

'I didn't expect to see you here,' Austin whispered to me quickly, 'but I'm very glad you are . . . I hope you're . . . bearing up . . .'

'I'm fine.' I was surprised, and afraid for a moment that I would cry, when he gave my arm a reassuring squeeze. Turning away I caught Malachy Woulfe's profile in all the drama of its aquiline nose, darkly glittering eye and velvet-ribboned pony-tail. The feeling that I should know him nudged me again. I would think about it later, when the business of Darragh's death had been sorted. Or not.

Liam came through the door wearing his uniform

just as things were about to start. He spotted me and marched upright in my direction.

'Are you all right?' He put a hand on my shoulder and I nodded. The others looked at us, curious, blank and indifferent in turn, and I introduced him.

'This is my brother, Liam Hopkins . . .'

They were polite but wary, all three of them. Funny the effect a garda uniform has on people.

Liam left us when the Coroner began, in the low, reasonable tones of a man giving a maths lesson, to explain the Court's procedures. The inquest would make inquiry into the causes of death, nothing more. He looked sadly down on us all. 'We cannot say here today that anyone is to blame, nor indeed that anyone is *not* to blame. To the immediate family I must say that the autopsy report can be upsetting. Are there members of the immediate family present?'

Alison sat mute. I touched her arm and said, 'Mr McCann's widow is here.'

The Coroner leaned forward. 'I am quite agreeable to your leaving the Court during the autopsy report, Mrs McCann.' He was gentle.

'I'll stay,' Alison whispered.

And so it began. Alison's was the first statement and it was read by the Clerk. It said Darragh had left the family home on the day after Christmas. 'That was the last I saw of him,' the Clerk read, 'until the gardai called to our home, early on the morning of December twenty-seventh, and asked if I would identify his body. I went with them to the morgue. The body I saw there was that of my husband, Darragh McCann.'

The Clerk stepped down and the Coroner turned

to Alison again. 'Had your husband ever attempted to take his own life, Mrs McCann, or expressed any intention of so doing?'

Alison looked at him blankly, then shook her head. 'I don't know. No. I don't think so . . . not that I ever knew about anyway.'

'Did he seem to you in low spirits, or unduly depressed in any way over Christmas?'

'No. He was himself.'

'Thank you, Mrs McCann,' said the Coroner.

Witness followed witness. A teenage boy told how he'd been walking home after spending the night in his girlfriend's flat at Fisherman's Wharf. The tide was low and he'd seen the back end of a car sticking out of the water, its nose buried in mud at the bottom of the river. He'd called the guards.

A garda from Pearse Street Garda Station told how he'd taken the call and Sergeant Redmond got up to tell, slowly, and in careful legal language, how, as the investigating officer, he'd 'seen the car and the body removed from the river Liffey by a sub-aqua team, using hooks and a crane'. The keys had been in the ignition, the ignition turned on. The body appeared lifeless and had been removed from the car immediately. Sergeant Redmond had felt for and failed to find a pulse. Artificial respiration had been administered but hadn't appeared to bring life to the body. The Sergeant had examined 'the deceased's clothing and found documents revealing his identity to be Darragh McCann, with an address in Ballinteer, Co. Dublin'. An ambulance crew had taken the body to the Meath Hospital where the Sergeant had seen a doctor again

70

administer artificial respiration before pronouncing the victim dead.

An overweight fireman gave evidence about taking the body from the car. A diver gave evidence, and so did an ambulance man. Nothing that any of them said explained how, or why, Darragh came to be there and how, or why, he'd gone into the water.

The Coroner looked at a sheet in front of him. 'I will be calling Dr McMahon next,' he said, 'and feel obliged to remind family members that they might wish to leave for this part of the proceedings.'

Malachy Woulfe cleared his throat and stood and announced, with the air of a man offering to go to the front, that he was willing to wait outside with his 'poor, dead friend's wife' if she felt she wanted to leave. Alison stood up.

'I'll wait outside,' she said.

She walked slowly from the Court on Malachy Woulfe's arm and the doctor rose to give evidence. Short and sixtyish, he had elegantly waved hair, a narrow, foxy face and rocked on his heels as he carefully positioned a pair of bifocals on his nose. He spoke in a raspy voice.

'There were no marks or injuries on the body of the deceased, just a lot of watery fluid in the lungs. The skin colouring, along with the wrinkling of the hands and feet, indicated that the body had been in the water some ten to twelve hours.' He looked at the Coroner over the gold rims of the bifocals. 'A sudden immersion in very cold water may cause immediate cessation of breathing and precipitate death by cardiorespiratory inhibition. This does not appear to be what happened

71

in this case. The evidence indicates that drowning took place. Water appears to have descended deep into the principal bronchi and thrust the residual air beyond it, causing gross distension of the lungs. This distension we call "ballooning". Also, in this instance, during the agonal struggle to survive, air and water were gulped into the oesophagus and both were found in the cardiac end of the stomach, along with silt, weed and other foreign matter.'

I let out a long, slow breath and wished to God I'd gone outside with Alison.

The Coroner intervened. 'It is your opinion then, Dr McMahon, that the fluid in the lungs indicated the immediate cause of death to have been by drowning?'

'Yes, Coroner, I was convinced of this.' Dr McMahon cleared his throat. 'There was proof of the victim's drowning in the fact that alcohol was found fouling the air passages and diatomaceous matter had entered the circulation. This would mean, of course, that the victim was alive when he went into the water. Serious disturbances of fluid balance and blood chemistry ensue immediately upon inhalation of water. The circulating blood was diluted and electrolyte concentration reduced. The red cells had swollen and burst and hyperkalaemia had ensued owing to haemolysis . . .'

'Thank you, Doctor.' The Coroner's interruption was curt. 'I wonder if you could tell the Court whether or not the amount of alcohol found was significant? Was it, in fact, a factor in the victim's death?'

'Both blood and urine samples proved positive as regards alcohol,' Dr McMahon spread elegant fingers, 'and both were very high – 459 milligrams in the blood level, reflecting between fourteen and fifteen glasses of spirit alcohol. There was also evidence of drugs having been taken.'

Beside me Austin Finn made a small protesting sound and put his head in his hands. I sat staring at the doctor, rigid with disbelief. He was wrong. Darragh had been too vain, too self-preserving, to do drugs. He would never, for the same reasons, have swallowed an entire bottle of any spirit.

Not unless he'd been intent on killing himself.

'The evidence,' the doctor went on, 'was of some valium or librium present. But it was the alcohol present which was of a high toxic range.'

The Coroner turned to Austin and me.

'In lieu of the presence of a family member,' he said, 'I must ask if either of you know of any difficulties the victim may have had with drugs or alcohol during his life?'

'None,' I said. 'He didn't have a problem with either.' I stopped, stricken suddenly by a vision of Darragh by my Christmas tree, laughing, a little unsteady, a week before he died. But tipsy was what he'd been, not drunk. And it had been Christmastime; everyone had been celebrating. 'He was a social drinker,' I said, 'and I was never at any time aware of him taking drugs.'

'You knew the victim well?'

'Quite well. He was the father of my seven-year-old daughter.'

'I see,' said the Coroner. 'And your name?'

'Norah Hopkins. I last saw Mr McCann about a week before he died.'

'I'm sorry to have had to ask you these questions,' said the Coroner.

Austin Finn put a hand on my arm. Muttering 'Excuse me' and 'This has to be said', he stood up.

'The . . . victim, Mr McCann, was my business partner and a friend. I feel constrained to tell the court that I too considered him merely a social drinker.'

'Were you aware of him taking drugs of any kind?'

'I was not aware of him taking drugs.'

'I see. I presume, Dr McMahon,' the Coroner studied a sheet in front of him, 'that the Court has heard the last of the details of your medical evidence?'

'Well, yes, I . . .'

'Thank you. I will ask then that the victim's wife be brought back to Court. I feel her evidence is a necessity at this point.'

Alison, again on Malachy Woulfe's arm, came palely through the door. She sat between Woulfe and Austin Finn and turned large, red-rimmed eyes on the Coroner.

'Did your husband have any difficulties with drugs or alcohol during his life, Mrs McCann?' he asked.

'Not really,' Alison whispered.

'Had he been drinking before he left the house on December the twenty-sixth?'

'Some whiskey. It was Christmas Day . . .'

'Forgive me, Mrs McCann, but I am obliged to ask if your marriage was experiencing difficulties?'

'No.'

'The fact of Miss Hopkins and her daughter wasn't causing undue distress?'

'I didn't know about any of that . . . about her . . . until after he was dead.'

'And your husband, according to the evidence,

didn't leave either a note or letter indicating a wish to end his life?'

'If he did it hasn't been found.'

'I see. Well, in that case . . .' The Coroner turned to the doctor. 'Your summation of the medical evidence, Dr McMahon, is that death was in fact due to drowning?'

'Indeed. There were all the signs of serious disturbances of fluid balance and blood chemistry which ensue immediately upon inhalation of water,' the doctor rasped along at speed, 'as well as the fact that the circulating blood was diluted and electrolyte concentration reduced . . .'

'But none of this tells us *how* the victim came to drown?'

'However the victim came to drown, Coroner – whether accident, suicide or murder – the actual process of drowning takes the same course. There were no injuries in this case and so no suspicion of foul play. Drink had been taken in large quantities, however, and some drugs had also been taken.'

The Coroner thanked him and said he would now begin his summing up. Malachy Woulfe cleared his throat and got to his feet.

'I would like to add something to the evidence given here today,' he said.

The Coroner gave him a politely assessing look. 'Would you care take the witness stand?' he asked.

'That won't be necessary, I would like to bear witness to the late Darragh McCann's commitment to life,' said Malachy Woulfe. 'He was involved with me in a . . . business venture of some importance. The production of a play, to be precise. It was an undertaking to which he was completely pledged and which he wanted very much to see to its conclusion. I cannot believe, given his commitment and enthusiasm, that he would have taken his own life.'

He inclined his head and sat down. The Coroner thanked him, said he would take what he'd said into consideration and went into his summing up of 'the evidence at this inquest into the tragic death of Darragh McCann . . .'

Tragic death. Darragh McCann. For just a minute I closed down my eyes, ears and heart. Life and the Coroner went on.

'. . . indicates that this young man's death was caused by drowning when he entered the river Liffey in his car. The evidence shows too that though death occurred in the river itself he was nevertheless aided by the fire ambulance team and pronounced dead in the Meath Hospital. The gardai have confirmed that there was no third party involved and no note or letter was found on or about the deceased. There is therefore no evidence that the late Mr McCann deliberately intended to take his own life.' He paused and went on more slowly. 'Normally, in a drowning case where there is no witness, the verdict is an open one. In this case, the evidence quite clearly points to death by misadventure. This is similar to an Accidental Death but, because of the alcohol level and what this indicates, I am obliged to record a Death by Misadventure.'

I felt an odd sense of relief, vindication even. Misadventure I could bear. Misadventure had a ring to it. Suicide would have been unendurable.

Alison began to sob. Austin Finn put an arm around

her while Malachy Woulfe, all manly protectiveness, stood and glared at the Coroner and gardai. The Coroner offered her his sympathies.

'You are left to bear the burden of his sad death,' he said. 'It will not be an easy thing.'

Chapter Eight

Wednesday, 5 January

It was dark when we came out. We'd been less than an hour in court but rain-clouds had killed off the daylight.

'The normal processes of life must go on,' said Malachy Woulfe as we stood on the pavement. 'A drink, if not two, is called for. Name your hostelry of choice, ladies, and we will repair there instantly . . .'

The mock theatrics finally jogged my memory cells. Malachy Woulfe was a theatre director who appeared more often in social columns than he directed plays. His work was well regarded though, and his fans legion.

'If either of you has a car nearby I'd appreciate a lift home,' I said. 'I'm sure Alison would too.'

'I haven't been introduced to this lovely young woman . . .' Malachy Woulfe worked his eyes from my feet to the tips of my damp, frizzy hair. Austin did the honours and we shook hands.

'Delighted.' He gave a despondent smile. 'Please forgive my earlier frivolity, Norah. It was inappropriate.' His boyishly contrite act was some feat given his Faustian appearance and age, which must have been at least forty-five. 'My suggestion that we share a drink together was intended as a celebration of our mutual friend's life.' He drew Alison to his side. 'I would like to talk a little about the play we were producing,' he gave her a look of great kindness, 'though today may not be the most suitable of times. Just say the word and I will deliver you both to your respective homes. We can always arrange to meet again.' He made it sound as if a postponement would be a personal and global disaster.

'I'd like a drink,' said Alison.

'Then let it be in the Gresham Hotel.' Malachy cheered up immediately. 'It's reasonably close and comfortable.'

I decided drinks were a good idea after all. Talk of a play had made me curious, to say the least.

Malachy Woulfe drove with more energy than skill and wrapped a protective arm around Alison as we walked along a sleety O'Connell Street to the hotel. We'd beaten the early evening customers by an hour or so and had the warm, plush burgundy bar to ourselves. We'd arrived ahead of Austin too, still apparently somewhere in traffic. Malachy's baritone ensured us immediate attention. I ordered a Pernod. Alison asked for a gin and tonic.

Stripped of his raincoat, the director was revealed in a tight, black roll-neck sweater and black jeans. Alison refused to take off her leather coat. The drinks arrived and we raised our glasses to Darragh.

'Your husband, Mrs McCann,' said the director, 'has left behind him something which will stand in times to come as a monument to his passion for life, his dedication to the arts . . .'

'What are you talking about?' Alison's small voice was impatient.

Malachy Woulfe coughed and took a breath and said, 'I will speak plainly. Darragh had planned to surprise you with the news of his investment in the play I am currently directing. It's a new work, and a fine one, and could very well become the play of the decade. Darragh believed in it passionately, and in the production, and was intensely involved. I feel privileged to have known him.'

Alison, staring at the table top, looked as if she was concentrating hard on not fainting. Malachy covered her hand with his.

'I'm sorry this has come as a shock,' he said. 'Darragh planned to bring you to the first night and to tell you then.'

Alison shifted her stare to his hand. 'What do you mean when you say he invested in a play? Are you saying he put money into it?'

'Yes.'

'How much money?'

'Quite a lot. He was the sole backer.'

'He was paying for everything then?'

'More or less. Yes. You could say that. He put cash in the bank and he let me get on with the job, didn't interfere.' Malachy lifted Alison's hand and touched her wedding ring gently. 'There wouldn't be a play without him,' he said.

'But we were in debt . . . he said we couldn't go on holiday . . .' Tears spilled silently down Alison's cheeks. 'If he had money why didn't he give it to us? To me and the children?'

Malachy Woulfe turned her hand over in his and studied its palm. Alison went on silently crying and he put her hand down, his braggadocio seemingly deserting him. He looked like a man suddenly uncomfortable in the role he'd set himself to play.

I was as shocked by his news as Alison, though for different reasons. The way I saw it, Darragh, a man of many parts, had finally managed to put his money where his mouth was.

'Darragh must have known what he was doing,' I said.

'He said nothing about it.' Alison lifted her drink. 'He never once mentioned a thing. Everything had to be a secret with him.' She sipped the drink. 'I was thinking to myself, the morning when they brought me to look at him in the morgue, that at least there would be an end now to all the secrecy, that there would be no need for it any more . . .' She looked at me. 'But it's worse than when he was alive. There's no end to it. God alone knows what's to come.'

I couldn't find a thing to say to her.

'Will the play make money?' she asked Malachy Woulfe. 'Does Austin know about this?'

I had to hand it to her. She was displaying more survival instincts than I'd given her credit for. Given the nature of their business it seemed natural to assume that Austin would be privy to any investments made by Darragh. But then Darragh had never organized his life along natural assumptions. Malachy faced Alison and assumed a no-nonsense role.

'The play opens in just over a week.' He was terse. 'It's one of the best plays I've come across in a decade. It's going to make money. For everyone.'

There was no need for him to spell out his predicament. His play's backer had died, suddenly and most likely without leaving a will. He had, however, left an

81

ill-provided-for widow and two children who might, just might, be entitled to lay claim to the money used to fund the play. Malachy Woulfe was deeply concerned.

'What theatre will it be playing in?' I asked.

'The Tivoli. Exactly the right venue for this kind of play . . .'

'What kind of play is it?'

'Powerful. A contemporary Dublin story that takes a look at where we're at, warts and all. More warts, in fact, than anything else . . .'

'Why did Darragh back it?'

'The playwright's a friend of his . . . was . . .'

'Are we talking about a play by Conal Bergin?'

'The very man. Do you know him?'

'Yes.'

'When Conal didn't come to us for his Christmas dinner I thought it was because last year's was such a mess.' Alison sounded bleak. 'Now I don't know what to think . . .'

'Where's Conal now?' I asked Malachy.

'God knows.' He poked a finger in the air to attract a waiter. 'I'm for another drink, if there's service to be had around here . . .'

'Shouldn't the writer be around for rehearsals?' I persisted.

'Yes and no. He was around for the first three weeks, then he cleared off. Got his school holidays and went. Best thing he could have done, really. There was a bit of tension building up, all very normal but he decided to take a break from it. Should be back any day now.'

'He hasn't been in touch?'

'No. But that's not important. The playwright's job

ends on the page. It's up to the director, and the actors too of course, to make it work after that. Conal knows the score . . .'

He stopped and made signals as Austin appeared and stood searching the growing crowd. Spotting us he approached, pulling up a chair as he came near. Malachy actually mopped his brow.

'How long did you know Darragh?' Alison ignored Austin.

'Darragh . . .' The director sighed. 'Hard to say, really. Some years. He was always around, you know how he . . . was. I used to meet him off and on. What'll it be, Austin?'

While Malachy ordered another round Alison stood, unbuttoned and took off her coat. Underneath, covering a body Kate Moss would have envied, she was wearing a short black dress with a chain belt. As an ensemble it did everything for her small, perfect body.

She was a nymphet, and there wasn't a man in the bar who didn't notice. Malachy Woulfe certainly did. Alison sat primly waiting for her drink.

'I hope I haven't upset you with all of this news.' Malachy rested warm, moist eyes on her. 'When you've had time to absorb things you'll see that it's a rather magnificent situation. This play will stand as a legacy to Darragh. We'll dedicate it to him, it'll be in the programme. I'm sure Conal will agree. It's called *The Eleventh Hour* and we're looking at the West End, maybe even Broadway. Darragh's left you a future, Alison, something that could grow for you and the kids . . .'

It was a Willy Loman-like performance, and it was wasted on Alison.

'You'd have to say that, wouldn't you?' she interrupted him wearily. 'I'm off to the ladies.'

Malachy's eyes followed her all the way out of the bar. Austin watched him watching her. When she was out of earshot he said, 'I'm sorry you felt you had to tell her today, Malachy. There was no need. It could have waited, been done more gently in a few days' time.'

'Done more gently by whom?' Malachy picked up his drink. 'By you?'

Austin's small shrug conveyed a hurt he attempted to hide by flicking fluff from the sleeve of his suit. Even suits have feelings, as Darragh could have told Malachy, especially when the person inside was Austin.

'Laughable or not, I'd planned to tell Alison this weekend.' Austin gave me a wry look. 'I was banking on a little help from you, Norah, after I'd filled you in on things first, of course. The idea came to me today, when I saw the two of you together.'

'What exactly were you planning to tell me?' I asked.

'More or less what you've found out from Malachy. That Darragh had put a considerable amount of money into backing his friend Conal Bergin's play before he died.' Austin loosened his tie, opened two shirt buttons and leaned forward with his hands dangling between his knees. His expression was perplexed, and hurt. 'There's something else too. Something that's looking very messy.' He rubbed a hand across the back of his neck as if to loosen the muscles there. 'I didn't bring this up at the inquest because it might have upped the ante on the suicide theory. Darragh's youngsters could do without a suicide for a father.' He paused. 'Thing is, it seems likely that the money Darragh put into the play, and maybe more that I haven't yet discovered, wasn't his to invest in the first place.'

'What exactly are you telling me?'

'Darragh, as far as we can make out in the firm, was playing around with clients' money. In simple terms, he wasn't making the careful investments in pension plans he should have been. It's looking as if . . .' he studied the toes of his shoes '. . . he dabbled in alternative investments quite a bit – and not just with money from his own clients' accounts either.'

'You mean he invested money belonging to people who were your clients as well?' Out of the corner of my eye I saw Malachy Woulfe had dropped all pretence at boredom. Austin hadn't dropped his voice so clearly wanted him aware of things too.

'All of this is very preliminary.' Austin's eyes met mine. Shattered about described the way he looked. 'We've only just begun to uncover these few . . . irregularities. Christ, Norah, you've no idea what a shock this is, what it means to me, to the company. It's looking as if we could be fucked, to put it bluntly. I trusted Darragh. I thought he was a friend as well as a partner . . .' His jaw looked rigid enough to crack.

'Take it easy, Austin,' I said. 'You don't know the full story yet. You said so yourself. Things might not be as bad as you think. Maybe there's an explanation . . .'

The sheer banality of this made me stop. The explanation seemed to be that Darragh, finally, had gone over the top and into fraud of some kind. I was shocked, but most of all I was angry. If he'd wanted to gamble and make money then exploiting clients who trusted him was a shabby way to do it. At the core of my anger there was a sense of betrayal. Like Austin, I'd believed he had a certain integrity.

'There's an explanation all right,' Austin said, 'and it's that Darragh was ripping off the company. What we don't know is by how much and if the ruin is total.' He pulled a ruefully apologetic face. 'You don't need to be burdened with all of this, Norah, and maybe I shouldn't have told you. It's just that things are going to be messy for the next while and I thought it better to be straight with you. Alison's a bit of a . . . hermit. Doesn't have many women friends. Maybe you'd help me out on this one?'

'I'm not sure what I can do . . . or what you want me to do . . .'

Austin had a wife, Sheila. I'd met her once, briefly. Beautiful after an icy fashion and a more acceptable person to explain things to Alison than the woman he'd been unfaithful with. Or maybe not, given the iciness.

'I'm not sure myself what I want you to do. Be available, I suppose,' he flashed his quiet smile, 'in case I need back-up and support with Alison. The youngsters need her. She's going to have to keep it together for them.'

This caring individual was a side of Austin I hadn't seen. 'What about money?' I asked. 'Is there any proviso in the partnership which looks after Alison in the event of Darragh's death?'

'Yes. That's all looked after.' Austin finished his drink in a gulp. 'We set up an arrangement when he came into the company. Alison will be taken care of.

The children too.' He paused. 'There's nothing in writing to provide for you, or your daughter. I'm sorry.'

This didn't surprise me. 'I'll do what I can to help you with Alison,' I said.

'You're great, Norah, a terrific woman. I appreciate it.' Austin said this with an intensity which made me uncomfortable. 'We weren't making money in the company. We were ticking over, just about, but we were safe and there were a few big accounts in the offing. Could be Darragh went ahead of himself on those too . . .'

'Look, this is all very tragic but there *is* another side to it,' Malachy Woulfe, who'd been indulging in some deeply noisy sighing, interrupted loftily. 'This is a damn good play I'm directing. All this talk about risking money isn't important, not when put in the context of the money which is to be made by this play. *The Eleventh Hour* will make more than enough to recoup everything Darragh put into it . . .'

'For whom?' Austin's tone was mild.

'What do you mean?' Malachy asked.

'Who gets the profits? Darragh's dead. Who's his beneficiary?' Austin was businesslike. 'Were the profits to go back into the production company, into an account of Darragh's own, into future plays? Or were they to go to Alison and the children? Do you know?'

'No, I don't know.' Malachy flicked an impatient hand. 'None of that is my concern. He came along, put the money up front for the production and, naturally, as far as we were concerned, he would have been the one to benefit. The money's gone, you do realize that? It's all gone into the production. There's no way you can take it back . . .'

Austin shrugged. 'I'll have to take a look at the way it was done, and where the profits go.'

'Fine by me,' Malachy said.

'Alison's taking forever.' I stood. 'I think I'll go and see what's keeping her . . .'

'Good idea.' Malachy looked around as if he expected Alison to be stretchered in. 'Could be she's . . . well, she's a delicate creature, isn't she?'

Alison looked anything but delicate when I found her in the ladies. Encouraged by a stick woman in a leopardskin skirt, she was leaning into the mirror and putting the finishing touches to a kohl job on her eyes. She'd already piled her hair wispily on top of her head and applied a ruby lipstick.

'We were worried about you,' I said. 'You've been up here a while . . .'

'You'd no need to worry.' Alison's eyes, hugely luminous in the centre of the kohl, met mine in the mirror.

'Poor pet,' said the stick woman. 'She was in ribbons about her husband dying so I said to her the only thing for it was to put a good face on things. Didn't I, pet?' The woman took a pin from her own hair and slotted it as extra security into Alison's topknot. 'There now, you look just smashing. No point in letting yourself go just because your fella drives himself into the Liffey, is there?'

'No,' said Alison.

The woman flashed me a wide smile. 'Doesn't she look smashing? Are you a friend of hers?'

'Yes, and yes,' I said. Thing was, Alison didn't look half bad, in a Spice Girl sort of way. Even allowing for the stick woman's obvious hand in things, the kohl, lipstick and hair dramatically emphasized her doll-like prettiness.

'If you've got it, flaunt it, I always say.' The woman toyed with her own platinum locks. 'My name's Lisa, by the way. The minute I saw your friend I knew she had to be saved from herself. I said to her that life is for the living and that she'd have to put herself first from now on, didn't I, pet?' She fussed around Alison, dusting stray hairs from the shoulders of the black dress. 'That's exactly what I said to you, pet, isn't it?' She nudged Alison who, still staring into the mirror, hadn't answered.

'You did.' Alison nodded with reasonable enthusiasm and Lisa turned to me. She was about thirty-five. As well as the leopardskin skirt she was wearing a black leotard top and several gold chains.

'I lost my own fella in tragic circumstances ten years ago,' she said, 'so I know what it's like. A bit of a push at the right time works wonders and she looked like she needed a dig out. She'll be grand now, won't you, pet?' Alison, in the mirror, nodded again. 'And you'll keep a good eye on her, won't you?' This to me. 'Make sure she looks after herself, keeps putting a face on things. The dress is great,' she touched the belt around Alison's hips, 'but no good having the body and the clothes if you don't do something about the face. Now,' she gathered the scattered make-up and wrapped it in a tissue, 'I'm making you a present of this lot. Until you get your own.' She handed the tissue package to Alison who, wordlessly, shoved the lot into the bag hanging from her shoulder.

'Remember all I told you,' said Lisa. 'Think of me and all that I said every day when you use these. Do you hear me now?'

'Thanks,' said Alison.

Lisa gave her a hug and picked a pale silver fur from a chair. Sweeping from the room on three-inch boot heels she stopped at the door to blow a kiss.

'Always remember, things could be worse,' she said. 'My fella threw himself on a knife. Now that was a real mess.'

'Do you think she was sent to me?' Alison stared at the closed door.

'I doubt it,' I said.

'I think she was.' Alison turned to her reflection in the mirror. 'I think she was sent to tell me to get myself together for a reason.'

'Sent my whom?' It was against my better judgement to pursue the subject but Alison was worrying me. 'And for what reason?'

'Sent by Darragh. I think all that's happened has happened for a reason. I've been thinking about it since I came up here and met Lisa. She's a part of what he's doing. The men are the rest of it. Darragh has arranged things so that they'll all look after me, make sure I'm all right.'

'I'm not sure I follow,' I said slowly. She looked quite sane but you never know. 'What men?'

'The men downstairs.' Alison spoke with infinite patience, as if explaining something to an idiot. 'Austin is going to sort out the money for me,' she counted off on her fingers, 'Malachy's doing this play and Conal wrote it. Don't you see? They were his friends and now they're all around me, carrying on what he was doing and looking after me. Darragh arranged it all. He put the money into Conal's play so as I'd have a nest egg and now,' she smiled, quietly confident and pretty, 'well, now he's sent Malachy along to look after me. I know I'm right. I can feel it.'

'You mean,' I stared at her, 'that you've decided to replace Darragh with Malachy?'

'I have to have someone to look after me,' she pointed out, 'and Malachy likes me. He's meant to, Darragh sent him.'

Clearly, I had not been sent by Darragh since he appeared to be sending men only to look after his widow.

'Darragh gave me this dress for Christmas, you know.' Alison smoothed the wool over her hips. 'He said things were going to get better. Now he's sent Lisa to point out to me that I'm still a woman . . .'

So women did have a place in Darragh's scheme: even if it was only for the purposes of heading Alison in the direction of the nearest man.

'Tell me, Alison.' I eyeballed her in the mirror as she smudged on more kohl. 'Why are you so certain Darragh took his own life? The police don't seem to think he did and the Coroner didn't think so either . . .' I took a brush to my hair. Some healthy pulling and tugging at the frizz relieved some of the rage building in me at Alison.

'Because I don't believe he'd have gone down the quays alone at Christmastime unless he had it in mind to drive himself into the river.' Alison turned from the mirror and put her arm through mine in a positively friendly way. 'There's no point in us worrying about it any more. The police haven't said one thing or the other and the Coroner more or less said there wasn't enough evidence to say definitely what had happened either.'

She stopped and I faced the facts. Alison for whatever reason, *wanted* to believe Darragh had committed suicide.

'But *why* would he commit suicide, Alison?' I asked her, softly.

Maybe the answer lay in Mollie's tale of a row on Christmas Day. Maybe not. I knew nothing of Darragh's other lives but taking his life seemed such an unlikely thing for him to do, no matter *what* the problem.

'I don't know,' Alison shrugged, 'there were a lot of things I didn't know about Darragh.' She paused. 'Now I'll never know.'

Amen to that, I thought and caught my hair back and knotted it. 'I'll just freshen up,' I said to Alison who, like an obedient child, nodded, sat on the chair, crossed her legs and studied the wine-coloured carpet.

What I thought about as I splashed my face and mopped it dry was that there were too many things which would never be known about Darragh. It could be that I was denying reality, that his life had become such a mess there was only one way out.

His death had to be either suicide or an accident. If it had been an accident then it had happened while he was blind drunk and drugged and driving along a part of the quays which went nowhere but to the sea. Why would he have got drunk and driven down there? Why would anyone do a thing like that unless it was to deliberately take their own life? Alison just might be right . . .

The other alternative, which opened a whole other can of worms, was that he'd been forced into the river.

'We should go back down to the bar,' I said.

The mood between the two men waiting for us was not good. Malachy, elegantly smoking a cigar with an ankle resting on a knee, had adopted a disdainfully indifferent pose. Austin was engrossed in the evening newspaper.

They stood when we came in and for a moment it looked as if they were both going to take to their heels and vanish through the door. Alison's metamorphosis froze them where they were. It lasted until Malachy seized the high ground of conviviality.

'Everything all right, ladies?' His beam was for Alison alone and she, not unaware of her effect on him, gave him a timorous smile and slid into her seat.

'Fine, thank you,' she said. 'We met a friend in the ladies.'

'It's time I was off.' I didn't sit down. 'I'm sure we'll all meet again soon.' I'd had as much of the fall-out from Darragh's death as I could take for one day.

'You'll be along to the play's opening night?' The impressive boom was back in Malachy's voice.

'If that's an invitation I'll be delighted,' I said. 'When's the opening?'

'Thursday, January the thirteenth. Curtain goes up at 8 p.m. sharp.' Malachy, having given me as much of his time as I was worth, focused his attention on Alison. 'It may all be more than you can deal with just now,' he took her hand, 'but it would hugely encourage the cast if you would come along to the opening too, Mrs McCann. I cannot tell you how delighted I would be myself to see you there.'

93

'I'm not sure . . .' Alison sounded a bit panicky. 'I'll see how I feel next week.' She fiddled with her hair and crossed and uncrossed her legs, showing them to great effect. 'Darragh's only just dead . . . it doesn't seem right . . . I never go to plays . . .'

Malachy, displaying great social agility, immediately backed off. 'You do what feels right to you,' he said. 'Just take your time and please, please don't feel under any obligation.'

Keen as I was to leave, the amount of loose ends abounding bothered me. I tried to tie up at least one.

'When is Conal coming back?' I asked. 'He'll have to be told about Darragh.'

'He's due back tonight or tomorrow.' Malachy, still holding Alison's hand in his, was peevish. 'He said he'd be back a week before the opening, for the last round of rehearsals.' He stroked Alison's hand. 'It was his wish that he be incommunicado and he refused to leave a number, or an address. Said he wanted to do some work on something new.'

'I'll give him a call,' I volunteered. 'Arrange to meet and tell him when he gets back.'

'I've already left a message on his answering machine,' Austin said quietly. 'I've asked him to phone me at whatever time he gets in.' He stood. 'Time I was going too. I need to check a few things at the office.' He took a pair of sheepskin gloves from his coat pocket. 'I'll take you home, Alison, if you want to leave now. Otherwise I can send a taxi for you in an hour or so . . .'

'No need,' Malachy was brusque. 'I'll drop the lady home when she's ready.'

'That's that, then.' Alison looked relieved.

'Fine,' said Austin. 'I'll be in touch about sorting out business details next week, Alison. Take care of yourself in the meantime. You have my number if you need anything, day or night.'

We crossed the lobby together in silence. At the bottom of the entrance steps we braced ourselves against the ever icier wind snapping its way up O'Connell Street. It was 4.30 p.m. and homegoing crowds scuttled about us. Austin was the first to speak.

'What a bloody awful mess,' he said. 'Let's hope it can be sorted . . .' he moved me out of the way of a group of threatening yobs as they jostled past '. . . one way or the other.'

'Do you know,' I spoke carefully, 'where Darragh got the money he paid me and Emma every month?'

'No. I don't know.' He was silent for a minute. 'It's probable he was funding it by giving private tax advice . . .' He didn't sound convinced and I knew that, like me, he was hoping Darragh's investment dealing didn't stretch back over the seven years of Emma's life.

'I take it you didn't know about the play until . . . recently?' I asked.

'Didn't know about it until Malachy Woulfe phoned me a couple of days ago looking for Darragh.' He hunched so that his coat collar came over his ears. 'That was what made me begin to look into things. I tell you, Norah, this has not been the best New Year of my life.'

'I know what you mean,' I said.

Chapter Nine

Thursday, 6 January

Delia was waiting. She appeared in the door when I was half-way up the path. 'What was the verdict? Did the widow give evidence?'

I put an arm around her shoulder and took her with me to her kitchen, where I slumped into the single chair.

'The Coroner decided it was misadventure.' I kept my voice low because of Emma. 'Alison's statement was read out ... Can we leave this for now, Delia?' I pleaded, 'please? I'm really tired ...'

My reluctance to talk about the events of the afternoon had more to do with my confused state of mind than with tiredness. All I wanted to do right then was grab Emma, retreat upstairs and be with her there as if nothing had happened. I wanted to talk, see how she was, reassure her with lots of tender loving care.

'You're tired, child. I can see that.' Delia frowned. 'But there's something you'll have to hear before you go ...'

I started to get out of the armchair again. 'Can't it wait?' I said.

'No,' Delia, shaking her head, gently pushed me back into the armchair. 'You need to know, Norah, that there's a young man in a grey car watching this house. I saw him yesterday and again last night. I'd have put him out of my mind only he appeared this afternoon too, about four o'clock. He sat outside, opposite the house, and smoked three cigarettes and spoke into a mobile phone.'

'Delia, why would anyone want to watch this house?' I didn't remind her of the time she'd had a group of young skateboarders arrested as burglars.

'I don't know why he's watching the house,' Delia snapped, 'any more than I know why you think I'm half mad and that I'm imagining all of this. He was out there, Norah, large as life and twice as bold, a young man wearing a bulky, dark jacket and smoking cigarettes, one after the other, in his car.'

'Maybe he was waiting for someone . . .'

'That's what I thought the first time I saw him. An assignation, I thought, a married man meeting some trusting young woman he'd seduced.' She brushed crumbs from the worktop. Women were always the innocents in Delia's versions of life. 'I kept an eye on him,' she went on, 'thinking that if he was about to cause trouble and some young woman came to harm then I'd at least have his car number and a description. That was why I noticed him when he came back and did the same thing again, just sat there smoking and throwing the odd look at the house . . .'

'How do you know it was this house he was looking at?' Because I was still refusing to accept that Darragh's death was anything other than an accident I chose not to think Delia's watcher had anything to do with me.

'Because I'm not a fool and I could see what he was doing.' Delia pulled her brows together. 'I watched him, carefully, this afternoon. There's nothing wrong with my eyesight that these new glasses haven't corrected.' She paused. 'What I'm telling you, Norah, is that he was watching *your* door and *your* windows. He drove away after a long talk into the mobile phone.'

'He'd been given the wrong address,' I suggested. 'He was waiting for someone and when he checked on the phone he discovered he'd got things wrong and headed off to wherever he should have been . . .' This sounded to me a reasonable and logical explanation. I stood up. 'I'm sure that's it. There's no reason for anyone to watch my place – not unless Patsy's got some numbers racket going . . .'

'Very funny.' Delia was mulish. 'You can fool yourself all you like, Norah my girl, but I know what I saw. I'll be keeping an eye out even if you won't . . .' She stood and, though I saw she was offended, I couldn't go along with her anxiety. 'Emma's watching a video with the old man,' Delia said. 'I suppose you want to take her with you?'

Emma and Patsy were in the sitting-room and there was a video showing but together they were not. Still, one of them was old enough and the other young enough to be comfortable about ignoring each other.

I took Emma home and we settled, like old times, in front of the fire with our food and the Cosby show. Emma seemed fine, relaxed and chortling away as she snuggled against me. I didn't mention the inquest until Emma herself brought it up. She'd had enough thrown at her lately and I didn't want to give her any more information until she was good and ready.

'What happened at the thing about Daddy you went to today?' We were in the kitchen by then and she was getting ready for bed.

'Oh, just what everyone expected.' I was casual, brushing her hair and tut-tutting about the straggly ends. 'The people there talked about what happened and decided that Dad's car going into the river had been a terrible accident.' I lifted her on to my knee and kissed her and spoke into her hair while she leaned, like the baby she'd once been, into the crook of my neck. 'It's just something that has to be gone through when someone dies in an accident, or when it's not clear how a person died. What you have to do now is remember your dad the way he was, and all the fun we had together . . .'

I carried her upstairs and watched while she fell asleep. It didn't take long and she appeared fine. But I would have to watch her, carefully, during the weeks to come. She'd had far too much thrown at her in a few short days.

Downstairs again I listened to telephone messages. Harry Gibson had left one querying my well-being. Liam had issued a stern warning to put 'this bad business' behind me and Maisie had phoned 'for a chat'. The fourth voice was Mollie's, asking to speak to Emma. I rang Maisie. She gave me the same advice Delia had.

'You've done what you could,' she said. 'More than. What you do now is pick up your life and move on. There's nothing to be gained by hanging on, becoming involved with his widow. Cut loose, Norah, get on with it. Believe me, in time your gorgeous Darragh will become a sad and wonderful memory.'

'You're right,' I said.

But she was right only up to a point because she didn't know the whole story. I'd told her about the play and about Alison's insistence that Darragh had driven himself into the river. I hadn't told her, yet, about his investment gambles and the state in which he'd left things at Finn and McCann. Austin was still examining the damage; time enough to spread the bad news when I had a few more facts.

I made the call I'd promised to Conal Bergin but got only a terse answering machine voice demanding my name and number. I was drifting into fitful sleep an hour later when my phone rang. Conal Bergin was terse as his machine had been.

'You rang, Norah, what's wrong?'

'You got back from holiday then . . .' I wished I'd rehearsed what to say.

'Twenty minutes ago . . .'

'How was it? Where did you go?' How was I to tell him his friend was dead?

'It was a good holiday, thank you. I went skiing.' He stopped, waiting. I'd never phoned him outside working hours before.

'Skiing's fun. I've never been myself,' I said.

'Why did you phone, Norah?' Conal asked again, gently.

'To tell you that Darragh's dead,' I said. 'He died on St Stephen's Day.'

In the silence I told myself that if he hung up I would head straight for his place with a bottle of Jameson, that I would talk and explain to him for as long as it took. Testing whether or not he was still on the line, I said, 'It was an accident. His car went into the river.'

'Funny, I knew your phone call had to do with

Darragh.' Conal made a sound a bit like a laugh. 'Didn't take a clairvoyant to figure that out, of course.'

'This is a lousy way to give you the news,' I said.

'I'm glad I heard it from you . . .' He stopped. This time I waited until he was ready to speak. When he did he said, 'Tell me a bit more about how it happened.'

I gave him the inquest version of things. Then I told him about Alison's visit. When replies at his end remained monosyllabic I congratulated him on the play. I didn't tell him about Darragh's investment gambling but I did suggest we meet for lunch the next day.

'He's been dead twelve days.' He sounded tired; he was probably in shock. 'I go away for three weeks and come back to find him dead and dispatched . . .'

'Lunch,' I persisted. 'Tomorrow?'

'Fine.'

We met in Slatterys of Bath Avenue, a decent pub half-way between the school he taught in and Razor-bill's offices. We sat close to the fire. His hair was shorter than I'd ever seen it and looked as if he'd cut it himself. He seemed younger without his usual untidy locks, and vulnerable. The latter might have had to do with his pole-axed expression.

'I've ordered you a pint,' I told him as he sat down. Close up he looked as if he needed it. Despite obvious and recent exposure to wind and sun his face was a shade of grey.

'Thanks.' He smiled, sort of. 'Think I'll order a bite to eat too. Skipped on the breakfast.'

'Gave yourself a hair-cut instead, did you?' I asked. He pulled a face and ran a hand through the longish stubble.

101

'It had gone way beyond what the school's head is willing to tolerate.' He buried his face in the pint, coming up for air when he was half-way down. 'So Darragh's dead . . .' he said. 'I spoke to Austin earlier, and to Malachy Woulfe for a few minutes as well.' He straightened his specs. 'Darragh wanted me to stay around for Christmas . . . I didn't . . .'

'It would have happened anyway,' I said. 'It had nothing to do with you being here or not.' I wondered, though, how things would have gone *en famille* with the McCanns if their usual Christmas guest had turned up. Would Darragh have stayed at home?

'I told him to go find some other stray to haul in for the Christmas Day dinner. He was hurt. I shouldn't have said it.' He looked into the fire. Its light softened his face a little. 'I'll miss him,' he said.

'I know. We all will,' I said.

'He was different. A bit of a mess but different. A good friend.'

'True,' I said. 'It's a friend indeed who'll put the money up for a play.'

'Yes,' said Conal.

He stopped a passing barman and ordered the pub's brown stew for both of us. We waited in silence for it to arrive. Outside, it was another day of winds and cold rain and Slatterys, all well-worn wood and civilized bar staff, would have in normal circumstances been just the place to be. Conal took off his glasses and sat looking at them on the table. He put them back on when the stew came.

'How's Emma taking things?' he asked.

'Seems all right,' I said. 'Hard to tell, though. You know how it is with children, they don't exactly pour

102

out their feelings. It's only later . . .' I stopped. A persistent, aching worry that Emma was affected in ways which would only become apparent as time went on was not something I wanted to talk about just then.

'I'll call round this weekend if you like. She knew me as Darragh's friend. I might provide a sort of continuity . . .'

'Sounds like a good idea.' I smiled. 'Call on Saturday.' The visit might help him, at least. While we finished the stew I filled him in on events.

'Sad the way his lives came together at the end.' He pulled a rueful face. 'The worlds of finance, the theatre and wom . . .,' he stopped and muttered a miserable 'Sorry' and fell silent.

'It's all right,' I said, gently. 'I thought myself we were like the cast list for a bad play. Even to the lousy ending.'

'He'd never have driven himself into the river,' said Conal. 'It's just not the sort of thing he'd have done. The man loved life. More than that, he was just getting it together.'

'The play . . .' I began, but he cut me short.

'The play was only part of what was happening with him. He had plans. He said he'd arrived at what he wanted to do and he was going to go for it . . .'

'Tell me about the play,' I said. 'When did you write it? And where,' I leaned my elbows on the table and got down to the nitty-gritty, 'did Darragh get the money to put into it?'

'Nothing mysterious about it, though miraculous is an adjective which comes to mind. Darragh had an elderly client who wanted a part of his wealth to be invested "creatively", as he put it, before he died. I'd written the play and was toting it around to the usual suspects, without much joy, when Darragh asked for a copy to show this client. Within a week of reading it this old boy gave Darragh the go-ahead to put up whatever it would take to get a production off the ground . . .'

'Sounds miraculous all right,' I said, 'and lucky for you. He did it because he believed in the play?'

'So he said. I've never met this man, though I have spoken to him on the phone. He lives in a nursing home. Darragh had been trying to persuade him to come to the opening.'

'Who brought Malachy Woulfe on board?' I asked.

'That was my doing, I'd met him over the years and admired his work. I rang him on the off-chance, once the backing was there, and he was free and read the play and got us the theatre . . .' He made finger signals for a second round of drinks to the barman. I didn't want another but decided to keep him company. Good friends don't die every day.

We talked about Alison, and how she hadn't known about the play.

'Told me he'd no choice but not to tell her,' said Conal. 'The money man wanted his name kept out of it so things were done discreetly. He planned to tell Alison just before the opening.'

The barman arrived with our drinks and I chose words for what I wanted to say carefully.

'Austin seems to think that Darragh was using clients' funds without their permission . . .' This was about as delicately as I could put it. 'No chance the backing money came about the same way, is there?'

Conal moved his chair back and drummed his

fingers on the underside of the table. I couldn't tell if he was angry or just shocked.

'None at all,' he said, finally. 'The man whose money went into *The Eleventh Hour* chose his financial adviser deliberately. Darragh had been his accountant for a long time and told me this wasn't the first . . . creative investment he'd made for him. I don't know anything about the other dealings you mentioned but this one's on the level.'

I felt a weight slip away. Things were falling into place, Darragh fashion. The other investments Austin had spoken about would all turn out to be like this one, made on behalf of clients willing to take risks. I felt sure of it.

It didn't, yet, explain how or why he'd gone into the river. But it did mean he wasn't a crook.

'He was a bloody loyal friend,' said Conal.

I lifted my glass. 'Here's to him.' We drank, and for several minutes I thought I would weep. When I was sure I wasn't going to I asked, 'What's Malachy like to work with?'

Conal gave a rueful grin. 'We were enjoying what could be called a robust working relationship before I absented myself from the scene. He's imaginative and intuitive and ruthless, a good combination for getting things done. I'm not worried about the play. He'll do his best by it.'

'He's talking about inserting a dedication to Darragh in the programme,' I said.

'Good idea. You'll be at the opening? I'll need all the support I can get . . .'

'I wouldn't miss it for anything,' I said.

The pub was very full now, suits and anoraks and

woolly jumpers all damply steaming as close to the fire as they could get. A barman piled the fire higher with logs and it roared up the chimney.

'You'll burn the arses off us,' a woolly jumper protested. Conal reached behind him for his coat.

'It's getting too crowded in here. Fancy a bit of a walk?'

I walked beside him along Grand Canal tow path toward Baggot Street Bridge. The rain was intermittent now and there was peace in the quiet canal waters.

'This wasn't such a bad idea,' I said. 'Now tell me how you came to know Darragh.'

He kicked, with some force, at a fallen branch in our path. 'It was a bit later in the year than this when I first met him. I was part of a student drama group rehearsing a play of mine in a room over a pub on the South Circular Road. It was a massage parlour when we weren't there so I suppose we gave the place a whiff of respectability. We were in the pub afterwards, discussing the Pinteresque aspects of my work, when Darragh walked in.' He stared into the water and went on tiredly. 'He was wearing a suit, some dark colour, and he looked completely out of place. My mistake. Darragh was just never meant to be ignored and the suit was a statement. I don't remember how but he became part of our company. It took only a couple of drinks for him to convince me the play would make money and that he was the promoter I needed.' He gave a short laugh. 'God knows how he did it but he got us three nights in the SFX hall. We didn't make money but, by Christ, we had a good time.'

We reached Mount Street Bridge and climbed up to

the road from the tow path. Waiting to cross the bridge Conal shook his head.

'Seems odd now,' he said, 'but he'd never been near a theatre until then. That undergrad play started the craving.' We crossed the road and rejoined the tow path. 'Christ, I wish the bugger was here,' Conal said. 'I want to talk to him. I want to *know*.'

'I'd like to know myself,' I said.

He picked up a stick and threw it into the water. It bobbed along for a while before it got caught in reeds. 'A man contemplating suicide doesn't make plans,' he said.

'Not usually,' I sidestepped an old woman whose dog was sniffing at my ankles. 'Darragh was full of surprises.' The truth of this brought on a desolate ache. 'And far too full of secrets.'

The best part of the walk was over. A gusting wind brought ripples to the canal surface and sifted the reeds along the bank. Someone had dumped a supermarket trolley in the water and litter drifted and gathered around it. It reminded me of Darragh's car, sunk in the Liffey bed. The thought brought a shudder and Conal put an arm around my shoulders.

'Let's get away from here,' he said. 'It's cold.'

Chapter Ten

Friday, 7 January

Emma was unhappy. She took to going silently about the apartment, holding Mac in a strangled embrace. She didn't cry and she didn't moan and she certainly didn't tell me what was wrong. When bedtime came I sat on her bed while she pretended to go to sleep.

'I know you're awake, Emma.' I stroked her hair and felt again the awful, helpless ache inside. 'And I know you're upset. The thing is, we've got so many good things to remember about your dad. He'll never really be gone so long as we remember the times we had together . . .'

'He was stupid.' She kept her eyes closed.

'Your father was not stupid.' I allowed myself some righteous indignation. 'He was different, it's true, but that's not the same as being stupid . . .'

'Why did he drive his car into the river then, if he wasn't stupid?' She opened her eyes and stared at me.

'He didn't drive his car into the river on purpose, my love,' I said. 'It was an accident. He didn't want to die. He loved life and he loved you and me and . . .'

'Love, love, love, love . . .' She sat up and shot the word like pellets around the room. 'Love is all adults ever talk about. What good is love? He said he loved me. He said he loved Mollie and Justin too. But he still went and drove himself into the river. If he loved us all the way he said he did then he wouldn't have left us like that . . .'

Her hands were fists on the bedcovers and her face was a steaming red. There was a frightening adultness about her distress and when I reached my arms to her she stiffened again, so fiercely that I dropped them. She did allow me to stroke her hair.

'It was an accident, Emma,' I said. 'The guards and doctor all decided that too. The word they used was misadventure, which is a way of saying things just went wrong . . .'

'Mollie said on the phone that he was a brilliant driver and that he was fed up and went into the river on purpose . . .'

I caught her chin in my hand and turned her face up to look at me.

'Mollie's wrong,' I said. If her half-sister had been there I'd cheerfully have strangled her.

'No, she's not. That's what her mother says too . . .'

'That was before it was all investigated, before the evidence proved it an accident. Now we know the truth, which is that it was a terrible accident. So will you try to get some sleep? Things will look much better in the morning, I promise . . .'

'How do I know they will? You always say that . . . you say that about everything . . .' All at once she threw herself into my arms and began to sob. I rocked her hot, convulsing body against me, the way I had when she was a baby. Which of course is what she was again, for that while; an infant who was terrified that her mother as well as her father was going to leave her.

'I'll always be here,' I told her. 'You know that, don't you?'

She nodded, gulping. 'I just got a bit worried.' She shook her hair out of her eyes; my resourceful daughter making a comeback.

'Perfectly natural,' I assured her, 'but that face is a sight. We'd better splash it with some cold water . . .'

Dabbing her face in the bathroom I decided to take up Maisie's invitation to spend the weekend at Duncolla. It would be good for Emma. It would be good for me too. Duncolla, a prison during my growing years, had become the place I escaped to when life acted up. We'd changed, of course, me and Duncolla both – but Duncolla had changed utterly.

'We'll go down to the farm tomorrow,' I promised Emma as I tucked her back into her bed. 'You can skip school and I'll take a day off work.'

I turned off the light and sat with her in the wintry moonlight while I pondered the Mollie factor. If Emma's strange little half-sister filled some of the space left by Darragh then so much the better. How she filled it might be a problem. Conal Bergin was another who might fill some of the space. He'd said he would call to see Emma on Saturday. I wondered if he'd meant it.

He'd meant it all right. He phoned next day as Emma and I were leaving for Duncolla.

'Sounds like a good idea, you two getting out of town,' he said when I told him about the change of plan.

'Why don't you call on Tuesday, let me feed you here?' This invitation was motivated largely by politeness. Conal wasn't keen anyway.

'I've a better idea,' he said. 'Why not let me buy you a meal that night?'

'Surely you'll be up to your neck in play rehearsals?' Dining *à deux* wasn't exactly what I'd had in mind; I'd been offering a bite with Emma and me.

'I'm leaving the last-minute hysteria to Malachy. He's much better at it than I am. How about it?'

I agreed. When he suggested a restaurant I agreed to that too, not one bit sure the idea of a meal together was a good one. I'd got used to thinking of Conal as Darragh's *alter ego*. I didn't want him playing his ghost for the rest of my life.

Maisie had transformed the house I'd grown up in, creating noise where there had once been silence, colour where all had been drab monochrome. I'd grown up with the bare essentials; Maisie had added rooms and heating and replaced every stick of 'heirloom' furniture. She'd have got rid of the house too, if there had been a way to do it. But age had made it venerable, if not beautiful, and the house stayed. She had the car door open before I'd turned off the engine. We hugged and she yanked the bags from the back seat, ruffling Emma's hair as we went inside. 'How's my favourite niece?' she teased.

Emma skipped ahead after her cousins and Maisie gave me a critical stare.

'You're not looking too bad either, considering.'

'How's Gerry?' I asked.

'Gerry's fine. He's having a tractor looked at. He'll be back for dinner. First things first.' She dumped my bags in my old bedroom. 'And that means drinks for you and me.'

In the kitchen I watched her, large and carrot-haired, as she filled a couple of wine-glasses. Maisie had freckles and a wide mouth. She wasn't beautiful but beauty was what you thought about when you looked at her. We sat at her scrubbed table, the bottle of wine between us.

'Never knew a man to make such an almighty fuss about everything he did,' said Maisie, 'even dying . . .' We raised our glasses to Darragh and I gave her an abbreviated update on events. She sighed when I'd finished. 'Aren't you lucky you're not the woman he married?' This being rhetorical I didn't answer. 'How's Emma taking it?' she asked then.

'Up and down. I'm worried about her. Being here will cheer her up.'

'It may cheer her up for now,' said Maisie, 'but the rest will take time. Or another father. Anyone on the horizon?'

'No.'

'You're not getting any younger,' Maisie reminded me. 'These are your best years. You *need* a bit of love and a bit of sex . . .'

'Oh, shut up, Maisie. Tonight's not the time . . .'

'Couldn't be a better time,' she snorted. 'Nothing like a tragedy for putting things into perspective. It was my father dying made me get on my bike and go after your brother.'

She topped up my glass and checked our dinner in the oven. She topped up her own glass and sat down again.

'Emma's father has been a hindering presence in

your life since before she was born,' she said. 'But he's gone now. Let him go. What is it you're waiting for?'

'I'm not waiting.' I was tetchy. 'I just haven't met anyone else that I cared for . . .'

'Why?'

'Because I haven't, that's all.'

'It's because you haven't let anyone within an ass's roar of you. I just do not know how you do it,' her exasperation was real, 'nor *why* you do it.'

'Do what?'

'Do without a bit of love and how's-your-father. I couldn't.'

'You don't have to,' I pointed out, 'and a seven-year-old daughter limits the options.'

'Have you, at any stage in the last seven years, tried to seriously get to know a man?' Maisie eyeballed and, when I didn't answer, pushed me. 'Have you?'

'There hasn't been anyone I wanted to . . .'

'How do you know when you've refused to get to know anyone? Look, Norah, for the sake of your child as well as yourself you're going to have to get back in there with the living . . .' She came round the table and gave me a swift hug. 'You know what I'm saying to you, girl, and you know that I'm right. Take a chance on men again. There's someone, somewhere waiting to cherish you the way you deserve.'

I wasn't as sure as she was about this. 'I'm fine on my own,' I said, 'and I have Emma.'

'Oh, give it a whirl, Norah.' Maisie became impatient. 'You've nothing to lose.'

I wasn't so sure about that either.

My brother Gerry, who is slight and fair and has the gentlest of smiles, arrived soon after that. My adult relationship with my brothers had happened thanks to Emma. First Gerry and then, more reluctantly, Liam, had defied my father in support of me and my pregnancy. Gerry had even sold off a field to give me a nest-egg. Now, before sitting down to eat, Gerry and I spoke quietly together for a while. Over dinner we all talked about everything under the sun except Darragh. It made a welcome change.

Later, when the fire had died and everyone was in bed, I went for a walk across the fields. There's nothing like the pitch of a moonless countryside for bringing memories, and what it brought to mind that night was the episode, years before, which had left me deeply distrustful of garda discretion.

It too had to do with Emma. Back in Dublin after my father's 'banishment' of me, hurt and anger made me go to ground. I changed flats overnight, took a month off work and refused even to give Harry my new address. My father would be sorry, I told myself, and so would my brothers, when they eventually came to look for me and found I'd gone. I had no doubt that my father would come round.

He didn't. My brothers did though. They fought with him on my behalf for two weeks, bitterly and miserably by all accounts, and at last came to Dublin themselves to rescue me. Finding I'd disappeared they called in the gardai.

It had never occurred to me they would do this and so, when a four-strong force of gardai came hammering on my door early one morning I was petrified. By the time I got out of bed and let them in, every other flat-dweller in the building was aware of their morning raid on the first floor.

'Why didn't you keep your family and workplace informed as to where you were living?' demanded the surliest of the guards.

'I'm not obliged to,' I said, foolishly. 'My life's my own . . .'

'It is indeed and we live in a democracy,' his sarcasm had a weariness about it, 'and your blow for human rights has cost the taxpayer and wasted our time. Unless you want to spend time in the nearest garda station you'll contact your brothers to tell them where you are and sort out your differences with them.' His eyes were on my clearly pregnant belly. 'Do I make myself clear, Miss Hopkins?'

'Clear as . . .'

'Good. We'll wait while you use the telephone.'

They did too, all four of them, the bulk and weight of their presence almost suffocating me as I dialled. Their visit made me the subject of gawping and rumour and gossip in that house until the day I left to move to Makulla Square. I swore I would never, ever, look for garda assistance where tact and discretion were needed. When Liam, well-meaning but blundering and insensitive, joined the guards my prejudices about the force were confirmed.

I walked further than I'd intended that night but felt relatively at peace with myself by the time I went to bed. When the phone went in the night I awoke from the best sleep I'd had in a week to hear Maisie getting up to answer it. When she arrived in my bedroom minutes later she was an apparition in sprigged Viyella.

'There's a bit of a problem at your place in Dublin,' she said. 'Your landlady's on the line.' She handed me the phone.

'Delia, what's wrong?'

'Are you sitting down?' Delia asked.

'I'm in bed,' I said. 'It's two in the morning. What's happened?'

'There's been a burglary, Norah, a couple of yobbos broke into your flat. They got away and the guards have been and had a look at things and all of that . . .'

'How did they get in?' I'd left a light on and radio playing. As a security system it had always worked before.

'They broke in through the kitchen window. I didn't hear a thing.'

'You couldn't be expected to . . .' A horrible thought struck. '. . . Did they try to get into your place too?'

'No. The gardai say they may have been intending to, until I frightened them away.'

'For God's sake, Delia, you didn't go up to them, did you?'

'Don't you go telling me what to do in my own house,' Delia snapped. 'I phoned the guards when I heard the noises, and then I went upstairs with the dog. They were through the back window and down the back garden before Woodie could get a whiff of their ankles. One of them cut himself on the glass.'

'Oh, God, Delia . . .' I closed my eyes and felt Maisie poking me in the ribs.

'What is it? What's happened?'

I shook my head to clear it and opened my eyes. 'Burglars,' I said. 'The apartment's been broken into. I'll have to get back.'

'Bastards,' said Maisie. 'There's not a place in the country safe these days.'

116

Delia's voice piped from the telephone. 'No point in you coming back before morning,' she said. 'I told the guards all they wanted to know and they've gone. I told them too about the fellow I saw watching the place. They paid great attention to that, took a great deal of notes.' She didn't actually say, 'I told you so,' but might as well have. 'They say tomorrow will be time enough for you to go down to the station with a statement about what's taken. There doesn't look to me to be much missing anyway. The TV's still on its perch, and so are the stereo and video. The guards said your thieves were most likely looking for drugs or money, given their age.'

'Well, they wouldn't have found either. Did they thrash the place?'

'Not much. I got up there with Woodie before they really got going . . .'

'Turn on all your lights, Delia,' I commanded, 'and lock your windows and doors *tightly*. Those little shit-heads might still come back.'

'What makes you think they were small?' Delia protested. 'They were bulky enough, and tall too. They could be down below now for all I know. I'm phoning from your place. It'll give the old man something to think about if they arrive back for a visit.'

I didn't sleep a lot after that. I lay thinking about Delia's watcher, trying to figure out what in the hell was going on. I couldn't shake a feeling that the man watching the house and the burglars were somehow linked to Darragh's horrible death and secretive life. When I got back to Dublin at 10 a.m. next morning I felt as if I hadn't slept for a week.

117

Chapter Eleven

Saturday, 8 January

'I've been expecting you since eight o'clock.' Delia, as too often these days, was fretful and waiting. Hauling mine and Emma's bags out of the car, I found it hard to be cheerful. Emma stood looking at the house as if she expected it to ignite.

'Did they go into my room?' she asked. Delia put an arm around her shoulders and led her up the steps.

'They hardly touched it,' she said. Either this was true or she had cleaned up the room. I gave her arm a squeeze.

She'd been busy everywhere. Books ripped from their shelves had been stacked into piles, clothes torn from the wardrobe laid across the bed and the contents of ransacked drawers put into piles for sorting. Even so, the place looked as if anywhere which might have been a hiding place for drugs or money had been savaged. The kitchen and my bedroom were worst hit.

'Go down and see if Patsy needs anything,' I said to Emma, 'while Delia and I sort things out a bit.'

She went and Delia, keeping a triumphalist tone fairly low, asked, 'Do you agree with me now that the house was watched? That this was planned?'

'Looks very like it.' I slammed shut the drawer I'd just refilled with knickers and bras. 'If they didn't know before they'd want to have been blind as well as bloody stupid not to suss that a woman and child live here. Shit . . .' I felt frighteningly exposed.

'You'll have to get an alarm put in,' Delia interrupted. 'These people often come back to the scene of their crime.'

'I know,' I said. I could have done without reminding.

The broken kitchen window and a kicked-in cupboard apart, there wasn't a lot broken. They'd had themselves a bit of a destruction spree in the kitchen and the place was a farrago of thrown-about food. I swept and mopped and fulminated.

'The guards said these youngsters lose their heads when they don't get what they're looking for.' Delia scooped up a mush of squashed fruit. 'They were very interested when I passed on my bit of information about the house being watched . . .'

'Did they actually *say* they thought the break-in was connected to the house being watched?'

'Not exactly,' Delia admitted, 'but they were *most* interested. They said they would be following it up.' She glowered. 'Whatever that means.'

The phone rang. I hesitated and looked at Delia who looked at me. Funny how easy it is to fill the mind with foreboding. All I could think of as it rang and rang was Delia's description of the man in the car using a mobile phone.

'I'll get it,' I said.

It was Liam on the line. 'Gerry gave me your news.' He was huffy. 'I'll be over there in twenty minutes.'

'There's no need . . .'

The line went dead and I sighed. I should have

phoned him with news of the break-in. Trouble was, knowing Liam as well as I did, I couldn't separate him in my mind from the old image of blundering, insensitive gardai. The idea of him surveilling Darragh, when I allowed myself to think about it, gave me the shivers and reinforced my prejudices.

Delia went down to Patsy and Emma went up to her room. I wandered into the living-room and picked up a broken-spined book. Delia had said the gardai wanted a list of what was missing so I sought, and found, my most valued possessions – my mother's watch, a couple of first editions, a Clodagh Thornton print, jade earrings given me by Darragh and the silver spoon he'd given Emma when she was a year old – before going through everything else. The TV, video and sound system hadn't been taken either. I gave Liam the good news when he arrived. He went through the rooms slowly. 'They were probably disturbed then . . .'

'Delia disturbed them.' I paused. 'Do burglars often make return visits?'

'It's not unknown.' He was policeman-cautious. 'But we can do something about it in your case . . .'

'Do you mean have the place watched?' Images flickered of Darragh dead in the river and Delia's man in the car . . . 'I'll get an alarm system fitted too,' I said.

'I'll see to it.'

'The alarm system?' I asked.

'Yes. Now get yourselves ready and I'll drive you and the child down to the station in Rathmines to make your statement.'

I was in the bedroom changing when I noticed the photograph missing from its spot on the mantelpiece.

Puzzled, I scrabbled about, searching, hoping it had fallen down somewhere. I went on my knees under the bed, poked with a pole behind the dressing-table and wardrobe, emptied the basket of unwashed clothes. When it failed to turn up in or about the armchair I accepted it was really gone.

'Shit, and shit again . . .' I sat on the bed feeling angry and sick. The photograph had been taken in Grafton Street early in December by a Santa Claus photographer. It was the only one I'd ever had of Darragh, Emma and me together. It didn't make sense for the thieves to take it.

An ugly, paralysing fear began to slither and insinuate its way to the core of me. Something awful was going on and I was being dragged into it. Emma was being dragged into it. We were being watched. We'd been burgled. A photograph of us both with Darragh had been stolen. None of it made sense but it felt truly terrible.

I crossed to the window and did some deep breathing. This, along with the familiar and reassuring vista of wintry back gardens, a dog on the prowl, a few stripped Christmas trees, brought a sort of calm.

At the garda station Liam insisted on seeing the police report from the night before. None of the guards who'd answered Delia's call were on duty so he sat down alone to study it. Emma sat beside him and a policewoman, civilized and sympathetic, took me into a quiet room.

'Nothing missing that you've noticed?' She double-checked what I'd written down.

'Nothing . . .' I hesitated – old prejudices die hard and I didn't want overt police attention on myself and Emma. But the policewoman waited, wearily persistent, until I told her about the photograph. I described it, told her about Darragh's death and the house being watched. She took notes.

She had a lack-of-sleep paleness about her. When she suggested a coffee I sympathetically agreed.

'I'll be a couple of minutes.' She stood, looking as if she needed the coffee a lot more than I did. 'But while I'm gone I'd like you to draw up a list of those who knew you'd be away for the weekend.'

Several people knew I was going to be away and they were all people I trusted. When the policewoman came back I gave her Gerry and Maisie's names, as well as those of Delia and Patsy, Harry Gibson and, remembered at the last minute, Conal Bergin. She said nothing about the possibility of a link with Darragh's death. I left the station feeling not a lot of hope and a good deal of desperation.

At least one more person was added later to the list of those who knew we'd been away. I was catching up on work I'd brought home when Emma asked if she could phone Mollie.

'She won't know I'm back unless I do,' she said.

'She didn't know you were away,' I pointed out.

'Yes, she did,' Emma said. 'She rang before we left, when you were out putting petrol in the car, and I told her.'

'Well, then.' I turned her gently towards the phone. 'You'd better tell her you're back.'

If Mollie knew then God knows who else did. A list had become pointless.

When Emma was in bed I worked until the fire died on a manual to do with physical chemistry. When I'd finished I did what I'd done many times in the past: wrapped myself in a blanket, turned off the light and sat in the window looking out across the square.

I liked the peace of it at night, the still, shadowy quality to the old trees and railings. That night all it made me think about was the cost and effectiveness of an alarm system. I was wondering about the possibility of moving Woodie upstairs for a week or so when a pale grey car drove into the square and stopped on the road opposite the house.

Delia's car was a BMW and its driver, illuminated briefly as he dragged on a cigarette, was a shorn-headed young man. He wound down the window and flicked the dog end on to the road. Too late I shrank back into the room. He couldn't have missed me there as he glanced, then stared, up at my window. Slowly, without taking his eyes off my window, he helped himself to another cigarette from a packet on the dash. I moved when he dropped his eyes to light up, but froze again as he took a long, long drag, squinting narrowly in my direction when he exhaled.

In the cigarette's burning glow I'd seen a broad, narrow-lipped face with a flattened nose. It was not the face of a suburban BMW-owner.

What I did next was reckless, but seemed right at the time. When I dropped the blanket and grabbed my coat in the hallway I was reacting to a gut urge, driven by anger and an overriding fear for Emma's safety.

The man watched me coming down the steps. He'd

closed the window and I knocked hard on the glass with my knuckles.

'Open this window.'

He looked at me, his eyes the colour of the bottom of a fish-tank.

When he made no move to open the window, I knuckled it again, next to his ear. This time he turned on the engine and gave me the benefit of a thin smile as he revved the engine.

It was his sheer audacity that did it. I kicked the car door, hard enough to wish I'd worn a pair of boots. The man's mouth moved, viciously forming words I couldn't hear. When his hand moved to the gears I landed another kick to the door, then stood back as it opened.

'What the fuck do you think you're doing?'

He wasn't much taller than me but he'd an awful lot more muscle. His neck bulged and his chest barrelled beneath a white T-shirt worn under a nylon zip jacket.

'Trying to get your attention,' I said. 'I want to know why you're watching my home and I want to know what you know about last night's break-in.'

This was a lot more than I'd intended to say but he'd bent down to examine the door and there was a silence to fill.

'I don't know what the fuck you're talking about.' He straightened up. 'But that's a £30,000 car you're lashing into with your foot. I should break your fuckin' face in . . .'

'Break-ins a speciality of yours then?'

His face took on a purply-red tone and for a minute

I thought he was going to carry out his threat. I couldn't have done a thing to stop him. But he turned off the car engine and stood facing me. Delia had taken a pill to get some sleep so I had to just hope that someone else, somewhere in the square, was watching from a window. I was feeling very alone with this thug.

'I should get the guards over here, have you fuckin' arrested.' He made a fist of one hand and punched it into his open palm. 'Are you fuckin' mad, or what?'

'Why don't you get the guards? Maybe you can explain to them why you're parked here, watching my home, and what you were doing watching it a couple of nights ago too . . .'

'I'll say it again, you fuckin' madwoman, and I want you to listen to me this time.' He took a step closer. He smelled of unwashed teeth and cigarettes. 'I don't know what the fuck you're talking about. You'd better get out of my fuckin' sight before I do something you'll regret.'

I took a step backwards. He followed. 'You know exactly what I'm talking about.' I stood my ground. 'I want to know what's going on, why I was broken into and why you're . . .'

He grinned at me then, a sudden and horrible sight. 'If you were broken into, sweetheart, then maybe it's because you've got something someone wants, or,' he gave a snickering laugh, 'maybe they were after the family fuckin' silver. Ever think of that?'

He stood, legs apart, waiting for me to answer. I stared at him, at his gingery stubble and fish-tank eyes and knew I was in deep trouble. Men like him didn't go away until they got what they wanted.

125

'No,' I said. 'I never thought about it like that . . .'

'Maybe it's time you did, Norah,' he said my name very softly. My heart stopped. I kept my mouth shut.

'If I was you, Norah,' he rocked on his heels, voice still full of soft menace, 'I'd take very good care of my daughter, that's if I was you, like. I'd look after little Emma night and day, just in case anything happened to her. Lovely child, lovely. You must be right proud of her, all those lovely dark curls like her dad.' He looked up at the bedroom windows. 'I'm not you, mind, so all I'm doing is giving you a bit of good advice.' He smiled. 'And if anyone comes calling, Norah, and wants you to do them a bit of a favour like, then my advice to you would be to do that too. It's all for your own good, believe me.'

'Are you threatening me?'

'Threatening you? I'm not fuckin' threatening you, I'm telling you something for your own good. You're the one came charging out of the house and tried to smash my door. All I did was stop here for a quiet fag.' He leered. 'You'd better get back to your bed now, Snow White, before I'm tempted to invite myself in with you.' He shrugged. 'Except you're not my type. I prefer my flesh younger. One last thing.' He leaned casually on the car door. 'Keep your stupid fuckin' brother the guard out of this. You've got nothing to fuckin' tell him, understand? We didn't have this conversation, got it? It'd be too bad if anything happened to Liam, alone in that bachelor pad of his on the dangerous northside, wouldn't it?'

My head nodded, up, down. When he reached and touched my face I couldn't even manage a flinch. He ran his fingers down my cheek. 'You go squealing to

126

the guards and there's a whole lot of shit going to hit the fan. You keep your mouth shut and everyone'll get things sorted out a lot quicker. Just mind your own business until the call comes. That way you and yours won't come to any harm.' He leaned closer. 'Play fuckin' ball, got it?'

He turned to look again at the car door and, like a rabbit set free, I bolted for the pavement.

'I don't understand any of this.' I stood at that relatively safe distance and bleated. 'I don't understand what you want from me, or my child . . .'

'Oh, fuck off.' Fish-eyes looked up. He sounded bored. 'You're a lucky bitch this door isn't damaged. You ever try a stunt like that again and I'll break your foot, as well as your face. Got it?'

He got into the car and pulled the door closed with a dull clunk. His exit from the square was smooth and slow. A message in itself.

I didn't call the guards and I didn't ring Liam. I was more scared of the thug's threats than of the possible consequences of keeping quiet. I brought Emma into my bed for the rest of the night. She slept on while I lay quietly in the dark, coming up with more questions than answers. They all came back to the same, unavoidable fact. Darragh's death had not been an accident. Murder, a deliberate killing, was the only thing which offered any logical explanation for the way in which Darragh had died.

What I wanted to know was why someone would have killed him and who that person was.

The why had to have something to do with his risk-taking investments. There must have been serious amounts of money involved for it to have ended in murder.

The who seemed just as obvious. The thug in the BMW wasn't alone, there had to be others involved. And if he wasn't alone then who else was out there watching and waiting to harm Emma? And my brother? And me?

For all I knew my enemy's face was one I already knew. It could belong to any one of the people who'd come into my life because of Darragh – Alison, Malachy Woulfe, Austin Finn, Conal Bergin. I didn't know any of them very well, Alison and Malachy hardly at all. But there wasn't one of them struck me as the murdering type.

There seemed no reason either why any one of them would have had Darragh killed. Alison might well have had a row with him on Christmas Day, but that didn't make her a murderess. Austin Finn felt betrayed and was faced with a business in disarray, if not collapse. But if he'd killed Darragh wouldn't that have drawn attention to the fact that his partner had been dabbling with clients' money and totally discredited the company?

Conal Bergin had been Darragh's friend, his *alter ego* and boon companion. Unless there was some terrible evil afoot to do with the play I couldn't imagine why Conal would have killed Darragh. One thing did strike me: a dead Darragh ensured that the money backing Conal's play stayed backing it. If Conal had known Austin was sniffing around discrepancies in the firm, had feared Darragh's partner was about to pull the plug on unauthorized investments, might he have feared enough for his play to murder the person who controlled the account? As a possibility this struck me as a very slim one.

All of which left Malachy Woulfe, an unknown quantity as far as I was concerned. His friendship with Darragh went back a few years, according to Conal Bergin, so maybe there was something terrible enough in the past to bring about murder now.

What all, or any of it, had to do with Emma and me was the really big question. At some time around 4 a.m. I decided I would talk things over with Harry next day. An objective view was what I needed. The thought helped me get to sleep.

Chapter Twelve

Monday, 10 January

Harry was blackly fuming when I arrived at Razorbill next morning. This was not the mood I wanted him in for our talk. The cause, an early morning run-in with a garda, was less than auspicious too.

'This city has become morally degenerate,' he thumped my desk. 'Time was when a man, or a woman even, could walk the streets at any hour. Time was too when a man could leave his car to get the morning paper and not be attacked by a young skut in uniform about holding up the traffic flow . . .' he snorted into a mug of Bewley's dark roast. God knows what the caffeine did to his already malfunctioning heart.

'Did you leave the car in traffic?'

'Don't push for an answer to that question, young woman. In any event it was a case of traffic flow my arse. This was not a case of traffic control,' he thumped my desk, 'it was just the old business of a man dressed in authority carrying on in a way that would make the angels weep. A boy in uniform is even worse. That youngster was corrupted, given a taste for power before he was dry behind the ears. He gave me a ticket . . .'

'Could have been worse,' I said. 'Could have been a wet morning.'

'Who was it said that corruption was the most infallible symptom of constitutional liberty?' This switch to pedantry, or philosophical musing as Harry called it, was a good sign. Harry was calming down. I was feeling more agitated than ever myself.

'I don't know who said it,' I snapped, 'but whoever it was hadn't been burgled and terrorized in the middle of the night. Those bloody great wisdom-makers were rarely touched by reality.'

'Are we speaking generalities here?' Harry sat down in the visitors' armchair. 'Or do I detect the bitter pill of specific experience?'

'I was burgled on Saturday night. Last night I had a visit from a thug who was most likely one of the perpetrators . . .'

'This is terrible.' Harry's shocked concern was reassuring. 'Really dreadful. It's just as I was saying, the city's become morally degenerate. You weren't there, I presume, since you were with the country brother for the weekend.'

'I wasn't there when they burgled the place. But Delia was downstairs and she disturbed them . . .'

'But you said they came back. Why did they do that?'

'One of them came back. I tried to find out but couldn't . . .'

'You spoke to this person?' Harry's voice rose. I nodded. 'And then you called the police?' When I didn't answer this Harry became very quiet. 'You didn't call the guards,' he said.

I shook my head. 'I was scared to,' I admitted. He drummed his fingertips on the desk between us. At last he said what I'd been expecting him to say.

'I need a cigarette. Have you got any cigarettes?'

131

'No.' Harry'd been told not to smoke.

'I have to have a cigarette,' he insisted.

'No, you don't,' I said.

He got up and went to the mantelpiece and rooted out my emergency supply, there for writers who needed a cigarette when it came to talk of corrections. The ashtray on my desk, which Harry pulled towards him as he sat down, was there for the same reason.

'Now that you've brought me to this state will you please tell me *everything* that's going on . . .' He lit a cigarette, held it between two of his great fingers and leaned back with his legs crossed. 'If, at the end, I am not satisfied then I am willing to put myself through a conversation with your brother the guard.'

'I'll tell you everything,' I said quickly. I'd arrived at a sort of rounded-out version of things to tell him. I took a deep breath.

'It's looking as if Darragh was keeping some dodgy company before he died. Liam had been following him, and them, around. It may be that Darragh's death was not an accident . . .' I couldn't bring myself to say the word murder. ' . . . From something the thug visitor told me last night said it looks as if he had something they wanted . . . as if they now think I have it . . .'

'Are you telling me,' Harry asked, 'that McCann may have been murdered for this something?'

'Looks like it,' I said.

'You were very wrong not to call the police, my dear. You cannot deal with this yourself.'

'What I haven't told you, Harry,' I took a deep breath and got what I had to say out quickly, 'is that last night's creepo warned me against going to the

132

guards. He wasn't messing. He knew my name and he knew all about Emma. He threatened to harm her. He threatened to harm Liam too . . .'

'All this if you went to the police?'

'Yes.' I was testy. I was beginning to worry about Emma, to regret having sent her to school that day. I should have brought her to work with me where I could have kept an eye on her . . .

'He's bluffing,' Harry said. 'All bullies bluff. You don't have a choice about this, Norah, you have to go to the police. I'll go with you myself, if that'll help.'

'I don't want you to do that.' I chewed on a nail. 'Thing is, Harry, I'm seriously worried about them not being discreet, you know – using a sledgehammer to crack a nut. I don't want them attracting all sorts of attention on to mine and Emma's heads. They might make things even worse . . .'

'They'll be discreet,' Harry said. 'They're not all arrogant young pups like my friend of this morning. You'll be dealing with grown men.' He gave a modest cough. 'I know some of the senior men myself. I've had drinks with them on occasion . . .' I took this to mean he'd met senior gardai in late-night drinking establishments. '. . . You can take it from me that they've more than learned how to deal with criminal skullduggery in recent years.' His tone changed. 'If you don't go to them, Norah, I'll go myself on your behalf. I will tell them everything you have just told me. Furthermore, I will tell them exactly what I thought of McCann.'

'You're bullying me.' I stood. 'I'll go, but I'll go in my own time . . .'

'I'd prefer it if you went in my time. Right now.

Better to deal with it than have murderous criminals take over your life. They won't go away, you know. It's far more likely that they'll become seriously dangerous. Also,' he pulled himself out of the armchair, his expression full of regret, 'I naturally enough don't want them coming round here. Razorbill has enough on its plate without the unsavoury types you appear to attract camping on its doorstep. Go now, Norah, and get it over with.'

Pearse Street garda station is an imposing pile of grey granite in an almost dead central city location. It's very large, and so familiar a landmark that it goes unnoticed for the most part. It being the station which had dealt with Darragh's death I reckoned the gardai there would have to be the ones to hear my tale.

I thought about something else too, walking down Grafton Street towards Pearse Street. If Darragh had been murdered then a killer, or two, was walking freely around the city.

Pearse Street garda station was busy, a regular Busarus of a place. Clearly refurbished – the colour scheme had a lot of powder-blue and dove-grey – I was several minutes in front of the curved, Art Deco-style reception desk before I got the attention of the guard on duty.

'Can I help you at all?' He was robotic.

'I'd like to speak to somebody . . . senior . . .'

'About what?'

Good question. 'About a drowning. And about threats made to me and my daughter . . .'

'You'll have to wait.' He wrote down my name.

I took my place with half a dozen other waiting

134

citizens. I'd been sitting ten minutes, and the surly teenager to my left had inched a bit too close, when a man wearing a plaid shirt and grey jeans appeared.

'Miss Hopkins? I'm Detective-Sergeant Liston.' He gestured to a door on our left. 'We'll be more private in here.'

I followed him into a small room. It was certainly private. It was windowless too, with a high ceiling, grey walls and touches of powder-blue on the skirting and door. We seated ourselves on two of three chairs at a narrow, grey-topped table.

I eyed the Detective-Sergeant cautiously while he waited for me to speak. He had his hands in front of him on the table and his face, with its firm jawline and steady eyes, was that of a good policeman. He gave me an encouraging, inoffensive smile.

'I want to report a man who harassed and threatened me last night,' I said, 'but I don't want him to know I've been to the guards, or that I told, you know, anything about him . . .'

The detective sighed. 'Why don't you tell me what the problem is, Miss Hopkins, and then we'll discuss the logistics.'

'Fine. Yes . . .' I took a deep breath and phrased the next bit carefully. 'I'm here because I'm frightened for my child and my brother, both of whom this man threatened to harm. And I came to this station in particular because all of this is somehow involved with the death of a Darragh McCann, who died in the Liffey on Stephen's Day. If I remember rightly from the inquest it was a Sergeant Redmond from this station who dealt with things at the time.'

Detective-Sergeant Liston had produced a notebook and was scratching with a dark green, gold-topped pen. 'Go on,' he said.

'I'm worried about confidentiality . . .' I began.

'Miss Hopkins, we cannot ensure your safety or that of your daughter unless you tell us what's going on.'

'Yes. I know that . . .'

'There is no reason for you to lack confidence in the gardai.'

'No. Will you keep me informed about what happens?'

'You will be given all the information you need,' he said.

'What does that mean, exactly?'

'It means, Miss Hopkins, that I want you to stop wasting my time and tell me why you're here.'

I began at the end and gave him the bare bones of things back to when Alison had appeared on my front doorstep eight days before. Darragh's widow, I explained, was unlikely to know anything and was in an extremely vulnerable state (I was remembering her off-the-wall summary of things in the ladies' room in the Gresham). I told him about the Grafton Street photograph going missing. Detective-Sergeant Liston didn't interrupt and, apart from writing down the odd word, appeared to doodle throughout.

There was a small silence when I finished and then he asked, 'Why did you go out to speak to this man last night?' He waited, doodling again, until I answered.

'I had to know what was going on. I was hoping that confronting him would bring an end to it all, put him off watching my home . . .'

136

'You might have put an end to things all right,' Detective-Sergeant Liston folded his arms on the table.

'There's one other thing I should tell you . . .' I said. He nodded encouragingly when I stopped. 'I have a brother in the guards . . .' I told him then about Liam, where he was stationed and how he'd taken to following Darragh in the weeks before he died. 'He was worried about me,' I said defensively, 'but now these people are threatening to get at him too. The thug I spoke to last night warned me not to tell Liam anything. He even knew where he lived and . . .'

'We'll talk to Guard Hopkins,' he abruptly cut me short, 'I take it from what you've said that you haven't told him about your encounter and the threats yourself?'

'No. I don't want him involved. I want him kept out of this, absolutely out of it.' I meant it. Liam was my brother first and a guard second. I'd enough problems without something terrible happening to him on my account.

'You can leave us to deal with that,' Detective-Sergeant Liston was off-hand. 'Would you care to give me a description of the man you met last night?'

When I put my mind to it I was surprised at the amount of detail I remembered. Things like him favouring his left hand when turning down the radio and opening the door.

'A young man, was he?'

'Yes. Not more than twenty-five or six. The car was a BMW. Grey. It looked new, though I didn't think to look at the number plates.' I stopped when he began to drum his fingers on the table. 'Does any of this indicate who he might be?'

'Sounds like someone we're familiar enough with. I'd say we're talking here about one Jamesy Collins. We'll show you some pictures but I'm fairly confident he's our man. Not the kind of company your brother would approve of . . .' He thought for a moment, still drumming the table. 'Did the man you spoke with make any specific suggestions as to what he might do to you?'

They were going to go after him. They would go after him and arrest him for threatening behaviour and Emma and I would be at the mercy of every one of his thug associates in Dublin. A cold sweat broke out on my palms.

'I should point out,' I rubbed my hand on my coat, 'that I provoked this man. I was abusive myself.'

'You provoked him.' Detective-Sergeant Liston gave a short laugh. 'You provoked our Jamesy. Difficult thing to do, that.' He restrained a guffaw. I could feel him doing it. He looked as if the restraint was causing him pain. 'And how did you provoke him then?' he asked.

'I kicked the door of his car.'

'You kicked the door of his car.' More restraint. Even more patience. The man was a saint.

'He was about to drive off. I wanted to stop him.'

'Kicking the door would've stopped him all right. Jamesy's fond of his cars.' He leaned back in the chair and studied the high ceiling for several moments. His honest-cop expression was back in place when he faced me again. 'I think, Miss Hopkins, that I should explain a few things to you at this point. When I've finished we'll look at photographs and I'd like you to make a statement.' He rubbed a hand across his brow. 'James

138

Collins and his kind are, as the saying goes, mad, bad and dangerous to know. I could give you chapter and verse but I'm not inclined to waste time on a litany of evil. You would be well advised not only to keep your distance from Mr Collins but to have someone move in to live with you over the coming weeks. Can that be arranged?'

'No. I can't think of anyone . . .'

He interrupted impatiently. 'We'll see what we can do about surveillance then. It could well be, Miss Hopkins, that you can be of assistance to the gardai, that we can be of mutual assistance to one another. We've been interested in the activities of Mr Collins and his friends for some time . . .'

'So you're going to charge him with threatening behaviour and expose my child and me to the vengeance of his friends . . .'

'I was merely giving consideration, Miss Hopkins,' his tone was patient, 'to the fact that our investigation into the affairs of Mr McCann and his connections with Jamesy could help our inquiries, nothing more.'

'Good.' I was curt. 'Because I'm not pressing charges against him for threatening me. I just wanted you to know what had happened . . . and to do something about him . . .'

'I understand,' he said, gently enough. 'But please realize that there's very little we *can* do. Your friend didn't use a gun, a weapon of any kind. He did nothing, in fact, for which he could be arrested. We could bring him in under Section 4 of the Criminal Justice Act and hold him for twelve hours. After that we'd either have to charge or release him and I wouldn't reckon your chances once he was on the street again. Better all round to give him enough rope to hang himself.' He paused and stuffed the notebook into his pocket. 'As far as Jamesy, or whoever, is concerned this meeting never took place. No one will know we've met until, and unless, they have to.'

'I wouldn't bet on it,' I muttered. 'The man I met last night wasn't exactly the Einstein of the underworld – but he was no fool either.'

'No, he's not a fool,' he agreed, 'but you have my word that the situation will be dealt with delicately and that you'll be given the best we can manage by way of protection.'

'The best we can manage' lacked a ring of confidence but I nodded an acceptance of reality. They would do what they could. I hoped it would be enough.

'We'll set up an unobtrusive surveillance.' He stood up. 'I'm going to bring a Detective Garda Lalor in to you now. He'll take a statement about all of this. Unless you'd be more comfortable with a woman garda?'

'A man will be fine,' I said.

Detective Garda Lalor took down what I had to say silently and at speed. While it was being typed up I studied a selection of photographs and confirmed that the man in the BMW was indeed one Jamesy Collins. The shorn head and dead eyes were unmistakable. I read and signed the typed version of my statement and, hoping I hadn't done anything I might live to regret, rejoined the innocent crowds in the street outside.

Liam came by that evening. Detective-Sergeant Liston had been in touch with him and, looked at from the viewpoint of male dignity and pride, my going behind his back to his bosses seemed to him a terrible betrayal. I argued that he was too involved, that things were better left to his more objective colleagues. He was having none of it.

'It was a terrible thing to do, Norah, going into Pearse Street like that, asking them to remove me out of the way . . .'

He followed me around the kitchen while I got him something to eat. Wearing a dark suit and tie he looked exactly what he was; he might as well have worn the uniform. If Jamesy Collins, or any of his friends, were still watching the house there was no way they'd have missed the arrival of my very garda-looking brother.

I put a glass of whiskey into his hand and looked him in the eye. 'I gave them the facts and identified Jamesy Collins as the man who'd threatened to hurt Emma – and you. They obviously think you're too close to things, that it's best for you to stay clear . . .'

'They think more than that.' Liam was angry.

'What happened?' I turned the steak under the grill.

'I was called into Pearse Street this afternoon. The Superintendent there, along with your Detective-Sergeant Liston, put me through the wringer. Questioned me like I was the one had committed the crime, instead of that little bastard Collins.' He spoke very quietly. 'Why didn't you ring me last night? What possessed you to go out into the street after that madman?'

I put the steak on to a plate. 'I just did it, Liam, that's all. Now eat.'

I sat opposite him and poured myself a glass of red. Liam doesn't drink wine. I watched him eat. His appetite was unaffected.

'You were telling me what happened in Pearse Street,' I reminded him.

'Liston had me make a statement.' The shock of this was still in his voice. 'Said he considered me hostile, on account of my "grave" concern for you. Said I was off-side on this one and that I was to keep out of it. The Super backed him, said it was an order.' He shook his head. 'I never thought I'd see the day when one of my own would do me in like this. My sister, at that.'

'I haven't done you in, Liam.' I wasn't about to give in to emotional bullying. 'It was for your own good. Mine and Emma's too. Collins threatened to hurt you, said I was to keep you out of things. I had to do it . . .'

'You shouldn't have done it.' He shook his head stubbornly. 'I'm your brother. It's my place to look out for you. You've put the shoe on the other foot and now it's you looking out for me and that's neither natural nor right.'

'People look out for other people,' I said shortly, 'and that's the way it is.'

'Hmn,' Liam grunted, and finished his meal in silence. He pushed the empty plate to one side. 'You and the child aren't safe here any longer. It'd be best if you went home for a few months. Maisie'd be glad of the company in any event.'

I could have pointed out that Maisie had a husband and four children for company. Or that Duncolla wasn't my home any more. I forbore.

'There's no security at all in this place,' Liam went

on. 'None in the world. Even with an alarm system in place I couldn't allow you to stay here. Couldn't allow it on any account.'

'Please try to understand how I feel about this, Liam.' I was very calm. 'I don't want to worry Emma any more than I have to and a move would upset her very much. Nor am I going to allow myself be intimidated out of my home. Not by you and certainly not by Jamesy Collins. I'm staying here.'

'Better to upset the child than have her hurt,' Liam said.

'Emma. Your niece's name is Emma. She has a life here, and so have I. Detective-Sergeant Liston didn't suggest I move out. He said he would put surveillance on the flat.'

'So he said. It might make a difference all right.' Liam conceded this with clear reluctance. 'But even so, I don't think you should altogether discount the idea of spending some time in Duncolla. It would put Collins's nose out of joint no end.'

He worried the subject for a while longer and then he went off home where he worried it a bit more and phoned Maisie. She called as I was getting ready for bed.

'It's not such a bad idea, you know,' she said. 'Don't reject it out of hand just because it comes from Liam. We'd love to have you, for as long as you want to stay. You know that. The door's always open . . .'

'Thanks, Maisie. If things get any worse here I'll bring Emma down. I promise.'

Chapter Thirteen

Tuesday, 11 January

I arrived home from work next day to find a taxi with a man in the back seat parked outside the house. It seemed to me unlikely that this was how the police would mount guard so I kept a wary eye on the taxi's passenger as I got out of my own car. It could be that Jamesy, unwilling to risk the BMW again, had come calling in a taxi. I shoved up a brolly against the teeming rain and marched briskly towards number 9, keeping close to the wall. I was almost at the gate when the taxi door swung open and Conal Bergin hopped out into my path.

'That was a stupid thing to do!' I jumped back, yelling and frightening myself as much as him. 'I might have attacked you.' To prove it I swung the brolly in a wild arc.

He stepped back and made the peace sign. 'I come as a friend. Sorry if I frightened you. I called at Harry's place, hoping to get you there, but you'd left.'

'I rarely stay there overnight,' I snapped, still jumpy. Plus, the rain was falling faster all the time, pounding and bouncing off the brolly, and I was hungry.

'Can I come in?' Conal asked.

Since the taxi had driven off this was a bit superfluous. Even so, I hesitated before leading the way inside.

Events had made me cautious, if not downright paranoid, about anybody connected to Darragh. I reminded myself that Conal arriving in a taxi two hours earlier than we'd arranged to meet was odd, but not necessarily menacing.

'I wanted to say hello to Emma before we went out to eat.' He shook himself like a dog when we got inside. 'You haven't forgotten our date?'

Date was pushing it a bit. 'Of course not,' I said. 'You caught me by surprise, that's all.'

Emma was pleased to see him. He went through some homework with her and they had a conversation in which Darragh's name featured a few times. He'd brought her a present too, a nicely gift-wrapped address book.

I changed into a russet-coloured silk blouse and the Mexican silver earrings Maisie had given me for Christmas. The effort made me feel better.

'Have a good time,' Delia called too loudly as we went down the path. I'd said nothing to her about the night before and going to the police. I badly wanted a rest from talking about things.

Conal had booked an Italian restaurant in Camden Street. I drove us there, which meant that I wouldn't be able to drink, or not much anyway. This suited me fine, since I didn't want to become loose and gabble-mouthed. The restaurant was very Conal: low key, stone walls and authentic food. The staff and *maître d'* all knew him and we were given a table close to the wood-burning fire.

An awkwardness descended when we sat down. We chit-chatted and chose our food, but the mood persisted through the selection of tortellini with *ragú bolognese* for him and *scampi alla griglia* (grilled shrimps with garlic butter) for me. Things got better when I asked him about the play.

'Shouldn't you be at the rehearsal tonight?' I asked.

'Probably,' he shrugged, 'but there's not a lot I can do at this stage.'

He smiled at the pun and I noticed that his hair had started to grow. In the silence while a waiter put down bread and rearranged our table I thought about telling him about my trip to the police. Maybe he should know that the guards, thanks to me, were going to investigate Finn and McCann and Darragh's various investments and would be looking at where the money for the play came from. But the waiter began to chat to us and the moment passed and I said nothing.

At work I'd been feeling bad about having told the police of the problems at Finn and McCann and had tried several times to get hold of Austin on the phone to warn him. His office couldn't say where he was, and a frosty Sheila, when I rang his home, insisted that he was out of town. I didn't believe her but since she wasn't going to get him for me he might as well have been on the moon.

I devoured some bread and went back to the play for conversation.

'How do you feel about it now? Is it the play you wrote?'

'More or less. More more than less, to be honest. Malachy ain't subtle, and he's a bully, but he gets the job he wants done.' He hesitated. 'I'd appreciate it if you came with me to the opening night. Will you?'

'I'd like that,' I said. 'I was going anyway.'

The food came. So did a bottle of Chianti. The

mood had warmed up and Conal leaned across the table. 'Look, Norah, you might as well know that Harry told me what happened at your place over the weekend. He's worried.' He paused. 'I wish you'd told me yourself. Whatever's going on, we're all involved. You're not a one-woman show. I want to help . . .'

'What I told Harry I told him in confidence . . .' I said and waited, wondering if Harry had said anything to him about my going to the police.

'I'm not trying to invade your life, Norah.' He looked wry. 'It's just that whatever's going on really does involve everyone who knew Darragh. Don't you think Alison should be told, if only to prepare her for a possible visit from Jamesy Collins? Don't you think I should?'

If he knew Jamesy Collins's name then he knew I'd been to the police.

'There's no reason to suppose Jamesy Collins is interested in anyone but me,' I said, remembering the photograph and what he'd said.

'You can't be sure of that.' He gave me a teacherly look and surprised me by saying, 'I wish you'd trust me, Norah. I owe it to Darragh to make sure you and Emma are OK. I want to be around. I want to help.'

'Thanks. But I really am on top of things . . .'

'Good. Your food's going cold.' He speared a forkful of his own. 'Better start eating.'

Chatter on my part about the high points in Razorbill's spring catalogue got us through to the coffees. We left without lingering and walked silently to my car. The rain had more or less stopped and I was rooting for my car keys when Conal said, 'I meant what I said about being around if you need me.'

'Yes ... thanks ...'

I felt awkward. The cold night air had cleared my head and allowed some fresh thoughts in. I remembered the times Conal had been there over the years, never interfering, leaving Darragh and me alone when we'd been in the throes of our affair, maintaining friendly contact after I became a mother and the affair ended.

The wine, a wave of sadness – something brought on a blur of tears, blinding me as I tried to get the car keys into the door.

'Take this.' Conal turned me to face him and handed me a paper napkin from the restaurant. 'It's all I've got.'

I took it and mopped. 'Thanks,' I said, 'and sorry.'

'Think nothing of it.' He drew me close and arranged things so that my head rested on his shoulder. Standing in the soft drizzle, leaning on his very familiar shoulder felt very, very comfortable.

'He's worth a few tears.' I felt Conal's lips in my hair.

I had a good cry then, sobbing into his shoulder for Darragh, for the end of friendship, most of all for the way he'd died. Conal's was a broad shoulder. He said nothing, holding me tightly and stroking my back. I'm not sure at what point things changed. One minute we were sharing grief, the next we were clinging together in what had become primal sexual need. I don't know whether it just had to do with one emotion leading to another or whether sex had been there, unacknowledged, all along.

Whatever the cause, the effect felt right and when we kissed it was for real and full of serious sexual intent. Conal's mouth on mine felt good as he cradled my head in his hands and I felt the warm inside of his mouth. For the first time for a very long time I felt a surge of glorious, life-fulfilling passion and went with it.

But the cold, the cursed habit of responsibility, caution, insinuated their way past my lurching senses.

'We can't.' I pulled away, quickly and suddenly. 'I have to get home to Emma . . .'

He stood back too, his shocked expression quickly becoming a cool one.

'I'm sorry,' I said. 'That was not a good idea.'

'Seemed like an excellent one to me.' He touched my mouth with a finger. 'But maybe you're right.'

He took the keys and opened the car door for me. He refused to let me drive him home.

'I feel like a walk,' he said, and kissed me lightly on the cheek, a passionless exchange between friends.

Chapter Fourteen

Thursday, 13 January

'Sorry I'm late.'

Conal, as playwright, stepped into my hallway two nights later looking very much the part. He was wearing a charcoal-coloured suit and ochre shirt. All very controlled chic and not bad at all with his glasses. He could have been Arthur Miller. I told him so.

'I wish.' He did a bit of fiddling with his glasses. 'This is a first play, Norah, I hope you're not expecting great twentieth-century truths.'

'I'm expecting some, at least,' I said.

'Oh, God,' he said.

I disentangled my best coat from the pile on the hallstand. Black and long and, after a brush down, resplendent with its own particular chic. I'd gone for black all over: jacket and trousers with my hair piled up. Understatement is best when your size makes a point of its own. Emma thought I looked beautiful.

'You look good.' Conal was more restrained as he helped me into the coat. I picked up my bag and for a moment we were pleasantly close and the kiss of two nights before very recent. A bit of warm, sexual attention from someone you like is not to be sneezed at when you're severely malnourished in that area.

'You look *very* good,' he said, and I stepped away, out of range.

'One careful owner, that's me,' I said, and immediately wished I'd kept my mouth shut. I called Emma and she came sulkily down the stairs.

'Why can't I come too?' she demanded of Conal. He handled it well.

'Not this time.' He pulled a programme from his pocket. 'I brought you this. It tells all about the play so you can see exactly how boring it is. You're not missing a thing.'

Emma looked blankly at the arty grey cover. 'Why did you write a boring play?' she asked.

'Because I'm a boring person,' said Conal and she sighed, recognizing a cop-out when she heard one.

'I don't want this.' She handed back the programme and picked up her night things. Guilt, weighty and relentless, tugged at my sense of anticipation.

'I won't be late,' I told her, 'so if you want me to carry you up to your own bed from Delia's when I come home . . .'

'No, thank you. I'd better go now.' She stiffened her back and walked silently to the door. On her toes, she tried and failed to open it. But then she'd known she wouldn't be able to when she'd made her brave-but-unbowed passage across the hall. I opened it for her.

'Be nice to Delia,' I said.

'You don't have to say things like that to me.' She stepped with dignity into the evening drizzle. 'I hope you have a good time.' She was a study in forlorn abandonment and it was a perfect exit. Her father would have been proud of her.

'We will.' I was upbeat. 'And you enjoy the video.'

'Delia will love it anyhow,' she sighed. This was probably true. In an effort to please both of them I'd chosen a Fred Astaire movie. With a deep sigh Emma turned and went slowly down the steps.

'Kids do it all the time.' Conal gave a low laugh. 'Performances an actor would kill for, aimed right at the heart of the parent wearing the guilt sign.'

This cheered me up nicely as we set off. It made me think too that constant exposure to the wiles and wicked ways of children could be the reason he had none of his own. Or maybe he had. I really knew very little about Conal Bergin.

In the taxi he gave me the programme Emma had rejected. The inside page was given over to a one-line tribute to Darragh 'whose belief and energy had made it possible to stage *The Eleventh Hour*'. A neat way of putting it. I couldn't find a thing to say but we managed a companionable silence as the taxi took us through the streets to the Liberties and the Tivoli Theatre. The incident of two nights before had been an aberration. This was what we really were; two people brought together by the dead friend we'd had in common.

We arrived ten minutes before curtain-up. The small foyer was crowded, filled mostly with self-conscious first-nighters and people who knew Conal.

'You're a bad, bad man.' One of the latter, a long-haired blonde with moulded cheekbones and thrusting bosoms, swooped as soon as we stepped into the foyer. 'What bolt-hole have you been hiding yourself in? I've been trying to get hold of you for days . . .'

'Haven't we all,' an infinitely smoother redhead

cruised into place on Conal's other side. I stood back and admitted to myself that I was shocked. Conal as man of the night was one thing. Conal as sex object was another. To be fair, he seemed a fairly passive object of desire though it could have been that his quietly besieged look was a front. I stood to the side for several minutes before he reached across the blonde and jerked me forward by the wrist.

'Norah.' He said my name loudly. 'I'd like you to meet Majella and Terri.'

I nodded and smiled, my coat's long, black austerity losing its chic beside the lycra and dazzle of Majella and Terri.

'I'll leave my things in the cloakroom.' I bolted for the stairs.

Alison was standing beside the cloakroom desk. The upstairs foyer in the Tivoli is not large – the place was built in 1936 as a cinema, went dark in the 1970s and reopened in 1987 as a theatre and was never intended to be anything but intimate. Its intimate qualities, however, were lost on Alison, who appeared so adrift she might have been rudderless on the ocean main. She'd clearly taken the advice of Lisa from the Gresham Hotel's ladies' room seriously, and hadn't stinted on effort for the night. Her hair was curled and sprayed so that it stood like a windmill about her head and shoulders and she'd gone to town on the kohl and with a lush, baby-pink lipstick. Under the inevitable leather coat she was wearing something white with her black boots. If I hadn't known her to be the mother of two children I'd have taken her for a slightly loopy sixteen-year-old.

'Hello, Alison,' I touched her arm and she jumped.

She was trailing a bag and white gauzy thing from one hand and had a lighted cigarette in the other.

'Oh, Norah, I've been wondering where you were. I've got a seat beside you. Malachy arranged it. He had to leave me here. To go backstage. I was afraid you wouldn't find me. That you mightn't come.' She looked nervously towards the auditorium. 'I couldn't sit on my own in there.' She might have been contemplating a couple of hours in hell's fire.

'I phoned you several times,' I said, 'but all I got was your answering machine.' With Darragh's voice still on it.

'I've stopped Mollie from answering the phone.' She looked blindly around the sea of faces. 'We need peace.'

She puffed on the cigarette and nodded towards the auditorium. 'They wouldn't let me smoke in there. Some stuffy little ponce told me to get out.' She took another drag, failed to find an ashtray and smartly flicked off the head before dropping the butt into her silver, linked-mail handbag. Her bitten nails were the same baby-pink colour as her lips.

'Give me your coat,' I said, 'and I'll check them both into the cloakroom.'

Her dress was a slip affair which gave her the look of a sexy ragdoll. Loopy she might be but Alison was ringing bells for the men around. Beside her I felt like a Sumo wrestler.

'We'd better go on down,' I said. 'Conal's got my ticket . . .'

'Oh, you're with Conal Bergin,' she said. 'He didn't tell me that when he called to see us . . .'

'Probably didn't think it important,' I said. Conal

154

hadn't said anything to me about calling on Alison, but then why should he? There were things I would have to tell Alison myself, but not now. With a bit of luck she might never need to know about some of them.

The Eleventh Hour was a good play. From the moment the curtain went up it grabbed and held its audience with its bitter story of vague hope. Bleakly funny, it told the sad, self-destructing tale of a group of inner-city inhabitants and was set, for the most part, in a fish'n'chip shop. The story was woven around supply and demand; the dealing and taking of drugs, the giving of love and the taking it back. What hope it offered was for the individual: its message for the community as a whole was bleak.

The audience stood to applaud at the end. Conal was encouraged on to the stage where, surrounded by the cast and Malachy Woulfe, he delivered a short, elegant speech. The play wasn't intended, he said, to be a moral horror show, merely a reflection of how a lot of people lived a lot of the time. Then he spoke of Darragh.

'None of you would have seen this play on the stage tonight if it hadn't been for Darragh McCann's belief in it. Because of that belief he sought and got backing. Much thanks tonight too to our anonymous backer, who chooses not to be with us. Sad to say, getting backing for *The Eleventh Hour* was one of the last things Darragh McCann did. He died on St Stephen's Day. This production is a tribute to someone who was unique, a once off.'

The first-night party was in a hotel in Temple Bar.

'It's hard that Darragh didn't say one word to me about your play,' Alison said sadly to Conal.

'He was going to,' said Conal. Alison said nothing.

'You managed some fairly close to the bone stuff,' I said lightly. 'Any of it personal?'

'I only wrote it,' Conal shrugged. 'I didn't live it and I don't even agree with some of its premises.'

'Like what?'

'I don't think people so willingly self-destruct.'

'Why did you say that they do then?'

'Because some people do, sometimes.'

Malachy surfaced from a sea of post-mortems and praise and swept Alison from my side.

'Thanks for taking care of her.' He kissed me on both cheeks and added one on the mouth for good measure. 'You are a queen amongst women. Be kind to our playwright.'

He gave a leering wink and vanished with Alison into the crowd.

Things geared up for a good party. The mood was exultant, laughter and talk feverish, body language promising. A jazz combo played in a corner and one of the actors grabbed the microphone and did a mean Mack the Knife.

All of it made me wish I'd gone home after the play. Nothing to do with the crowd or with Conal, who did his best to stay by my side in the face of a lot of coy flirting on the part of Majella. Darragh's absence killed the party mood in me.

'You're meant to smile at parties.'

Austin Finn, when he touched me on the shoulder, wasn't doing a lot of smiling himself. Dressed in accountancy grey, he looked as out of place as a cat in water. I found I was delighted to see him.

'I hoped you'd be here,' I said. 'Were you at the theatre too?'

'We got there just as the curtain went up.' He straightened his tie. 'Sheila wasn't feeling well and we were delayed. She's a lot better now so I persuaded her along here. I'm not a great judge of these things,' he gave a deprecatory shrug, 'but I'm told by those who are that this is definitely a party with something to celebrate . . .'

'Oh, I think there's something to celebrate all right,' I said. 'It's a good play. I'd be willing to bet, Austin, though I'm ignorant as sin about these things, that it'll cover itself. Could be that this is one investment of Darragh's you don't need to worry about.'

'On its way to Broadway, is it?' he raised a gently sceptical eyebrow. 'The play investment is not major and doesn't look as if it'll be a problem anyway.' He helped himself to a drink from a passing tray and raised it in salute. 'Here's to *The Eleventh Hour*.'

'*The Eleventh Hour*.' I drank with him, hugely relieved to hear that Conal had got it right and that the play's backer had been a willing investor.

'He'd have enjoyed all of this,' Austin said, and I knew I was going to have to tell him I'd gone to the police. He was decent and solid and deserved to know I'd dropped his firm in it. It could be that he knew already but I didn't think so. He looked reasonably relaxed and I hated to spoil his night. Still, better the news came from me than the police.

'There should be messages from me on your office

157

system,' I said carefully. 'I've been trying to contact you for days.'

'Didn't get any.' He took my arm and moved us against a wall, clear of the slip-stream of swirling bodies. 'Things are in something of a shambles at the moment. The investigation is going on and all of that. Sheila did mention you rang, though . . .'

He looked at me expectantly. I'd have preferred a more intimate setting for what I had to say but, with Conal coming through the crowd at me, that moment was all I was going to get.

'I had to go to the police, Austin, about something that happened over the weekend. I had to give them a lot of background detail . . .' I stopped and Austin looked at me, puzzled and waiting. Conal was several people away, involved in a touchy-feely conversation with a Majella clone. 'The thing is, Austin,' I went on quickly, 'the police needed to know things which led on to my telling them about Darragh's investment ventures, how he'd left a few problems behind him in the company. I'm sorry. I hope it's not going to cause you a lot of hassle . . .'

Austin wasn't looking hassled at all. The puzzled look had cleared and he looked quite benign.

'That's all right, Norah, we'll sort things out when the guards call. If they call, of course. I'm more interested in this something which happened over the weekend. What's been happening to you?'

Conal reached my side, full of apologies for having left me alone.

'I haven't been alone,' I began. 'I've been . . .'

'Norah's been telling me about her weekend.' Austin, interrupting me, was himself interrupted by a lofty, south Dublin female voice.

'The playwright himself! Congratulations on the production.' Sheila Finn was looking a lot more beautiful than I'd remembered. Tall and dark, with diamond-shaped eyebrows, she looked smoothly elegant in olive green.

'Thank you, Sheila.' Conal smiled at her pleasantly and touched my arm. 'You know Norah, of course?'

'Hello, Sheila.' I held out a hand and she touched my fingertips.

'Sad about Darragh,' she said. She'd said nothing about him when I'd telephoned her looking for Austin. I asked her how she'd enjoyed the play. I shouldn't have.

'Very cleverly put together, I must say,' she turned to Conal, 'though the point of it all escaped me.'

'You can't please all of the people . . .' Conal began.

'For myself I found it intellectually disappointing.' Sheila all but yawned.

'It simply takes a look at the lives lived by some in our times . . .' Conal said mildly.

'It did that.' Austin was hearty. 'It certainly did that.'

'It did nothing of the sort.' Sheila was dismissive. 'It tried very hard to to be sympathetic to a certain sort of person. Overall though, I thought it duplicitous in the extreme.'

'In what way?' Conal looked genuinely interested.

'Those people, that sort of life, are in no way typical of how we live today,' Sheila said. 'They're marginals, their sort always have been . . .'

'You're wrong.' Conal shrugged. 'Those people, as

you call them, Sheila, are a huge part of the community we live in. But let's not get too wound up about this.' His smile was general, for everyone as much as Sheila. 'It's just a play.'

'It purported to deliver great truths.' Sheila was enjoying herself far too much to let go. 'It was . . .'

'Oh, come on, Sheila, it was good, entertaining stuff.' Austin's tone was placatory. 'It was well written, too . . .'

'What would you know about good writing? You haven't opened a book for twelve years.' Sheila threw an idle, cold look around the room. 'Probably longer, for all I know.' She turned to me. 'We've been married twelve years, Austin and I.'

'Congratulations,' I said.

'Were you one of those who enjoyed the play?' she asked.

'Absolutely,' I said. 'Every minute of it.'

The diamond eyebrows came together. 'You don't really have to be loyal to a dead man, you know.'

'The playwright is alive and well,' I said.

'Indeed.' Sheila Finn turned to Conal. 'Do you intend writing other plays?'

'Probably.'

'We must all pray then that this one is a success.' Sheila smiled. 'Though I would have thought the drug thing had reached saturation point as a subject for books and plays.'

'A lot of people feel it's still pertinent.' Conal wasn't so mild any more.

'Of course it's pertinent.' I was feeling defensive of Darragh's judgement as well as Conal's play. 'Given its effect I don't see how the drug culture can be dismissed as . . .'

'You don't?' Sheila's eyebrows rose to her hairline. 'You don't see that something more original would have enlightened us all a lot more tonight?'

'I don't see that it's an either or situation,' I said.

'Tonight's play should never have been written.' Sheila spoke loudly and her voice carried. She yawned into the stilling of voices around us. 'I do wish you well, Conal, and I'm sure the writing of tonight's play was a learning experience.'

'Let's hope so,' said Conal.

'Lovely party.' She patted him on the arm. 'Do enjoy the rest of the evening.' She smiled at Austin. 'We really should leave now, it's late.'

Austin had moved from beer to whiskey. 'The night's young yet, Sheila,' he said.

'I've got a busy day tomorrow,' Sheila was sharp, 'and I'm sure the party will swing without us. I would like to leave *now*.'

Austin sipped steadily at his whiskey. 'Soon,' he said.

'You can't leave, Austin.' Alison, intimidated by Sheila until now, came suddenly to life. 'You're representing Darragh . . .'

'What fanciful nonsense,' Sheila snapped. 'Austin knew nothing of this play until after Darragh's death. Really, Alison, I . . .'

'Really, Alison . . .' Alison's mimicry was viciously accurate. Sheila stared. Alison smiled. 'He certainly wouldn't have wanted *you* to be here,' she said in her normal voice. 'He didn't like you. He said you were a jumped-up bitch from Dolphin's Barn and that you

might have got out of the barn but you were still a cow
. . .' She trailed off, wilting. It was as if her sudden
outburst had taken all her energy.

Sheila was breathing deeply. Even with her mouth
tight and cheeks furiously pink, she was lovely. Some
people have it every way. 'Your husband was a dangerously foolish man,' she said.

Austin was eyeing the door. Majella laid a slender,
supportive hand on Conal's arm. People began to talk
again and it looked as if a crisis had passed. Sheila
wasn't about to give up so easily, though. She wanted
a fight and she was going to have one. I felt a rush of
sympathy for Austin, his business in disarray and his
wife behaving like a bitch. Sheila went with icy precision for Alison.

'Your husband, Alison, was a pitiful creature. His
investment in this play was typically irresponsible and
a betrayal of *my* husband's trust. He created the most
dreadful difficulties for Austin and myself and . . .' She
stopped as Alison, with a couple of quick steps, stood
in front of her, her hands fisted by her side and eyes
narrowed to purple, glittering slits.

'Why? It wasn't your money he used, was it?'

'Did he use yours? Did he use his own?' Sheila
demanded.

'God knows what money he used.' Alison faded a
little. 'For as that same God is my judge I don't know.
All I know is that what's done is done and he should
be let have this one night, at least.'

Sheila went for the kill. 'It's a little late to play the
innocent now, Alison. Your husband had nothing that
didn't come from his partnership with *my* husband.
What little credibility he had was because of their

162

partnership. I have no doubt that whatever money went into tonight's play rightfully belonged to the company . . .'

'Prove it.' Alison's voice was like thin ice cracking. 'Prove he took money from the shaggin' company!'

'Oh, that's easily done,' Sheila was cool, 'but you're forcing me to say publicly something which was going to be said in private.' She turned her cold anger on Conal. 'A decision has been made to, as it were, let sleeping dogs lie. We, that is the company, will not be pursuing the money invested in this play. It's not of great consequence anyway.'

She stopped and looked around her audience, a smile uncurling like a warm day across her lovely face. I stared in astonishment. The company wasn't pursuing the money because, according to Austin earlier, the play was an above-board investment. What *was* Sheila playing at?'

'I agree with Alison,' Sheila went on, 'in as much as I think it's best we all forget and let things go. The production seems set to at least cover itself.'

'Let's drink to that,' Conal raised his glass, 'at least.'

In a relieved, chatty buzz, glasses were raised all round, including Alison's. But not, in her case, to drink. Too late to do anything about it, I watched as she lashed the contents into Sheila's face.

'There.' She was calm satisfaction. 'That's for being a stupid, snotty bitch and trying to spoil Darragh's night.'

Sheila blinked and spluttered. There were titters, a barking laugh from someone, a few murmured sounds of shock as Austin mopped his wife's face and dabbed at her drenched green dress.

163

'I'll have you in court,' Sheila hissed at Alison. 'You won't get away with this.'

'See you in court then.' Alison shrugged.

'I'm leaving,' Sheila snapped. 'Alone.' She glared at Austin. 'Don't dare to follow. I don't want you anywhere near me.'

He didn't. It would have taken an armour-plated warrior to go anywhere near her as, head high, she made a straight line for the door. No one tried to stop her.

'I should go after her.' Austin looked sick.

'Better to leave these things to time.' Malachy clapped him on the back. 'There will be sunshine later. Women are mercurial creatures. She'll have forgotten everything in the morning.'

'Oh, no, she won't,' said Austin with conviction. He was glassy-eyed.

'Let us proceed with the party,' said Malachy. 'These things happen and must be put aside.'

Alison was limpid against his chest and I felt a twinge of uneasy concern. If Malachy wanted Alison, and getting her meant exploiting her vulnerable widowhood, then I was willing to bet he would do just that. It wasn't my concern, but . . .

'The man of the night is being neglected.' Majella kissed Conal redly on the cheek and caught his hand. 'I want to dance . . .'

'The night grows old,' Conal gave a rueful grin, 'and the day job awaits in the morning . . .'

Majella shrieked. 'You can't even *think* about leaving,' she cried. 'You need food and nourishment. Come with me, my darling, and I'll see you replenished, body and soul.' She pulled at him, quite forcefully to judge by his resistance. I waited for him to extract his hand from hers, but he didn't.

'Care for something to eat, Norah?' he asked me.

I shook my head. I didn't fancy a threesome with Majella, which was what he seemed to be offering. I told myself I wasn't jealous, that the problem was simply that whatever she meant to Conal, Majella just wasn't my type. The truth was, though, that I was hurt by Conal's near-dismissiveness. The nastiness of the last twenty minutes had exhausted the last of my party mood too. I wanted to go home.

'I'm not hungry,' I said. 'But don't let me stop you.'

I looked around for Austin. He was slumped in an armchair, gloomily studying the tips of his well-shone shoes. Conal, following my gaze, went to him and gave his shoulder a small shake.

'Food, Austin?'

Austin grunted and shook his head. 'Don't think I could stomach it,' he said. 'Not the best of times in my life, you know. First I lose my partner and now I've lost my wife.' He looked unbearably wretched, and very drunk.

'God, this is ridiculous.' Majella, voice raised, arms akimbo, tapped an impatient foot. 'Half the world is waiting talk to you in the other room, Conal. This is meant to be a celebration, for God's sake . . .'

'I'll take Austin home,' I said quickly.

'You're right. He has to be taken home,' said Conal. 'We'll leave now . . .' He deposited his glass on a passing tray.

'No need for you to come.' I was firm, rude even. I was damned if he was going to make a martyr of himself and leave the party for me. 'I'll grab a taxi and get him home,' I managed a smile. 'This is your night.' I leaned over Austin. 'Up you get,' I said, 'I'm going to grab us a taxi.'

'You're a good sort, Norah.' Austin staggered to his feet and I stood back, warily. He wobbled but remained reasonably upright. 'Darragh didn't deserve you.' He leaned on my shoulder. He was not light. 'But then again, maybe he did.'

Conal's goodnight peck on the cheek as we left was cool. I was too tired to care.

Temple Bar was its usual, teeming self, not a hope in the street of getting a taxi. The hotel got us one however, when Austin asserted himself with the porter, pretty niftily too, I thought, for a man who'd been mixing his drinks. He lived in Blackrock: coastal suburbia and quite a distance from my nest in deviant Rathmines.

'We'll drop you off first,' he said as we cruised slowly out of Temple Bar and down the riverside. 'No sense dragging you out of town.' He looked ashen, but our brief brush with night air seemed to have sobered him a bit.

'How do you feel?' I asked.

He rested his elbows on his knees and put his head into his hands, a move which brought his knee in contact with my thigh. He jerked back as if the contact had been with a red-hot poker. I couldn't decide whether to be insulted or flattered.

'I feel fine,' he said. 'Couldn't be better.' He sounded like a New Age positive thinker on a frantic day.

'You don't look fine,' I said, 'but it's nothing terminal. Lotsa water when you get home should do the trick.'

'I always envied Darragh having you . . . a woman like you . . .' Austin's voice was a bit croaky but the words were clear enough. I kept my mouth shut. To encourage him seemed a bad idea. He went on anyway. 'You're a fine woman, Norah.' As passes went it wasn't what you'd call abandoned.

'It's late, Austin,' I said, 'and alcohol is a killer on the judgement . . .'

'I'm sorry, I'm an embarrassment.'

He was sitting with his hands dangling between his knees and his head down when the taxi lurched and he was thrown against me. He shifted away quickly and I felt a stab of pity. Marriage to Sheila could hardly be a barrel of laughs and he'd never struck me as the philandering type. He was probably lonely.

But pity was one thing: being an available comforter was another. I'd been there, worn the lover-of-a-married man T-shirt, and as a way of life *it* wasn't all that much fun either. I kept my distance.

We stopped at the traffic lights at Portobello Bridge and Austin, as a police car pulled up alongside us, remembered our earlier conversation and jolted back to life.

'What happened last weekend? You didn't tell me . . .'

I told him then about the burglary and about how Jamesy Collins had come calling, and threatening. He didn't interrupt and I kept things as concise as possible.

'God, Norah, what a bloody awful experience for you. And all because you've a brother in the guards.'

This was an angle I hadn't thought of before. 'Do you really think that has anything to do with all of this?' I looked at him doubtfully.

'I think it has a lot to do with it,' Austin said. 'If your brother was following Darragh, and his friends, before he died then it seems to me that they could be worried about what he may have seen, or discovered. Looks to me as if they're trying to frighten him off, using you.' He paused. 'The irony is that it's unlikely Darragh was up to any serious wrongdoing. He craved the alternative life, that's all, and liked to brush up against it now and again.'

There was reason and logic to this. It explained why I'd been singled out for intimidation – and it explained a burglary in which only a single photograph had been taken. Jamesy Collins watching the flat and coolly returning after the burglary had been intended to frighten. Now that I thought about it, the main thrust of his little speech had involved threats to Emma if I didn't keep Liam away from things.

As a scenario it changed everything and explained a lot. I gave silent thanks for Austin's uncluttered, linear mind.

'You're right.' I didn't dare risk a hug. 'And now that the guards are on to him, and Liam's been told to leave things alone, there's no reason for them to get at Emma, or Liam.' I let out a deep breath. 'I'm home free.'

'I wouldn't say that, exactly,' Austin said cautiously, 'but I do think you might relax a little.' The driver turned into Makulla Square and he touched me lightly on the hand. 'You're a fine woman, Norah, I meant that. I'd hate to see anything happen to you. I'd like to think you'd get in touch with me if anyone . . . If you've any further problems.'

'If your theory is right then I won't have any more problems, will I?' I gave the house number to the driver and we drew into the kerb. The rain had got worse so I slipped off my precious, low-heeled Italian leather pumps.

'Better cold wet feet . . .' I began to search my bag for the fare.

'Oh, for Christ's sake, Norah, don't be ridiculous.' Austin put his hand over mine in the bag. 'I'll pay this.' When I tried to pull away he held on. 'I mean it,' he said. 'If ever you need anything, it doesn't matter what, call me.'

'Thanks,' I said gently. He clutched my hand tightly between two of his. 'Goodnight, Austin.' I opened the door with my free hand and swung my feet out of the car and into a running stream by the side of the road. The cold took my breath away.

'I'll come with you to the door.' Austin let my hand go and was on the footpath beside me before I could protest, covering me with his coat and rushing me up the steps. He went on holding the coat over me while I found my key and opened the door. Then he stepped after me into the hallway.

I kept moving, putting space between us. Austin kept moving too. When I came to a natural full-stop at the end of the stairs he was right behind me.

'You shouldn't have left the car, Austin.' I was as distant as I could manage. 'You're all wet now.'

'That's a point.' He sighed and leaned against the wall. 'I really am wet.'

Rain had made his hair curly and lingering drops

slid down his face. A less threatening male I had rarely seen. I relaxed.

'I'm safely home, Austin.' I moved past to the open door. 'So thanks and don't keep the driver waiting any longer.'

'You're quite safe from me now, Norah, I'm sobered up as well as wet.' He shrugged into his wet coat. 'I behaved badly in the car. The demon drink . . . I wouldn't offend you for the world, please believe me.'

I believed him. It was hard not to as he stood there, stiffly dignified and in definite discomfort. I was discomfited myself.

'Don't give it a thought.' I gave him a nice smile.

'I wonder if you would . . .' He stopped, looking even more uncomfortable, then went on quickly, '. . . Why don't you let me take you for a meal, feed you up by way of apology?'

'Now?' I looked at him in surprise. Such impulsiveness was definitely out of character in the Austin I thought I'd known.

'No, no, not now, of course not.' He protested so much that I knew he really had had it in mind to rush me off for food there and then. 'Maybe tomorrow, or the day after, the weekend maybe . . .'

'Give me a call,' I said. I was feeling rather touched at the way the men from Darragh's life kept wanting to feed me up. It probably had to do with a perception being that someone of my proportions needed plenty of food.

'Take care then.' He leaned forward and pressed damp lips briefly on to my forehead. A drop of rain fell from his hair on to my face.

'I will,' I said.

It was much too late to go down for Emma so I turned off the lights and started upstairs to bed. In the dark the message light flickered redly on the telephone answering machine. My instinct was to ignore it until morning but, worried it might be Delia and that something had happened to Emma, I turned it on.

I was sorry I had.

The voice was a woman's. The accent was pure Dublin. The message was clear as mud.

'Great play, wasn't it?' the woman said. 'Hope you enjoyed it. Take care, now, Norah, of yourself and of Emma.'

Chapter Fifteen

Friday, 14 January

If I hadn't listened to the answering machine. If I hadn't allowed myself to be seduced by Austin's explanation of events. If I'd phoned Detective-Sergeant Liston straight away after listening to the woman's voice. If I'd kept my head . . .

But I didn't. I allowed my wary vigilance to be relaxed by Austin's explanation and didn't immediately phone Liston. This might not have made any real difference, but then again it might have. As it was, the calamitous sequence of events carried on uninterrupted.

Emma, at breakfast, was full of school plans and schemes. She produced a newsletter with details of a proposed pantomime outing, a museum trip and a school open day to which parents and friends – the entire world from the sound of it – were invited. I was filled with panic. Emma would be exposed, away from the security of the school's normally enclosed routine. I decided it was time to take Maisie's, and Liam's, advice and send her down to the safety of Duncolla. But for now, and until I got the trip organized, I would have a word with her headmistress about the need for extra vigilance. I'd already told Ann Fox that Emma's father had died but had spared her too much detail.

I dropped Emma at her classroom and sought out Ann Fox. Devoted to her school and pupils, she was defensive with parents and would have to be handled delicately. Told too much, she might become fearful for the school, worry about the city's criminal confraternity threatening other pupils. I didn't want Emma singled out either, made to feel different and isolated. She was having a hard enough time.

'I hope this won't take long, Miss Hopkins.' The headmistress wasn't encouraging. 'Our school day is a busy one.' This was a reminder that she preferred parents to make appointments to see her outside school hours.

'I'll be brief as possible,' I said. 'I'd like an especially careful eye kept on Emma. Do you think she could be kept within the school boundaries at all times?'

'None of the children are allowed go beyond the school grounds unsupervised,' she reminded me. 'We are, as you well know, most careful with *all* of the pupils in our charge . . .'

'Of course. It's just that, since her father's death, certain individuals have been paying more attention than is healthy to Emma . . .'

'What exactly are you saying, Miss Hopkins?' Her small face went still as she scented a threat to the school and her charges.

'The circumstances of Emma's father's death, as you know, were particularly tragic,' I was businesslike, 'and have led to a garda investigation which has involved both Emma and myself. Naturally, I'm anxious that Emma be kept away from anyone who might question her or . . .'

'I see. You are not, I presume, referring to the gardai?' She was looking paler than I'd ever seen her.

'No, though the gardai have the situation well in control.' I hoped this was true. 'I simply thought it better to tell you what was going on . . . as a courtesy . . .'

'And a precaution.' Some colour returned to her face. 'I'm glad you did, Miss Hopkins. We need to be aware of anything which might endanger any, or all, of our pupils. Emma will be carefully supervised.' She pulled her sandy brows together. 'As will every other child. I take it this means you will be collecting Emma yourself today?'

'Mrs Brophy will be collecting her, as usual,' I said.

'I see,' Miss Fox said, sadly.

As soon as I arrived at Razorbill I phoned Maisie.

'You said you'd take Emma for a while,' I reminded her. 'Is it all right if I bring her down tomorrow?'

'We can do better than that.' Maisie sounded relieved. 'I'm coming up to Dublin today so I can collect her and bring her back down with me tonight.'

'Maisie, you're a darling. My brother isn't half good enough for you . . .'

'You could be right about that.' Maisie laughed. 'I'll be at the flat around six.'

I rang Ann Fox and told her I'd be taking Emma out of school for a while. She sounded relieved too. I felt an awful lot better myself.

Harry, when he arrived late and with the second hangover of the week an hour later, made a production out of reading aloud the reviews of Conal's play. They weren't raves, but they were good. The *Irish Times*

174

saw *The Eleventh Hour* as 'unashamedly theatrical', the *Independent* said it had a 'strong social context'.

'Not bad.' Harry, in spite of his peaky appearance, glowed with an I-gave-him-his-first-break smugness. 'Not bad at all.' He hadn't been at the first night. Such occasions, he maintained, were for the *arriviste*. Half-way through the morning the playwright himself rang. He was between classes and rushed.

'We're in the middle of a working day here at Razorbill too,' I said tartly.

'You're annoyed about last night,' he said.

'Why should I be annoyed about last night?' Hurt more accurately described how I felt but I wasn't about to tell him that. I was going to be adult about this. He'd invited me to his play. He'd said nothing about taking me home afterwards.

'Look, I'm sorry you had to leave with Austin. There just didn't seem any way I could decently leave at that time . . .'

'I am not annoyed about leaving with Austin. I was happy to leave with Austin. And now I've got work to do . . .'

'What *are* you annoyed about then? What's wrong?'

'I'm busy and I'm preoccupied, nothing more.' Down the phone I could hear a bell ring in the background and a lot of high, childish yells and screams. 'How was Alison after I left?' I asked.

'Fine.' He paused. 'Alison was fine.' He didn't sound convincing. The bells got louder and he said, 'I've got to go. Talk to you again.'

It was a day for phone calls. The one that really cranked the day up to fever pitch came around midday. Detective-Sergeant Liston of Pearse Street garda station was all polite no-nonsense.

'If you could spare the time, Miss Hopkins, I'd like you to call in to see me,' he said.

'What's happened?' Emma . . . I kept calm. It wasn't easy.

'Nothing you need alarm yourself about, Miss Hopkins,' Liston said. 'If you could get here quickly we'll discuss things then.'

'I'll call by on my way home from work.'

'It would be helpful if you came now. I'll wait.'

'I'll be there in twenty minutes,' I said.

There was no waiting about when I arrived at the curved desk this time. As soon as I gave my name a uniformed guard appeared to take me out of the public domain. I followed him along a corridor hung with some good pictures until we came to a door with Detective-Sergeant Liston's name on it. While he knocked I stared at where someone had scribbled 'aliens and refugees!' under his name.

'That's what passes for a joke around here,' the guard grinned.

'Very funny,' I said.

A voice called and the guard opened the door into a room even smaller than the one in which I'd had my first meeting with Liston. It too had no window. A woman garda, delicately pretty as Liston was solid, sat with him. She smiled at me and stood up.

'I'm Garda Waters,' she said.

'Glad you could get here,' said Liston, implying I'd had a choice. 'Garda Waters will be keeping us company.'

Garda Waters sat back down and I dropped myself

into the third seat by the plastic-topped table. The lack of colour, or a window, gave the room a vaguely sinister aspect. At Liston's elbow there were several files and a large, buff envelope.

'You said there was nothing to worry about,' I reminded him. 'Have you discovered something . . . useful?'

'We're hoping that you can help us there.' He reached for the brown envelope. 'I must warn you, Miss Hopkins, that you may find the pictures I'm going to show disturbing. You will certainly find them unpleasant. Even so, I would like you to look at them carefully and, if you can, identify the people in them for me.'

He spilled a series of photographs from the envelope across the table and, spreading them like a pack of cards, arranged them so that they faced me.

'Do any of the people look familiar to you?' He straightened the nearest one. I'd already got glimpses of what they were about but I dutifully leaned forward, head in hands, to examine them carefully. I knew one of the people all right. I knew the main player in all of them. Not immediately and not easily, but it came to me who she was, along with a sick feeling in the pit of my stomach, the longer I stared at them.

It had nothing to do with the way she looked, because she was quite different now. She was a lot older than when the pictures were taken, for one thing. It was the tilt of her head, the vacant, forlorn look on her face in one of the photographs, that alerted me. The blonde hair threw me initially, and the heavy make-up might have thrown me off altogether if I hadn't seen her tarted up recently. Then there was the situation. Jamesy Collins caught in some despicable act wouldn't have surprised me. Alison McCann as porn queen was the last thing I'd been expecting to see.

But there was no mistaking the woman straddling the pictures, in poses variously ludicrous and obscene, no mistaking the limpid gaze and slight, perfect body. Her partners were a mixed lot and she was helped out by another woman in some of the situations. But this was Alison's portfolio. In two of the pictures she was in bondage, in one tied to a bed and in the other hooked up to a wall while her male partner enjoyed a masterful role. In others she was equally pliant, a child-woman between two men.

It was Garda Waters who broke the silence. 'Would you like a coffee?' she asked.

I nodded. 'Two sugars, please,' I said.

In the room alone with Detective-Sergeant Liston I went on studying the photographs. He didn't push me and once the shock and disgust passed I felt pity. Alison was little more than a child in the pictures. Who was I to judge how she'd got herself into the situation? Whatever she'd done then, she was someone else now. She was Darragh's widow, the mother of two of his children.

'What makes you think I might know any of these people?' I asked, carefully. There was too much I didn't understand here. I needed time to think.

'They arrived marked property of Darragh McCann.'

'Oh . . . Have you shown them to anyone else?' I asked, meaning Alison, wondering if Liston was merely using me to confirm something he already knew.

178

'Gardai have visited and shown them to his widow.' He was matter of fact. 'She was unable to help us.'

Unless they'd seen her recent make-over *à la* Lisa they certainly wouldn't have identified Alison themselves. If I hadn't been so sure that Emma was going to be all right, that she'd be safe from whatever was going on in Duncolla, I might not have done what I did next. I pushed the photographs away from me. When in doubt, don't . . .

'I don't know any of these people,' I said.

'You're sure?' Liston asked, mildly enough. I flashed a quick look over the pictures and lied again.

'I'm sure.'

Liston sighed. 'It was a long shot, on our part, bringing you in, but it was one we felt we had to take. The pictures arrived in this,' he laid the buff envelope face up in front of me on the table. As well as Darragh's name in large block capitals it had 'Personal property of' scrawled over it.

'Were you at any time aware of an involvement on Mr McCann's part with prostitution?' Liston's expression wasn't what you'd call a probing, or even searching, look. It missed nothing either.

I shook my head. 'No.'

The pictures were ten or more years old, taken before he'd known Alison. He hadn't been her pimp. It was inconceivable and it was also impossible.

'He didn't mention any money dealings he might have had outside his work as an accountant?'

'No.'

Liston began to put the photographs back into the envelope. He did so very neatly and slowly, giving me plenty of time to reconsider what I'd said about not

179

knowing anyone in the photographs. Garda Waters came back with the coffees and I thought about Alison as she handed them around, the woman Darragh had never been able to leave, now derelict without him. She wasn't evil, merely frail and flawed and, now that the guards had pictures of her prostitution past, probably terrified she was going to lose her children as well. I wasn't going to be the one to make the identification. Alison would have to do it herself. I would see that she did it too, after we worked something out together. I owed her that much, but that was all I owed her.

'You've been very helpful, Miss Hopkins, and we're grateful for your assistance.' Liston looked at his watch.

'Have you come up with anything on Jamesy Collins?'

'We thought that these,' he tapped the envelope thoughtfully, 'might have had something to do with what's been happening to you, that maybe McCann had been involved in a prostitution – a vice racket. We'll continue to pursue that line of inquiry, along with others. But for the moment the answer to your question is no, we don't have any concrete news for you.' He sipped at his coffee, grimaced at Garda Waters and pushed it away. 'What sort of man *was* Mr McCann?'

'He was interesting,' I stopped. Liston was likely to interpret this as deviant. It would be the police thing to do. I began again.

'He was generous and witty . . .' I stopped again; was Liston hearing big spender, flash merchant? I shrugged. 'I'm not sure exactly what it is you want to know about him.'

'Did you ever think Mr McCann was leading a double life?' asked Liston.

'Of course he was.' I was terse. 'He was married.'

'A life outside the law was what I was referring to.' He was impatient.

'No.' I looked him in the eye. 'It never occurred to me that Darragh McCann was a crook or a criminal.'

'Well, that's it then.' The detective stood up, overwhelming the room with his bulk. 'We'll be in touch if there's anything you need to know. Thank you for coming in.'

'There's something I should mention.' I stood and so did Garda Waters. With the three of us standing the room was a very tight fit. 'A woman left a message on my phone answering machine last night. It was fairly innocuous but, well, I felt it was threatening all the same. I'd been to the first night of a play written by a friend of Darragh McCann's. The woman said she hoped I'd enjoyed it and that I should look after myself and Emma. That was all.' I paused. 'But why would someone I don't know bother to leave that sort of message?'

'To intimidate you.' Liston was curt. Garda Waters had taken a few notes while I was talking. 'We have surveillance in place, Miss Hopkins. Be assured we are doing everything we can to safeguard you and your daughter . . .'

'I'm sending Emma away for a while.' I cut him short. 'She's going to stay with my brother and his wife. They've got a farm near Portlaoise. She'll be safe there.'

'We'll alert the nearest station to be on the lookout

for anyone suspicious in the neighbourhood,' said Liston, 'but it would be better all round if you kept quiet about where you're sending her. What dates will she be away?'

I gave them the details and left soon after. I collected my car and pointed it in the direction of the Dublin mountains, Ballinteer and the McCann family home.

Chapter Sixteen

Friday, 14 January. Afternoon

Ballinteer is in the Dublin mountains. In what were once the green and lovely foothills, to be precise, but is now an area overrun by an epidemic of housing developments. Number 331 Rathbourne Drive was in one of these, no better and no worse than any of the others I'd passed on the way. If it was remarkable at all it was for its absolute anonymity. It was hard to imagine Darragh living there.

Like its neighbours, one half of the façade was grey pebble-dash, the other red brick. Like its neighbours too it had net curtains on the windows and a low grey wall surrounding a small garden.

Yet there *were* differences. The bald and muddy state of the garden struck an individual note. None of the other houses had dark curtains pulled tightly closed inside the net ones. It was a desolate mess in an indifferent row of houses. A few small children cycled their Christmas bikes in circles on the road. Otherwise, the place was quiet, with a chill, wintry calm over everything.

It took Alison fully five minutes to answer my banging on the door knocker. The bell didn't work. The journey from Pearse Street hadn't taken long and though it was early, just after noon, I reckoned it was time for her to be out of bed. Unless she was ill, of course. While I waited I divided my time between studying the flaking dark green paint on the door and futile attempts to see something through a gap in the curtains. I waited because I knew, just knew, that Alison was inside.

I'd lifted the knocker for a fourth assault when I heard the bolt being drawn on the inside. The door opened an inch.

'What do you want?' Alison's eye appeared.

'Can I come in?' I would kick the door in if she said no. The cold had gone right to my bones.

'Oh, Norah.' Alison seemed only then to register who I was. 'I was having a rest. Could you come back some other time?'

'No. I could not.' My foot itched. 'I'd like to talk to you, Alison, now. It's important.' She looked as if she was about to close the door so I put my foot against it and pushed. 'I'm not going until we speak,' I said. Her face disappeared and for several seconds there was silence. She was tying a pink cotton dressing-gown around herself when she at last opened the door enough to let me slip through.

'Come in, quickly, quickly,' she urged.

I was barely through the door before she slammed it shut and slipped the bolt into place.

'What's wrong?' I asked. 'What are you afraid of?'

She didn't answer, just turned and hurried into the room with the closed curtains. I followed and found her curled into a couch which took up the length of a wall.

'I don't really feel up to seeing people,' she said.

184

I parked myself in an identical couch opposite. They were brown couches, with the one I sat in taking up the space in front of the curtains. These too were brown, a darker shade than the couches. Cheerful the place was not. Alison's sitting-room, which had once been Darragh's too, was a cold, stale space. One central light bulb hung without a shade and the browns of curtains and couches coordinated dully with the beige cigarette-burned carpet. There was enough ash in the fire grate to account for a small volcanic eruption and scattered toys and a stack of videos were the only evidence that children ever used the room. There was a transient air about it, as if people visited but didn't actually live there.

'Mind if I open the curtains?' I stood up.

'Yes, I do.' Alison sounded panicky. 'But you can switch on the light if you want to . . .'

I flicked the switch by the door and we were bathed in the dirty yellow of a 25-watt bulb. Its glow did nothing at all for Alison. The childish vamp look had disappeared and her small face appeared merely thin and strained. Her hair, falling lank on to the dressing-gown, could have done with a wash. So could the dressing-gown.

'How've you been?' I asked.

She shrugged and shivered before unfurling her feet and placing them, in their dark blue woollen men's socks, neatly on the floor. Darragh's socks, no doubt. They were the only reminder of him in the entire room. Alison studied her feet in the socks when she spoke.

'I was having a rest,' she said again. 'I don't sleep at night. I don't like being alone.'

185

The implication was that Darragh had been an attentive night-time companion. I didn't believe it.

'It can be hard,' I agreed, 'at times. How are the children?'

'They're not bad. Justin's in a crèche down the road. Mollie collects him on her way home from school. They miss their father. They miss the fuss. He played with them . . .' She sank back into the sofa and closed her eyes. The blue socks stayed side by side on the floor.

'The play's doing well so far,' I said. I wanted Alison a little more alert before I launched into the reason for my visit.

'Who gives a shit?' Alison's voice was low and harsh. 'The play's just something else I didn't know about. Like you were. Could be there are more plays, more women with his children. How am I to know? How am I to know anything, stuck in this house with no man and no money and two children depending on me?'

She leaned forward and wrapped her arms tightly around herself. She looked about to collapse.

'Don't you have any women friends?' I was genuinely curious.

'No.'

'Neighbours?'

'No.'

'Relatives?'

'All dead, as far as I'm concerned.' She opened her eyes. Anger gave them a spark of life. 'Malachy hasn't been in touch since the night of the play. He said he would and I thought . . .'

She'd thought he would be attentive, maybe more. A man in her life to tide her over the emptiness while she got used to there being no Darragh. But Malachy would be attentive only when it suited him. Anyone could have seen that. Anyone but Alison.

'It's a busy time, the first week of a play,' I said. 'Maybe it's better to spend some time alone, anyway, give yourself a chance to adjust . . .'

She looked at me as if I'd gone mad. 'What I need is a man to be nice to me.' Restlessly, she jerked her feet up under her. 'Someone to make me feel better again.'

Didn't we all. 'It takes time,' I said. 'It stops eating at you after a while.'

She stared at the curtain behind me as if I hadn't spoken. Maybe, as far as she was concerned, I hadn't. People who trot out wisdoms are hard to take when your life is a pool of misery.

The sheer strength of her apathy, the determination of her unhappiness, was unnerving. I could think of no way to get through it, no way to create an opportunity to bring up the subject of the photographs.

The cold in the room was almost numbing and I was still wearing my coat. An image of hot sweet tea flashed across my inner mind, and stayed there. Hot sweet tea would do us both good. There had to be a kitchen even in this bleak house, had to be water and sugar and tea as well.

Alison began to speak in a low, crooning voice. 'I wasn't very happy in my marriage,' she said. 'Darragh didn't love me. But you knew that. There's no good me pretending any more, or you pretending for me. The love was dead, for a long time, so it's not as if I've lost some great passion. There's nothing so dead as dead love, I heard that somewhere, once, and it's true.'

She stopped and we sat there, the sad truth of what she'd said like a dark cavern between us. God, but it was cold in that room.

'You can love more than once,' I said, hoping she wouldn't ask how this could be arranged, or why I hadn't gone about getting a life-saving second love for myself. I needn't have worried. Alison had been doing some thinking and had come up with her own conclusions. She had faced reality, after a fashion.

'What I've lost is a husband, though he was that in name only. There was no way he was going to start loving me again, ever. I'm not saying he was going to leave me, because he wouldn't have done that. Ever. He promised he'd stay with me the day he married me and that was one thing I believed in, that I'd have him until death. I was right. He always said that he'd look after me and the kids. And he would've too. I was sort of like his cross.' She gave a sour, bedraggled smile. 'I was the burden he had to bear. He thought he could do whatever he liked as long as he was doing his duty. He called me that once, said I was his duty. He laughed when he said it but he meant it and there was no taking it back.'

'Where did you meet him?'

Now, I thought, now I could begin gearing things towards an explanation of the photographs. Except that Alison changed tack. She began to pluck agitatedly at the brown Dralon, picking and smoothing, picking and smoothing as she went on quickly.

'He married me and he put me into this house and then he went back to living the way he always had. I thought a child might do the trick, make him love me again the way he did before he married me, and so I had Mollie.' She sighed. 'Only by then he'd met you and you had a child too, another girl, and a prettier one ...' She trailed off. Her picking had created a small, bald patch on the Dralon and she smoothed over this, trying to make it go away.

'I don't think he would have seen things like that,' I said carefully, 'I'm certain he loved both Mollie and Emma in the same way. And he wouldn't have stayed around simply out of duty ...' I reached a surreptitious hand towards the radiator and confirmed it wasn't on. It was January and Alison had no heating in the house.

'But that's what he did. He stayed out of duty.'

'What about Justin?' I told myself all of this was going somewhere, that though the route to the explanation of the photographs was proving circuitous it would all come out in the round.

'Justin was an accident, that's what about him. An accident.' She paused. 'Justin changed nothing.'

She bit her lip and looked as if she was going to cry. Time, I thought, to get down to business. She could cry later. I would even lend her my shoulder.

'I was shown some photographs of you this morning,' I said. 'You were younger then. I hardly knew you, at first. I think you know the ones I'm talking about ...'

'You must be talking about my wedding pictures. I don't know of any others. Where could you have seen them?' She stopped her plucking of the couch covering. 'I suppose it would have been hard for you to recognize me all right. I was different then. I wore my hair in curls.'

My patience snapped. I'd had enough of the game-playing, enough of people all around me giving me bits and small pieces of the truth. Alison had been a live, if not exactly lively, participant in the photographs and I didn't for one minute believe she'd forgotten them. I sat up straight and barked at her.

'I'm not talking about wedding pictures, Alison, and you know it. You *know* the pictures I'm talking about. The guards were here with them showing them to you. You told them you didn't know yourself in them. You were lying. So tell me about them. Now.'

'I *don't* know what pictures you're talking about . . .'

'Yes, you do. There are about a dozen and you're in all of them, in a variety of working situations . . .'

'You're mistaken.' Alison looked at me with eyes that were blank, denying and cold. 'I haven't worked since I married Darragh and that was nine years ago. I . . .'

'Cut the bullshit, Alison,' I was suffering from frost-bite by this time. 'I'm talking here about pornographic poses and you know damn well what pictures, and working situation, I'm talking about . . .'

'You think you know everything,' said Alison child-ishly. 'You think everything's easy, don't you? But you don't know anything, about anything . . .' All at once she was shouting at me, out of the couch and standing in the middle of the room and clawing the air with her hands. The dressing-gown fell open to reveal a black transparent negligee.

'Sit down, Alison.' I raised my voice but kept it calm. 'Sit down and listen to me.' That was all it took. She deflated immediately and slipped with a sound like a kitten mewing back on to the couch.

'You don't understand,' she whimpered.

190

'I know I don't,' I said, 'but there's a good chance I will if you tell me about those photographs.'

'Where did you see them?'

'In Pearse Street garda station . . .'

'Oh Jesus, Oh sweet God . . . they're showing them to everyone then . . .' There was real terror in her whisper.

'Not everyone,' I said. 'Just a few people they think might know the people in the pictures.' I very much wanted for her to tell me the truth so gave her a couple of minutes for this to sink in before I said: 'I put my neck out for you this morning, Alison. I told the guards I didn't recognize anyone in the photographs. But I swear to you, if you don't tell me what's going on, or was going on, I'm going straight back to Pearse Street to tell them I've had a memory flash. It's up to you.'

She began to cry. Like a small child she stuffed her fists into her eyes and howled, her mouth wide open. I let her at it, but kept my distance, feeling that such abandoned, wholehearted howling must be good for her. She stopped fairly quickly.

'I don't remember them being taken. I don't remember much about that time. I was taking a lot of stuff.' She paused. 'Drugs. Darragh got me out of it.' She dragged the words out of herself, one, two at a time, sniffling as she did so. I didn't interrupt.

'It was all in the past, another life, until a bunch of photographs like the ones you saw today arrived in the post one morning about six or seven months ago. They were addressed to Darragh and there was a letter with them. The letter said the photographs were going to be sent to the school and crèche, that the teachers would get a set each. It said that other people would get them too. Darragh nearly went crazy at first but after a while he said there was nothing for it but to meet the people who'd sent the photos and come to some agreement with them. So he did and they said they wouldn't do anything, that they would leave us alone. I don't know what agreement he came to with them, I swear to God I don't. He didn't tell me.'

She shuddered. 'And now they've sent them to the police. Oh, God, Oh, God!' She was wild-eyed. 'The police can't do anything, can they? All of that happened more than ten years ago. They can't lock me up for things that happened that long in the past, can they? They can't take away my children?'

The fear of losing her children was more than she could bear and she fell apart, sitting hopeless and broken, crying silently. I went to her and she turned and sobbed, her arms wrapped tightly around me, like a small child when it doesn't want you to leave. I held her until she was all cried out, making reassuring noises, feeling infinitely sorry for her and, because I'm nothing if not pragmatic, putting together the couple of questions I still wanted answers to.

Like: What were the photographs being used to blackmail Darragh about?

And: Would she please try to figure out what he had done for the blackmailers to make them back off?

A third question suggested itself on the heels of these. It was about the phone call which had come on Christmas Day. I wanted to know if it had anything to do with the photographs.

I stood and pulled her up with me. 'I want to sort

this thing as much as you do,' I said, 'and a cup of something hot would definitely help. I don't know about you but right now I'd kill for some hot sweet tea. I'll make it while you're getting dressed . . .' I steadied her and she leaned on me like she was used to leaning on someone, which of course she was. 'You *have* got tea in the house?' I asked.

'Only coffee.'

I got her into the bathroom and under the shower. She was pliable as dough, limply allowing everything to be done for her, until I turned on the cold water. That woke her up. I shoved a bar of soap into her hand and left her to it.

While she dressed I rooted about in the kitchen. It wasn't quite as lifeless as the sitting-room, mainly because of a large, curtainless window and a television set showing cartoons. Three of everything sat draining by the sink. There were four chairs around the table. The sharp wintry light from the window focused on breakfast debris and a couple of dead plants. I helped myself from a jar of instant coffee, loading it with sugar to kill the taste. The cupboards revealed breakfast cereals, tins of beans, biscuits and not much more.

'I need to shop.' Alison came silently into the kitchen and began to drink from my mug of coffee. In black leggings and grey sweatshirt she was, if anything, more ashen than before. I made myself another mug of coffee.

'I'm sorry about all that in the other room,' said Alison. 'I'm not myself at the moment.'

Wildly guessing, I'd have said she was herself to the power of ten.

193

'It's freezing in here, Alison. Why isn't the heating on?'

'No heating oil.' Alison warmed her hands around the mug. 'It ran out a couple of days ago. I'm not sure how to order it. Darragh used to do those sort of things. I light a fire in the evenings.'

'How're you managing for money?'

Like it or not, I was involved in the mess that was Alison's life and, before deciding where to go from here, I wanted to know the score. For all I knew Alison and Darragh might have been a part of a vice ring which was still operating. For all I knew too, and in as much as it was any of my business, the money which Darragh had got to put into the play had come from the wages of sin. I doubted it, but anything was looking possible.

'Austin gives me money,' said Alison. 'It's from the company, a sort of pension.' She sat at the table and produced the inevitable pack of cigarettes. 'Sheila would get the same if Austin died.'

'What time do the children get home?' I asked.

'About four,' Alison said. 'The school is just down the road.'

'That gives us a little over three hours,' I said, 'to get to work on what I'm about to propose. I want you to listen, carefully.' I leaned against the draining-board. 'I've had threats and nasty visitors. Sending those pictures to the police looks as if someone's trying to get you too. I meant it when I said that the guards don't know, yet, that you're one of the women in those photographs. But they're going to find out, sooner rather than later if I go back to them. And that's

194

exactly what I'm going to do if you don't level with me. If we're straight with one another we could speed up the garda investigation by passing on whatever information we come up with. We've both got children to protect. So – if you fill me in on what's been happening to you, and what's gone on in the past, we might just come up with some insight into what's going on . . .'

'That's a deal?' Alison gave a dismissive sniff. 'I don't want to talk about things that are done and over with. Honest to God, I don't. Don't ask me to. It wouldn't do any good, you knowing all about the terrible mess my life was at one time . . .'

'The deal is about a bit more than you talking.' I was as patient as I could be. 'What I'm proposing is that, when you've filled me in as much as you can, I take you shopping. We'll stock the cupboards. We'll also drop by the oil heating suppliers and badger them into getting round here straight away. Things will be much easier to deal with when you and the kids are comfortable again.'

She looked doubtfully around the kitchen. 'I was managing so well,' she said. 'I thought Malachy . . .'

'Malachy's not going to pick up the pieces.' I wanted to shake her. 'No one is. And no one's going to look after your children for you either. It's up to you, Alison, so come on, give.'

For a minute I thought she would cry again but she just shrugged and said, 'What do you want to know?' in a resigned voice.

'To begin at the end,' I said. 'Did the row you and Darragh had on Christmas Day have anything to do

195

with the photographs? And don't, please, tell me you didn't have a row on Christmas Day because I know you did.'

Alison debated with herself for a few minutes. I was getting used to the workings of her mind by this time, and could see evasion written all over her face.

'I'm out of here and back to the guards if you don't tell me the truth,' I warned.

'We had a fight,' Alison conceded at last, 'over the photograph people ringing and asking him to go off and meet with them there and then. I didn't want him to go, he'd been out most of Christmas Eve night and that had maddened me and I didn't want him to go out again. He wasn't keen to go out himself but whatever it was they said to him he said he'd no choice but to go. So he went.' She stopped and looked at me defiantly, cheeks flushed, eyes glittering. 'He did it for me, you know, he drowned himself for my sake, so that the mother of his children wouldn't be disgraced and so that they wouldn't have to live with everyone knowing what I'd been. He might have stopped loving me but he never broke a promise and he'd promised to take care of me and them so that's why he did it.' She stopped, breathless. 'Now you know.'

I stared at her, my head whirling as I tried to grapple with what passed for logic in her head. Alison, clearly, was a lot dippier than even I'd given her credit for.

'I'm sorry, Alison,' I said eventually and very gently, 'but I'm not sure what it is you think I know . . .'

'You know now why he committed suicide,' she was patiently matter of fact, 'and why I've been so certain about that. When he was leaving the house Darragh said that he was going to sort things out, get the photographs and put a stop to the blackmail, one way or another. Then, when the guards came and told me he'd drowned in the river I knew that was the way he'd sorted it. He'd gone into the river so as they couldn't get at him any more and so as we'd be safe, the children and me.'

'But, Alison . . .' I stared at her pale, half-smiling face and knew that, in the maddest of ways, she believed everything she was telling me. She had decided on what she'd just told me as a version of events because it was what she could live with. To accept that Darragh had gone out into the lonely quiet of Christmas Day to face down murderous criminals for her sake and been killed for his trouble was more than she could live with.

'You really believe he died for you and the children?' I asked and she nodded, vigorously, yes, that was what she believed and that was what he had done.

'If he wasn't around to blackmail then they couldn't touch us, could they?' Her eyes were hard and bright and so was her smile.

'Of course not. There would be no reason to, once he was gone,' I said. This was not a point on which to disagree with her. There was no way she was going to accept even the possibility that Darragh had been murdered. Once she did that she would have to accept some blame, some responsibility for his death. Darragh taking his own life placed the responsibility firmly with him, as she saw it. Suicide, in Alison's view, was simply his way of fulfilling his pledge to protect her, and the children. She was teetering on the edge of a break-down and couldn't, and wouldn't, accept any other explanation. Not now anyway. Maybe she never would.

It wasn't the time to point out to her either that she'd perverted justice by lying to the guards about when and why he'd left the house. Or that she'd obstructed that same justice by not telling them about the blackmail and the photographs.

It most definitely wasn't the time to point out that the blackmailers had not folded up their tents and gone away.

I did not reckon my chances of getting any more information out of her just then.

'Grab your coat and we'll go shopping,' I said, gently.

In the car, wearing her leather coat, she swung into a mildly elated mood, the mood she'd been in with Malachy when he'd played his consort/protector role. It looked like I'd been assigned the part for the afternoon.

'You said this was a deal, that I was to tell you about myself.' Alison crossed her legs and leaned back. She was paid up on her part of the deal, as far as my interest in anything else she had to say went. I'd had enough of her sad, convenient 'truths' to last me a lifetime. The real truth had become more complex and elusive than ever and all I wanted to do now was get Alison sorted so that I could go home and get Emma packed and off to Duncolla with Maisie.

Maybe then, with the decks cleared, I could get down to a bit of serious detective work on the situation I found myself in. If that failed I'd at least be able to sit things out free of worry about Emma.

But first there was food to be bought for Alison's empty cupboards, an activity which would take a good hour by my reckoning. If Alison wanted to talk about herself I could hardly stop her.

'You know, Norah, I thought all of that past stuff was behind me for ever when I married Darragh.' She was just short of cosying up to me. I kept my eyes on the road and the signs for the shopping centre and grunted. 'I'd put it out of my mind, decided to myself that it had all happened in the life of some other person. You know how it is.' I grunted again and forbore from saying that I didn't really understand how a stint in the pornography business could be blanked from one's mind. Alison shook out a cigarette and lit up.

'Things didn't work out so well for me when I came to Dublin.'

Smoke from her cigarette drifted in front of my face. I opened the window.

'You can't imagine how lonely I was. It was not having anyone started me on the drugs. I couldn't help myself. It began in the hostel. A girl from Belfast called Miriam shared some stuff with me one night. She said it would make us feel good and save us having to eat the hostel food, and I said why not? Miriam let me be her friend after that. She was bigger and older than me and she got us into bars and clubs. Then one day she moved out of the hostel. Just went. I was on my own again and it was worse this time because I'd got used to having a friend.' We came to an intersection and she waved her cigarette to the right. 'It's that way.' She turned up the collar of her coat. 'I'm cold. Can't you close the window?'

'I will if you stop smoking,' I said, deciding to give being tough a whirl.

'I couldn't,' Alison sounded genuinely shocked.

'Fine. I have fresh air and you have your cigarette. That's the deal.'

She continued smoking, and talking. 'I went round to Miriam's flat one night. I was really sick and desperate and I'd no money for gear. There were two men there and Miriam said if I did what one of them wanted he'd pay me and she'd see me all right. It wasn't too bad, what the man wanted, and that's the way it started. It was a lot harder to stop than start.'

I could believe that. I said nothing, just drove slowly and waited to hear where Darragh came into Alison's everyday tale of a life on the skids.

'You don't really have to do anything, you know, just let the men do what they want. They like that.' Alison shrugged. 'I liked the drugs.' I shot a quick look at her profile. She seemed to be concentrating hard, carefully piecing together a landscape of how she'd got to where she was. I grunted again, an encouraging grunt this time. In the wintery daylight her skin was frighteningly translucent.

'Darragh wasn't a client, you know. It was nothing like that. Miriam got me work in a massage parlour. That's what they called it anyway. All it was was two rooms with cubicles around the beds over a pub on the South Circular Road. Darragh was working out a business plan for the landlord.' She gave a short laugh. It wasn't without humour. 'The business didn't go far but Darragh got talking to me one day. I was eighteen and he was nineteen and we got married five months later. I'd still be on the game but for him marrying me. Once I got pregnant he said there was nothing for it but for us to get married . . .'

'Pregnant?'

'An accident. Anyway, I lost the baby. But we were married by then. Darragh got me off the drugs. They said in the hospital it was the drugs lost me the child and he made a prisoner of me after that until I was right off them.'

It was all so easy to imagine, Darragh playing a knightly role to Alison's distressed damsel, not even the ghost of reality between the two of them. I couldn't look at her any more, I didn't want to hear her any more. I would never have thought I could feel so sad for my poor, lovely, misguided Darragh.

'Would you have married him?' Alison asked as we drew into the shopping centre. 'If he'd left me would you have married him?'

'He wouldn't have left you, Alison, you know that.'

He wouldn't have left her because he'd have been fearful of her going back on drugs and neglecting their children and destroying her own life. He wouldn't have been able to live with that. What I couldn't figure was the miracle of Alison the limpid and Darragh the boy-hero producing someone like Mollie.

'What am I to do with myself? How am I to live now?' said Alison as I bundled her along towards the shops. I couldn't think of anything to say.

The shopping centre was cheerful and warm and half empty. I filled a trolley with necessities, as well as a few extras, in thirty minutes flat. I whinged and made the case for Alison-the-widow in the oil heating centre and got them to promise a delivery next day. Just in case, I had Alison buy an electric heater. In the car, on the way back to the house, I made one last stab at poking something like real information out of her.

'Do you have any idea who had the photographs?' I asked. 'Or why they would have given them to the police?'

'No. I'm out of all that. It's gone, in the past. I want nothing to do with it.'

'Yes, I understand that, Alison. But what about Darragh? Did he get dragged into something?'

'How should I know? He didn't tell me things.' Her voice became shaky. 'I told you before, I never knew what he was up to. If you want to know, we hardly spoke a lot of the time. Except about the children. None of what's going on now has anything to do with me. I didn't know what Darragh was up to and I didn't want to.'

'Listen, Alison, I know you're frightened, but I need some help here. I need . . .'

'You're damn right I'm frightened!' Her voice rose to a shriek which, in the confines of the car, was ear-piercing. 'I don't want to talk about this. I don't . . . I don't . . .'

She began to shiver and shake and I pulled into the kerb and stopped the car. She looked at me with eyes like a beaten dog and it would have taken a Rottweiler to keep on at her. As dogs go I'm a Labrador.

'I'm sorry, Alison,' I said. 'Let's just forget it. Now, tell me where the school and crèche are and we'll pick the children up.'

Chapter Seventeen

Friday, 14 January. Evening

Maisie, in a lambskin coat and red beret, arrived hard on my heels at the apartment.

'Bit of luck, my coming up to town today.' She followed me into the kitchen, arms around a cardboard box filled with enough vegetables to feed a large household for two weeks. She dumped it on the table and looked round. 'Emma'll be the better away from all of this,' she said. Her eyes moved from the fresh putty around the kitchen window to the rough repair job I'd done to the cupboard doors. Maisie had not come casually to town. She'd come for a front-line, post-burglary inspection.

'I thought maybe a few weeks . . .' I began.

'Three. At least.'

I didn't argue. Maisie fed the cat while I poured us a couple of glasses of wine.

'Those yobs gave the place a right going over,' said Maisie. 'I don't know how you can stay on, really I don't. I wouldn't myself.'

I could see where this was going, and see my brothers' over-protective hands in what was coming. I cut her off at the pass.

'I'm not going down to the farm, Maisie. Emma's one thing but I've got a job and a life here. And don't tell me you'd pack up and leave the farm if there was a break-in because that's nonsense.'

'Maybe not,' Maisie conceded. 'But the boys are worried and they . . .'

'The boys! Jesus Christ, Maisie, my brothers are grown men and I'm a grown woman.' I calmed down and gave her a hug. 'I know you're all worried but I really am able to look after myself.'

Maisie went on looking worried. 'I'm just telling you the option's there. Why so ratty and over the top, Norah? Things not so fine as they might be?'

'You could say that,' I sighed. 'Nothing life-threatening, though.' I hoped I was right about this. 'And nothing a bit of time and work on the part of the gardai won't sort out.'

'I see.' Maisie cast a calculating eye at the black night beyond the window. 'Do me a favour, Norah, and stay out of this thing yourself. Charging into the night to take on a criminal yob wasn't the wisest action you've taken in your short life. It'll stay a short one if you . . .'

'I'll be good,' I promised.

Maisie folded her arms on the table and looked at me hard. 'Maybe you're right about staying here,' she conceded. 'Some time on your own might give you a chance to come to terms with the death.'

'Yes,' I said.

And then it was time to say goodbye to Emma. Maisie, tactfully, went on ahead to the car and we stood in the kitchen, Emma and I, holding hands and putting off the moment.

'Be nice to Maisie and . . .' I began.

204

'When will you be down to see me?' Emma asked.

'At the weekend. I was thinking I'd paint your bedroom while you're gone. Would you like that?'

'Will you come on Friday or Saturday?'

'Oh, Emma.' I opened my arms and she came into them. 'You'll have a lovely time in Duncolla. And I'll come on Friday. Now give me a kiss goodbye. Maisie's waiting.'

She kissed me and picked up her schoolbag and held my hand while we walked to the front door. She hopped down the steps, only stopping when she got to the bottom.

'See you on Friday,' she called, and ran to Maisie in the car.

The flat took on a spooky, silent emptiness after they'd gone. I read for a while, then did some work, then had a bit of a think. The latter proved not to be a good idea. Fantasies about Darragh and what he'd been involved in came thick, fast and wild, all of them centring on him having been some sort of vice over-lord with Alison as his handmaid and me a naïve novelty on the side. Maybe everything Alison told me had been true. Problem was, I was damn sure she hadn't told me everything.

By ten o'clock I was a pacing, strung-out basket case. I'd been to Emma's room twice to tidy it up and straighten her bed. I'd phoned Duncolla to check they'd arrived safely and then phoned again to check she was in bed and hadn't forgotten me.

By 10.45 p.m., having worked myself into a frenzied need for company, and some more answers, I phoned Conal Bergin. He might just provide both. He might provide more. I tried not to think how nice it would be to go to bed with him but my imagination had gone into overdrive and it was hard. Impossible, in fact.

Conal made pleasant, if surprised sounds, at hearing from me. When I asked if I could call over to see him he gave immediate and precise directions.

'Just give me a half hour to clear the mess,' he said. 'I'm up to my armpits in copybooks.'

I'd never been to Conal's place before but Darragh had told me about the small, two-up two-down he'd bought in Ringsend.

'Are you sure you're OK?' His greeting was warm and reassuring.

'I'm fine.' I held up a bottle of red. 'And this is by way of an offering for the ear you're going to lend.'

He hadn't exaggerated about the copybooks. There were great stacked piles of them in his living-room, which took up almost all of the ground floor space. He took my coat and led me to a wing-backed chair before disappearing to get glasses and an opener. Even allowing for the copybooks the place had style. The fireplace was in curving cast-iron and the bookshelves were of the palest, honey-coloured wood. The floor was covered in polished flagstones. This assured taste was a side of Conal Bergin I didn't know. It made me uncertain.

He reappeared and we began on the wine. He was wearing a truly awful green jumper and he sat down in a chair opposite me.

'I went to see Alison today,' I said, Nothing like beginning at the end. 'And I spent the morning in Pearse Street garda station.'

'Alison's going to need help getting her life

206

together,' he said quietly, and, then, 'What were you doing in Pearse Street?'

I launched into and told him, briefly as I could, the tale of events. He didn't interrupt, though he did look at me sharply a couple of times, once when I told him about Alison's early working life and again when I told him Alison's theory that Darragh had committed suicide, and why.

'Did you know how Alison and Darragh met?' I asked at last.

'No.' He gave a small groan. 'This is all news to me . . .'

I went back to the puzzle of the photographs. 'They weren't just titillating sexual poses, Conal. This was porn, and pretty graphic at that. Alison looked totally stoned in them. What I don't understand is who gave them to the police and why . . .' I shook my head. 'In fact, what I do understand is bloody minimal. Except that I'm sure Darragh wasn't pimping, or part of some vice ring . . .'

'No. Vice wasn't Darragh's thing. He adored women too much to exploit them . . .'

'Neglect is a harshness, an exploitation,' I said.

'It can be.' Conal looked at me. 'Though I doubt he saw it like that. He saw you living your own life, getting on with it . . .'

'I wasn't talking about me,' I interrupted. 'I was talking about Alison and their children. Oh, I know he put a roof over their heads and that they were clothed and had enough to eat. But that was it, from the looks of things. There isn't a trace of Darragh in the house they live in. You must have seen that for yourself. He paid the bills and left them to get on with it, taking the children on splashy outings, the big treat dad. Now *that's* harsh, and it was an exploitation of their affection for him too.'

'Yes, it was,' he said, 'but by default. It wasn't calculated.'

'No,' I agreed sadly, 'it wasn't calculated. He was simply doing what suited him.'

He gave a bewildered shake of his head and stood up. 'Christ, Norah, I don't know why I'm defending him. I didn't agree with things he did when he was alive so God knows what I'm doing defending the same actions now.'

He paced for a minute then sat down again and quickly finished his glass of wine. 'I suppose I'm defending him because he was my friend and it appears to be open season on him now that he's dead.' His tone was subdued. 'The view seems to be that he was either a waster, a messer, a user, an opportunist, a thief, a philanderer,' he pulled a wry face, 'or a vice king. OK, he was some of those things. But he was other things too and he was my friend and I cared for him. I still do.' He looked away from me. 'I loved him, and that's not an easy thing for one man to say about another and be understood. He was what he was and I accepted him, critically. It's harder for me to be critical of him now he's dead and has become a sort of field sport.'

We sat in silence. 'You're right,' I said after a while. 'There's not much point in doing an open surgery job on him now. But things do need to be sorted. I thought we might talk . . . All I'm doing is intruding on your grief . . .' I put down my glass. 'I'll go . . .'

He shook his head. 'Please don't. I want to listen.

Go ahead, sound me out.' When I hesitated he stood, threw a log on to the fire and said, 'Bottle's empty, I'll get another.'

The log crackled and I got on to the floor and hugged my knees watching the flames. If I was honest with myself I hadn't just come to talk. Conal wasn't a fool: surely he must sense the need in me . . .

He was back with the wine in no time.

'Talk.' He refilled my glass and sat on the floor beside me. We watched the fire together.

'Did you know Darragh met Alison in the massage parlour rooms you used to rehearse your first play?' I asked.

'No,' he shook his head, 'but it doesn't surprise me. It's likely he met massage parlour people in the pub too, the way he met us.'

'But why would someone give those pictures to the guards? Why would they want to blackmail a dead man?'

Conal put his glass on the ground between his feet. 'My guess is that Darragh got into some money dealing that went wrong. Leave it to the guards to discover what it was, Norah. You're upset and in no state to go charging into the jungle on your own.'

'I should go . . .' I didn't want non-committal advice. I wanted information, facts about Darragh's life which would make sense of what was happening. If he couldn't give me those then all I wanted was for him to hold me, kiss me the way he had a few nights before.

'I like having you here,' he said. 'Why don't you stay the night?'

I closed my eyes and enjoyed the heat of the fire on my face. 'Sounds like a good idea . . .'

'What about Emma?' he sounded closer, almost as if he were peering into my face. I kept my eyes closed.

'Emma's away,' I said. 'My sister-in-law Maisie's taken her to the farm. It'll do her good and she'll be safer there, with dogs and alarms and fencing and all sorts of things protecting the place . . .'

'In that case you can relax,' his voice was in my ear, 'and it might as well be in the bed.'

I felt his arms go under me and then his breath on my forehead as he lifted me up. I opened my eyes and made a mild protest as he carried me across the room to the stairs. My size and weight didn't seem to bother him and a part of me was deeply impressed. At the bottom of the stairs I increased the protest levels.

'Be quiet.' He began climbing.

I was too big for him to get me through the bedroom door. Laughing, holding on to one another, we made our way to the bed. I fell across it, and while Conal removed my boots took lazy note of the books and folders everywhere, a littered writing desk and moribund-looking word processor.

'Norah.' He smiled down at me, looking pleased.

'Delia . . .' I had a sudden stab of conscience. 'She'll be worried.'

'Delia's not your keeper . . .'

'No. She's not . . .'

He took off his glasses and held my face in both of his hands and said to me, very softly, 'You were the one thing I always envied Darragh. God, how I envied him having you.' He smiled. 'Now you know,' he said. 'My secret's out.'

'Conal . . .'

210

'It's all right,' he said, still smiling. 'That's not a proposal. You're quite safe.'

'I know that,' I said and moved closer to him and held my mouth up to his to be kissed.

He held me gently, loosening my hair as he touched his mouth to mine. The kiss developed nicely and became long and hot and probing in no time. We came up for breath and I shook my hair free of his hand and thought how gentle his face was. He said my name, 'Norah', again, making it sound like a caress as he pulled me close and began, with a slow luxury, to touch the parts of me that wanted to be touched. I felt the old, familiar melting process begin, a treacherous softening take over as the excitement moved from my belly up . . .

I twisted away and put my hands against his chest.

'Do you think this is a good idea?' I said, suddenly uncertain.

'It's a brilliant one . . .' he grinned.

'You're right.' I put my mouth against his again.

He was no novice, thank God, and the sex was great; a purging, liberating, wonderful thing. We made love too fast the first time but with a great deal of slow, wonderful, exploring care the second time. He was thoughtful and he was imaginative and he was not, thank God again, one of those men who're afraid to talk in bed.

'You're a goddess,' he assured me, moving his hands thoughtfully in all sorts of ways and along parts of me that set up welcoming tremors even before he got there. He knew it too and grinned and gave me a long kiss and said, 'You're an Aphrodite, made to be loved.'

'Then love me,' said Aphrodite and he did, for a good two hours until, in wonderful tiredness, we fell asleep.

I woke to the light of a grey, January morning coming through the skylight window and the smell of fresh coffee coming from below stairs. I lay there and took time to really look around and saw that the bedroom and bathroom made up the entire upstairs. It looked to be where he did a lot of his living and I liked it. I'd liked the Conal who'd inhabited it with me the night before too.

But sharing good sex and some tender loving care in the night was one thing. A lukewarm shower sobered the senses and brought an old, self-preserving caution into play. I liked Conal. More than liked him . . .

But the timing was all wrong, though. I couldn't think straight and my feelings were on an emotional seesaw that was going to take a while to balance out. Maybe when the turmoil created by Darragh's death was over, when I was less frantic about Emma, when grief had abated . . .

I dressed in the bathroom and came out into the bedroom to face a tray-carrying Conal.

'Breakfast,' he said. His dressing-gown was a sludgy shade of brown, definitely not a good morning colour. I found myself thinking of replacing it with a more positive blue, or even a stripy model, and caught myself on quickly.

'I didn't feel you getting up,' I said, awkwardly. 'You should have woken me.'

'I don't like sharing my kitchen.' He put the tray down on the desk. It held orange juice, brown bread, marmalade, a coffee pot and two mugs. He handed me a juice.

'Black or white coffee?' he asked.

I sat carefully on a chair by the desk with the juice. 'Black,' I said and fixed a smile to my face. 'Look, Conal, I don't want to sound presumptuous but I can't stay. Emma will be ringing me and I've got a job to finish for Harry this morning . . .'

'You still have to have breakfast.' He put the coffee beside me on the desk and sat on the bed with his own mugful. 'Help yourself,' he nodded at the brown bread.

'Thanks.' I spread some marmalade. If he'd made a move to touch or kiss me I'd have been lost again. He didn't. He went on being polite, as if the night before and now was all part of a bed and breakfast deal. It looked as if he felt much as I did about the timing of things between us. I felt irrationally peeved.

When I stood to go he immediately got up too.

'Thanks for last night,' I said. 'It was . . . lovely.'

'I'll get your coat.' He kissed me lightly on the forehead as he passed. In the hallway he helped me into the coat and turned me to face him.

'Give me a call,' he said. 'Any time.' He kept his hands on my shoulders.

'Yes,' I said. The sludgy dressing-gown didn't seem so awful any more. He touched my face. He looked even nicer. 'You'll get cold.' I nodded at the dressing-gown. 'Better get out of the hallway before I open the door.'

'I meant it about calling. Don't be alone and don't be frightened, or worried.'

'Things will work out,' I said, 'somehow . . .'

I meant things in general, but I meant us too and was aware of sounding a little desperate. Conal hesitated fractionally before opening the door and stepping back to let me through.

'Thanks for everything,' I kissed him lightly on the lips and stepped into the street.

'Take care,' he said.

The car started straight away. When I turned to wave he'd already gone back inside.

The horrible thought occurred that sleeping with me might, for Conal, have been some sort of weird extension of his friendship and loyalty to Darragh. I hoped not but, given the events of the last weeks, anything was possible.

214

Chapter Eighteen

Saturday, 15 January

Austin Finn turned up on my doorstep late that Saturday afternoon. I'd had a bellyful of domesticity and was pleased to see him. It was five o'clock and a hard night frost was settling in.

'Hello, Norah.' He was diffident to the point of appearing faded when I opened the door. 'I could say I was just passing but of course that would be a lie. May I come in?'

'Of course, Austin. Nice to see you.'

I went ahead of him into the living-room. 'How are things?' I asked. I had in mind things with the beautiful Sheila.

'Things . . .' He pulled a rueful face and began to peel off a pair of fleece-lined gloves. 'Depends what you mean. Things in general aren't great.' He put the gloves into the pocket of his navy blue Crombie overcoat. 'But some things in particular are doing fine.' He shrugged out of the coat and stood like a polite dinner guest with it and his gloves over an arm. His impeccable grey suit and waistcoat were a bit over the top for weekend wear.

'You can tell me about the good things.' I took them from him. 'And about the rest only if you have to.'

He followed me to the kitchen, where I got us drinks, and then obediently back to the living-room where I'd been working by the fire. We had a desultory kind of conversation while this went on, with me finding it hard not to pounce and demand why he'd come.

'A woman's work is never done.' Austin looked at the manuscript pages spread across the floor. 'Looks as if I've disturbed you . . .'

'I'm behind with a few things,' I admitted. 'It's been a fractured couple of weeks.'

'That it has.' He sidestepped carefully around the pages and sat down in an armchair. 'I should have phoned.' He sipped his drink.

'I like surprises.' I sat on the floor, gathering up the pages. 'But take me out of my misery anyway. Why are you here?'

He cleared his throat. 'Because I want to take you and your daughter out for the night. I reckoned my chances were better if I caught you on the hop.' He looked apologetic. 'And if you were free, of course.'

I was touched. 'It was a lovely idea, Austin, and I appreciate it. But Emma's not here at the moment,' I said. 'I've sent her down to my brother's place in Duncolla for a while.'

He looked a bit taken aback but nodded approval. 'Good idea,' he said. 'You need a break, with all that's going on.' From his pocket he took a clutch of tickets. 'One should never be presumptuous. These are for tonight's Gaiety pantomime.' He dropped them beside him on the floor. 'Seemed like a good idea at the time, and worth the chance.'

'It was. Emma would have liked it very much.' I was feeling uncomfortable. 'If she'd been here.'

'Maybe I could take you for that meal I promised instead?' His expression was slightly pleading and, when I didn't immediately respond, he added, 'I've got something to celebrate and no one to do it with.'

I gave in to curiosity. 'What are you celebrating?'

'Sheila's left me.' He looked at his watch. 'She is, as we speak, airborne, on her way to a time-share place we own in Florida. I always disliked it there, Sheila's always loved it. She'll stay for the foreseeable future, which is to say three months or so. By that time our solicitors will have sorted something out. It should be all fairly amicable. No love lost on either side and it's been coming for a long time.' He became apologetic. 'I know that I should have checked with you about the pantomime but please come out to eat with me instead. No need to dress up, you're fine as you are.' He paused. 'I could do with the company.'

The latter was obvious. His need of company was the real reason he'd come calling, unannounced, on a Saturday afternoon.

'I'm sorry about Sheila,' I said. News of her defection wasn't the surprise it might have been prior to her Thursday night performance after the play.

'I'm not looking for sympathy,' Austin said hastily. 'I don't need it. But nor do I want to go back to the house any earlier than I have to. How about if I take you across town to Howth? We could find somewhere with a view of the harbour . . .'

'Sounds nice.' I was vague because I was uneasy. 'Except that I was planning an early night.' This was

217

true. There really hadn't been a lot of sleeping done the night before. There was also the fact that I wasn't one bit keen on being caught up in Austin's rebound from his marriage. I liked him. He was a nice man, probably a good one. He was attractive. It was just that I'd never thought about him in *that* way and we were both alone. The night had all the makings of a situation I didn't want to have to deal with.

'Indulge me.' Austin stood up. 'I haven't eaten. Don't send me out into the night to eat alone.' He looked morosely around the room. 'Nice place. Comfortable. I can see why you wouldn't want to be tempted into the night by a boring old accountant.' He loosened his tie and sighed. 'Look, Norah, I'm obviously going to have to come clean. This call isn't just to do with pleasure and I didn't come entirely on impulse either. Fact is, something's turned up on Darragh's side of things at the company which drags you right into this mess. We actually *need* to talk. It doesn't have to be tonight, of course, but it would probably be better to get it out of the way. I'd hoped we might be able to sort something out in the course of a pleasant evening, take the sting out of things so to speak. But if you'd prefer we can talk some other time . . .'

'The suspense would kill me.' I smiled.

We went to Howth. Remembering the advice of Lisa from the Gresham's ladies, I put a 'face on things' with make-up and my best black dress. I'd never be Sheila but I did have a certain presence.

Austin hadn't mentioned Alison and I decided, driving along in his smoothly purring Merc, that I wasn't going to mention her unless he did first. This

218

was the same unease I'd felt about levelling with the police, a feeling that she deserved the chance to sort her early mistakes with the guards herself. I'd told Conal about the photographs because he'd seemed to me the one person likely to know about Darragh and Alison's past. Austin was different. He'd only known Darragh four or five years and then not that well personally. I'd told Alison I would give her a chance to tell the police about the photographs herself and it seemed only fair to keep that promise. Broadcasting her story to everyone who knew her seemed to me just what the people who'd sent the photographs to the gardai would want.

Austin's choice of restaurant was subdued and very expensive. The sort of place I could imagine Sheila at home in. Austin was known there and we were given a table by a window with views of the harbour.

'Do you like it?' he asked.

A piano played softly and waiters padded discreetly between linen-covered tables. The cream and dark blue décor had subtle pools of roseate light and a mood *intime*. Diners spoke in murmurs and gave stifled laughs, a pianist played Gershwin and, outside, boats bobbed merrily on the icy waters of the harbour. There were no prices on the menu.

'It's very nice,' I said. 'I hope your news isn't too grim. I meant it about needing an early night . . .'

'I'll have you home by ten o'clock,' said Austin. I'd heard the line before but from Austin I believed it. We ordered and marked time until the food and wine came. As I began to eat Austin asked, 'How are you managing for money?'

'I'll be okay,' I said.

'The company may be able to help out,' Austin said. 'All you have to do is say the word.'

'I'll remember that,' I said, 'and you might live to regret saying it. But since we're on the subject of money, what is it you've turned up about me in Finn and McCann?'

'We could talk about it after the dessert ...' He started to refill my glass but I covered it with a hand.

'Please, don't. Just tell me ...'

'Right ...' He topped up his own glass. 'You may already know something of what I'm about to tell you, Norah, you may not. It's got me reeling ...'

'Darragh didn't discuss company business with me,' I said, 'so you can safely assume whatever it is will be news to me too.'

'Right. Well, the fact is that I've uncovered a lot more about the sideline business Darragh had going ...' He paused and looked at me as if, in spite of what I'd just said, I could somehow enlighten him. When I said nothing he went on. 'I've followed a fairly exhaustive paper trail and come to a full stop with a company called NOMA, which appears to be the umbrella company for all of his dealings.' He fiddled with his glass for so long I thought he would break the stem. 'Darragh had been making investments on behalf of this company for several years, putting money into high-risk, high-yield new ventures, that sort of thing. Some of them have paid off, others were less successful. Conal Bergin's play was only one such venture. The money he put into it came from the NOMA account ...'

'Apart from the fact that you didn't know about this account, what's so terrible about it?' I asked, carefully.

'What's terrible, Norah, is that the money he's invested for NOMA, redirected from clients' accounts without their knowledge, has risen to very serious figures . . .'

'What you're telling me is that the buck stops with this NOMA crowd? That whatever money came from Darragh's investment gambles was to be paid to NOMA and not back into the accounts he'd lifted the money from?'

'That's it, more or less . . .' He poked aimlessly at his lobster. 'NOMA appears to be the only account to benefit. If there are others I've yet to find them. It could be that he intended straightening affairs, paying the money back in the fullness of time . . .'

'But you don't think so. And as things stand, whatever profits are made from these ventures all go into this NOMA account?'

'Yes.'

'Well, now that you've uncovered all of this can't you have the bank close NOMA down and pay the people back their money? Do they even have to know?'

'It's not that simple.'

Of course it wasn't. There hadn't been a simple breath drawn around me since Alison's arrival in my life on 2 January.

'Tell me,' I sighed, 'but do the complicated bits slowly.'

'It's not complicated, just a mess.' Austin gave a rueful smile. 'We're in the stupid position of knowing where and with what bank the account is but are without legal access to it. Darragh arranged things so that he and one of the other directors were the only people with access. To say that I'm reluctant to expose

Finn and McCann and the state it's in to the bank is putting it mildly. We'd be totally ruined, left without any chance of salvaging the company. What I need to sort things out are either the original set-up papers or an agreement in writing from one of the directors of NOMA . . .'

He stopped, but I had the picture anyway. It didn't take genius to figure out where I came in. Austin may have felt himself reeling from the shock of his discoveries but I was fairly well in orbit myself. I was also, instinct told me, far from a safe landing.

'I don't have any papers, Austin,' I said quietly. 'Whatever Darragh did he did without telling me. NOMA is an anagram of Norah and Emma, isn't it? And I'm a director, aren't I?' He gave a worried nod and I went on. 'I've never signed anything. If my signature is there it's forged. Maybe he was going to square it with me, I don't know. I don't know anything about any of this. But what you've just told me does explain a lot . . . sort of . . .' A thought occurred. 'Did he mean us to have the profits? Or was he simply using our names and nothing more?'

'I don't know.' Austin shook his head. 'It may be that he thought he could look after both his families *and* put the original money back into the clients' accounts without anyone ever knowing it had been taken in the first place.'

'What sort of money is involved?'

'Upwards of a million and a half, over the last three years. The company's ruined if we don't get this thing sorted out.'

'Does Sheila know?'

'Yes.'

222

'Is that why she left?'

'The two events are not entirely unconnected.'

I had another horrible thought. 'Can I be held responsible? Can I be prosecuted if the people whose money was moved around like this decide to go after me for it?'

'No. Certainly not. I'll see to it that you're not involved.'

'And where,' I took a deep breath, 'does my new friend Jamesy Collins come into all of this?' The awful fear growing in the pit of my stomach was that some of the invested money had belonged to Jamesy.

Austin sighed. 'Darragh dabbled with all sorts and types but I'm reasonably sure Collins had nothing to do with Finn and McCann. I'd have come across the name by now. Could be Darragh had him bring a car into the country for him, something like that. God knows what else Darragh was up to.'

I relaxed again, but not a lot. Austin could be right. He knew more about it than I did. But he didn't know everything. No one did.

'Consider yourself lucky, Austin,' I raised my glass, 'that all you have to contend with is a little embezzlement on Darragh's part. He's left me to deal with a threatening thug and menacing phone messages . . .'

Austin touched my hand shyly. 'You don't have to be on your own, alone with Emma I mean. The house in Blackrock is big, far too big. Always was.' He smiled, a fairly wonky effort. 'It's bigger than ever now Sheila's gone. You're welcome to stay, the pair of you, for as long as you like. No strings attached.' He added the last hastily and with a shrug.

'Thanks, Austin.' I thought this really nice of him.

'But no thanks. I'll go with the arrangement I've made and hope things sort themselves out over the next few days. The guards are bound to come up with something. They know this Jamesy Collins, they say they're looking into everything to do with him, everything to do with Darragh's life which might have involved him too.'

They were probably, as we spoke, finding out about Alison's life of porn. Linking it up with the NOMA account for all I knew. I hoped I was doing the right thing not telling Austin about the photographs and blackmail. If Alison didn't go to the police on Monday I would tell him. There wasn't a lot he could do if I told him now anyway, given that the next day was Sunday and not a working day.

'Have the guards been on to you yet about Darragh's connection with Jamesy Collins?' I asked.

'Briefly,' said Austin, 'to make an appointment to see me during the week. I might have come up with something to help them by then, but I doubt it. There's nothing I'd like better than to help nail that bastard Collins but there's nothing, anywhere that I can see, to link him with Darragh's investing activities.' He swirled the contents of his glass and added, with a bitterness I hadn't heard in him before, 'You'll have to take it that I'm right on this, Norah. About money, at least, I know something. Even if I'm a lousy judge of human kind.'

'Darragh would have made things come right, somehow,' I said. 'I know he would.' I could find nothing consoling to say about Sheila. The piano was silent and, out in the harbour, boats were beginning to bob uncomfortably in a rising wind. It seemed a good time to leave.

'Can we go now?' I said.

'Not until you've been properly fed.' Austin, displaying a bit of imperious steel, signalled a waiter and got us a couple of dessert menus. He decided on cheese and I went for a chocolate concoction which promised more calories than was decent to eat in a week.

'You do realize you could help with this mess, Norah,' Austin said while we waited for my calories and his cholesterol.

'Because I'm named as a director on Darragh's fictional account?'

'Yes.'

'You want me to sign something, don't you?' The waiter arrived with Austin's cheese and my dessert. 'Tell me what it is,' I said.

'With Darragh gone you're it, Norah, you're NOMA. There are a set of papers which, if signed by you, could get us all out of this thing . . .' He hesitated. 'Signing them would also get you off the hook if any complicating factors arise . . .'

'What complicating factors? You said there wouldn't be any. That I wouldn't be in any trouble . . .'

He was keeping something back, I just knew it. As liars went Austin wasn't very good. I didn't like the way this set of papers had suddenly come into the picture. I'd believed him when he'd said he'd see to it I wouldn't be involved. I'd been a fool. Either he hadn't meant it or he couldn't do it. Hysteria caught me by the throat.

'Tell me what the implications of my name on that account are.' I paused. 'Please.'

'It doesn't matter what they are, Norah.' Austin's smile seemed to me less reassuring than it had been. 'I'll see to it that this thing never becomes a problem for you . . .'

It wasn't that I didn't believe him any more, more that I didn't believe he could do it. 'What you're really saying is that it *could* become a problem for me,' I said, 'and that you'll do what you can when it does. Well, that's very kind Austin, and I appreciate the offer, but I *haven't done anything wrong* . . .'

'None of us have done anything wrong, Norah, and you're getting this thing way out of proportion . . .'

'Nearly a million and a half pounds embezzled and and my name's on the crooked account and you're telling me I've got things out of proportion. I could be facing fraud charges, years in jail . . .'

'I'm telling you I'm going to look after it . . . after you . . .'

'How?'

'This is my business we're talking about, Norah, the bit of the world I understand. By signing you'll get yourself out of all this, dissolve that account and give me access to our clients' money so it can be paid back . . .' He stopped. He was looking relatively cheerful. 'We can get things sorted tonight, if you like. Everything I've been working on is in a briefcase in the car. I'll show you what I've done and you can sign . . .'

I was taken with a fatal-feeling calm as a further complication darted from my unconscious. 'Let me think about it, Austin,' I said quickly, 'while I take myself to the loo.'

The loo, unfortunately, was occupied by two skinny,

middle-aged women in black who were engaged in a noisy row about someone called Douglas, seemingly the husband of one and more than a friend to the other. I locked myself into a cubicle, stuffed my ears with soft, pink toilet paper, and had a think.

Austin really didn't know whether the NOMA account had anything to do with Jamesy Collins and Co. The thought that it might be had scared me into a paralysing calm and filled me again with fears and horrors for Emma's safety.

If I went along with Austin's plan for dismantling the account, then I might very well screw up whatever the police were doing about Jamesy Collins. Much as I would have liked to sign myself out of things, the risk of creating an even greater mess was too great. I needed time, and to give the guards more time, before I signed anything.

If I was right, and logic as well as instinct told me Jamesy and NOMA were linked, then Austin would surely be in the clear anyway once the guards got things sorted out.

If I was right, and what Darragh had been up to at Finn and McCann was part of a bigger scheme of things, then Austin prematurely drawing money out of the NOMA account and handing it back could bring the wrath of all sorts of corrupt types on his head too. I needed time to breathe and the guards needed time to get on with whatever they were doing.

Austin stood as I arrived back at the table.

'Are you all right?' He held out my chair for me. 'I don't want you worried about this.' He patted my shoulder as I sat. 'The whole idea was to take the pressure off you and sort things out. I've done the thinking, Norah,' he smiled, 'and this is the way to do it.'

'Give me a few days,' I said.

'Oh, God, Norah.' He sat down, rubbing a hand across his eyes. 'We don't have a few days. Things are moving, client inquiries are piling up . . .' He let out a deep breath. 'But that's not your problem. Come on, I'll take you home.'

We drove back across town in silence. I felt I'd let Austin down by not signing but knew he'd see the sense to what I was doing in time. I didn't ask him in for a nightcap. I wasn't sure how much comforting he might need if he had a few more drinks.

Chapter Nineteen

Sunday, 16 January

I was too exhausted to sleep. After Austin had gone, after I'd had a long soak and watched the last thing watchable on television, I lay in my bed with the cat and willed my mind to turn off. But the dull, low density buzz in my skull went on, unreliable theories and half-formed conclusions circling and coming round to meet each other. Two weeks of having my world stood on its head had taken a toll. I missed Emma and the cat was no comfort at all.

There had been a message from Conal asking me to give him a ring. When I'd done so his number had rung unanswered in my ear, making me feel even more miserable. Quite bereft in fact. It had left me wondering too where he was at nearly midnight on a Saturday night. Not that it was any of my business.

A knocking on the front door woke me at 9.45 a.m. precisely next morning. I know because I checked the bedside clock and also because the bells were ringing out for ten o'clock Mass in the Three P's. I thought at first that I was having a *Groundhog Day* nightmare in which Alison repeated her visit exactly and everything started all over again. The persistence of the knocking, and Mac's disgruntled hiss when I rolled over, got rid of that illusion.

The cat went ahead of me down the stairs, tail moving in a high, annoyed arc.

'Miss Hopkins?'

The man on the doorstep looked like a shrunken adolescent, with a head that was all lumpy nose and protruding cheekbones above an anorexic body. I couldn't remember ever seeing a man so small and, when I looked closer, so delicately formed. He looked up at me out of a pair of cloudy blue eyes and removed his peaked cap with a tiny, white hand.

'I'm Norah Hopkins,' I confirmed.

He quickly replaced the cap. He needed its protection against the elephant hailstones bouncing off the granite steps. 'If you're not too busy I'd like a few words.' He looked skywards and gave a small, polite cough. 'Unfortunate weather we're having. Perhaps I could step inside? If you don't feel too nervous about strange males entering your home, that is.' This faintly archaic language added to the Dickensian quality about him. As I stood there, tightening the cord on my dressing-gown, he smiled, his face folding up like a corrugated, blue-toned potato. But it was a beguiling potato, full of elfin charm. Whatever he was selling he was trying hard, knocking at doors at this hour on a Sunday morning.

'I'll risk it,' I said and he hopped inside, so quickly I had to spin to check where he'd gone before shutting the door. He'd seated himself on the bottom step of the stairs.

'I'll not intrude any further than this.' He was still smiling, but had taken the cap off. He turned it round and round in his little hands. 'I'll say my bit from here.' He gave a small, throat-clearing cough and it was only then that I acknowledged a sense of vague foreboding about who he might be, and why he'd come calling. I later put my heedlessness down to lack of sleep.

'Have we met?' I asked.

'Indeed we haven't.' He smiled ever more widely, cocking his head to one side. 'I am an emissary from one who wishes you nothing but good, Miss Hopkins. He has asked me to give you this package.' One of the white hands flushed a bulky envelope out of his anorak pocket. 'My friend describes it as a token, a little something to help you get on with your life and put the unfortunate events of this year so far behind you.'

He put the envelope into his cap and extended it my way as if it were on a platter. He might have been offering me the Eucharist host, so reverential were his movements. I reached down and took it.

'Does your friend have a name?' I studied the envelope. It was long and brown, the kind used in legal offices. It was also without writing or an address of any kind. The little man hadn't answered and I looked down at him. 'Who sent you with this?' I asked again.

'Someone who wishes you well but wants to remain anonymous.' He nodded at the envelope. 'Open it,' he said, and I did.

Inside there were banknotes, red and blue ones, £50s and £100s. I'd never seen a £100 note before and I took one out to look at it more closely. Reasonably sure that it was the real thing, I put it back into the envelope and waited for the little man to explain what exactly was going on.

'There's £20,000 in there,' said the little man.

231

'Count it if you like.' He sounded eager, as if he really wanted me to.

'I don't like.' I handed him back the envelope. 'I can't take this.'

'Of course you can.' He looked disappointed. 'My friend wants you to have it. You'd be a very foolish woman not to take it.'

'I am a foolish woman,' I agreed, 'but I'm not an entirely stupid one. Money never arrives without strings attached. Why are you giving me this? What do you and your friend want from me?'

His smile disappeared and he looked earnest instead. Earnest and a little anxious. 'My friend, and yours, would like you to relinquish your rights to any profits which may be made from the play at the Tivoli Theatre. Our friend is the person who financed this play and he is upset at the late Mr Darragh McCann's arrangements about the profits going to an account called NOMA, of which you are the sole remaining director. Naturally enough, he would have preferred them to be paid directly into an account of his own. He would like you to sign a waiver which will enable him to put things in order himself.' In a move so fast I was barely aware of it, he took a second, long brown envelope from another anorak pocket.

'My instructions,' he said, 'are to exchange one envelope for the other.'

I took the second envelope. Looking down at my messenger, I thought wildly about picking him up and throwing him out the door. I felt surrounded by people wanting me to sign myself out of things – and the £20,000 on offer this time round made me feel worse, not better about it.

There was a single sheet of closely typed paper in the second envelope. The name of the play, and something about profits going into the NOMA account, were all that registered. There was a space for my signature. I'd always suspected the play's backer of being mad, bad or crazily generous. Now I wondered if he'd simply been shrewd. He certainly wanted his profits from the play. The little man was smiling merrily. I'd half expected him to have grown horns but he remained himself, beguiling and unchanged.

'Your friend seriously wants me to have the £20,000 for signing this?' I asked.

He bobbed his head up and down. The bobbing worried me in a way that nothing else about him had, made me aware of the lonely, echoing silence in the house. It was time, I thought, to show my visitor the door. Nobody threw envelopes with £20,000 in them at women they didn't know. Not unless there was something funny going on.

'I can't take it,' I said. 'It doesn't seem right.' I handed the envelope back and he slipped it into his pocket with a sigh.

'Miss Hopkins,' his tone had become as weary as I felt, 'I would like you to consider my friend's options. He can get his money back this way, with a relatively small payment to you, or he can go to law and have things dragged through the courts for years and end up paying ten times as much to get what is legally his in any event. Think about taking the money and signing, Miss Hopkins, I implore you. It makes common sense.'

It did too, of course. It made common sense and it was logical. I could see that getting my signature was the worldly wise thing to do. None of it made me feel any better about taking the £20,000.

'Would you like a cup of tea,' I asked him, 'or something else to drink?' I was in dire need myself of tea and he looked as if he could do with one too.

'Don't mind if I do.' He left his perch at the end of the stairs and skipped ahead of me to the open kitchen door. By the time I got there he was sitting on one of the high stools and looking around him with an eloquently silent interest. He commented eventually on the garden and 'how hard it was to make anything of a place in the month of January' and went on to give his views on winter gardening. I let him prattle on while I filled the kettle and considered the situation. The kitchen was warmer, at least, than the hallway, which helped a return of my presence of mind.

'You have the advantage of me in that you know my name,' I interrupted him as I scalded the kettle, wryly aware that I was falling into his formal speech patterns. 'You haven't yet told me yours.'

'My apologies.' He crossed his legs and extended a hand. 'I'm Timmy Dargan.' When I took his hand it was like holding a child's. 'Please tell me who sent you here, Mr Dargan,' I said.

'Timmy.' He wrapped his hands around his knees and chortled. 'No one's ever called me Mr Dargan in my life, not in an entire lifetime.' I could believe it.

All at once I found I was past being entertained by his oddness. 'And I, in my lifetime, have never been involved in dealings that weren't above board,' I said. I saw no point in telling him that this had as much to do with cowardice as morality on my part. 'I'm not about to start now. If I take that money I become involved immediately in something I'm not sure about. I don't want to do that . . .' I paused to choose my words as carefully as I could, '. . . it's just that I'm not sure where this whole thing could end. You're telling me that by taking this money I'm helping your friend get hold of his money and get out of the play situation cleanly. Which sounds fine, only I'm not so sure it would be like that. The situation is more complicated . . .'

I turned off the whistling kettle and made the tea. When I turned with the pot my visitor was standing beside the worktop, neatly laying the two envelopes side by side. He placed his cap beside them and turned to me. The crassness of my response seemed to have grievously saddened him.

'The person on whose behalf I am here is a thoroughgoing gentleman.' He spoke even more stiffly than he had before. 'He merely wants to help you.'

'If he really wants to clear things up then I think he should go to the gardai.' I said this reluctantly, partly because I felt sure the police had already been rejected by the 'friend' and partly because I was beginning to have nightmare visions of a raid on the Tivoli and the curtains coming down on Conal's play. I put biscuits, sugar, milk and the mugs on the worktop. Without asking Timmy Dargan what he'd like, I popped bread into the toaster.

He leaned against the worktop all the while, looking into the back garden and saying nothing. Pouring the tea I broke the silence.

'What's really going on, Timmy?' I asked, more in hope than expectation. It could be that as far as Timmy Dargan and his friend were concerned there was nothing more involved than the version of things he'd presented me with. On the other hand . . . 'Why won't you tell me?' I pushed for an answer, just in case.

'You're better off not knowing,' Timmy said gravely. 'I'd be a happier man if I didn't know myself.' He pulled an empty mug towards him and poured milk into it. 'I like my tea weak,' he said, so I poured his first and then my own. 'Couldn't take any of this when I was riding.' He spooned half the sugar from its bowl into his mug. 'No sweet things allowed at all in those years. Can't get enough of them now and I don't put on any weight anyway.'

'You were a jockey?'

'I was.'

'Any winners?'

'A few.'

'What happened?' I put the question gently. He was a man remembering, and not happily.

'What happens to too many.' He avoided my gaze, focusing instead on wrapping his hands around the mug of tea. 'It's a miserable tale and not one you'd want to hear.' The toaster threw out the toast and he watched while I sat at the table and spread it with butter and marmalade.

'Tell me anyway,' I coaxed. His miserable tale might include the name of his friend and/or how he came to be running errands like that morning's. But he shook his head and sipped his tea quietly and silently. I offered him toast and he shook his head to that too.

'It really wouldn't do you any good to know, Miss Hopkins,' he said again, 'and you'd be a wise woman to take what's in that envelope and sign the bit of paper. That would put an end to it and you and your daughter could get on with your lives.'

I wished, with every sinking feeling in my body, that he hadn't mentioned Emma. It wasn't that I thought he was threatening us, exactly. What he said even made sense.

'If it's so easy why don't you get yourself out of whatever it is? You don't seem so very happy to me. Is it about drugs? Are drugs what this is all about?'

He winced and I thought, Oh, my God, I've been too harsh: now he'll never tell me what I want to know. But I couldn't help myself, the horror of getting myself caught up with drugs and their wretched subculture kept me standing there, hoping for an answer.

Timmy Dargan straightened up. Standing like that, he was just a little taller than I was sitting, which is to say about Emma's height. His face was closed and pinched now, and very tired-looking.

'Drugs lost me my livelihood, Miss Hopkins.' He put down the mug and studied his small hands on the worktop. His wrist bones protruded like white marbles from the ends of his sleeves. 'You could say, indeed, that drugs cost me my life, for I don't care a lot about what's left to me to live.' He looked up at me and the cloudy eyes had turned grey as water in a gutter. 'No one ever offered me a way out. No one ever offered me £20,000 to walk away and mind my own business. I'd have had the sense to take it if they had.'

So it *was* about drugs. My stomach turned over, once, then settled uncomfortably into a dull acceptance. I leaned across and pushed both envelopes his way.

'Take it now, then,' I said. 'Take that money and go. Fly to France, somewhere you can get work with horses. Your friend will understand. You can pay him back . . .'

He picked up his cap, slowly, and looked at me with dislike. The speed at which he changed, became hard and distant, frightened me more than the change itself. I didn't know this man. He could be anyone, anything.

'God, but you're ignorant, Miss Hopkins.' His voice too had hardened. 'I am not a child and neither you nor I inhabit fairyland.' I felt dismissed and when I tried to say something he waved a silencing hand. 'I have chosen my life.' His shrug was infinitely jaded. 'We all choose, in one way or another, and we must live with those choices.'

His gaze roamed around the kitchen, stopping to study a drawing of Emma's on the fridge door before coming back to rest, still coldly, on my face. He didn't meet my eyes. 'When I made my choice I made it for myself, alone. I had no one else to consider. No one in the world. The same cannot be said of yourself. Seven years is a very vulnerable age in childhood.'

He picked up the envelopes, holding them in one hand and seeming to weigh them against his cap in the other. I was close to screaming but sat where I was, rigid, feeling an iron claw close around my heart as I looked at him. He seemed to me now to be evil personified: a tiny, warped, perverted messenger from the devil.

'Is there any point offering you these again?' The cold voice chilled the air in the kitchen as he held up the envelopes.

238

'No,' I said.

'Pity.' He stuffed them back into his anorak pocket and turned immediately for the door. I didn't get up to let him out and didn't move either when I heard the front door slam behind him. When I was sure he'd gone I finished my mug of tea, cold now, but I wasn't fussy any longer.

Chapter Twenty

Sunday, 16 January

Timmy Dargan's visit had unnerved me to the point where I couldn't sit, or even stand still, after he left. I hovered by the phone, debating whether to call Conal or Austin. In the end I didn't contact either of them. I didn't go down to Delia either. I decided that what I needed was movement and that meant getting away from the apartment.

The roads were too icy for the sort of speed I felt like doing and it took me more than two hours to get to Duncolla. But the frost-tipped, spiky clarity of the countryside as I drove along did a calming job on my soul and lightened my mood. I didn't come up with a definitive solution to things, but by the time I was driving through the farm gates I'd managed to fool myself with the notion that the aggravations of the past two weeks were moving towards a resolution. Optimism is, of course, only ever valid if based on real possibilities.

I met Emma on the avenue. She was riding a bike with the dog alongside and two of the boys running behind. She leaped from the bike and pulled open the car door.

'I'm collecting the eggs every morning.' Her face when she kissed me was pink and tingling with health. 'It's my job while I'm here.'

'Great,' I said. 'Do you want to follow me up to the house and tell me more about it?'

'No. We're going to our friend's house to see his pups.' She looked worried. 'I'm not going back yet, am I?' she demanded. 'You can't take me back yet. I'm going to a birthday party tomorrow and on Tuesday Maisie's taking us to . . .'

'Only visiting,' I assured her. 'Just came to see how you were getting on.' Her cheerful indifference as she rode off with her cousins told me she was getting on fine.

'Don't know why I came,' I grumbled to Maisie in the comfort of her sitting-room. 'She made me feel like an intrusion.'

Maisie snorted. 'Would you prefer to see her wasted and wailing?'

She poured me a large gin and tonic which I gulped gratefully. The drive hadn't completely obliterated the feeling, created by Timmy Dargan, that sands were shifting uncontrollably under my feet. I felt better as the day with Maisie went on. Removed from the scene of the crime, and with the help of a great meal and second gin – Timmy Dargan *et al* became part of another world.

I left Duncolla as dusk descended on a luminous day. I was much too lightheaded from gin to be driving, but bolstered by the good food I felt I could have driven the Paris–Dakar. It was this buoyant mood that led to my decision to detour and pay a visit to Alison along with a twinge of guilt that I hadn't been in touch with her since Friday.

The lights were on in several of the rooms when I got to Ballinteer and from the doorstep I could hear the reassuringly screechy sounds of television laughter. Mollie answered the door at my second ring.

'Hello,' she said. 'Did you bring Emma with you?'

'I'm afraid not,' I said, and for a minute I thought she was going to shut the door in my face. I stepped quickly into the hall. The house felt warm. 'Is your mother about?' I asked as Alison, in pink leggings and black top, appeared in the kitchen doorway. Even from ten feet away I could see that this was a relaxed Alison, a woman to whom something good had happened.

'Norah!' She beamed and took my arm and led me into the kitchen. It was warm in there too, the table littered with the remains of a pizza meal. 'I'm glad you called.' She looked up at me, her eyes outlined in kohl and her smiling mouth a becoming, deep pink. 'I have a huge favour to ask of you.'

'You have . . .?' Life in the McCann household seemed to have improved dramatically since Friday afternoon. 'Things seem to be better here,' I said.

'Yes,' said Alison. 'We're fine. The kids are fine. Look, Norah, what I wanted to ask you, and since you're here and everything it just fits so well, was if you would baby-sit for me?' Malachy called and he'll be arriving in a half hour and, well, I was going to leave Mollie in charge for an hour or so while we went down to the pub but it would be a lot better if you could stay with them.'

I pulled my arm free. Mollie came into the kitchen and looked at me carefully before going to her mother's side. Alison, with the instinct of the truly selfish, clutched her daughter to her side and looked at me pleadingly.

'I'd feel so relaxed if you were here with the children, Norah,' she said. Clearly, there was no question of her not going whether I agreed to stay or not. 'And Mollie is so fond of you.'

This was news to me, and to Mollie too from the look on her face. But with the child's eyes fixed on mine I could hardly refuse.

'I can't stay very long but yes, I'll wait with Mollie and Justin.' Aware of Mollie's acute antennae I kept my voice, and words, carefully neutral while I made what amounted to a subtle demand to be told what Alison had done about the photographs. 'I really called to see how you were managing things since we spoke on Friday,' I said.

'We're very well, aren't we, Mollie?' Alison put a hand on her daughter's head, effectively keeping the child beside her. 'The heating man came and we've been getting ourselves organized all over the place, haven't we Mollie?'

Mollie shook her head free of her mother's hand and stood in front of me. 'When can I see Emma?' she demanded.

'She's gone to spend a while with her aunt and uncle in the country,' I said, 'but I'll bring her over to you as soon as she gets back . . .'

'When will that be?'

'Oh, in a week or so.' I was vague. 'I'll give you the number and you can phone her.' I scribbled the Duncolla number on the side of a pizza carton.

'Thank you,' said Mollie gravely.

'You should phone now,' I smiled with shameless encouragement. 'You'll get her before she goes to bed.'

Alison wasn't pleased to see her protective shield

disappear to the phone and when I closed the kitchen door after Mollie she looked as if she would yank it open again. I towered over her and became firm and purposeful.

'Tell me what's happened, Alison,' I demanded. 'Did you speak to the guards? Has anyone been on to you about the photographs?'

'Malachy will be here soon and . . .'

'Bugger Malachy.' My patience snapped and I hissed, 'I want to know what's happened since Friday. Tell me!'

She looked up at me with great swimming eyes and trembling chin and I hardened my heart before it could give in to her. Alison's instinct for finding shoulders to lean on was her great survival tool: mine was not available that evening. I'd been pushed just too far. Alison didn't need my shoulder, in any event. Malachy's much broader model would be arriving any minute.

'I mean it, Alison,' I said. 'I want to know and I will not budge from this kitchen, and nor will you, until you tell me. Do you want Malachy involved in all of this when he arrives?'

'He knows already.' Alison sat sulkily on a chair and cleared a space for her elbows on the table. 'He phoned yesterday and I told him everything. He said it was fascinating. He said it would all make a great play.' She actually giggled. 'He said that was how I must look at things, as a drama in which I was the tragic heroine.' She gave me a wide-eyed look. 'So that's what I'm going to do from now on. I'm not going to get myself upset about things any more.'

Not until Malachy Woulfe disappeared from the

244

scene anyway, I thought. But he was at least a port in a storm and keeping depression, or worse, at bay for the moment.

'Have the guards been to see you?' I asked.

'Oh, yes, they were very nice,' said Alison casually. 'I told them it was me in the photographs and they said that since it was all so long ago nothing would happen to me now. They said they were only interested in knowing where the photos had come from. Of course I couldn't help them with that so they went away.'

What *had* I been worried about? As long as she had a male prop this woman would survive in a sardine can buried six feet deep in the desert.

'That was it?' I asked.

'No. They said they'd be sending me a social worker, someone to help me out over the next while. She arrives tomorrow.'

That was that, then. Alison had been picked up by the system. She would be all right, hopefully.

Malachy, when he arrived, expressed great delight at finding me there. I wasn't convinced by the excess of his pleasure but went along with it, returning his hug and telling him how fine he looked.

'We try,' he preened, 'especially in what are difficult times for us all.' He laughed at what was apparently a joke and gathered Alison into the crook of his shoulder. 'This brave little creature deserves a cosseting drink or two.' He gave me a soulful look over her head. 'Life's thrown her a few nasty turns, and not just over these last weeks either.'

'Have a good time,' I said, 'and don't worry about the children.'

I put a sleepy Justin to bed in a room full of football hero posters and Batman paraphernalia. 'My daddy got me . . .' He held my hand and toured the room pointing out his treasures to me. 'My daddy got . . .' Sitting with him until he slept, on his grubby Batman duvet, I thought my heart would break for him.

Two and a half hours later, when I went to her room with Mollie, I was given a similar tour of all that Darragh had done there for her. Mollie had a desk and a lot of shelves filled with animal books and stuffed creatures.

'I'm going to be a vet,' she announced. 'My dad always said I could.' She lay watching me with wide-awake eyes after I kissed her forehead and said goodnight.

Darragh had obviously put his domestic energies into his children's rooms then, creating retreats filled with their special passions. They would need them. There was more of him in their two rooms than in the entire rest of the house.

Alison and Malachy Woulfe got back at 2 a.m. I was asleep on one of the brown couches when they arrived and didn't dally over goodbyes. Malachy looked to be settling in for the night.

I arrived home, at three in the morning, to a dark, cold flat and the realization that people I'd been having the jitters about, Emma and Alison, were in blithe and happy shape compared to my own irritable and confused exhaustion.

Chapter Twenty-one

Monday, 17 January

I'd been getting round to ringing him myself when Detective-Sergeant Liston called me at Razorbill next morning. He was businesslike.

'We'd like your assistance. I'll send a patrol car at once.'

'Right away?' My pulse rate began to speed. 'What's happened? Have you caught Jamesy Collins?' I kept my voice low. Harry had a hangover, not a condition to be taken lightly.

'Events have taken a turn about which we must ask you some questions,' he said and the line went dead. I had another coffee and brightened up my lipstick. I was in the laneway when the garda car arrived.

There was no shuffling me into little rooms off the reception area this time. I followed my garda escort past a great many more powder-blue doors in another dove-grey corridor, then on up a short flight of stairs into a long room where there was a large table, many chairs and a map of the city on the wall. The mood of the dozen or so gardai occupants was seriously industrious. Detective-Sergeant Liston rose when I came in. A couple of burly types in plain clothes turned from a survey of the map to look me up and down.

'We can talk here or use an interview room, if you

prefer,' said Liston. He was wearing a navy suit and dull, green tie and had the look of a man whose breakfast had been taken from him before he could eat it.

'This is fine,' I said. The prospect of another windowless room lacked appeal.

'Right.' He loosened his tie, pulled a chair up to the table and we sat. 'Tell me if you will, Miss Hopkins, when you last saw Mr Austin Finn.'

It seemed to me as if everyone in the room held their breaths for my answer. Not that they looked at me, or even turned around: nothing so obvious. It was the vibes. Something had happened. My heart stopped and then began to hammer like mad. Any more of this and I would suffer a cardiac arrest.

'Is he dead?' I asked.

Sheila had gone, the business was collapsing. Austin's life had had all the classic reasons for suicide.

'Unlikely.' Liston looked stern. 'It's far more likely that Mr Finn has fled the country in advance of a visit to his offices this morning by members of the Criminal Assets Bureau. The offices were locked when the CAB officers got there and when they did gain entry they found the premises stripped of all files. Mrs Finn would appear to have left with her husband. She is not to be . . .'

'That's not how it happened.' I sat up straighter. A glass of water appeared from somewhere in front of me. I turned it round on the table, avoiding Liston's gaze. Maybe Austin *had* fled the police investigation. Maybe he'd taken the files hoping to start up business somewhere else. It sounded like a panic-stricken move.

Which didn't sound like Austin. Unless he'd had something to hide. 'The problems in the firm were created by Darragh, by his dead partner,' I said. 'Austin had no reason to run away . . .'

'Let the gardai be the judge of that.' Liston was becoming more informal by the minute. He'd taken off his jacket and was rolling up his shirt sleeves. 'Now tell me about the last time you saw Mr Finn.'

He knew. I knew by looking at him that he knew I'd had dinner with Austin on Saturday night. He was playing the policeman's game of catch-the-suspect-lying. But what was I suspected of? A gust of anger passed through me, circled back and settled into a gentle gale.

'I had dinner with him on Saturday night,' I said, 'in a restaurant in Howth. He ate lobster. I had prawn. We talked about his wife, Sheila, about how she'd just left him. We spoke of Darragh McCann. I think we may have discussed the wine.'

This wasn't true. Austin had ordered without consulting me. Belatedly, this angered me too. But my real anger was at his having dropped me in things like this. 'I think we at one point discussed the view from the window,' I went on, 'and I certainly remember asking Mr Finn for directions to the ladies toilet . . .'

'Thank you.' Liston cut me short mildly enough. Someone brought both of us tea and for a calming two minutes nothing more was said. Then Liston asked, 'Did Mr Finn at any point indicate that he might be thinking of leaving the country? Imminently?'

'No, he certainly did not. Quite the opposite in fact. He suggested that my daughter and I might come and stay for a while at his home in Blackrock. He said we would be safer there, because of his security system, than in Makulla Square.'

'Did you make plans to move to Blackrock?'

'No. I had already sent my daughter to stay with my brother and his wife. I told you on Friday morning that she would be going there . . .'

'Yes. Yes, indeed, I remember.' He looked harassed and rubbed a spot between his eyes – and I knew immediately and instinctively that he'd forgotten to tell the local garda station to keep an eye on the farm. 'Mr Finn said his wife had gone that very day?'

'Yes.' I paused, then decided to tell him what I knew of their marriage. 'They hadn't been getting on. They'd had a very public row earlier in the week at the party on the opening night of the play I told you about . . .'

'I see.' His tone indicated complete disinterest. 'Did he indicate where Sheila Finn had gone to?'

Something about the way he said the name rang a warning bell for me. Sheila wasn't just the wife of someone the guards were interested in. Liston was interested in her in her own right. I was all at once at sea again, adrift and with rafts all around me which floated away as soon as I seemed to find one to cling to. I couldn't stand it any longer.

'You're going to have to tell me what's going on.' I took a deep breath and leaned forward. 'I'm right bang in the middle of this shit-awful situation and I'm dammed if I'm going to be treated like a letter-box any more, or like a bloody rubbish bin into which everyone pours their needs and half-baked bits of information and then walks away leaving me to wallow in confusion . . .'

I stopped to draw breath and was heartened by the benign way Liston was sipping his tea and nodding in what seemed to be sympathetic understanding. 'If I'm to help you then I have to know what I'm helping you with,' I said more calmly. 'I have to know what's going on, where I *am* in all of this.' An idea came, so brilliant I couldn't understand how it had evaded me before. 'I could tell you what you need to know if I knew what you needed to know, if I knew it,' I said.

'Yes.' He rubbed the spot between his eyes again, with four fingers this time. Fearing I hadn't been clear enough, I drew breath to explain further but he held up his hand.

'It's all right, Miss Hopkins, I understand what you're trying to tell me. There's no need for you to repeat yourself. Now,' he began to speak slowly, 'we have evidence to indicate that a money-laundering operation may have been going on through the firm of Finn and McCann.' He signalled with his empty styrofoam and two fingers that more tea was needed. 'Our investigations indicate too that both Mr McCann and Mr Finn were involved and that laundering has been going on for a number of years.'

A woman guard came and said something to him too softly for me to hear. Not that I wanted to. It was enough to concentrate on the fact that Liston was telling me Darragh and Austin had *both* been criminals, that they had for years been running a money-laundering operation. The woman garda departed and Liston went on without missing a beat.

'The money-laundering side of the business might have gone on undisturbed were it not for Mr McCann's unfortunate drowning. This, we are now convinced, was in some way connected to problems with some of the people they were dealing with . . .'

'Jamesy Collins?'

'We're not inclined to think so,' said Liston, surprising me. 'Not Jamesy personally at any rate. He has an alibi for the whole of the Christmas period.' Liston paused thoughtfully. 'So do his closest, uh, associates. They'd taken themselves to the Canaries for a holiday, three of them with their families. Nice for the Canaries, having that crowd on board for the Christmas . . .'

Sourly, he took a styrofoam cup from a garda. I gratefully sipped the hot sweet tea in the one he handed me. 'No doubt it'll all come out in the wash. Mr Finn's disappearance would seem to be part of ongoing problems, which is why we're hoping that you can help us . . .'

Of course they were – except that I had a few questions of my own to ask first.

'Was Sheila Finn involved with all of this?'

'We have reason to believe she was . . .'

'Is Conal Bergin's play being used to launder money too?'

'It would seem, from our investigations, that the money backing Mr Bergin's play did indeed come from criminal sources . . .'

'Is Mr Bergin also a suspect?'

Liston raised his eyebrows, then lowered them again into a frown. 'I cannot reveal information of that nature, Miss Hopkins,' he looked at me crossly, 'for obvious reasons . . .'

'What do Alison McCann's porno pictures have to do with all of this?'

If he was surprised that I now knew the identity of the woman in the pictures he didn't show it. 'We haven't quite tied that one up yet,' he admitted, using what I thought an unfortunate metaphor. 'It seems they were being used to blackmail Mr McCann' (I could have told him that myself) 'but we're not sure to what purpose. Maybe you could enlighten us?'

'I'm sorry. I don't know any more about them than you do . . .'

Except that I knew the story of the woman involved and that she'd been hooked on drugs. I thought about telling Liston this but couldn't quite get the words out. I asked another question instead.

'Are there drugs involved? Do these criminals make their money from drugs?'

'Drugs, protection, robbery, they're not fussy, any-thing to turn a dishonest bob.' Liston gave a sour half-smile and leaned forward across the table. His eyes, at that closer range, were slightly bloodshot. 'That, Miss Hopkins, is as much information as I'm in a position to give you. I don't need to tell you that time is of the essence. Time, or the lack of it, is the reason I sent a car to bring you here. Consider: one of the men running this operation is dead, the other, within two weeks of that death, disappears. You have information which may help us. I would now like you to give me detailed answers to questions I'm about to ask you.'

He gave me a look which I felt he'd have been better keeping for homicidal maniacs. Pitiless hostility about described it. He was finished humouring me.

'You should bear in mind, Miss Hopkins, that with-holding information from the gardai in the course of their inquiries can be a crime.'

I knew enough about the law to feel reasonably sure that the onus would be on the guards to *prove* that I was withholding information. But the expression on Liston's face dispelled any notions I might have had about getting any more information out of him before I told him all I knew. I nodded, agreeable and under-standing, and answered his questions as they came at me. He set up a tape recorder and installed another garda at the table to take notes. I asked if I could eat something and when Liston nodded I took a bar of chocolate from my bag.

What had Austin Finn said to me *exactly* about problems within the company? Had he ever suggested I might be privy to the details of accounts set up by Mr McCann?

Yes and yes, I said, and told him all that Austin had told me about Darragh's use of clients' monies for risky investments and how all of this money, including that which was backing Conal's play, seemed to be circulating in and out of the account of a holding company called NOMA, whose directors were Darragh and myself.

I assured him that I'd known nothing of this while Darragh had been alive and had only learned of the existence of the NOMA account from Austin on Saturday.

'Why did Mr Finn tell you all of this now?' With one question Liston cut to the heart of my doubts and confusion.

'He'd prepared some paperwork which would allow

him access to the NOMA account and needed my signature . . .'

'Go on,' prompted Liston.

'He was keen to get things sorted out at Finn and McCann, put the money quietly back into clients' accounts. He wanted to save the company, didn't want everything exposed to the guards and in the courts . . .'

'I'm sure he didn't.' Liston was caustic.

Now that the shock of events had worn off I was beginning to wonder if Austin hadn't just vanished because things really had become too much for him. How could the guards be so *very* sure that he hadn't just run away from it all, innocently and fearfully? So very sure that he hadn't taken another way out . . . I didn't want to think of him dead, a suicide. I put it out of my head.

'Mr Finn has absconded.' Liston seemed to have been following my thoughts on some antennae of his own. 'And Mrs Finn was seen boarding a London flight on Friday morning. Her husband sent his staff home on Friday at lunchtime and evidence suggests the place had been cleaned out by lunchtime Saturday. He did not return to his Blackrock home after leaving you on Saturday night and appears to have slipped out of the country some time yesterday.' Liston drummed his knuckles on the table top. His impassive expression didn't do a lot to hide his anger.

'You'd been watching him and he got away? Is that it?' I asked.

'He hasn't got away yet,' Liston gave me a full-frontal glare.

'And it was because you were following him that you knew he'd been to see me on Saturday night?'

'He was under surveillance on Saturday night, yes,' said Liston.

I digested this for a minute and found that it wasn't so much the knowledge that we'd been watched on Saturday which upset me. It was more the realization that I hadn't noticed. Not a thing, all evening. Small things took on new meanings: like Austin telling me he'd left his car around the corner and had walked along the square 'looking for the house'. He hadn't wanted to risk the gardai spotting his car outside my place, it now seemed like . . .

It was looking too as if the guards had missed someone else. Because they'd been trying to keep tabs on Austin they didn't appear to have kept a proper watch on my place. Clearly, they hadn't seen Timmy Dargan arrive on my doorstep on Sunday morning.

'Do you know of a man called Timmy Dargan?' I asked.

'Timmy . . .' Liston's eye quite definitely brightened. 'Timmy Dargan is known to us, yes. Does he have something to do with this?'

'Looks like.' I shrugged and told him about Timmy's visit. He frowned a lot as I spoke; Timmy's role in things was clearly news which didn't quite fit the forming scenario.

'Don't let him inside your place if he comes back.' Liston was blunt when I finished. 'Call us immediately, even if you see him around or about the house. Is that clear?'

I told him it was and then said, 'What happens now?'

'We will continue with our inquiries, Miss Hopkins.' Liston got out of his chair and smiled at me in avun-

256

cular fashion. 'No doubt someone from the Criminal Assets Bureau will contact you with questions of their own but for the moment there's nothing else I want to ask you. Thank you for coming in.'

I was on the street again within minutes, this time with answers to some of the questions which had been churning in my head for the two weeks. But only some.

There were far too many incidentals which didn't fit an overall pattern: the porn pics, whether or not Darragh had been involved in solo laundering activities. Then there was the Austin factor. I was having a problem, which had nothing to do with the facts, accepting the idea of Austin as arch, money-laundering criminal. Either he was a better actor than Darragh had ever been or I was an even more hopeless judge of the male character than I'd given myself credit for.

Of the two options the latter seemed the most credible. But accepting it meant accepting Austin as a lying, cheating, cold-hearted, traitorous, low-down snake. In a world far from perfect this was possible. But improbable.

There was the problem too of my inability to believe that Darragh had been motivated by an evil greed. I would not, and could not, believe that he had ever meant Emma and me – or Alison and her children – any harm. All of this left yawning gaps in the garda landscape of events.

There was always, of course, the possibility that the gardai had got things wrong.

Harry, recovered somewhat from the toxic, dehydrating effects of what he swore was 'only a couple of whiskeys', came down totally on the side of the forces of law and order – and went to town on his prejudice against accountants.

'Blackguards and scoundrels, the lot of them,' he snarled, and paced around my desk in a good imitation of a nobbled lion.

'The keepers and inspectors of accounts . . . they're what's turning this country into a parody of itself . . . making us the court jesters of Europe . . . milking the country dry . . .' He stopped and looked at me sadly. 'Of course your Mr Finn is a crook, my dear, and the father of your child was his accomplice. The stakes became too high and the people they were dealing with too rough. It's an age-old story that the greedy, unimaginative types in the accountancy profession should learn from but never do. Fancy a lunch? We can pop over to the Shelbourne if you like.'

We walked across Stephen's Green, had a large and satisfying lunch in the Shelbourne and afterwards put in a productive afternoon's work. I was at home later that evening, managing to keep things nicely at the back of my mind, when Liam arrived. In a few short minutes he pulled my cocoon apart.

'This fellow Finn going missing is not good, not good at all.' He helped himself to half the cheese I had in the fridge. 'He'll have left a lot of dissatisfied customers behind him. They'll be looking for their money and they'll be making plans to get it back. They'll be willing to do anything. You don't know these people . . .'

'Well, I haven't got their bloody money,' I said, 'so that gets me off the hook. Anyway, I thought you were to keep away from this whole business? Seems to me you know an awful lot about what's going on for someone who is not supposed to be involved.'

'I have my sources.' He tapped the side of his nose and gave a silly, secretive smile. 'Doesn't do to leave everything to the lads in Pearse Street, you know.' He became sombre. 'The Criminal Assets Bureau are to repossess the house in Blackrock. They don't do the likes of that easily, I may tell you. I'd still feel a lot better if you would take yourself down to join the child in Duncolla for a few weeks. This thing'll be over soon now . . .'

He left around ten o'clock, by which time I was once again severely agitated and back to tossing things around in my head. All of which meant I was having another fitful night's sleep when the phone got me out of bed at close to 2 a.m.

'Norah . . .' It was Maisie's voice, faint and hardly there but still her voice. 'Oh, Jesus, Norah . . .'

An awful stillness crept into me. My body closed down. My breathing stopped. My heart ceased to beat. I closed my eyes and stiffened myself against the wall and made myself function again.

'Tell me what's happened, Maisie,' I said. 'Just tell me, please.'

'Emma's gone.' My brother's voice came on the line, harsh and torn. 'It happened not ten minutes ago. The guards are on their way out here and they've put the word out all over the county. The bastards who took her will be caught, Norah, they won't get far. She's going to be all right. The guards will be with you there any minute now too. I . . . we thought it best to talk to you ourselves first . . . Not to have the news come from strangers . . .'

Chapter Twenty-two

Monday, 17 January

Gerry was taking up valuable time. I needed to know what had happened, how it had happened, to be able to plan what I could do to get my baby back. I cut across him.

'Who were they? How did they get her?' I slid down to the floor, keeping my back against the wall for support. I kept my voice calm.

'They came in here with a gun, three of them. We could do nothing, Norah, nothing . . .' My brother's voice broke and Maisie's voice came back on the line.

'One of them was a woman, Norah. From the sound of her she was Dublin. The two of them who spoke sounded Dublin . . .'

'You didn't see their faces then?'

'They had masks on . . .' She was crying now. 'Walt Disney masks. The woman wore a Goofy, the other two were Mickey and Minnie Mouse . . .'

It was pouring outside. The wind had blown the rain in under the door and it had formed a pool there.

'Did they let you get her into some warm clothes?' I asked. Please, God, I prayed, please don't let my baby be frozen and wet on top of everything else.

'Yes, she was fine and warm when she left here.' Maisie's voice was getting stronger. 'I put a couple of jumpers over her pyjamas and a pair of heavy socks on with her boots. Oh, and her anorak and a hat on her head. I insisted on the clothes . . .'

Thank you God, thank you for keeping her warm and for Maisie. Hang in there God, hang in, please.

'Was she frightened?' I regretted the question as soon as it was asked and rushed on before Maisie could make up some lying answer. 'Did you tell her it would be all right? That we . . .' Useless questions, all of them. I shut up.

'We told her everything would be fine,' said Maisie, so quietly businesslike now that I knew something else was coming. 'They told us to tell you to go out to your car, Norah, that there would be a message there . . .'

'My car . . .' In the high old hallway my voice was a shriek.

'Go and look, Norah, quickly. I'll hang on here. Quickly, go quickly . . .'

I dropped the phone on Maisie's shrill bidding and hit the steps outside, stumbling.

The message was in an empty Coca Cola can, flattened to fit under a windscreen wiper. I started to read as soon as I'd freed it but the rain streaked across the words and threatened to waterlog the paper so I stuffed it into my dressing-gown pocket and rushed back inside. Kneeling on the floor I spread it so that every inch was clear to me. Maisie's voice crackled from the dangling phone but I ignored it.

The paper was A4 size, torn unevenly from a pad. They'd used a blue biro to write on it. The message was very clear and very to the point and absolutely terrifying.

'We want to know where Austin Finn is. Tell us and

you can have your child back. We will be in touch so do not leave the house. Do NOT talk to the guards. The child gets it if you do.'

It was written in well-formed capitals, without any spelling errors. There was no signature.

I reached for the phone.

'Gerry said he called the guards! Did he call the guards? Did he? Did . . .' I was screaming and waving the note around and it was all useless anyway. Maisie's voice was talking to me, telling me something, but all I could hear were the background sounds, male voices, several of them, asking questions, doors banging, the dog barking at the gardai as they piled into the house in Duncolla. I clamped my lips together to stop the screams getting out and bit into the bottom one. The blood felt thick and sweet as I listened to what Maisie was telling me.

'He called them.' Her voice was flat. 'They warned us not to and they pulled the phone out of the wall and said Gerry was to drive into town and ring you about the message from a phone box. But he had the mobile hidden away from the boys so they didn't find it and and once he got himself free he used it . . .' She took a deep breath. 'I tried to stop him, Norah, but . . . maybe it's for the best. The guards would have had to know anyway . . .'

No, they wouldn't. I'd never have told them. I'd have got my child back from the kidnappers myself and I'd have ripped their hearts out with my bare hands in the process.

I closed my eyes and willed the frenzy in my head to be still. But the black-red world behind my lids filled with images of a petrified, grey-faced Emma, with darkened rooms and cold, evil faces.

I opened my eyes as feet pounded up the steps outside and a knocking came on the door.

'We should have done what they wanted. Gerry shouldn't have told the guards . . .' I said and went to answer the door to the gardai outside.

As they piled into the hall I remembered that I hadn't even asked Maisie about my nephews. I turned to find a guard hanging up the phone. I would have to hope they were all right. Liam was with the guards, Gerry having phoned him too, and so was Detective-Sergeant Liston. Computer coordination is a wonderful thing. I hoped it was capable of more than just bringing people together, that it could get Emma back too.

Liam was ashen as he put an arm around me and Liston filled with a stony calm. I heard myself ask if they all wanted tea.

'We'll do without the tea,' said Liston, 'but I'll take that message, if you don't mind . . .'

He took it from me, holding it carefully by a corner, mindful of fingerprints, I supposed. I remembered that I'd dropped the rest of the evidence, the Coca Cola can, into the running water by the kerb-side. It had probably been swept away by now. I said something about this to Liston, who passed the word on and called over a young policewoman.

'You're soaked through,' she said to me. 'I'll go upstairs with you while you change.'

'Why?' I was shivering uncontrollably so maybe I did need to change out of my sodden nightclothes. But why should this woman want to accompany me to my own room?

'It's just to be company for you,' she said firmly. 'You've had a shock.'

In my room the policewoman asked me for pictures of Emma. I gave her the most recent school poses.

'There was a photo of her taken at Christmas, with her father,' I told her, 'but it was stolen . . .'

'These will do fine,' she said.

Delia was coming up the stairs as we went down. Part of me registered that she was looking her age in a way she never had before. I was glad the guards had told her about Emma's kidnap. I don't know how I would have told her myself.

'I put the kettle on,' she said, 'and the old man says you're to spend the night below with us.'

This, a supreme sacrifice on Patsy's part, would have in normal times been something to celebrate. But to have left the flat that night would have been to abandon Emma.

'I have to stay here,' I told Delia and she nodded, understanding.

Things became hazy after that, blurring into a fog of unrelated events which seemed to be happening in spite of me. The shock acting as an anaesthetic, I presumed.

The woman guard sat with me on the couch while Delia fussed with tea and sugar and Liston, like a lumbering horse in a brown overcoat, asked me questions. I had difficulty concentrating and he had to keep prodding me, reminding me what the question had been. My teeth chattered, and shuddering attacks of the shivers overtook me every few minutes. These were nothing like so overpowering as the desperate, compulsive urges I kept having to rush from the house, into the night, and search for Emma myself. They would never find her, I was convinced of it. No one but me could ever find her.

'Who knew where your daughter was staying?'

Of all the questions Liston asked me this seemed the most significant. It was also the one I needed most prompting to answer because it really needed me to think back. All my mind wanted to do was focus on the horror of what if? and on images of Emma terrified and calling for me from the dark unknown.

'Liam knew where she was . . .' I began. My brother, sitting watchfully opposite, became very calm. 'And you knew where she was . . .' Out of the fog the expression on Liston's face when I'd mentioned Emma and Duncolla the day before appeared clearly before me. 'You forgot to tell the local gardai to keep an eye on the farm, didn't you?'

Liston coughed, looked quickly at Liam and back at me and agreed. 'I omitted to pass the word on, yes,' he said, 'but I assure you, Miss Hopkins, we will be using every means at our disposal to get your daughter back. Can you remember who, apart from immediate family members, knew where your daughter was staying?'

Delia's voice, somewhere to the right of me, answered. 'I knew,' she said, 'and so did my husband, Patsy Brophy.' She waited while this was written and until another attack of shivering had passed through me. 'Mr McCann's wife Alison and their children knew also. I'm right about that, Norah, am I not?' I nodded and she came up with another name. 'Harry Gibson,

Norah's employer, knew. She may have told Conal Bergin, the young man who has written a play and . . .'

'Did you tell Mr Bergin?' Liston interrupted Delia.

'Yes,' I remembered, 'and I told Austin Finn too and Malachy Woulfe, the director of the play . . .'

Great, I thought, good girl, Norah. You told half the city where you'd discreetly and secretly sent your seven-year-old daughter to be safe.

'Quite a few people knew then?' Liston confirmed, looked at the names he'd compiled.

'I assumed she was safe,' I whimpered. 'That the local guards knew . . .'

'Of course.' He was surprisingly humble. 'This note, Miss Hopkins, the one left on your car. Does the handwriting look in any way familiar?'

'No.'

'And you can't remember anything which might be helpful in locating Mr Finn? He gave you no indication at all, didn't mention a favourite holiday spot or anything of the like?'

'No. Yes.' I remembered something. 'He said they had a time-share in Florida.' He wrote this down. I wished he would leave and let me go, out into the night where Emma was. I wished they would all leave.

'Clearly, Miss Hopkins, the people who abducted Emma are convinced you have knowledge of Mr Finn's whereabouts and want to make contact with him.' He spoke slowly, looking at me hard. 'Clearly too they had planned to intimidate you into telling them.'

'Yes,' I said. Did the man think me a fool, that I couldn't work this out for myself? Emma could have worked it out and she was only seven.

Liston cleared his throat. 'Our involvement means

that their plan has misfired, very badly,' he said, 'so we can't be sure of their moves from now on. I am of the opinion myself that these people will not want to hold on to your daughter now that the gardai are involved. The consequences have become more than they'd bargained for.'

This was probably his way of saying they'd bitten off more than they could chew. It was small comfort.

'Are you saying they're going to drop her back here, or at the farm, any minute? Is that the sort of ludicrous thing you're suggesting?' My voice rose. 'I'm not a fool, Detective-Sergeant Liston, I know that's not going to happen.'

'They'll await their opportunity,' he spoke patiently, 'and release her somewhere safe. They won't want to hold on to her.'

'They could kill her. That would get rid of her. Anything could happen, these are crazy people, not rational . . .'

'They won't kill her. That's not their style . . .'

'Not whose style? Are we talking here about Jamesy Collins and his friends? Because if we are then the man I met is capable of a great deal . . .'

'We may be dealing with Jamesy, yes. And please believe me, Jamesy will not want things to get any worse. He will not want the combined strength of the garda and his own community against him. Because harming a child will do that – put him both outside the law and the support of his own people. He can't operate without support.'

I didn't believe a word of this, largely because Liston seemed to me to be indulging in the national pastime of telling people what they wanted to hear. In his place

I would have been saying the same consoling things to me myself.

But I didn't believe him too because I knew, contrary to all he was saying, that if the kidnappers had gone this far they were capable of anything.

'Are you telling me that all I have to do is sit and wait for Emma to be returned, unharmed?' I said.

'I'm asking you to stay here, yes, and to be available if we need you.' He stood, sombre and sad-looking. 'Everything humanly possible will be done, be assured of that. I must ask, Miss Hopkins, that you on no account attempt to make contact with these people yourself.'

I don't know how he thought I proposed to join up with Jamesy and Co., but he wasn't light years away from the wild plans running through my head.

The main body of gardai left soon after that, Liston taking the note from the kidnappers with him. It was odd how powerless, impotent and even more bereft this made me feel. It was as if a last, thin link to Emma had been severed.

Liam stayed with me. Liston had wanted to leave the policewoman in the house too but I'd been adamantly against it. Liam was my brother and he was Emma's uncle and he might just understand my need to go after Emma myself.

It wasn't until they'd gone and we were alone in the forlorn house that I thought to ask about my nephews.

'The boys . . . are they OK?' I asked Liam. 'They weren't hurt?'

'They're fine.' Liam walked to the window and opened the curtains. 'The bastards locked them into their bedrooms but they're fine. Frightened, but that's only natural.'

I didn't think any of it was natural. What was natural about making innocence pay for the crimes of the heinous? About tearing a blameless child away from her life because of the sins and evil of the adult world?

But I knew what Liam meant and that he wasn't thinking any of this. I was relieved to hear the boys hadn't been hurt.

I banished Delia back down to Patsy and made a bed on the couch for my brother. I couldn't bring myself to offer him Emma's bed. He half lay down and, because I wanted to be alone, I told him I was going back to my own bed for a while. He had enough sense not to question me, or suggest he check on me, though I knew he wanted to.

I sat by the window in my room and looked across the square and saw, unfolding in the dark, the seven short years of Emma's life. In the small, remembered sorrows and great joys and ten million everyday things I saw the close sweetness of the first years and the growing, changing person she became as she got older. She had never been more real to me, never closer. I could feel her skin, touch her hair if I wanted to, listen again to her howls as I tried to untangle her curls.

The terror of what might be happening to her, could be happening to her, assaulted me in waves of nausea which made me gag and lean my forehead against the icy glass of the window. But all I saw behind my closed eyes was a deep, spinning blood-red colour.

I opened them and put the palms of my hands, pleading, against the glass. And then I wept.

I wept until there was nothing left in me but a dull, dry emptiness and a hollow in the part of me that Emma had filled with life's hope.

Chapter Twenty-three

Tuesday, 18 January

I sat through the night. How could I have slept? If I closed my eyes, dropped my vigilance for even minutes, anything could happen to Emma. I had to remain awake, alert, be ready for the call when it came. I didn't phone the police during the night. I was afraid to hear she'd been found, afraid to hear she hadn't.

The wintry dawn began to come into the sky some time before seven o'clock. Like dirty linen spreading across the blanket of dark, it crept up over the rooftops and brought in another cheerless January day. There had been sixteen such days now since Alison had come visiting, twenty-two since Darragh had been found dead in the river. The house was deathly silent all around me. There wasn't a sound from Liam, who I presumed to be sleeping, and not a tinkle from Delia, who was no doubt intent on allowing me to get some sleep. It couldn't last. If nobody else did it I would have to disrupt the terrible quiet myself. The cat would have to be fed. The police would have to be harried, plans made, a strategy for rescue arrived at. As I sat by the window, nothing useful by way of ideas presented itself. Standing up brought on a great wave of desperation, but I had to begin somewhere.

I went along to Emma's room. I'd been unable to

go in there in the night but I went in at about seven-thirty, the time I would have been getting her up for school.

I opened the curtains and, as the light fell across the room, looked at the everyday things I'd taken so much for granted: the wall she'd had me paint a dark blue so that she could draw on it, the ever-growing family of furry animals, her favourite book . . .

This was my child's life, it wasn't in whatever grey, threatening place she'd been taken to. I'd never questioned but that our shared dreams would be there for us when tomorrow came, and all the tomorrows after it.

Standing inside the window of her room, I tried to dimly imagine a future, but nothing came. There was only fear, icily severing the birth of every other feeling. My child had been my centre of gravity and now that she was gone I was falling apart. I didn't care whether I lived or died: I only wanted my baby to live, for her to have *her* life. Because if my loss was terrible then Emma's was so much more: she'd lost her innocence and blameless hope and her childhood.

I would have to see to it that she didn't lose her life too.

And it was that, a primitive force in me deciding that my child *would* live, which drove the paralysing fear away. It went quite gently, dissolving as the resolve formed. I wouldn't collapse. I couldn't collapse.

I arranged Emma's woolly toys the way she did herself each morning before school. Then I had a shower, dressed myself in jeans and jumper, and went downstairs with a slowly forming plan in my head. Liam would need to be brought on side. He knew me

271

and would be alert to the possibility of my taking unilateral action. I would have to convince him that I knew what I was doing. Otherwise he would stick to me like a limpet, be my shadow wherever I went. Hearing me come down the stairs, he appeared, groggily, in the sitting-room door.

'I fell asleep.' He was shame-faced.

'One of us was enough to be awake,' I said. 'I've finished in the bathroom. Go on up and have a shower.'

And so the sixteenth day got under way.

Mac was angry in the kitchen, his tail high and moving in a slow, threatening arc as he glared at me. He'd been locked in there by Liam, who didn't like him. I fed him and put him outside and got together something for myself and Liam to eat. Maisie rang. Her concern and fury bolstered my own, filling me with enough anger against Emma's abductors to give me strength to carry on for another while.

Through it all, though I worried it like a dog, the plan remained a mere germ in my head. Nothing I did fertilized it and it refused to grow past the point where I got out of the house and went into the streets in search of Emma. The one other thing I knew I had to do was get in touch with Jamesy Collins, convince him the police hadn't been my idea and tell him I'd no idea where Austin Finn was.

I rang Pearse Street who told me they'd no news, 'so far'. Detective-Sergeant Liston, they said, would be in touch within the hour. I took this to mean he hadn't yet come in to work and wondered if he had children of his own.

Delia arrived up and, proving that adversity does

indeed make strange bedfellows, so did Patsy. The sight of him, hobbling irritably through the door on his stick, almost reduced me to further tears. The steps had proved a colossal effort and he collapsed into an armchair. Liam, never a great fan of Delia's, any more than she was a fan of his, seized the opportunity to go out to get the papers.

'Haven't been up here for years.' Patsy wheezed and began to cough like a drain emptying.

'I told him to stay below. I told him there was nothing he could do for you, that you had enough to be dealing with besides having to listen to a diseased old man . . .' Delia fussed about him worriedly but he shook her off.

'Are the guards doing anything?' he demanded. 'Because by God if they're not . . .' Overtaken by another fit of coughing, he doubled over in the chair.

And that was the moment when God, or Fate or something omniscient anyway, delivered a fertilizing flash and the plan moved into gear. I needed a messenger, a go-between. I knew someone who was just that but not where he was to be contacted. But Patsy, with his prodigious memory and obsessions, might be just the person to help me.

'The guards are slow enough.' I sat down in the armchair opposite him. 'They suspect a man called Jamesy Collins but if they've been talking to him then they certainly haven't told me about it. I've no idea what they're doing . . .' I worked on an expression that mingled annoyance with indignation and disgust, a mixture guaranteed to appeal to the anti-Christ in Patsy.

'I never knew them to be anything but thick and

lumbering as a force,' Patsy said. 'They grew out of the Civil War, you know, and out of the old Metropolitan Police and that's always been their trouble, not knowing whether they're fish or fowl . . .'

'Oh, will you shut up, old man.' Delia's rebuke lacked heart. She was wearing her gold track-suit and her hair had been gathered into a tight knot and tied with a purple scarf. As an attempt at braggadocio it worked not at all. She looked withered and worried and very much an old woman. She patted my shoulder awkwardly.

'Isn't it enough that Norah's distracted with the pain of the child going missing without you feeding her guff about the incompetence of the guards . . .'

'It's all right, Delia,' I said. 'I've accepted that the guards can't be expected to do everything. I'm trying to figure out a way I can help, do something myself. If I don't I'll go mad. I can deal with this thing better if I'm involved . . .'

'We'd all like to help . . .' Delia said gruffly. 'Wouldn't we, old man?'

'She knows that,' Patsy snapped. 'The woman hasn't become a fool because her child's been stolen from her . . .' He was overtaken by another fit of coughing and I could see in Delia's face that she wanted to get him back downstairs. I gave thanks for the stubborn contrariness which had brought him to me.

'There's something you might be able to help me with, Patsy.' I spoke slowly, as if the thought had just come to me, when Patsy's coughing began to subside.

'What's that then?' Patsy gave me a sharp look but I didn't answer immediately, letting him get good and curious. A rushed Patsy, even that morning's concerned Patsy, could very well go all contrary and clam up. Delia crossed to build up the fire started earlier by Liam.

'What was it you wanted to know then?' Patsy asked again, frowning as the fire leaped into life.

'There's a man I met might be able to help the guards, a man I think might know something about all of this. He seemed to me to have a handle on the city's criminal life . . .' I stopped and Patsy's head snapped up impatiently.

'Well? Who is he? Is he someone you think I know?'

'More like someone I think you might know *of*,' I said, 'or *about*.'

'God Almighty, woman, would you say what you have to say and be finished with it . . .'

'Did you ever hear, or know of, a jockey called Timmy Dargan? He'd be about fifty years old now, a Dubliner by the sound of him.' I watched Patsy closely for any indication that the name rang a bell. There was nothing. I prodded him a bit further. 'He rode a few winners in his time, so he says, but I suppose that would have been thirty years ago or more . . .'

'Be quiet and let me think.' Patsy plucked irritably at his scarf and, though I could see that his physical discomfort was great, I couldn't let him off the hook. He was my only hope of contacting Timmy.

'Who is this Timmy Dargan?' Delia's voice was quiet, reminding me that there were gaps where I hadn't filled her in on events. This had partly to do with things happening so quickly there hadn't been the time but had more to do with saving her the anxiety of constant involvement.

'He called here on Sunday morning.' It seemed

impossible that this had only been two mornings before. 'He said he was a messenger, from Austin Finn it looks like now, though I didn't know that at the time. He had money to give me if I signed papers to do with an account set up by Darragh. It was a lot of money.'

'In that case, and if it was that big a sum ...' Musingly, Delia got right to the possibility I'd been avoiding. 'He's more than likely gone off with that Austin Finn. Or taken the money and gone somewhere on his own. He's hardly likely to be hanging around if what's happened is an indication of how desperate some people are to get hold of Finn.'

Exactly. Timmy Dargan, Austin's faithful gofer, would have seemed the most likely person to know where Darragh's partner had gone. What I was hoping was that Jamesy Collins didn't know about Timmy and Austin and that I'd been his only, and obvious, target.

I had, after all, been one of the last people to spend time with Austin.

'I remember the name.' Patsy coughed into life. 'But nothing about the man. Delia,' he glared at his little wife, 'help me out of this chair. I'll have to go down and look at the racing calendars for the seventies.' When she seemed about to object he expelled an exasperated breath. 'Help me out of here. There isn't the time for debate.'

Delia helped him up and I went with them to the front door. I badly wanted to go with them but knew I had to play things carefully or Patsy's mood of cooperation might change. I was also afraid to leave in case the phone rang, afraid not to be there when news of Emma came.

When they'd gone, and on the off-chance, I checked for Timmy Dargan in the phone book. There were quite a few Dargans but no Timothy, or even a T. Dargan. Even so, in the event of a no-joy situation with Patsy, I was prepared to ring every Dargan in the book.

With nothing else that I could usefully do I sat and waited an agonizingly long five minutes until Liam came back. He'd got us fresh bread and milk.

'I have to do something about Emma myself.' I faced him in the kitchen. 'I can't just sit around and wait . . .'

'There's nothing you can do, Norah,' he interrupted me gently enough, 'except be here when you're needed.' He put a hand on my shoulder. 'And that'll be soon enough, don't you worry.'

I knew that by this he meant me to believe the gardai would be bringing Emma home to me. I didn't have his faith.

'I can't wait here. You must understand that, Liam. I'm going to do something . . .'

'*What* are you going to do, Norah?'

If he hadn't interrupted me I might have gone on to tell Liam what I was planning. As it was, his interruption put me on guard, told me as clearly as if he'd spelled it out that he would stand in the way – forcefully if necessary – of me leaving the house.

'I don't know.' I shook my head in deflated fashion. 'But what I would like to do, right away, is go downstairs to Delia for a few minutes. Is that all right with you?' When he looked doubtful I added. 'It's either that or she comes back up here. I want to talk to her.'

Liam, reluctantly, agreed to my going downstairs.

In the basement Patsy was working his way through

the contents of an old binder, impeccably detailed and dated 1965–75 on the side. He was working slowly, carefully scanning the thin pages.

'All of this is for the museum when I go,' he muttered at me when I came in. I didn't want to know. I just wanted him to turn the pages more quickly: I had to sit on my hands to prevent myself doing it for him.

Patsy still hadn't come up with anything when Liam came knocking at the door. Detective-Sergeant Liston was on the phone for me.

'We've spoken to Jamesy,' he said, 'as well as to several of his associates.'

'And?'

'Protests his innocence, of course. They all do. Say they'd never touch a hair on a child's head. We're holding Jamesy and a friend of his here for as long as we can. We'll continue to question . . .'

'How long can you hold them?' I would go in, face Jamesy, deal with the man who'd taken my child myself . . .

'We're holding them under Section Four of the Criminal Justice Act, which means we'll have to let them go after twelve hours unless we've something to charge them with. We've already had them here more than four hours . . .'

'I'll be there in twenty minutes . . .'

'I can't let you see him.' Liston was curt. 'We'll deal with getting any information he has out of him.' He didn't exactly say, 'We have ways,' but the implication was there. Or maybe I just wanted to think it was. I had to believe they were doing everything possible, even if

278

it meant more than everything possible. The liberal in me was dying fast.

'He might be persuaded to remember something if I was to remind him of what he said to me that night . . .'

'No. Any persuading that's to be done we'll do it, Miss Hopkins,' said Liston. 'We're working on a particular line of our own, playing things down and not going to the press, just yet. This way Jamesy, or whoever has your daughter, has the opportunity to return her quietly, without losing face.'

'I see,' I said and I did. The insight didn't make me feel any better.

'I'd like a word with your brother now,' Liston said, 'if you don't mind.'

To tell Liam not to leave me out of his sight, no doubt. 'You'll let me know if there's anything I can . . .'

'Of course. It might be a good idea if we sent a policewoman around there to be with you too, to act as a liaison . . .'

Act as a back-up keeper to Liam, more like, 'No, thank you.' I was polite. 'I'd prefer just to have my brother here. I'll get him for you now.'

Whatever chance there had been of my staying put, going along with the 'garda line of inquiry', was blown in that conversation. The idea that officialdom wasn't going to allow me any role, not even the chance to eyeball Jamesy, was more than any mother of a missing child could have been expected to bear.

I would find Timmy Dargan, with or without Patsy's help, and I would get to Jamesy Collins if and when the guards released him. The alternative was to sit and wait and imagine the worst. Or, nightmare scenario, sit and wait while the worst actually happened.

Patsy was staring into the fire when I got back downstairs. Delia had disappeared to the kitchen.

'I was right.' Patsy didn't turn when I came in. 'Your man had a few decent races in the late sixties and early seventies before disappearing from the scene. Rumour had it he was involved in some doping racket. That's why the name rang a bell. There were a few other of the lads went down with him.'

'What happened to him? Where did he go to?' I was full of controlled delirium. Things were moving.

'Bring me the phone and I'll find out for you . . .'

Patsy, for Patsy, displayed an almost lively interest in the prospect of some detective work. He actually rubbed his hands together when I put the phone into his lap. He dialled and waved me away while he proceeded to have a bizarre, and highly coded, conversation with someone called Valentine.

'That Val character!' Delia, shaking her head and arms folded, reappeared from the kitchen. 'I remember that lad. Sold his soul, if he could be said to have had a soul, to the horses and dogs. I had to run him from the door more than once.'

Patsy, with a muttered oath, put his hand over the mouthpiece. 'Will you be quiet, woman.' He spoke with such ferocious intensity that I knew he was on to something.

'A glass of port, Delia,' I said. 'A glass of port is what I need.'

Anything to get her out of there, give Patsy free rein.

Delia poured me close to a quarter-pint of port.

She'd baked scones and piled a plate of those in front of me too. When in doubt or pain have some carbohydrate, was Delia's philosophy. We'd got through half the plate before Patsy called irritably from the living-room.

'The word on Timmy Dargan is that he spent a few years in Hong Kong, then came back to this side of the world and got work in a stable outside Newmarket.' Patsy was brisk and important. 'From a few other of the details my contact gave me I'd say that we're talking about your man all right, Norah. The Timmy Dargan my contact is familiar with had a problem keeping on the straight and narrow . . .'

'Is familiar with? He knows where he is now then?'

'He knows a man who knows your man and knows where he is.' In Patsy's animation I glimpsed, for the first time ever, the man Delia must have married. There was a contrary edge about Patsy Brophy which could have been, in youth and good health, invigorating and fun to be around. I was very glad it had come to life on Emma's account.

'Where is he then?' I was careful to keep myself from leaping at Patsy. 'Did he give you an address?'

I wasn't careful enough. 'Restrain yourself,' Patsy snapped. 'We must make haste slowly. My informant has given me a Dublin address. No telephone number. That we will have to look up . . .'

'He's not in the book under Timothy, or T,' I said.

'He wouldn't be,' said Patsy. 'He lives with his mother, an old woman called Mary McCauley, McCauley being the name of her second husband, a man who had nothing to do with the fathering of Timmy.'

I brought him pen and paper and, in a wonderful

copperplate hand, he wrote down an address in Drum-condra. I knew the houses. They were solid and red-brick and overlooked the Tolka river. I found Mary McCauley's number in the phone book and dialled. I let it ring for fully five minutes. No one picked it up.

'Send the guards over there,' Delia suggested.

'Waste of time,' I said. 'He won't talk to them. I'll be very lucky if he talks even to me, *if* I can get hold of him . . .'

'You can't do this thing on your own.' Delia was aghast. 'I wouldn't have been a party to it if I'd thought that's what was in your head to do. Leave it to the guards . . .'

'He has no criminal record,' said Patsy, 'and there's no indication in anything my informant told me of any kind of violent activity on Dargan's part. I can see no harm myself in your talking to him.'

'She can't leave the house. The guards don't want her to leave, that's why they left the brother upstairs with her.' Delia's small face was strained and distressed-looking. 'And what if . . . *they* phone, those animals who've taken the child. You can't be away from here, Norah. It wouldn't be right.'

'Liam has a mobile. I'll take it with me. I'll keep in touch.'

They were looking at me now, Delia and Patsy both, their faces wearing identically wretched expressions. There was something else too: in that moment I could see that their hearts were aching with mine and that Emma and me meant more to them than I'd ever accepted. I moved closer to them and held out my hands and they took one each and we stood like that, holding hands, close together, saying nothing. Everything we wanted to say was in the feeling between us.

'You'll cover for me while I go?' I asked Delia after a while, 'I don't want the guards on my tail the minute I leave here.'

'I've got a better idea.' Delia hushed me with a quick frown. 'Just listen to me before you say anything. It's a good idea.'

Delia's idea was that *she* would go, seek out Timmy Dargan and arrange for him to meet me at an agreed venue. On the face of it it seemed a terrible idea. Delia was seventy years of age and one of the best people ever to come into my life. If anything happened to her . . .

'You could go all the way across there and find he's not at home, that he's flown with the other character. Why risk being out of contact unless it's to some purpose?'

It wasn't easy but I allowed her to persuade me, mainly because I could see the sense of what she was saying. The phone wasn't answering in Timmy Dargan's home so maybe he *was* gone. If I was to leave Makulla Square, take myself away from possible contact, then it had to be to some purpose.

I wrote a note for Delia to give to Timmy Dargan and went back upstairs.

From my front window I watched as Delia, purposefully and with a shopping bag as decoy, walked down the front garden path and turned in the direction of Rathmines. She planned to get a taxi there. Delia dashing off by taxi from the house would have raised suspicions in Liam.

The wait became agonizing as soon as she disappeared from sight. Without activity my mind became again filled with frenzied imaginings. Standing by the window I wanted to howl Emma's name at the indifferent day outside, pound on the glass till it shattered. As I paced the room my mind spun crazily between remembered moments and panic-stricken fears. Emma was so trusting, so innocent, so ill-prepared for life's ability to mistreat.

I tried not to think about how she was feeling, the blank terror which must have become her existence and about how she was dealing with it.

And through all of it, like pinpricks of light shining through a colander, there came moments of forgetfulness. I would suddenly feel lighthearted and everyday, as if my mind had rejected the fact that Emma had been taken and that this nightmare existed. But these were crazy flashes, blazing for seconds only before the iron trap that was reality reasserted itself and dread returned leaving me even more disabled than before.

I prayed to my dead mother. 'Send her back safe to me. She has done nothing. You died before you could be a mother to me so, please, wherever or whatever you are do this thing now for my child, your grandchild. Keep her safe until I get to her.'

Delia was gone two hours. I'd stopped pacing by then and had used the time to catch up on neglected chores – a scrub-out in the bathroom, clean-up in the kitchen, a polish to a couple of windows. In between I'd phoned Pearse Street twice, Maisie once and took calls from Harry and a hysterical Alison.

'The guards were here.' Her voice was high and piercing. 'They told me about Emma. They wanted to know all sorts of things. Mad stuff. Do they think I've got something to do with the people who took her? What's it all about . . .' She broke into a wild sobbing. I let her at it for a minute, or perhaps two, while I stared blankly at the wall, thinking about nothing at all, just wishing she wouldn't cry.

'Stop crying, Alison,' I said at last. 'Please stop. The guards have to gather all the information they can, from everyone involved. Is there anyone there with you?'

She sniffled and sent a shuddering sigh down the phone. 'There's a woman guard here. She's going to collect the children for me and stay a bit of the night too. I couldn't stay on my own . . .' Her voice rose again. '. . . Suppose they come for *my* children. Oh, my God Almighty, suppose they do that . . .'

I cut her short before she got into full, primal scream. 'When did you last see Austin Finn?' I asked.

'Austin?' She was silent for a moment. 'I don't know. The night the play opened, I suppose. The guards asked me the same question . . .'

'So you don't know where he's gone?'

'No, I don't.' She was, for Alison, quite robust when she said this.

'Why would I know where he's gone?'

Because you're his dead partner's wife, I thought but didn't say it. 'Well, since you haven't seen him, and don't know where he is now, the kidnappers are unlikely to bother you or the children . . .'

'Unlikely! What do you mean unlikely? Do you mean they *might* come after us? Is that what you mean by unlikely?'

'No, that's not what I mean.' I lost patience. 'Look, Alison, why don't you get your children's dinner and be thankful they're all right? Better still, and it's what I would do if I were you, why don't you get down to the school and mount guard outside their classrooms yourself until they get out?'

The call ended soon after that, with Alison more teary than ever and me unrepentantly impatient.

It was ten minutes past two when Delia walked briskly into the square. She didn't once glance towards my window as she walked up the garden path and side-tracked on to the smaller pathway to the basement. As she all but disappeared from view she straightened her hat a little on her head. A signal, I thought, and a good sign.

I gave it seven minutes before I told Liam I was going down to Delia for the aspirins I'd asked her to get me in the shops. Even if he'd wanted to I doubt he'd have had the heart to question me; I was strung out as a wire and liable to attack at the slightest provocation.

Delia opened the door and scurried wordlessly ahead of me back to the living-room. She stood by Patsy's chair and they both looked at me, their old faces strained and unhappy and deeply worried.

'I met him,' said Delia. 'An insect of a man. I spoke to him and he listened to me. When I'd finished he read your note and then left me standing in the door-way for fully ten minutes. I don't like that side of the city. Never have. The northside people were always and ever an ill-mannered lot. They haven't changed . . .'

'Timmy Dargan isn't a northsider. The man's from bloody Kildare. Just tell Norah what he said.' Patsy was remarkably controlled. His skin was white and thin as ash though, and he seemed to have shrunk a couple of inches in the hours since I'd last seen him. I silently berated myself for leaving him alone while Delia had been away.

'His mother's from the northside,' said Delia. 'She yelled down the stairs. No mistaking . . .' She pulled herself up short. 'When he came back there was the smell of drink from him. Whiskey. He made me step outside, into the street, with him. He said . . .' Delia paused and a slight, becoming pink blush spread and faded across her cheeks. I recognized one of her quick flashes of temper. 'I took issue with him but it was all he was willing to say to me . . .' She paused again and I closed my eyes tight and made fists of my hands by my sides.

'Please, Delia, please tell me what he said . . .'

'He said that you should be on your knees praying. He said that you would have to be closer to God before he could give you any help or guidance about the whereabouts of your child.'

'That's all he said?' I felt sick. 'You told him I was willing to pay him? You told him he could name his sum? You told him everything I . . .' Useless to push her like this. I'd said it all in the note anyway.

'I told him,' Delia came to me and put a hand on my arm. 'I told him everything we discussed and that was all that he said to me. He went inside then and closed the door. I made it my business to memorize his words while I went looking for a taxi. I knew you'd understand what he meant better than me, Norah, and that I'd have to have the words right. The words are a message, Norah, they're a message . . .'

Her familiar voice, nasally and precise, cracked. I put my hand over hers. She was right. All I had to do was calm down and figure out what Timmy was really saying.

'He didn't want to incriminate himself,' I said, 'make a definite arrangement that could be used against him. It'll come to me in a minute what he means.'

It came to me all right, but took five or six minutes.

'On my knees, praying . . .' I yelped, gave Maisie a hug. 'God, it's so simple! He wants me to go down to the church in Rathgar. He came yesterday, Sunday. The bells were ringing when I opened the door to him. He means me to remember those things and . . .'

'You're right. He means to meet you in the church.' Patsy was tart. 'But when? Did he say anything about a time to you, old woman?'

'I told you what he said, and I told you all of it.' Delia flashed with her old energy.

'I'll go now,' I said. 'He'd have added something about time if he didn't mean to follow you immediately. He's probably down in the church right now.'

'What're you going to do about the brother?' asked Delia.

I'd covered that. Liam was the reason I'd put on boots and an anorak to come down to Delia's place.

'I'm going to leave over the back garden wall. Apart from Liam there's a good chance the guards have someone watching the front of the house.' I zipped up the anorak and fished in the pockets for my gloves. 'I want you to go upstairs, Delia, and keep Liam out of the kitchen for ten minutes at least. Ask him if there have been any calls, news of any kind.'

'That wall's five feet high,' Delia said. 'You're not

going to be much good to anyone, or any help either, if you fall from that height and break your back . . .'

'I won't fall.' I put a hand on her shoulder and turned her towards the door. 'And go now. Go.' She walked down the corridor to the front door. 'Delia,' I called and she turned. 'I can never thank you . . .' She waved a hand dismissively and opened the door. As soon as it closed I hurried through the kitchen and out into the back garden.

The wall, as I'd told Delia, was no problem. Long limbs have their advantages. The misty, early afternoon light was an advantage too: it was probably the reason no one saw me and yelled from a window somewhere.

I walked quickly once I got back into the back laneway. At a couple of minutes to three o'clock I was standing on the footpath outside the church of the Three Patrons in Rathgar.

As buildings go, the Three P's has presence but not much style. A large, squarish, grey pile on the outside, it has vast, soaring spaces inside. I went there on occasional Sundays with Emma without ever getting any great feeling of spirituality from the place.

There was no sign of Timmy Dargan outside so I pushed through the cream and glass doors and walked into the nave of the church. Muted lighting threw shadows and nothing, not the prayers of the few souls on their knees nor the old woman moving with her rosary between the stations of the cross, broke the vastness of the echoing silence.

I walked slowly up the aisle, turning to examine the faces of those praying in the pews as I passed. There were five of them in the main body of the church and Timmy Dargan was not one of their number. Near the altar I slipped into a pew myself, knelt on the soft navy vinyl of the kneeler and studied the altar and surrounds. The painted plaster walls looked blandly back at me. The altar itself, with white flowers in bunches to either side, looked serenely functional, and empty. I hadn't really expected Timmy to be perched there anyway.

I knelt for a while, figuring that if Timmy did arrive in the church then he couldn't fail to spot me in the front pew. I felt starkly exposed to the unfriendly gaze of the saints in their lofty niches above me and when I couldn't stand the plaster eyes of Patrick, Columba, Brigid, Laurence O'Toole and Rumold any longer I got up and, childhood training dying hard, genuflected to the tabernacle before moving off to the side.

My boots thudded softly on the rubbery surfaced floor as I went around the back of the main altar. I paused by a side altar where St Joseph sat with the child Jesus before moving slowly on to another devoted to the Holy Family. I stopped there too, this time putting 50p in the box, lighting a candle and, eyes closed, sending out a prayer of such fevered intensity that God could only have ignored it at his peril. Fifty yards further on, sitting in a pew under the Seventh Station of the Cross – the one where Jesus falls for the second time on his way to Calvary – I came upon Timmy Dargan.

'You took your time finding me.' He didn't get up so I slipped into the pew behind him. He did turn to face me. 'I don't know how you thought I'd be up at the altar. I'm no Pharisee.' He grinned without mirth and I didn't even attempt a merry response.

'I need your help, Timmy,' I said. He was sitting

with his hands in his pockets and hunched forward. He looked like a toy man.

'Your friend told me the story.' He looked past me, letting his gaze rest on a statue to the Sacred Heart behind me. 'My own friend wouldn't have cared for this turn in events. He wouldn't have cared for it at all . . .'

I noted the past tense and pounced. 'Your friend's gone away, Timmy, hasn't he?'

He turned and his face was caught in the red light from a vigil lamp by the statue. 'It's not your place to ask questions, Miss Hopkins.' He was all red planes and shadows. I tried not to see him as a small devil but it was hard. 'You're here to ask a favour, nothing more.'

'Will you take me to the people who have my daughter?' I asked.

'What makes you think I can do that?' he countered and I wanted to catch him by the small neck buried in his anorak and shake and shake him.

'You said I was to ask for my favour, nothing more,' I reminded him.

'So I did,' said Timmy, very softly, 'so I did.' He smiled his mirthless smile again. 'But humour my inconsistencies, Miss Hopkins, and tell me why you think I can take you to the child.' He shrugged. 'Apart from doing it for the money you're going to give me, that is.'

I took a deep breath and put together the jumble of thoughts which had convinced me Timmy Dargan could help.

'Because it's my belief that the friend on whose behalf you came visiting yesterday morning was Austin

Finn. It's my belief too that you feel a loyalty to Austin and would want to protect him . . .' I spread my hands to indicate my helpless feeling in all of this. '. . . You know too that I don't know where he's disappeared to. What you don't know is how far the people who've taken Emma are prepared to go to find him, though it does look as if the answer to that is any lengths . . .'

'They're desperate, right enough.' Timmy was watching me closely but I looked away, avoiding his red gaze and looking up instead to where Jesus, clad in a pink gown, had fallen under his Cross. 'Taking the child was an evil thing to do.'

'It was,' I said and fell silent.

A new thought had occurred to me. It was that Timmy Dargan wanted me to think his motives were altruistic, that he was in the Three P's because he disapproved of what had happened to Emma and wanted to help.

What I actually believed was that Timmy was there because he wanted the people who'd taken Emma locked up. It was the one way he could be sure they wouldn't find Austin Finn.

But if Timmy wanted me to believe he was the good Samaritan then amen to that, and so be it.

'I felt sure, because of your friendship with Austin and knowing he cared for Emma,' this affection was pure invention on my part, 'that you wouldn't have wanted these people to get away with it. That if you could at all then you would help . . .'

'I didn't say anything about knowing an Austin Finn,' he reminded me. His narrowed eyes had an impossible number of darkly webbed crows' feet around them.

'No, you didn't,' I agreed, 'and no one will ever hear me say you did . . .'

'I'll deny any such knowledge anyway.' He took his hands out of his pockets and joined them as if in prayer. 'I'll do what I can, Miss Hopkins, but I won't deal with anyone but yourself. I inhabit a small, nasty and brutal world,' he held his joined hands in front of his face, 'and it's one in which bad news travels fast. I'd heard word earlier in the day, before the arrival of your emissary Mrs Brophy, of your daughter's kidnap. Harming a child,' his expression was righteous, 'is not approved of, even in the world of villains and low life. There is not a lot of sympathy for what's happened. And not much loyalty to the perpetrators.' He paused, turned sideways to look at the Christ statue, and went on, 'I've heard whispers about where your child is . . .'

'Whispers . . .' My mouth went dry. Timmy jerked his head round to look me in the face.

'Loud whispers,' he said, watching me again with his wrinkled, squint-eyed look.

'Can you take me there? Please?' I was harder put than ever to keep my hands off him. 'I'll give you £20,000 . . .'

'You must be a wealthy woman, Miss Hopkins . . .'

'I'm not a wealthy woman,' I hissed. I couldn't help it. 'I can get you that amount, no more.' The £20,000 was what I had in the bank from the money I'd got from the sale of the field at Duncolla. I'd been keeping it for the future and Emma so it would be damn all use if I didn't have her.

'When can you get it for me?' Timmy was cool.

I looked at my watch. 'Now, if we hurry. The bank

closes at four. I'm not sure how much of it they'll give me on demand, just like that, probably all of it . . .'

'I'm not a greedy man.' Timmy stood up. 'I'll take £15,000 from you. Cash. Delivered when we get to where the child is being held.'

I looked at him for long moments, trying to slow my racing thoughts into some sort of order. Timmy was most definitely a greedy man. Agreeing to take less than I'd offered said an awful lot about his devotion to Austin and I wondered at its root cause. Simple affection didn't ring true, and I would have put money on Timmy's, and Austin's, heterosexuality. There had to be a reason why Timmy Dargan felt obligated to Darragh's partner.

I wished I knew what it was. If I knew where Timmy was coming from then I would know whether or not to trust him. As it was I was flailing in the near dark, hoping my arms would come in contact with something solid.

I didn't actually care about the money. Timmy Dargan could have had every penny and every thing I had in exchange for taking me to Emma. What bothered me was the fear that I was allowing myself to be conned, that Timmy had no idea where my child was and would lead me, a willing victim, into some criminal cesspit.

In the end, of course, it all came down to one reality. If there was any chance at all that he could lead me to Emma, then I had to go with him. I stood up.

'Let's go,' I said.

Chapter Twenty-four

Tuesday, 18 January

The day outside had turned bad tempered, full of low cloud and spitting rain. Cars splashed by with their headlights on, and people passing on the footpath kept their heads down against the sniping wind. I stood, towering over Timmy, by the railings of the church. He was wearing riding boots and a pair of leather gauntlets.

'My bank's in Rathmines village,' I said.

'I'll give you a lift there,' said Timmy.

He had a motorbike in the street next to the church. It was large and black and would have looked more in place on a battlefield. From a box attached to its side he extracted two helmets.

'Put this on.'

I crammed my hair into the helmet and managed to close the strap. It wasn't easy. Timmy meanwhile sat briskly astride the machine and settled the other helmet on to his head. When he kicked down to start I climbed on behind him and he began, gingerly but smoothly to manoeuvre into the traffic. I was glad he was being careful; we were conspicuous enough as it was and even the slightest traffic misdemeanour could have the police on to us before the completion of business.

Though it was obvious Timmy was in control of his bike I felt insecure, a Gulliver being transported by a Lilliputian. I couldn't find anything of Timmy to get a firm grip on either, and had to keep my balance by holding his anorak with one hand and the motorbike seat with the other.

'Tens and twenties, if you don't mind,' said Timmy as he pulled up in front of my bank in Rathmines. 'I'll wait down the road a bit.'

It was coming up to closing time and the bank was crowded. I went to a teller who knew me and smiled and told her how much I wanted to withdraw. She looked seriously uncertain.

'I'm making a short-term emergency loan to a friend.'

Even as I lied I reminded myself that it was none of her business why I needed a withdrawal. Then I lied again.

'It'll be back in the account in less than a week,' I said.

'Would that we all had friends like you,' said the teller archly as she busied herself with a screen. 'It's usually best to give notice for a cash amount like that . . .'

'It's an emergency,' I repeated, sharply enough for her to give a nervous little cough and apologetic nod of the head.

'As it happens,' she'd become cool, her eyes fixed on the screen, 'we do have enough money on hand in the branch to pay you that amount. What denominations would you like?'

I told her and stood, feeling like a bank robber and resisting an urge to tell her it was *my* money and not the bank's, while she counted out neat piles and slipped them into a brown pouch. She hadn't warmed to me before I left.

'You took your time,' said Timmy when I rejoined him. I slipped the money inside my coat and climbed on to the bike.

'Time's moving on while we sit here,' I reminded him.

Now that we were on the serious leg of the journey Timmy Dargan showed just how excellently he was able to handle a motorbike. He had nerves of steel, which was a help, nipping between buses where there was just enough room for the passage of my knees, clearing the sides of lorries with inches to spare and firing off from traffic lights like a horse from the starting line. He seemed not to care about getting us noticed any longer, if he'd ever thought about it in the first place.

'You'll get us bloody arrested,' I yelled as we zipped between stalled traffic on Dawson Street. He didn't answer. I don't think he even heard me. I don't think either that he was capable of riding the bike any other way. Timmy, the demon rider, was ridden by his own demons and took them out on horses and motorbikes. I didn't speak again until we were forced to halt by a bottleneck on O'Connell Bridge.

'Where are we going?' I tugged at his anorak.

'Don't do that,' he pulled free of my hand, 'and don't ask questions.'

He revved the engine. 'You'll see soon enough.'

We were nearly there then. O'Connell Street he treated like the Le Mans race track and Parnell Square like Mondello. It was raining heavily now, and the street lights had come on, dazzling on the wet of the road and on the streaming cars.

It reminded me of Christmas, of being in town with Darragh and Emma before any of this had happened. Grief for both of them, so desolate it took my breath away, swept through me. I closed my eyes, tight, and let it go from me. I didn't open them until I felt us slowing down.

Timmy was drawing in to the kerb by a block of flats. The building was grey, relieved only by occasional brickwork and windows, many of them either broken or boarded up. Unwholesomely verminous about described the appearance and mood of the place. In the distance I could see Temple Street children's hospital, which landmark placed us at one of the Gardiner Street flat complexes, an area in which armoured tanks have been known to seek protection.

A group of youngsters materialized from an archway leading into an inner courtyard. They were all boys, aged between eight and twelve, though assessing stares indicated that several at least had advanced early into adulthood. Like small, territorial animals they slouched to within twenty feet of us before standing in a straggly row, watching. I unwound my legs and put my feet on the ground.

'Stay where you are.' Timmy Dargan hopped off the bike and tucked his helmet under his arm. 'Don't leave her,' he slapped the seat of the bike with one of the gauntlets.

From the back, as he moved in on the group of children, he looked like a child himself. A nasty, strutting child with a fetish for riding boots. He stopped in front of the youngsters and spoke too quietly for me to hear what he was saying. They listened to what he had to say without apparent enthusiasm, then broke ranks, some of them drifting away to disappear through the arch. A hardcore group of three remained, listening as Timmy Dargan went on in low, persuasive tones.

The real thaw didn't come until Timmy put his hand into his pocket and pulled out some notes. From where I sat they looked like tenners; Gardiner Street twelve-year-olds don't sell information cheap. The boys looked at one another and the tallest of them shrugged, saying something which made the other two snigger and drew a harsh, barking reprimand from Timmy. The boys jostled about self-consciously. One of them reached for the money and I heard Timmy's voice come clearly for the first time as he snapped, 'Watch it!' and pulled his hand back.

The conversation became even more earnest then, and it was short. When it was finished Timmy handed over the money. The boys had disappeared back to wherever they came from by the time he got back to me and the bike.

'Your daughter's here all right,' he said. 'We'll have to move fast.' He got back on to the bike.

'Where are we going?' I asked. 'If she's here . . .' I grabbed the seat as we took off, cruised slowly to a pub at the corner and pulled in. 'Get down. Wait inside the door.' He took my helmet. 'I'll be back in a couple of minutes.' He sounded quite kindly.

I stood in the doorway, wet and cold and prepared to murder the first man, or woman, who as much as frowned at me. Timmy was as good as his word and reappeared beside me, *sans* bike, in a matter of minutes.

'Couldn't leave the bike where that shower of little bastards could strip it, could I?' he said.

Presuming the question to be rhetorical, and not inclined anyway to dwell on the reality of the lives lived by the 'little bastards', I didn't answer. Timmy Dargan began walking quickly back the way we'd come. I fell into step beside him and asked, 'Where are we going? Did those youngsters say they'd seen Emma?' I had to trot to keep up with him; for such a small man he moved with real speed.

'We're headed for flat 307 on the third floor. The kids I spoke to haven't seen your daughter but they know the woman who is holding her and where *she* is . . .'

'In flat 307?'

Timmy was curt. 'That's right. Now I don't want another word out of you until I say so.'

We went under the arch and began climbing a stone staircase smelling of urine. The only light came, dimly, from the dull wattage shining along the balconies we passed. The place echoed with misery and abandon, with the turbulent sounds which came from behind the closed doors and a fulminating rant by a woman alone on one of the balconies.

On the third lot of steps we heard a laugh, soft and happy sounding, before a man and woman appeared round a bend in the stairs. They passed us cheerfully and when I turned to look after them the man had his arm around the woman and their heads were close together. I had to stop myself running after them, just to touch their blessed normality.

The graffiti got worse as we climbed, visible in all its anger and wretchedness in spite of the bad lighting. It told us what to do with ourselves, invited us to take part in ludicrous obscenities, cursed life and politics and glorified drugs and the country's men of violence. The fury and frustration I could understand. The lack of imagination was another thing.

We reached the third floor and stepped on to the balcony. Far below, in the courtyard, a group of children played in a disused car and a couple of women walked with babies in pushchairs. I turned to look along the balcony and saw that Timmy Dargan had gone ahead of me and was already half-way down, leaning to the side of a door while he lit a cigarette in cupped hands. I'd never seen him smoke before. He was taking a deep drag by the time I got to him. The number on the door was 303 and the window next to it was boarded up.

'She's two doors down,' Timmy spoke very, very quietly.

I hugged myself, whispering, 'She's really in there?'

'That's where she is.'

He dragged again on the cigarette and I saw, with a shock, that he was nervous. Anger, irrational and futile, bubbled and died in me and left me filled with fearful doubting. Timmy Dargan's granite-like self-containment had been my rock and ballast until now. He'd no right allowing it to crack.

He'd said nothing either about the £15,000 since I'd come out of the bank. Maybe this was all bluff, maybe he didn't really know whether or not Emma was in the flat behind the door, maybe he'd an agenda I hadn't even begun to imagine yet.

'How do I know she's in there?' I asked.

Slowly and silently Timmy ground the cigarette

beneath the heel of his boot. I was formulating plans for a terrible revenge on him when he began to speak in a low, slow voice.

'You don't know she's in there, Miss Hopkins, *I* do. And I know because I know the people who've taken her and why. They were wrong, and some of them know now how wrong they were, but that won't stop the rest of them behaving like the mad fools they are. I was sure the child was here somewhere.' He shrugged. 'All I needed was the flat number. Now,' he took a breath and signed me to stand behind him, 'I'm going to knock on that door. The woman we want to meet may be on her own with your daughter or she may have company. One way or another I want you to step past me and inside as soon as the door opens. Go through the place until you find your child. I have a thing or two to explain to her keeper. Once I've sorted things out you can give me the . . .'

'No!' I cut him off with a hiss. 'I'm not going blundering in there just like that.'

I moved closer and stood over him, all five foot ten inches of me. He put his head back and looked up, unblinking, his nose bigger than ever and his eyes smaller at that angle. An urge to grab and shake him raged in me and to stop myself I stood back again.

'How do I know who, or what, is in there?' I demanded. 'What if I go charging in and . . . what good would a dead mother be to my child when she gets through all of this?'

'She's not going to have much need of any kind of a mother if you *don't* go in there. You're the only one can convince those lunatics things have gone far enough. You're going to have to tell them, Miss Hop-

302

kins, that their one hope of getting out of this thing lies in damage limitation – and that that means giving you back your child.'

He said all of this in a reasonable, quiet voice. 'If you don't manage to do that she's lost,' he sighed, 'we're all lost.'

The fate of Timmy and his friends failed to move me. They could stay lost for ever as far as I was concerned. But they were not going to have Emma for company. Or me as willing victim.

'I've met Jamesy Collins already,' I reminded him. 'He's a violent, sadistic brute. If he's in there then I'm not going to be given much chance to convince anyone of anything. You have to give me some idea of what to expect . . .'

'Jamesy Collins . . .' He interrupted me with a disbelieving shake of his head. 'Do you really believe Jamesy's the one behind this? That Jamesy has your child?'

The balcony spun around me. When it settled a little, and I was fairly sure I wasn't going to faint, I said, 'If Jamesy doesn't have Emma then who has her?'

'Jamesy Collins,' Timmy spat on the ground between his boots, 'is a small-time shit and big-time scab. He's finished in this town. I've seen to that.' He freed a hand and smoothed his hair back at the sides. He was very calm, in control again. 'You need to understand, Miss Hopkins, that Jamesy Collins is nothing but an insignificant piece of vermin, a retrograde without a future.' He allowed himself a small smile. 'Not only is he a greedy and vicious man, Miss Hopkins, your Mr Collins is also an incompetent and foolish one. If Mr Collins and your friend Mr McCann

303

had remained in their boxes the unfortunate Mr Mc-Cann would be alive today and his daughter would not have suffered this distressing trauma . . .'

'Look, just tell me without the flourishes what's going . . .' I realized I'd raised my voice when Timmy fluttered a little hand in a silencing gesture.

'Briefly then, Miss Hopkins, and because I have no axe to grind with you, I will explain. For some years past my regrettably absent friend looked after the financial arrangements for some business people in this town. Entirely his own affair, you understand, and nothing to do with the firm of which he was a partner, nor indeed with your Mr Darragh McCann. All went well until Mr McCann, for reasons of greed, one must suppose, decided to set up a side-line operation of his own. I have no idea who approached who but the net result was that Mr McCann took on the said Mr Collins as a client . . .'

'What you're telling me,' I spoke slowly, aware that Timmy had finally revealed Austin as his mysterious 'friend' and focusing furiously on the core of what he was saying, 'is that Austin Finn was laundering money for one lot of criminals and that Darragh, for some time before his death, had been laundering money for another lot, namely Jamesy Collins and company . . .'

'Crudely and simply put but more or less how things were,' Timmy agreed.

My mind was working overtime. I just wanted a few points sorted out, fundamentals which would help me see this nightmare more clearly. I couldn't take any more of Timmy Dargan's tripe about 'friends' and 'business'. All I wanted were a few questions answered.

'Did Darragh McCann's death have to do with him

getting caught between rival criminal gangs? Jamesy Collins's lot and whoever Austin Finn was laundering money for?'

'That's one way of putting it . . .'

'So Jamesy Collins's lot weren't the ones who murdered him?'

'Only indirectly, in that Mr McCann's dealings with Jamesy brought the situation about . . .'

'Did Austin Finn condone the killing of his partner?'

Timmy looked, I thought, genuinely shocked. 'Certainly not. It was entirely without his knowledge.' He looked sulky. 'I have not, Miss Hopkins, at any time in our acquaintance mentioned the name Austin Finn . . .'

'Of course you haven't.' I'd really had it with Timmy's gameplaying.

'But would it be true to say that when Darragh McCann was killed control of the situation went from Austin Finn's hands into those of his criminal associates? And when things became impossible and Austin went AWOL it was Austin's associates, and not Jamesy Collins, who assumed I would know where Austin had gone?'

'That's it.' Timmy sniffed.

There was a lot in between that I didn't understand but for now I wanted to be clear about the bottom line.

'So it is Austin Finn's criminal associates who were responsible for killing Darragh McCann?' I asked.

'Yes,' said Timmy.

'And they are the same people who have kidnapped my daughter?'

'Yes.'

So, now I knew. Timmy wanted revenge. Austin's criminal associates had turned on Austin and Timmy wanted them punished. I was being used.

'Will you knock on that door or will I?' I asked.

Chapter Twenty-five

Tuesday, 18 January

Timmy knocked on the door, twice and sharply on the glass panel with his little knuckles.

For minutes it seemed that nothing would happen. He was about to have another go when a door opened somewhere in the flat and light filled the hallway behind the glass.

A blurry shape moved slowly towards us. An arm separated itself from the blur and was raised to open the door.

'Brace yourself,' said Timmy. I did.

The woman who stood in the doorway was no more than twenty-two or three with shoulder-length red hair and a heavily pregnant belly over which she held a protective hand. Pregnancy apart, she was no sylph and her bulk filled the entire doorway. There was no way I would have been able to rush in past her. She ignored me and looked down at Timmy.

'Yeah? What do you want?'

She seemed to be either tired or bored and was probably both. If I'd been asked I'd have said her time was imminent. Her voice sounded like that of the woman on the phone.

'We want to come in and talk to you,' said Timmy.

'Yis want to come in and talk to me . . .' She put

one hand where there would normally be a hip and the other against the door jamb. Talk about putting up defences. 'Well, you can't come in and talk to me. Who are you, anyway?'

'You know who I am, Jacinta,' Timmy was cool as snow falling, only not so gentle. 'And Charlie would not be pleased to hear you'd left me outside where I can make a lot of noise and attract attention. Charlie wouldn't want the mother of the child you're looking after in there kept standing out here either . . .'

'Let them in.' The male voice came from behind the woman. The words belied the tone, which was flat and unwelcoming. Jacinta without moving either of her hands, turned her head in its direction.

'Why the hell should I let them in?' she demanded. 'I'm the one'll have to deal with them. You'll do shite all about it. They can go talk to Charlie in the fuckin' pub.'

'No, they can't. Let them in.' The voice was closer now and more lethal. Jacinta, after a few seconds' silence and an angry toss of the red hair, turned back to Timmy.

'You heard what he said.' She stepped away from the door and Timmy pushed it open and hopped inside. I was there on his heels, fast, before anyone could change their minds about letting me in. The small hallway was stacked with cardboard boxes, in front of which stood a man with a broad chest, thick neck and large, suspicious face. Beautiful he was not, though there was a certain youthfulness to his round cheeks. He looked like a bouncer but my guess was that he was most likely a middle-management criminal type. He avoided my gaze.

'Say your bit and be quick about it,' he told Timmy. 'This isn't a hotel we're running here . . .'

As sarcasms went this wasn't just cheap, it was unfortunate in that it gave Timmy Dargan the opening he needed.

'Well now, Mick,' he drawled, 'it's my information that you are indeed running a class of a hotel here. The word is that you and your lady Jacinta are keeping a guest, a very young guest.'

His voice and demeanour changed without warning and he leaned forward, tapping the man called Mick on the chest. I have to say that he was fearless, a terrier snapping in the face of a Rottweiler.

'Bad move, Mick, abducting a child like that. But I'm sure you know that by now. I know Charlie's not pleased.' Mick's face had turned puce and Timmy, wisely, took a step backwards to the door. 'I've brought the mother. Give her the child and let them be off. Then you and me'll have a chat about a few things.'

This sounded a lot better than Timmy's original plan to have *me* remain after *he* had gone. Timmy had obviously reassessed the situation. The man called Mick wasn't too impressed, however.

'Fuck off out of here, you twisted fuckin' midget . . .' Mick's colour was getting worse all the time. He advanced on Timmy who, albeit with the open door at his back, stood his ground. Jacinta, a look of boredom on her face, had retreated to stand by a closed door at the end of the corridor. From behind it there came the everyday unmistakable sounds of a television. I willed Emma to be in there watching it.

'You know I'm right.' There was an insidious menace about Timmy's tone. 'Taking the child wasn't

Charlie's idea at all, was it Mick? It was your brainwave, wasn't it? Only it turned out not to be such a great idea and now the shit's hit the fan and you've got a real situation on your hands.' He paused. 'Well, I'm here to help.'

Mick, surveying Timmy with a pair of remarkably unintelligent-looking eyes, folded his arms and struck a belligerent pose. 'I don't know what the fuck you're talking about. What child . . .?'

Timmy, quietly sinister and confident, shook his head and cut him short. Mick wasn't convincing anyway. His heart wasn't in the denial. My own heart rose hopefully.

'Don't be a total eejit and make things worse than they are, Mick,' said Timmy. 'How do you think Charlie's going to react when he hears I brought you a solution and you fucked that up too? And he'll hear about it Mick, old son, all about it, because I'll be telling him.'

Leaving Mick time to ponder this, but no time at all to respond, Timmy spun on the increasingly languid Jacinta. 'I'm surprised at you,' he was reproachful, 'about to become part of the miracle of motherhood yourself and you lend assistance to a caper like this. How would you feel if . . .'

'Are you going to deal with this creepin' little retard or what?' Jacinta, without raising her voice, fired the question at the now very agitated Mick.

Myself, I'd have taken Mick more carefully than either Timmy or Jacinta; everything about him screamed powder keg and short fuse. I was surprised when he took Jacinta's barb quietly enough.

'Shut up, you,' he said. 'I've a bit of thinking to do here.'

'Look, I feel sort of in the way.' I knew I sounded feeble but I had to get in on things somehow. 'Why don't I go on in there and have a chat with Emma? You can tell us what you've decided when you . . .'

'This is my place and you're going nowhere in here unless I say so.' Jacinta met my gaze coolly.

'And you're not giving the orders around here.' Mick's head jerked bullishly in her direction. 'And I'm still thinking about the best thing to do . . .'

'You already did your share of the thinking,' Jacinta's lip curled, 'and look where it's got us. Jesus, I'm sick of this shite and carry-on. I warned you, Mick Brennan, that the whole thing was fuckin' stupid. But would you listen? Would you?' She advanced on the rigidly defensive Mick. 'No, of course you didn't listen, you stupid fuck. You never listen. Well, I'm telling you something now, Mick Brennan, and you better pay heed this time.'

She was standing in front of her by now choleric consort, her belly pinning him against the wall and her finger stabbing his chest. 'If you don't come to some arrangement, fast, then I'm going to fuck you and that kid in there *and* her mother and that withered little runt, out of here. The lot of you'll go. More than that, you'll have nothing to do with *this* child.' She tapped her belly. 'I've put up with you this far but no more. And you know I mean it. I told you before; I'm sick of the shit.'

What struck me while Jacinta was speaking was the expression on Timmy's face. Satisfaction about described it. He'd known the set-up, had gambled on things developing like this and it was now looking as if he might win the £15,000 bet he'd placed with himself.

Mick pushed his face into Jacinta's. 'I told you before, you'll do what you're told if you know what's good for you . . .'

Jacinta, whether acting on instinct or desperation I'll never know, then did something which changed the whole mood of things in the hallway. Slowly, deliberately – and before he realized what she intended – she reached for one of Mick's hands and held it against her belly. He stared at her, anger, bluster, awe and what looked like fear all chasing across his face.

'It could happen tonight, Mick, you could be a father tonight. Feel him, feel him . . .' In a silence broken only by howls of television laughter Mick allowed his hand to be guided over Jacinta's swollen stomach. 'There,' Jacinta breathed, 'and again . . . can you feel him? He's jumping around. Can you feel? You've upset him, with all of this . . . It has to stop, Mick.'

'Do you really think he could come tonight?' Mick moved his blunt-fingered hand under hers.

'He was due a week ago.' Jacinta shrugged. 'I'm not going to hold on to the little bugger much longer . . .'

'Emma came early,' I said. 'Her father wasn't there . . . He's not around now, either.'

I stopped. I wasn't accusing anyone. Just grabbing the moment to remind them about another child and the nightmare she'd been thrown into because of them. They didn't look like murderers. But how did I know what murderers looked like?

'You can go on in to her,' Jacinta jerked her head

at the door, 'but you're not leaving here, any of you, until things are sorted out. I'm not taking the can for this.' I was reaching for the door handle when she stepped in front of me. 'It wasn't me that took her. I'd nothing to do with any of that. I didn't know a thing until him,' she nodded at Mick, 'and another clown and his woman brought her here to me. If I hadn't taken her from them,' she took a deep breath, 'then Jesus knows what would've happened to her.'

She made it sound as if taking Emma from them had been a corporal act of mercy.

'Thank you,' I said and opened the door and walked into the room behind it.

There was one, central light, covered with a pink frilly shade. There was a table with glasses, beer cans and the remains of a burger and chip meal. The curtains were yellow, the three-piece suite covered in a brown, floral design. There were two sound systems, a TV and video. It was reasonably clean. All of this I saw, with absolute clarity, as my eyes travelled to where Emma lay, apparently asleep, on the settee. She was curled up and someone had thrown a plaid rug over her. She looked very beautiful and very, very alive.

I knelt beside her and touched her face. She was warm, breathing normally. I pushed the hair back from her face and gave thanks to the God who had delivered her to me twice. She stirred under my hand.

'Emma? It's Mommy, I'm here. Wake up, Emma . . .'

She stirred again and sighed in her sleep but didn't waken. Relief gave way to cold fear and I gathered her to me, rocking her in the way I always did, crooning as I kissed her hair, her face, praying for a response. She slept on. They'd given her something. This sleep wasn't natural. Even allowing that she'd had no sleep the night before it wasn't natural.

'She'll be all right.' Jacinta's voice sounded behind me. 'They gave her something in the car, to make her sleep like. It was a bit strong and she got sick after they brought her here to me. I gave her milk and biscuits and after a while she went back to sleep again. She's sleeping it off now.'

'This is *not* natural.' I looked up at her over Emma's head. 'It's not natural when a child who's been abducted doesn't wake on hearing her mother's voice ...' Our raised voices did what my soporific crooning had failed to do. Emma woke up.

'Mommy.' Her arm came up and curled around my neck. 'I didn't know you were coming. They didn't tell me you were coming ...' She wrapped her other arm around my neck too and we held each other, half-laughing, half-crying, making a multitude of reassuring sounds, both of us. Timmy gave us a few minutes before he tapped me on the shoulder.

'I have to be on my way now, Miss Hopkins, so I'd be obliged if we could complete our business arrangement.'

I disentangled myself from Emma's grip and stood. 'I'm not going anywhere,' I assured her, 'I've just got to give this man something.'

She didn't believe me, of course, and got groggily up from the sofa to stand beside me. I took the money from the inside pocket of my jacket and handed it to Timmy. 'Thank you,' I said.

He stuffed it inside his anorak. 'Note that I am not counting it. I trust you absolutely, Miss Hopkins. It's been a pleasure doing business with you.' He made a small bow and smiled at Emma. 'You be good for your mother now, Emma. She's very fond of you. You only get one mother, you know.'

'Of course you only get one mother,' said Emma.

I held her against me. In the kitchen, which was off the sitting-room and no more than a galley really, I could see Mick helping himself to a beer from the fridge. Jacinta had disappeared.

'What happens now?' I asked Timmy, hoping Marge Simpson's voice on the telly would prevent Mick hearing the question.

'Now?' Timmy looked up at me in surprise. 'Now I depart and you make your case to Mick. He won't have the balls ...' He looked apologetically at Emma. 'Excuse my language, Miss Emma, the word I should have used was courage. Yes, indeed. Courage is what Mr Brennan lacks. He won't take unilateral action.'

He studied Mick in the kitchen for a minute. So did I. He had the beer in one hand and appeared to be making a sandwich with the other. He lacked grace and charm but he looked more inadequate than dangerous.

'Isn't he afraid we'll just go, run off?' I asked.

Timmy looked at me pityingly. 'Go, Miss Hopkins? Go where? Down those stairs and out of here? You must be joking. You'd get no further than the first flight before the tom-toms had the word around and the neighbours were obligingly picking you up. This is not Rathgar, Miss Hopkins. This is a reservation.' He grinned. 'People look out for one another around here. You're as safe in these flats as you would be in any secure prison. Now,' he looked at his watch and gave a whistle of surprise, 'it's time I was off. I've discussed things with Mick and it's my impression that he's keen to have a few words about things with a man called Charlie, who is by way of being his employer. The fair Jacinta is, I believe, trying at this very moment to make contact with him via the telephone in the bedroom. Things will work out. I have every faith in your persuasive powers, Miss Hopkins.' He held out his hand and, after a minute, I took it. 'We may not meet again,' he said, 'but my very best wishes to you, for now and in the future.'

'Thank you,' I said.

He marched smartly out of the room, no goodbyes to Mick or Jacinta, and pulled the front door firmly after him when he exited the flat. And so we were alone, Emma and me, with the people responsible for her father's death. Timmy Dargan had brought the lot of us together and abandoned us to our own devices.

'Can we go now?' Emma tugged at my arm. 'Is it over now?'

'Not yet.' I sat with her on the sofa. 'But it soon will be.'

She nodded and yawned, unworried and confident things would be sorted out now that I'd arrived.

'I'm sleepy all the time,' she said. 'They gave me a tablet in the car. They said it was to stop me getting sick but it was to make me sleep, wasn't it?'

'Yes, it was to make you sleep,' I said and cursed *them*, whoever they were, and swore that never, ever would I leave her out of my sight again.

'I got sick anyway,' Emma said with some satisfaction. 'But that was here and I did it all over Jacinta. Jacinta's nice, she didn't mind a bit. She's funny. She has nails like a witch. I didn't like it in the bedroom

and she said I could stay out here at the television . . .'
She yawned and curled into me. The spate of words
had tired her and her eyelids drooped again. I pulled
the rug about her. She felt warm, and relaxed, the
residue effects of the sleeping tablet acting as a seda-
tive. Her senses had been dulled enough to take the
edge off her fear, blunted enough to neutralize a full
awareness of her predicament. Realization would come
later.

'They didn't hurt you, Emma, did they?' I heard the
anxiety in my voice and lightened up, 'because I'll sort
them out if they did . . .'

'I told them that, I told them you would.' Emma
found my hand and held it. 'I told them my mother
would make them sorry.' She paused, remembering. 'I
was frightened in the car. They were horrible in the
house to Aunt Maisie and the boys and . . .' Her eyes
filled with tears and I smoothed her hair from her
forehead.

'Aunt Maisie and the boys are fine,' I said, 'and
we'll talk about things tomorrow.' There would be
plenty of tomorrows, when this was all over, to talk
things out of her system. 'The boys are making a big
thing of it in school . . .' This distracted her and she
jumped in gleefully.

'I'll bet they don't tell how scared they were. I'll
really have something to talk about when I go back to
school, won't I?'

'You certainly will.'

I looked at her and soaked some of her confident
belief into myself. If Emma could do it, then so could I.

'I'm going to have a word with Jacinta in the bedroom.' I eased her hand out of mine and tucked the

rug around her. 'So you can have another bit of a snooze while I do that. Don't worry,' I said when she made as if to hold on to me, 'I'll just be in the bedroom. You can come in to me if you feel afraid here.'

Jacinta was sitting on the bed scowling at a phone beside her on the pink coverlet.

'Nice mess you've landed the lot of us in,' she looked at me sourly when I came in.

'I didn't start this,' I snapped.

'And I suppose I did?'

'No, you didn't start it either.'

I sat on the bed, the phone and our miserable exchange between us, wordlessly sharing the fact that we'd both been dropped in it by the deeds of men, by machinations and events neither of us had desire to be a part of. In my case the catalyst had been Darragh, in hers the rabid Mick.

'What happens now?' I asked eventually. 'Did you get in touch with the boss-man, Charlie whatever?'

'I got him,' Jacinta said. 'He's on his way.' She gave me a bitterly resentful look and threw herself back on to the bed, her red hair alarming against the pink spread. 'He's not happy about things, I can tell you that for nothing. Not one fuckin' bit happy. So prepare yourself.' She closed her eyes. 'Jesus, I'm tired.'

She hadn't given me his full name and I took this as a good sign. She didn't want me to know, which could mean that she felt the less information I had when I left there with Emma the better. Which in turn indicated that she believed we *were* going to walk out

318

of there. I was clutching at straws, I knew, but had to have some hopeful foundation on which to work.

Even so, opportunities for escape should be seized. As now, with Jacinta asleep and the phone sitting on the bed beside me waiting to be used. I watched her round, white face for a while to be sure the sleep was for real. Her eye shadow was too mauve and her roots needed doing. Pallid, indoor looks apart she was a pretty woman, with an oval-shaped face and good mouth. The hands clasped atop her belly ended in curved, purply-black talons. Her breathing was regular and peaceful. I reached and picked up the handset.

For a pregnant woman, one coming to the end of her term at that, Jacinta moved with the speed of greased lightning.

'Don't even think about it.' The talons closed dangerously tight over the vein in my wrist. She was sitting so close I could smell tea on her breath. I opened my hand and let the phone drop.

'I'm warning you, and I'll only do it the one time.' Her breathing was laboured but I didn't for a minute doubt she meant what she was saying. 'Don't mess with me. That man out there might be thick but I'm not. There's no way I'm going to get myself landed with a jail sentence on account of you and your daughter. Is that clear?'

I nodded and she threw my hand away from her in disgust.

'Right, that's that then.' She stood up. 'The man you need to talk to will be here soon.' She paused and muttered something which sounded like 'better be' before beginning to brush her hair. The roots really were in a terrible state. 'Go and keep the child company until then.' She waved the brush at me. 'And try not to aggravate Mick. He's not in the best of humours at the moment and he might be inclined to blame you and the kid if you give him cause. Now, go on, get out of here. I don't want to have to look at your fat face any more. I'm sick of you and your kid and this whole fuckin' thing.'

Mick was drinking a beer and had rejected *The Den* for an American legal series. Emma was half sitting up and half asleep.

'Won't be long now,' I told her. 'We have to wait for another man to get here and then, after I have a bit of a chat with him, we'll be off.'

'Why do you have to chat with him? I want to go now.'

'There are a few things to sort out before we go.' I kissed her forehead. 'Don't worry. Everything's going to be fine.'

'Will I be able to sleep in my own room tonight?'

'I hope so . . .'

'I hope so too,' said Emma, softly, and took my hand. Whoever said children were cruel?

The boss-man Charlie arrived two hours later, at exactly eight-thirty.

Chapter Twenty-six

Tuesday, 18 January

In the hours before Charlie's arrival I held Emma and tried to piece together a scenario into which everything which had happened would fit.

Only I couldn't get it to work. I was having severe difficulties with Timmy Dargan's news about there being two opposing criminal gangs involved. Each time I got the players into position they switched roles and the rules changed.

Jacinta came out of the bedroom once only, and then for a cup of coffee.

'Make something for yourself,' she said, with a carelessness I wasn't about to be taken in by after the telephone episode. Jacinta was one player who was on the ball even if Mick, sipping beers and flicking channels, didn't appear to be. He didn't speak once during the two hours' wait.

The boss-man Charlie had his own key and I didn't know he was in the flat until Jacinta came bustling out of the bedroom, prodded me unceremoniously and told me to 'Put the child into the small bedroom, Charlie doesn't want her hearing what's going to be said.' I didn't want her to hear either, so I did as I was told and tucked an unprotesting Emma into the bed in a box bedroom.

Charlie was in the living-room when I got back there. He was dressed in a navy-blue overcoat and black scarf. A green baseball cap covered what appeared to be a bald head. His face was good, verging on hand-some, with wide-spaced grey eyes, straight nose and a moustache. The baseball cap gave him the appearance of an off-duty accountant indulging a flamboyant streak.

Mick woke up when he turned off the television set. 'Charlie, we wasn't expecting you so soon ...' He leaped from the armchair with the agility of the extremely fit. 'Jacinta's having a bit of a kip in the bedroom.' He looked worried. 'She gets tired a lot, but you'd know all about that, Charlie, wouldn't ya?' Mick laughed, an embarrassingly ingratiating sound.

'What Mick's alluding to,' Charlie gave me a brief look, 'is the fact that I'm the father of six children.' He paused. 'Which is why you can understand that this abduction had nothing to do with me.'

His voice was deepest Dublin and easy on the ear. Charlie was the sort of man, I would have been willing to bet, who was used to having his way with women. Men would have done what Charlie said too, but for different reasons.

'I'm glad to hear Emma's abduction had nothing to do with you,' I said, 'because I'd like to discuss a way out of this, one that will cause the least trouble for everyone.'

Charlie gave a loud laugh. 'If it suits me, Miss Hopkins, then it will have to suit you.' The laughter ended. 'Get into the bedroom, Mick, and get that dozy bitch of yours out here. I told her already to get herself out of the bed. I don't want to have to go over things twice.'

322

Mick hurtled out of the room and Charlie scowled at the sitting-room and kitchen. 'Place is like a fuckin' tip,' he said, and included Jacinta in the scowl when she appeared in the doorway, tying back her hair.

'Get rid of this shaggin' mess, Jacinta. Now.' With one hand he swept the table clear of uneaten food and dishes.

I moved out of the way of flying cutlery and plates and so did Jacinta. As the clatter and crash of breakages subsided, she said coolly, 'I'm tired, Charlie. I was woken out of my sleep early this morning and I've had the kid to care for all day . . .'

'Yeah, it's tough on you.'

Charlie, with an expression of dismissive disgust, sank into an armchair and took out a cigar. He'd taken off the overcoat and, in a Nike sweatshirt, looked in good shape for his age, which must have been about forty-five. He lit up and gave Jacinta a sour look.

'You're not a patch on the woman your sister is. She's got six of them to look after and you could eat off the floor in our place.'

'Fat lot of good it does her.' Jacinta's quiet fury was impressively intimidating. 'Doesn't keep you by her side, does it? Doesn't stop you puttin' it out all over town, does it?'

'Wash your mouth, woman, or I'll wash it out for you.' Charlie looked moodily at the top of his cigar, his heart clearly not in the argument. 'Now, you,' he shot me a cold look, 'sit over there, opposite, where I can look at you. We've things to discuss. Make us tea and a few sandwiches, Jacinta. I could eat the lamb of God, I'm that hungry. Now, Norah.' He squinted through the cigar smoke. 'It's all right for me to call you Norah?' His tone, as I scuttled into the chair vacated by Mick, was friendly. 'We have here a situation, created by mindless eejits like our headbanger friend Mick here, which has created a lot of difficulties for me in my work. It is in both our interests, yours and mine, that we come to an arrangement which will allow me to continue my business operations in this town. Do I make myself clear?'

'Absolutely,' I said, 'and now I'd like to make a point, and it's this: The kidnapping of a child is one thing. The kidnap and *murder* of a child would bring every guard in the city down on your case. The murder of that child *and* her mother would bring out every guard in the *country*.'

I paused. Charlie sighed tiredly but said nothing. I went on. 'We have, as you say, a situation, and I'd like to work out a deal.'

Charlie gave an even more tired sigh and stubbed his cigar in the empty grate. Still he said nothing, a tactic which put him in control. Jacinta arrived and put four of everything on the table – cups, saucers and plates. It looked like we were all going to eat together, a happy quartet over the tea cups. She piled the table with sandwiches too. They were filled with jam.

'You've got a point in what you're saying, Norah.' Charlie broke his silence as Jacinta retreated to the whistling kettle. 'There'd be no living in this town for anybody who did in a mother and child, given as we're a people that puts great store on the family and all of that. You being a single mother and not a proper family would take the steam out of things a bit, naturally enough,' he gave me a sad smile, 'but things'd go rough all the same.' His expression became that of a reflective and reasonable man. 'The thing we have to consider here, Norah, is whether I actually want to stay working in this town. Things have changed. They're not the way they used to be and, to be honest with you, I'm not altogether sure I want to stay around any more. If I decide, on balance, that it's time for me to go then that changes everything, doesn't it?' His smile became broad and happy.

'I can see that you deciding to leave would affect any arrangement between us,' I agreed, 'but what about your wife and children, and your friends?' I threw a quick glance at the morose-looking Mick and at Jacinta, now at the table with the teapot. 'You don't strike me as the sort of man who would abandon his family. There's also the reality of computer communications to think about. The guards are having people extradited and brought back every other day . . .'

'You've been busy inside that blondie head of yours, Norah,' he interrupted me softly, elbows on his knees, 'but I won't hold that against you. I'd do the same in your place. Only don't make the mistake of trying to be too smart.' This time when he smiled I was frightened. 'It would be fatal for you to think you were smarter than me, Norah. Fatal.'

'I'm trying to be helpful . . .'

'And that's the way it should be.' He sat back, reflective once more as he looked at me. 'What we discuss here, Norah, will decide my mind for me about whether I should go or stay. If I stay I have to be sure there's nothing the guards can pin on me. But then I was never here. It's your word against mine. Jacinta and Mick'll say what they're told to say. And you can forget about Timmy or anybody else speaking for you because they're not going to put their necks out. Nothin' in it for them but grief. Am I making myself clear?'

'Yes.'

'Good. If I go the guards'll make it hard on those I'll be leaving behind, but that'll pass. What I'm saying here, Norah, is that a tragedy happening to you and your child would make my life difficult, but not impossible. So don't make the mistake of thinking you're the one calling the tune here, because you're not. Got it?'

'Yes.'

'Right. Now you know your place we can begin to talk business. Them sandwiches look grand, Jacinta. Bring them over here and a cup of tea with them. Maybe Norah would like a cup too?' I said I would and he nodded approvingly. So much for tea *à quatre*. 'A cup of tea's a great reviver,' Charlie went on amiably. 'I never touch anything stronger myself. The hard stuff's a mug's game. Same as the drugs. Ruining family life, they are. Thanks, Jacinta, you're a good girl. How're you feeling? Ready to pop anyday, are you?'

'Any minute, more like.' A subdued Jacinta handed us two cups of milky white tea. Charlie seemed to like it that way. He offered me a sandwich from an over-loaded plate. 'Want one? No? Can't say as I blame you. Wouldn't go near so much carbohydrate myself if I wasn't suffering from starvation.' He bit into the layers of white bread and jam and, between munches, came slowly to the point.

'You have to understand, Norah, that none of this has anything to do with me. I'm just by way of a fixer in all of this, trying to get things sorted as best I can

326

for everyone concerned. There's no one wants to lay hands on Austin Finn more than I do but *I* know that you're not acquainted with his whereabouts. How do I know? Because I use my fuckin' loaf, that's how. Finn tried to rip you off, same as he tried to rip everyone else off, so why would he tell you where he was going? If Mick and his Einstein mates thought about it they'd never have gone after your daughter.'

He wiped crumbs from around his mouth. 'They'll pay for it too. By Jesus they'll pay for it.' He picked up another sandwich. 'I want to let you and your child go, Norah. My feeling, now that I've met you, is that you're an honourable woman. The sort of woman who'd go straight to the police if I was to let her walk away from here without conditions. You wouldn't be able to help yourself. You'd go straight to your friends in Pearse Street and tell them all sorts of things about Charlie and his mates.'

He held out his cup to Jacinta for a refill. She didn't offer to refill mine and carefully avoided my eye when I looked at her. Mick was manicuring his nails by the table. Charlie sat back into the armchair with the tea.

'Like yourself, Norah, I've been thinking. I've been thinking about what you can do for me in exchange for me letting you go. I haven't come up with much but there is one small thing . . .'

He fell silent and everyone looked at me. I looked from Jacinta to Charlie, ignoring Mick, who didn't seem to me worth the trouble. I cleared my throat and croaked, 'If I can do it I will.'

'Good girl,' said Charlie. 'Now,' he examined the bottom of his tea cup, 'there's some bits and pieces of information I need, and I think you might be able to help me out. Nothing major, just some things that'll help me plan the future.' He stopped and waited and I nodded.

'If I can do it I will,' I assured him, praying he didn't want me to draw a map of the inside of Pearse Street garda station or give him the low-down on Detective-Sergeant Liston's insights on the city's criminal confraternity. But if that's what it took . . .

'Your dead friend, Darragh McCann, was dealing with people I don't like, people who've been very nasty to me and mine over the years.' Charlie shook his head in disbelief. 'They've stolen from me, lied to me. Now I want to get back what's mine, no more. Trouble is, I can't do that until I know what the score is. That's where you can help me out, Norah.' His expression was one of profound sincerity. 'Tell me, if you would, what you know about an account with the initials NOMA.'

So that was it. Charlie, I was certain, already knew all about the NOMA account, that it was where Darragh had directed the gains from laundered money. Charlie's request was only a lead up to his real agenda: I was to be used in a war between two criminal gangs, enlisted to help Charlie's lot appropriate the illegal gains of Jamesy Collins's lot.

I played along with Charlie's request for information, telling him what I knew about the NOMA account – as well as giving him some news I didn't think he was going to like. The banks and the police would have to sort things out later. My priorities that night had nothing to do with law and order.

I told Charlie that I'd refused to sign a form which would give Austin Finn access to the account. I didn't bother telling him how Austin had gone on to try bribery and exploit my interest in Conal's play to get me to sign the same form. He didn't need to know.

'Not that it matters now.' I was casual – this was the bit Charlie wasn't going to like. 'Because the Criminal Assets Bureau have moved in to go through everything at Finn and McCann. I think you'll find,' I cleared my throat, 'that the offices and everything in them are being gone through fairly thoroughly even as we speak. The NOMA account will have been appropriated . . .'

'These things don't happen that quickly,' he looked amused, 'but you've been a good girl, Norah, and you've been straight with me. What you say ties in with my own information. Jacinta,' he snapped his fingers without taking his eyes off my face, 'bring me the bag I left in the bedroom.'

Jacinta left and Mick, the effort to appear keen giving him a strained look, asked Charlie if there was anything he wanted him to do. Charlie looked at him reflectively.

'Tell you what, Mick,' he said slowly. 'You could give a bit of a scout around outside, see if there's anyone knocking about as shouldn't be.'

Mick, shoulders squared and knuckles crunching, left at once. Charlie shrugged. 'Better to have him out of the place for a while anyway. Don't want loose talk about what's going to happen here.' He caught my expression and gave a merry chortle. My skin crawled. 'You're right to be worried, Norah, right not to take a thing for granted until, and if, you get out of here.'

Jacinta arrived back with a sports bag which she

dumped at his feet. From under a pile of clothes Charlie lifted out a large, manila envelope. He scrutinized the contents briefly before passing them over to me. I knew, even before I looked at them, what they were going to be.

'The NOMA account's in a Cayman Island bank,' said Charlie, 'and the money in it is mine, by rights. McCann tied things up in your name but he wasn't quite clever enough and possession,' he pointed to the documents in my hand, 'is nine points of the law. No one knows that better than the guards because they don't have the papers, do they?' He grinned and stretched his legs in front of him. 'They'll have found enough other bits and pieces in Finn and McCann's offices to keep them busy for a while but they won't have got what they really wanted. It's all down to contacts and that's what I've got, contacts.' The grin got wider. 'Contacts and luck, Norah, that's what it's about. You being here is the devil's own luck and I'll tell you why. I'm getting on a plane in the morning with those papers, Norah, and I'm going to put things right with that account. It won't be a problem because your friend McCann signed things over to me a few weeks ago. I didn't have your secondary signature on things but since McCann forged that in the first place I figured that a friend of mine could do the same thing again on the dotted line. The child's name was only a formality, a McCann touch to things so's he could give the account the name he wanted. The handwritten letter from McCann, along with a phone call he obligingly made for us, was the big thing. But now that you're here,' he leaned forward and patted my knee and I shivered, 'it seems to me that we could

330

foolproof this thing with a letter from you too.' The smile vanished. 'I'll tell you what to write. Jacinta, get writing paper and a pen.'

'Where the fuck do you think I'd get stuff like that?' Jacinta, at the table, was looking strained and sulky. Charlie went silent. He didn't even look Jacinta's way but I saw her change from sullen to nervously eager in ten seconds flat.

'I'll go out and get it. I know a neighbour can lend me some,' she said.

'You do that.' Charlie closed his eyes and leaned back. 'And be quick about it.'

So now I knew at least what had happened to Darragh. The man reclining opposite me, a father of six wearing a baseball cap on his bald head, had killed him. Or had had him killed, the details didn't really matter that much. The facts were that he had been killed after being forced to relinquish control of the Cayman Islands account he'd set up to handle the money he was laundering for his client Jamesy Collins.

And if I was to get our daughter and myself out of there I was going to have to do the same thing, all over again. Darragh had written and signed the release letter believing it to be the price of his getting out of the whole mess. He probably thought he'd got everyone else out of it too – his wife and other children, Emma, me . . .

I had to believe things would be different if I wrote the letter Charlie wanted. I couldn't afford not to. Panic tightened my chest and I took a few slow, deep breaths to calm myself.

'You'll let us go if I write the letter?' My voice was loud with fear.

'Of course. You have my word.' Charlie sounded surprised. 'I don't harm women and children. It's not my style. You write that letter for me, Norah, and I can get my money out of that bank before the guards move on it. That'll make me one happy camper.'

I wasn't tempted to ask what his style was. A practical question did come to mind. 'What about Jacinta and Mick? They're . . .'

'I look after my own, Norah.' Charlie spoke softly. 'Jacinta and Mick'll be out of here in the morning and on their way. Clean break, new life for the child. No good you blabbing anything to the guards about Jacinta and Mick.'

Fear continued to worm its way through me. Did Charlie mean to leave me and Emma in the flat? Did he mean to leave us alive, or dead?

Maybe he hadn't decided yet. Maybe if I went on talking to him . . .

'Look, Charlie.' I made my voice even, tried not to shrink away as I looked at him. 'I didn't ask to be involved in any of this but in one way or another all that's happened is going to be with me, and Emma, for the rest of our lives. I'd like to have a clearer picture but there are a few details have me confused. If I ask the questions will you fill in the answers? Nothing that would incriminate you, of course.' I added the last hurriedly, slavishly keen to appease.

Charlie looked steadily at me. He seemed amused. 'You ask the questions, Norah, I'll decide which of them I'll answer. We've got time to kill anyway.' He laughed.

I asked my first question, quietly. 'Tell me about Timmy Dargan,' I said. 'What's his connection with Austin Finn?'

'Timmy's a devious little fucker.' Charlie settled himself with the air of a man who liked the sound of his own voice. 'He's been worming his way in and out of things all his life but the only winner he ever backed was Austin Finn. They suited one another. Finn liked to do favours, make people beholden to him. He looked after Timmy's mother when Timmy was locked up, made a bit of money for her. Timmy was his after that. Does that tell you what you want to know?' I nodded and fed him another question.

'It was Alison McCann got me into all this – where does she fit into it herself?'

'McCann's dingbat wife, you mean? She doesn't.' He shrugged. 'She was just there, a tart who married an asshole who thought himself smarter than anyone else. Saving your presence, Miss Hopkins,' he flashed his even, yellowing teeth, 'and not saying you're a tart too . . .'

'Thanks,' I said, 'but someone sent photographs of her to the police. What was all that about?'

'Ah, yes. That was a case of maximizing an opportunity, that was.' He stopped, relishing the phrase. 'Anyways, them pictures was floating around waiting to be used. First off we sent them to McCann himself, trying to cure him of the error of his ways in working for the likes of Jamesy Collins. He didn't back off though. We would've given them back to him on Christmas Day only he went all thick and wouldn't play ball . . .'

He fell briefly into reflective mode and I saw, too clearly, what he was remembering: the Christmas Day call to Darragh promising the photographs, God knows what torture and intimidation, the forced letter and signature and Darragh, literally and every other way in over his depth, drugged and drowning in the Liffey on St Stephen's night. My head throbbed. My mouth was parchment dry. I sipped the cold tea dregs.

'It was Finn's idea to send the pictures to the guards. Seemed like a good one at the time. He said it would shift the focus of garda attention on to McCann's wife's past life, get them believing he was a suicide. He said this would leave him free to sort out exactly what McCann had been doing for Jamesy Collins. He found out all right, only he tried to take what he found for himself. What's in that account in the Cayman Islands is by rights mine. It was earned on my patch. It wasn't enough that I'd paid Finn well to make investments for me over the years.' Charlie's voice had slowed down, become incredulous. 'I trusted that bastard. I trusted him and he fuckin' betrayed me . . .'

The disbelief was twofold then. Charlie had trusted and Charlie had been betrayed. It was a mean one and he would be avenged. Whatever mine and Emma's position, I wouldn't have been in Austin Finn's for any of the money floating around in any of the accounts.

'I'll kill him. I'll squeeze the life out of the bastard.' Charlie said this quietly, a simple statement of fact. Purply-blue veins throbbed in his neck, another snaking across his temple. Austin Finn would have to spend a lot of the money he'd appropriated hiding from this man. Operating in the shadow of Darragh's dazzling bit part he'd stolen the show – but by God, he would pay for it, for the rest of his life.

'Is Darragh McCann's friend, Conal Bergin, involved in any way?' I whispered this question, not at all sure that I wanted an answer. Ignorance on this one could very well prove to be bliss. Charlie sighed and shook his head. He knew. He might have been taken in by Austin Finn but Charlie could still read people.

'Conal Bergin . . .' He repeated the name thought-fully, mockingly. 'What do you think yourself, Norah?'

I looked away from him. Feelings of sick despair are very hard to hide.

Charlie sounded weary. 'You'll have to decide on that one yourself, Norah. But take my advice and trust no one.'

We sat in silence until Jacinta came back in with a writing pad and biro in her hand.

'That's the best I could do.' She threw them on to the table. 'And the shops is shut so there's no good you sending me out again.'

I wrote what Charlie told me to write. He was very clear, precise words in precise order telling the Cay-man Island bank that, as per a communication from Mr Darragh McCann, I was relinquishing my director-ship of the NOMA account in their bank.

When I'd finished I slipped everything neatly back into the manila envelope.

'Mick's taking his time,' he said.

'Probably having a pint in McCluskay's.' Jacinta began to clear the table.

'I'm moving the two of you out of here,' Charlie told her. 'You're no use to me any more, not in this gaff anyways . . .'

'I like it here . . .' Jacinta stared down at the table.

'Start packing your things now, Jacinta, and con-sider yourself fuckin' lucky I'm still looking after you at all. You're moving out of here in the morning, the both of you. Things are arranged.'

'Just like that.' Jacinta sat at the table with heavy tears rolling unheeded down her cheeks. 'Where are we going?'

'You're going, that's enough for you to know.'

'Mick'll . . .'

'Mick'll put up and shut up. He's lucky I didn't shove his prick up his . . .' He stopped, sighing. 'You're getting me upset, Jacinta. Don't get me upset, I'm warning you. Don't let Mick back near me either when he gets in. Get him in there packing and tell him the score.' Jacinta went. I could hear her sobbing in the bedroom. I hoped she wouldn't waken Emma.

'Why did Jamesy Collins wait so long to come after me about the account? He must have been . . . upset when his accountant . . . died. Yet it must have been two weeks before . . .'

'Because Jamesy doesn't know what day of the week it is unless it's fuckin' spelled out for him,' said Charlie. 'It was the inquest began putting the letters together for Jamesy. He knew nothing about you until he saw you there with Finn. He's slow but that got him thinking and he put some pieces together. Your brother the guard showing up there was a bit of a shock too. Jamesy and his friends had spotted him following them around in the weeks before Christmas. They didn't like that. They liked it less when they figured out that McCann's connection to you was the reason he was taking an interest in them. Your brother the guard was what made Finn take his softly, softly approach to getting you to sign.'

'Jamesy Collins burgled my apartment and took a

photograph of Emma with her father. Was that because he'd planned to kidnap her too?'

'Taking the child was a mistake, I told you that.' The vein was back in Charlie's neck, popping purply-blue and ugly. 'Jamesy doesn't have the wit to organize taking a doll out of a pram. If he took a picture then he did it to frighten you. And it worked, didn't it?'

Charlie was looking irritable, becoming bored with the storytelling game. I asked the next question quickly.

'How did the people who took Emma from the farm know where she was?'

Charlie looked at me contemptuously. 'You're a sad case, Norah, and I'm going to give you the best advice you'll ever get, only four words to it.' He paused and proclaimed, slowly, 'Don't ever trust anyone.' There was a cold, malevolent chill about him. 'I trusted Finn with my money and look what he did to me. You trusted him enough to tell him where your child was and look what he did to you . . .'

'Are you saying Austin Finn set up Emma's abduction? That's crazy.'

'He didn't. He was *planning* it as a way of getting you to sign his bit of paper. When he realized there wasn't going to be time for any of that he sent Timmy Dargan round to you instead. And that's how it happened.' He yawned. 'The plan came from Finn in the first place. The lads just used it against him when he fucked off.'

There was nothing more to say. It was all pathetically plausible; the greedy dealings of a couple of villainous accountants rebounding with deadly consequences all round.

Only Darragh had been much more than a villainous

337

accountant. It was just that he'd been that as well and that, in the end, had been all that had mattered.

'When can we leave?' This was the only question I wanted an answer to and I asked it with an even calm which belied the hard, cemented fear in me.

'In the morning,' Charlie said, 'early. We'll all leave together.'

He said nothing else, nothing to comfort or reassure. He turned up the television, loud, and flicked through the channels until he arrived at a game show which he sat watching, moodily, ignoring Mick when he arrived back and ignoring the raised voices from the bedroom when Jacinta told Mick their futures had been decided in his absence. I would have to believe he meant what he'd said.

I took myself to the other bedroom and lay with a fitfully sleeping Emma, holding her and covering her ears against Mick's pained and futile protests.

The night passed. Unbelievably, I slept for some part of it. Emma clung to me in the bed and maybe it was the relief at having her near that allowed me to sleep. But I was awake when a grey light came sluggishly into the sky around six o'clock. The hour between then and when we left was the most terrible I have ever spent. When, finally, all five of us left the flat together fear was still lumpen inside me.

A blistering, easterly wind nipped round us on the stone steps as we went down. It was crueller still as we went through the arch on to the street. I held Emma close to me. Charlie had hardly spoken since getting up, Jacinta and Mick hadn't spoken at all.

There was a car waiting in the street, but not for Emma and me. It wasn't until it drove off with Charlie,

Jacinta and Mick inside that I began to believe Emma and I might really be free to go home.

It was Wednesday, 19 January, seventeen days since Alison had come knocking on my door. It was also trying to snow.

'Do you think there'll be enough for a snowman?' asked Emma.

'I don't know,' I said, 'we'll have to wait and see.'

We held hands and began walking toward O'Connell Street.

Chapter Twenty-seven

Wednesday, 19 January

Snow was settling peacefully on the early morning pavements by the time we reached Bewleys in Westmoreland Street. They'd just opened for breakfast and the sheer familiarity of the white-aproned staff and good-food smells filled me with absurd pleasure. And relief.

I rang Delia. It was time to let the world know we were safe. She was tearful, then overjoyed, then brisk. She was exactly how I thought she would be.

'Don't explain. Don't say anything. Just get yourselves home . . .' she said.

'We're going to have breakfast . . .'

'There's someone here wants to talk to you.' Delia's voice became muffled, as if someone was taking the phone from her. 'He's been here all night . . .'

'Norah? Tell me exactly where you are.' Conal's voice was harsh, shaking a bit too. He promised he'd be with us in minutes. I put down the phone and Emma and I went ahead and ordered breakfast.

Knowing Conal was on his way was the second best thing to have happened that morning. I wanted him there that very minute and was surprised at how right the feeling felt. It had been a long time since I'd felt myself approaching love for a man.

Maybe it would work, this time. My judgement

hadn't been great in the past but I'd come a long way in a long couple of weeks. Charlie would be disappointed in me; against his best advice I was going to trust, again.

Up to a point, anyway.

In Secret Sin

Acknowledgements

Much thanks to a couple of the good guys in Pearse Street garda station. To detectives Joe Dempsey and Jerome Twomey, my gratitude for the data on police procedure and the tour of the building.

To Assumpta and Arthur Broomfield, my thanks for a night on the farm.

And to Graeme Byrne, for his endless patience with my technological illiteracy.

Chapter One

Victor Francis Baldacci died on a morning in June while listening to a patient whose marriage was on the rocks.

It was 10.37 a.m., he was fifty-eight years of age and Constance Brady was his third patient of the day. Victor Baldacci had worked hard and his psychotherapy practice was large and successful.

Because his consulting rooms were in the family home his wife, Bridget, was close at hand when the fatal cardiac arrest occurred. Even so, her husband was well and truly dead by the time she got to his side.

'It wasn't my fault.' Constance Brady was beside herself, more ashen-faced and stricken than the peaceful-looking corpse. 'I was just telling him the usual things . . . there was nothing new . . . nothing for him to go and die about . . .'

Bridget Baldacci, standing over her dead husband, thought that never, in their thirty years of marriage, had she seen so serene an expression on Victor's face. He had not been a tranquil man and, though he hadn't been an angry one either, he'd been someone with a lot of unspoken disquiet about him. While Constance Brady clutched at her and wept, Bridget stretched out a hand and touched Victor's long lashes and gently closed the lids over his beautiful brown eyes.

She felt shock and she felt disbelief. Victor hadn't been the sort of person to do anything without warning, least of all die.

'Of course it wasn't your fault.' She helped Constance Brady into an armchair opposite Victor and looked again at his peacefully folded dead face. 'It must have been his heart . . .' though his lips weren't blue and he didn't appear to have had pain, '. . . he smoked such a lot . . .' sixty a day at least, never even trying to give them up, 'but he never complained, never said there was something wrong . . .'

Victor keeled over slightly in the armchair as, very gently, she rested a pillow under his head and put a rug about him. He was still warm.

'Sweet mother of God, why did you do this to me?' Constance Brady threw herself from the armchair to her dead therapist's feet. 'He was the only man who ever listened to what I had to say and you took him from me . . .'

'Listening was his job,' Bridget observed.

She felt detached and calm. In shock, she supposed. Victor would have approved of her demeanour. Raw emotions unnerved him, though he had indeed been an excellent listener. He'd been less good at talking, a reticence ideal in a therapist. He had appeared, and often had been, wise and consoling and unnaturally patient. He'd been so handsome too. Her lovely Victor.

'You've had a shock. I'll make you some hot, sweet tea,' she tucked the rug gently around Victor's knees as she spoke to Constance Brady. 'But first I must ring for an ambulance.'

'An ambulance! What's the good of an ambulance? He's dead! The man's dead!' Constance Brady embedded her hands in her hair and seemed about to tear it out by its blonde roots.

Bridget slapped her hard, twice, once on each cheek.

'It's the thing to do,' she said.

Constance Brady sobbed quietly, her face buried in her hands, as Bridget first dialled an ambulance and then Victor's doctor from the phone on his desk. Constance, in the meantime, seemed to shrink in the armchair.

'I'll make the tea.' Bridget, sighing, gave her a reassuring pat on the head as she slipped past and into Victor's kitchenette.

The consulting rooms were well equipped; Victor had sometimes spent days at a time alone in their quiet, cream-painted spaces. Bridget chose camomile from among the herb teas.

Bridget Baldacci, née Durcan, was a woman who trusted her feelings and instincts and was not much impressed by psychotherapy. Victor's knowledge and training hadn't, after all, helped him release his demons. 'My gut,' Bridget often half joked, 'is the most accurate barometer of tides and events round here.' Her stomach, depending on the circumstances, turned, sank or felt queasy. It never let her down.

Much later, when the events of that morning were memories and Victor had been long cremated and she'd put a great deal of distance between herself and his consulting rooms, she would blame shock for the fact that she'd had absolutely no premonition of the terrible consequences his death would bring.

But on that bright, sad June morning, as she filled a couple of mugs with the tea and laced them with whiskey, she was glad not to have whispers of foreboding, to be without knowledge of any kind about the sickening truths and other deaths Victor's passing would lead to. All she felt was mildly bereft as she sat with Constance and Victor and quietly sipped the tea until the doctor and ambulance arrived. That was when she discovered that Victor had died instantly from a huge coronary thrombosis.

'It simply interfered with the pacemaker function of the heart,' said the doctor. 'He didn't feel any distress.'

Bridget could have told him that herself.

In the weeks which followed she dealt with the business of death efficiently: with the funeral, the acknowledgements, the closing down of Victor's practice. She was a rock for their two grown children, listening and consoling her beloved Anna and Fintan as they talked their way through grief.

She contacted Victor's family in Seattle, his mother and his sister who he hadn't seen, or wanted to see, for thirty years. They sent flowers. She had Victor cremated because of a confused feeling that his homeland should have something of him and ashes were a movable feast.

And through it all she kept thinking that when it was over and she was alone she would collapse and weep and slowly die a bit herself.

Grief didn't come quite like that. She missed things about Victor: his hard, questioning mind, his body turning to hers in bed at night. The problem, as she saw it, was that her entire adult life had been lived within the framework of her marriage. Now that it, along with Victor, had been so brutally taken from her she had nothing against which to measure or identify herself.

Memories of their first meeting, on a summer afternoon in the west Canadian city of Vancouver thirty-one years before, had replayed themselves in her head. She went with them, reliving that time and understanding, all over again, how she had come to give her all to a handsome American nearly nine years older than she'd been and about whom she'd known nothing at all. But their meeting was all she could remember.

When she tried to call up other memories they wouldn't come to her so she stopped trying, understanding that it was her mind's way of protecting her from too unbearable a pain. At times she couldn't even remember his face and had to keep checking photographs to see how exactly he'd looked.

She still felt no aching pain or loss, existing in a fog in which only certain realities had substance and in which all thoughts were a blur. When she met friends she found she

4

had nothing to say to them. Watching television she was bemused and puzzled by the lives of the people she saw there. Everything except her beloved garden appeared to her shapelessly indifferent and beyond her understanding.

The garden saved her because there she was needed. Its paths and bowers and rampant plant life were her creation, she knew every corner and stone. She had been the one to coax life from the barren, stony field which had passed for a garden when she and Victor bought what became their first, and last, home twenty-five years before. It had to be got ready for winter, couldn't be ignored, and so became the place where she spent her days, and a lot of her nights too, in the months after Victor died. She wasn't unhappy.

What she felt most of all was suspended, caught in the calm before a storm.

But by the end of October the fog had lifted and she knew what she had to do.

It was at the end of October when her daughter and first born, Anna, said she felt Bridget was suffering from Post Traumatic Shock Syndrome and should talk to someone, a therapist of some kind. A decent psychologist might do the trick Anna said or, better still, a psychiatrist.

She came to her mother in the garden, in a navy-blue suit and full of sharp, city energy. Bridget, who by then had started to form a plan of her own about what she was going to do, was not encouraging.

'Don't be ridiculous,' she said, though gently, 'there's nothing wrong with me.' She knew far more about PTSS than Anna, who was twenty-eight years old and a steadily achieving lawyer with a good firm. Constance Brady was indulging in a rash of treatment for PTSS on account of Victor dying in front of her eyes.

'All I'm suggesting is that some counselling might help,' Anna said.

5

'Of course it wouldn't,' said Bridget. 'It didn't help your father, did it? With all that he knew he couldn't heal himself.'

Anna and her brother Fintan, who was twenty-five years old and a sculptor in west Cork, knew their father had gone to the grave with the secrets of his early life intact. Acceptance of his silence about his family and his youth in Seattle had been a family thing.

'You're in shock.' Anna backed away from any probing about her father. 'You need to acknowledge your grief so you can move on . . .'

'You'd be surprised how much movement I'm a part of just by being out here.' Bridget, on her knees planting tulip bulbs and anemones, looked thoughtfully about the garden. The day was shining and warm, one of many that autumn fine enough for Bridget to need a straw hat. The decision about what she would have to do to make sense of her life and marriage had germinated and taken root and grown, over days such as this in the garden. She wasn't ready to tell Anna yet, mainly because she didn't want to deal with her objections. These would be loud, when they came.

'This isn't enough.' Anna, pacing the flag-stoned path, dismissed the garden with a sigh. 'You need to do something *focused*, something you can rebuild your life around, structure a future – '

'These are for the early spring' – Bridget shoved another bulb into the warm earth – 'or is that too near a future?'

'Oh, for God's sake!'

Anna, pacing on her thin, elegant shoes, stopped and killed an instinct to tap her foot. She stood instead with her ankles crossed, studying her mother and thinking how interesting she looked, in spite of everything, with her red hair straggling loose from under the straw hat (the red, she knew, was helped along these days, though her mother

6

would never admit to such a thing), her small bones and wistful, sheepdog eyes seeming not much different than they'd always been. 'Your mother's eyes,' her father had once said to Anna when she was young, 'are the colour of the Atlantic ocean in March. She's a bit like the Atlantic herself. Unpredictable.'

The unpredictable bit worried Anna. Interesting-looking, age uncertain, unpredictable, that was her mother.

Interesting was, of course, far more useful than beautiful now she was getting older. She was hardly going to be looking for lovers, at her age, which was at least fifty.

But that's where the unpredictable came in. Because maybe she would take lovers, might even be planning to. Bridget Baldacci might do a lot of things – but Anna hated surprises and wanted to know what, exactly, her mother might do.

'I'm talking about *you* getting a life' – she snorted at the general selection of growing things – 'not the frigging plants. You're still young . . .' she hesitated, 'youngish, anyway. You've got a life to live. What're you going to do with it? You can't go on like this for ever. I'm worried about you. So is Fintan . . .'

'There's no need.' Bridget, separating the bulbs into groups, didn't for one minute believe her son was worried about her. Fintan rarely thought about anyone but himself. Anna didn't mean to be insensitive either. It was just that she had no interest in gardening and no facility much for understanding others. Bridget looked up with a sigh and saw with surprise that storm clouds had gathered in the clear sky.

'You both know I'm more than able to look after myself. I'm biding time, is all.' She smiled at her beautiful daughter, so very like her father to look at. 'To every thing there is a season.'

Anna gave an impatient toss of her head and a clump of

7

black hair, Victor's hair, fell loose onto her collar. She wound it sleekly back into its coiled topknot. Tumbling locks were not the thing in court and Anna, who specialized in family law, spent a lot of time in the courts. The fact of her being here, in the garden, in the middle of a working day, said a lot about how sincerely worried she was about her mother.

'You need more than a seasonal change,' she said, 'you're too alone here. Have you thought about going back to work?'

'I've resigned, you know that.'

Anna knew but preferred to think that Bridget's resignation from her job as a school secretary had been an aberration. It had been no such thing. To Bridget, in her new circumstances, it had made complete and logical sense.

Victor, no surprise to Bridget, hadn't made a will. He'd been so obsessively private that the idea of detailing his affairs for another to see would have brought on an even earlier coronary. Victor, when all was said and done, had trusted no one. Not even her. But he'd been clever about investments and Bridget had given up her job once she had realized she wouldn't have to struggle financially, at least. The job had become routine, in any event.

'You need to retrain for something,' Anna caught herself tapping her foot and stopped.

It was hard to know exactly what her mother should retrain for. She'd never been easy to categorize and as children Anna and Fintan had been mortified by her difference from other mothers. Bridget had always been too something – exuberant, colourful, opinionated. She'd never been the sort of obligingly background figure their father had been.

'You must have some idea what you want to do.' Hating the limp, ineffectual sound of her own voice she finally gave in to the urge to tap her foot.

8

'So much for the bulbs,' her mother, ignoring her, stood up, 'now for the montbretia. It's lost the run of itself altogether.'

Trailing Bridget to the end of the garden and the montbretia Anna dallied with the notion that perhaps her mother was glad to be a widow, was relieved to be free of her husband, glad to be on her own.

The intensity of her own grief had been a surprise, given her father's reserved temperament and the fact that he'd been difficult to get close to as an adult. She knew she was like him in many ways, and when he died she'd become swamped in memories of the loving care he'd surrounded her with as a child. Until they'd grown old enough to question him he'd been besotted with herself and Fintan. He'd lived for them during their childhood years, only growing cautious when adolescence and defiant questioning began.

He'd always lived for their mother.

By the fiery blaze of the rampaging montbretia Anna hunkered down beside Bridget. Not easy, in her straight skirt, but it didn't look as if her mother was going to stop what she was doing. Bridget was catching the flowers low, pulling the bulbed roots briskly out of the ground.

'Have you thought about selling the house? It's far too big for you.' Anna turned a calculating look on the grey stone pile she'd grown up in. 'You'd make a killing. You've never really liked it anyway.'

'No, I haven't thought about selling my home.'

Sitting back on her heels Bridget also turned toward the house. It was true that she'd never liked it. She'd felt herself devoured by its Victorian pedigree and too many rooms. Victor had liked it though, a lot.

'And I'm not going to think about it, yet.'

She wished wearily that Anna would make some concessions to the shining day. An open-necked shirt would have been a start. 'Might as well give those roses the chop while I'm here.' She got off her knees and marched to a clump of rose bushes. 'There's a time to pluck that which is planted' – the secateurs advanced and stems fell – 'and my time isn't right yet, Anna, for a lot of things . . .' she handed her daughter a vermilion rosebud, 'one of the last of the summer.'

'You're being evasive and sentimental and you know it,' Anna took the flower and turned it irritably between her fingers.

'Give it back.' Bridget took the rosebud and slipped it into her daughter's coiled topknot. Anna became Carmen in a suit. 'You look lovely.' Bridget touched the young woman's face, in a wistful gesture. Love had long resigned Bridget to an impatience she sometimes felt with her first born. Because Anna was so darkly beautiful it was easy to assume she was passionate about life. People usually did. She was, in fact and by nature, a pragmatist. 'I'll get you a bite to eat,' said Bridget, 'I don't suppose you've had anything all day.'

The clouds grew suddenly heavier as she led the way briskly back to the house. When a low tree snagged the straw hat from her head she left it where it fell and shook her hair loose. Anna, walking behind her, picked it up.

'I don't want anything to eat.' Anna hung the hat on a hook in the sun room. She didn't want to be in the sun room either. It was where her mother insisted on keeping the casket with her father's ashes and she couldn't quite reconcile herself to sharing space with them.

'You need nourishment.' Bridget, angling the casket more firmly into its niche in the brickwork, resisted what had become a regular urge to flush the contents down the lavatory. One quick, businesslike gush and they would be gone, dispersed for ever into the city's sewers, all decisions and maybe even Victor's pain gone with them. The urge was irrational, she knew, as well as wrong-headed, futile and horribly appealing.

'Any word from Seattle about the ashes?' Anna, calling from the kitchen, broke her train of thought.

Going into the kitchen and closing the windows against the approach of evening, Bridget didn't immediately answer her daughter's question. When she went on evading it, pulling back her hair to catch it in a rubber band, Anna tried again.

'Well? What about Seattle?'

Bridget, hair secured, began to wash her hands at the sink. 'I got a reply to my letter last week.' She removed and studied her wedding ring before, with infinite care, placing it on the window sill.

'You could have told me before now.'

'I suppose I could.' Bridget's mildly apologetic tone, as she dried her hands, didn't do much to mollify her daughter.

'I have a right to know.' Anna, abruptly and stiff backed, left the kitchen.

The sun room was no less inviting than before but if she'd stayed in the kitchen she'd have rowed with her mother. She touched the casket. Just because she couldn't bear to be around the damn thing didn't mean she didn't care about her father's ashes. How could her mother not know their fate mattered to her? She hated the way Bridget took things on herself and to herself, and didn't share. It had always been a problem between them.

'I'm sorry,' Bridget, standing in the doorway, spoke quietly, 'the letter wasn't what you'd call encouraging, exactly . . .' She paused. 'They don't want his ashes, in part or in whole, for scattering or otherwise—'

She stopped, choking back a sudden urge to howl at the cold, malign cruelty of it, as the same sense of impotent rage which had swept through her when first she'd read the letter, engulfed her again. She'd given in to the urge then, in Victor's rooms, systematically ripping every book on psychotherapy he'd owned from the shelves, kicking at them where they fell, cracking the spines of some of them. The rage had moved on, taking her detachment with it, and she'd been thinking ever since, memory piling upon memory, as her plan had started to form.

For a long time after they met, Bridget had wanted to meet Victor's mother. His evasiveness, then his obdurate refusal to arrange a meeting, had forced her to face the reality of his flawed and secretive nature. But by then she'd been hopelessly in love and couldn't imagine a life without him. They married when she was twenty and Victor twenty-eight and his secrecy about his family had continued relentlessly.

When Anna had been born, and then Fintan, Bridget had sent cards to Seattle. She'd got back printed, unsigned acknowledgements. The cold indifference had angered her and made it easier to accept Victor's rejection of his family. In time she'd even stopped wondering why.

Until now. Until his mother had written to say the family didn't want anything to do with his ashes.

'You don't look great, mother, are you all right?'

Anna's voice came to her as if down the shaft of a tunnel. 'I'm fine,' Bridget turned a sigh into a rueful smile, 'and I *am* sorry I didn't tell you about the letter.'

She was certainly sorry she'd told her today. In time she would have shown Anna the letter just as, in time, she would have discussed her future with her. The way this visit was developing she was going to have to tell Anna what she planned any minute. 'I really am OK' – of its own accord, and as she tried for damage limitation, Bridget's smile became even more rueful – 'and the letter, in its own way, wasn't so bad. Reasonable, really. She simply said that she saw no need to divide the ashes into two parts . . .'

'Who saw no need? Who wrote to you?'

'Victor's mother . . . your grandmother, Veronica Baldacci.' Bridget hesitated. 'It was in one sense quite a civil letter—'

'Can I see it?'

'Of course,' Bridget said. Reading it wasn't going to do Anna one bit of good. 'Make yourself a sandwich while I go and get it.'

In the bedroom she'd shared with Victor, Bridget re-read the letter. Its condescension and its discouraging tone struck her again. It began with a 'Dear Bridget' but that was about as familiar as it got.

> Your letter, together with its suggestion that a portion of my son's cremation ashes might find a resting place in Seattle, came as a surprise. Victor made certain, early, decisions about his life. This family did not feature in those decisions. He chose to live in Ireland and I think it more fitting that his ashes remain, intact, with the life and family he created there.

Her signature, black and very bold, took up most of the rest of the page. Clearly, Veronica Baldacci was not a woman to be cast aside, by anyone and for any reason. But then Bridget had sussed as much when she'd telephoned Seattle to tell the woman her son was dead.

'He died at home?' The elderly voice had been coolly disinterested.

'Yes, in a manner of speaking . . .' Bridget explained about the consulting rooms.

'I see,' said Victor's mother. 'Had he been ill?'

'No.' Bridget hesitated. 'He'd been having some discomfort is all. He'd talked to his doctor about it . . .' But not to her. More secrecy. Dr Russell had had to explain to her that Victor had been to see him about chest pains.

'His father had a stroke when quite a young man,' Veronica Baldacci sounded businesslike. 'He died as a result.'

'I see,' said Bridget. Veronica, in Seattle, did not volunteer any further information. Bridget told her about the funeral arrangements. 'Victor will be cremated. The ceremony can be delayed a few days if you or any of the family would like to—'

'That won't be necessary. I myself do not travel and Victor's sister would be unable to go to Ireland. Please convey our sympathies to . . .' When she stopped Bridget decided against reminding her of her grandchildren's names. Veronica, with an audibly impatient sigh, carried on, 'Our sympathies to the young people. Our thoughts will be with you.'

When a grotesquely large wreath arrived on the day of the funeral Bridget went to the end of the garden and carefully took it apart. She buried the flowers, lilies and white roses for the most part, and foliage. As compost it had an honest function.

But it wasn't good enough. Dealing with Victor's family had left a large, unresolved pain in her gut. For peace of mind alone she would have to do something about it.

Downstairs, in the sun room where Anna was eating a sandwich, Bridget gave her the letter from her grandmother. She sat and watched while the younger woman read it, anticipating the words, wishing she could change them. Anna read it twice before, without looking at her mother,

14

tearing it into careful pieces which she scattered across the glossy, cherrywood table.

'She doesn't want his ashes. We don't want her letter.' With a stabbing forefinger she manoeuvred the scraps into a neat pile. 'You don't need her either. But she's quite right, about one thing at least. *We* were Dad's life. He *should* stay here.' She took a deep, shaky breath and faced her mother. 'Bitch,' she said, 'rotten, lousy old bitch.' Tears ran in a flood down her face.

Bridget went to her and held her, silently and hard, until the wave of tears and neediness had passed. Anna's long, thin body felt no less fragile to her than it had when she'd been a child, and no more secure in the world. She patted her daughter's face dry before letting her go.

'I should correct myself,' Anna picked up and began to nibble again at the sandwich, '*you* were Dad's life, not us.'

'No.' Bridget shook her head as she gathered the scraps of letter and let them fall again, like confetti, on to the polished wood. 'I was his retreat from life.'

Victor had used his love for her to create his own, private world. That was one of the things which had become clear to her since his death. She'd been his cover, the children his insurance, this house his personal island. Even what he did – all the probing and the listening – had been on his terms. People came to him, into his lair, and there he took them apart and rebuilt their lives. As a defence it had been perfect, and impregnable.

'Well, it's over now,' Anna's voice was harsh. 'He's gone and his mother's rejected him, even in death.' Hearing the courtroom drama of her phraseology she allowed herself a half smile. 'So it's time to get on with the rest of our lives. Yours in particular, mother.'

'You're right,' Bridget said and Anna, surprised, sat forward.

'I'm right?' She leaned her elbows on the table.

15

'I've decided on something.' Bridget stopped to listen as rain began falling gently on the glass roof. She'd always liked rain, its power to soothe, wash clean, absolve. She was sure its beginning to fall now was a good omen. 'This is probably as good a time as any to tell you—'

'Don't do me any favours, mother,' Anna said dryly. 'I've only been trying to get sense out of you all afternoon.' Her eyes flickered involuntarily towards the wall clock as she stood up. 'You need a drink. So do I. Don't go away.'

Her heels made precision clicks on the Valentia slate of the sun room's floor before the door to the kitchen swung closed behind her. Bridget hadn't missed the glance at the clock, nor the inference that the time Anna had allocated to this visit was running out. Not a bad thing. If they dealt with the subject quickly then Anna's lawyerly mind would have less chance to cross-examine.

'Drink.' Anna handed her mother a liberal measure of whiskey. Her own glass held white wine with ice. 'Now talk to me,' she poked at the ice with a finger and watched Bridget carefully.

She's worried, Bridget thought, that's why she got us the drinks. She's afraid she's going to lose a mother as well as a father. And she is in a way.

'I've decided to go to Seattle,' Bridget said.

'You've decided to go to . . . Seattle.'

'Yes. I'm going to visit the Baldaccis, get to know a little about them. I plan to go after Christmas, very early in the new year.'

'You're going to Seattle in the new year.'

'It's time I met your father's family.' Bridget's tone was reasonable.

'I would have thought the time for that long past and gone.' Anna carefully extracted a piece of ice from her drink and began to suck it. 'Doesn't sound to me like a spectacular way to move on' – she shrugged – 'more like a step backwards, into the past.'

'Perhaps,' said Bridget, 'but then perhaps I need to do that too.'

'I don't see why . . .' Anna stopped.

She looked from her mother's quietly smiling face to the darkening garden. She'd wanted her mother to open up but now that she had Anna realized that she'd been afraid, all along, that Bridget would do something like this. Going to Seattle wasn't the answer to her grief. It would just prolong the holding on to her father. She had to be talked out of it.

Her father's family wouldn't want to see her anyway, any more than they'd wanted his ashes.

The rain, she saw, was falling heavily now, the sun room becoming cold as the heat of the day escaped fast through the glass.

Anna had never shared her mother's love of growing things. As a child garden shadows had held unnamed terrors for her, though she'd never said anything about such fears to Bridget, who would have laughed. Anna had talked about it to her father though. He'd stroked her hair, gently and for a long time, and assured her over and over that there was nothing in the garden which would ever hurt her. She'd believed him. She wished he was here now.

'As a family lawyer,' Anna took a deep breath, 'I feel I should point out that Dad may have been married before. It's fairly common you know, in situations like this.'

'Situations like this . . . Like what, exactly?' Bridget asked.

'Situations where there's been a lot of secrecy about the past. I've seen—'

'If he was married before then I want to know about it,' Bridget cut her short. 'I want to know everything there is to know.'

17

She meant it. She was fifty years of age and for thirty of those years had lived with a man about whose background she'd known hardly anything because he had decided it was his secret and none of her business. But now he was dead and she wanted to know everything. He'd been her sounding board and her ballast and she'd loved him for the way he'd brought her to life and given her an awareness of herself that first, golden afternoon in Vancouver, BC. She'd loved him for loving her from that beginning, when she had thought herself so very unlovable.

And it was because he'd been all of those things that now she needed to know who the real Victor had been.

'Why?' demanded Anna. 'You've lived without knowing all these years. What difference does it make now?'

'The difference is that your father is dead . . .' Bridget paused, 'and I'm alive.'

'And that's a reason for going to Seattle? For prostrating yourself in front of people who don't want to know you? Who never did?'

'Yes, that's a reason. And I'm not just going to Seattle. I intend to visit Vancouver too. A sort of pilgrimage, you might say.'

Anna ignored this and tried another tack. 'You respected his decision to put the Baldacci part of his life behind him when he was alive. I really think you should afford him the same courtesy in death.'

'No, you don't.' Bridget was resignedly dismissive. 'You don't believe that at all. But you think *I* believe it and that you can work on my guilt.' Ignoring Anna's protest she got up and walked to where Victor's ashes sat in their bright casket. 'The thing is, Anna, my love, I don't feel guilty. Not one bit. The dead have no right to judge and dictate to the living.' She stood over the casket, looking at it, but not touching it. 'I *would* feel guilty, however, if I didn't go to Seattle.' She turned to her daughter. 'On the positive side it'll mean you'll finally get to know about your paternal relations.'

'You know I don't give a fuck about them.'

'I would have preferred your good wishes.' Bridget smiled at the familiar, Victor-like intensity in her daughter's dark eyes. 'I'll take half the ashes with me.'

'They don't want them. They said so . . .'

'I'm going to give them a chance to change their minds.'

'Has it occurred to you that they may not even want to meet *you*?'

'Oh, yes. But they're not going to have a choice about that. I want to meet *them*,' Bridget's smile became rueful, 'for better or for worse.'

Chapter Two

It was raining in Seattle. The one thing everyone had said
about Seattle was that it would be raining. It's a watery city,
they said, in the way that Dublin is, with mountains and sea
and lots of rain.

Bridget found the grey, misty views of the city reassuring.

Vancouver, where she'd spent three days, had been full of
bright sunshine and sharp, wintery air. But it had refused to
surrender anything of the girl who'd fallen for and given her
all to an American lover there, thirty-one years before. She'd
found nothing much of Victor in Vancouver either. Memories
had come faintly and been so inert they might have belonged
to someone else. Since the city hadn't changed, was as
ordered and naturally stunning as ever, she was forced to
acknowledge that it was she herself who had changed.

There were times when, even more than at home, she
couldn't recall how Victor had looked, could see only the
peaceful, unsurprised face he'd worn the morning of the
cardiac arrest. She missed not having Victor to think about;
he'd made up so many of her thoughts for so long.

By the time she climbed aboard a Greyhound bus for
Seattle she'd been impatient to be gone.

First impressions matter and Bridget's of Seattle were
mixed. Afterwards, whenever she tried to capture her uncer-
tainties, the things which came to mind were the way the air

smelled of cinnamon and coffee, the hordes of stylishly cool downtown winter people, the shining spires of skyscrapers against ever-changing skies – all of it juggling with a darker, unsaid something she couldn't pin down.

It was as if there was a blemish, an unacknowledged evil or wrong of some kind, hovering about the life of the city.

At the time Bridget put such confusions down to her nervously dire expectations of Victor's family. But it was not long before, her expectations proving right, the city came to have an even more aberrant edge for her.

The Greyhound bus cruised into Victor's home town just after one o'clock. By the time the passengers had been unloaded at 1150 Station Street the low-lying cloud had turned the city as dark as early evening.

'Enjoy your stay,' the bus driver, who had fought in Iwo Jima, handed Bridget her bags, 'and enjoy the weather.'

He said the same thing to everyone. On the bus he'd told Bridget that people were people, wherever you went, if you gave them half a chance. Even the Japanese were people. Bridget had agreed that people were people and hoped it was true.

The bus station was full of people. She hadn't expected to be met but now that she'd arrived, and was tired, she found herself searching faces, and hoping. She had no idea who, or even what, she was looking for. She'd written to Victor's mother about her visit and had got back a letter which wondered about 'the wisdom of such a trip' and reluctantly encouraged her to 'get in touch when and if' she arrived in Seattle.

There had been no invitation to stay, no welcoming encouragement.

The taxi which stopped for her was driven by a pale, infinitely miserable-looking Pole. As it drove on the look of the city improved, the streets becoming wider and the buildings higher and more elegant. Bridget, hoping the taxi driver knew where he was going, wondered why people so often felt compelled to tell her their life story. Maybe the reason she'd fallen in love with Victor was because he'd never told her anything.

The driver was talking about his girlfriend.

'She has my children too,' he said. 'Fine children. I never will see my children in Poland again. Now I don't see my American children. My girlfriend will not allow it . . .'

'Is the hotel much further?' Bridget was losing her patience.

She was wet and cold and 9,000 miles from home. She did not want to listen to a Polish taxi driver with a dandruff problem and offspring on two continents mangle the English language. She should never have got into his car. This came of being out of travelling practice. God knows where he was taking her. She'd read a lot, in her research on Seattle over Christmas, about the city's serial killers. There were several of them currently on the loose, notably the Green River Killer. It was said too that one in four citizens of the area was classified as a sociopath, that the low-lying cloud, stormy nights, dark days, mist and fog gave cover to, and attracted, any amount of evil doers . . .

'Not far now,' said the Polish driver, 'only a cupla blocks.'

'I'm in a hurry,' said Bridget.

'The world is always in a hurry. Me, too. I hurry so much I never have time to learn American, never.' The driver's eyes on her in the mirror were like wet cement and full of tears. 'I just work and work for a few dollars. Sometimes, life is such a bitch to me that I drink a little bit . . .' A tear fell and he sniffed and blinked.

'Everyone needs to relax now and again,' said Bridget.

Relax. She was sitting in a car driven by a depressed drinker who might very well be the Green River Killer, forty-nine victims so far and presumably on the lookout for more since he hadn't yet been caught.

The rain had slowed to a drizzle.

'I'll get out here.' She leaned forward and tapped the driver's shoulder. His jacket felt cold and sticky. 'Please stop the car and get me my bags.' She was polite and she was firm.

'You're a nice lady. I take you to de door.'

He didn't turn around. In the mirror she could see his eyes fixed on the road ahead. He seemed to be perspiring and the taxi seemed to be for ever going downhill, passing high, glass emporiums and coffee houses. The bottom of the street came in sight, and an expanse of water. Seattle's waterfront, the Puget Sound. Bridget felt ridiculously relieved.

'I'd like to walk the rest of the way.' She didn't touch his shoulder this time.

'Bags too heavy for you.' He was firm. They stopped at a red light and he lit a cigarette. He didn't speak.

'There are people waiting for me at the hotel,' Bridget lied.

'We get there soon.' Ash fell from the cigarette as the car moved forward again.

'Tell me about an area called Madison Park,' Bridget said. 'Truly upscale' and 'extravagantly wealthy' were the words used to describe it in the guidebooks. 'Do you know it?'

'I don't go up that neighbourhood much,' his short laugh was like a stone hitting a grating, 'and the kind live up there don't much pick up cabs in the street.'

They drew up in front of a small hotel. It looked reassuring as it had in the brochure from which Bridget had made the booking.

'Thank you,' Bridget said. 'How much do I owe you?'

'Seven dollars.'

Far too much. Only a fool would have paid without a quibble. Bridget told him to keep the change from a ten-dollar bill and clambered out. The wet air felt cold and invigorating.

'My bags . . .'

He jerked his head and she saw that he'd opened the boot from inside the car. She retrieved the bags. The car was lost in the traffic before she got to the door of the hotel.

The Hotel Pacific Nights, which had advertised itself as 'European in style', was chintzy and brocaded with a log fire burning in the lobby. But this was Seattle, after all, and there was also a bank of coffee-dispensing thermos flasks and newspapers stacked beside reading lamps.

'And how are you today?' The Filipino woman at reception flashed a gold front tooth. Her eyes didn't quite meet Bridget's. 'You'll be with us for two weeks, is that right?'

'I hope so. It depends on—'

'We've put you on the fourth floor. You'll like it up there.' The tooth, flashing again as she studied her computer screen, looked like an accessory to the hotel's gold-braided uniform jacket. 'Hold it,' she said, 'seems we've got a special delivery correspondence here for you. Arrived yesterday. Also your keys, of course, and our very helpful guide to the hotel and city.' She made a hand signal and an elderly porter appeared. 'Mrs Baldacci will be going to the fourth floor.' She didn't smile at him.

'The elevator's this way, ma'am.' The man picked up Bridget's bags and headed briskly across the lobby. His silver hair was crew cut.

'Enjoy your stay with us.' The receptionist turned away.

'My letter,' Bridget reminded her. 'You did say you'd some correspondence for me?'

'One letter.' Without looking at her the woman put a manila-coloured envelope on the desk in front of Bridget.

'Thank you,' Bridget said.

She decided against opening it straight away. She was too tired, and far too wound up, to absorb whatever Veronica Baldacci had to say with any sort of equanimity.

If it was rude she would lose her temper, if it was kindly she would be embarrassingly grateful.

After the porter had departed with her dollar tip and a laconic nod, she leaned against the door and allowed herself a quick study of the envelope. Oblong, in decent quality paper, it had her name, Mrs Bridget Baldacci, printed in blue-inked, block capitals. Her fingers itched.

'Now now, Bridget,' she told herself, 'first you pour a drink, then you unpack. After that you will top up your drink and sit with it and slowly absorb your special delivery. It may need all your concentration.'

Her room was filled with dark furniture: desk, armchair, chiffonier and high-backed bed. The wallpaper was embossed, the bed covering tasselled and the roller blind had a lace trim. It was a sombre room, overshadowed and made gloomy by the taller building opposite. Bridget turned on all of the lights and, deciding against Scotch – the only whiskey in the mini-bar – poured herself a gin and tonic and topped up the glass with ice. Unpacking took twenty minutes; boots, rain gear and woollies had been the general advice of friends and family and, with a few exceptions, these were the sort of clothes she'd packed. It had helped eliminate decisions about what to bring.

She put the casket in which she'd carried half of Victor's ashes on the desk. It was small and plain, a gun-metal grey colour, and immediately became the only thing she could see in the room. She shoved it into the desk drawer and felt at once both guilty and relieved.

The envelope, when she opened it, held a single folded sheet of cream-coloured paper. Its message was written in block capitals and was not from Veronica Baldacci. The style was not right, the wording all wrong. There was no indication who it was from, no signature of any kind.

Dear Mrs Bridget Baldacci,

  It is unlikely, since you have come this far, that you will leave Seattle without meeting your dead husband's family. It was unwise of you to come here and I would advise you to turn about and go back to Ireland immediately. Victor Baldacci's family do not want the past disturbed and therefore do not care to meet you. There is nothing unnatural in this; mistakes are best left in the past where they can cause less pain.

  Meeting his family will not bring the dead man back. Neither will you be helped to find peace or understanding. I cannot be of assistance if you decide to stay; no one can. The best help I can give you is my advice to you to go home as soon as you read this letter.

Bridget put the sheet of paper down, flattened it on the desk and sat looking at it while she finished the gin and tonic. She picked out phrases over the rim of the glass.

'It was unwise of me to come, was it now? You'd advise me to turn about and go home, would you? I won't be helped to find peace and understanding? Well, in that case, you anonymous shit . . .' she picked up and tore the letter in two, then tore it in two again, 'I'll have to settle for trouble and strife.' She dropped the pieces into the bin. 'Because you're dead right, my friend. I didn't come all this way for nothing.'

She stood looking at the scraps of paper for a moment, willing them to tell her something, give a hint even of why so many people wanted what had happened in the past in Victor's family forgotten. She hadn't expected a red-carpet welcome but the basic civilities would have been nice. The letter could, of course, be the work of a crank, either a family member or a jealous friend. One way or another, she wasn't going to give it too much credence. Not unless something else happened.

She rang Anna, then Fintan. Given that day was just breaking in Ireland they were quick calls to say she'd arrived. She joked about her minor hysteria in the taxi, said nothing at all about the special delivery letter.

'When do you plan to see Dad's people?' Anna was a morning person.

Bridget hadn't planned. She did now.

'I'm going to give your father's mother a few hours to make contact. If I haven't heard by then I'll take a taxi out to the house. Five o'clock seems to me a respectable time to go calling, anywhere in the world.' She looked at herself in the mirror. Her wet hair resembled seaweed and her face looked pale and tired. 'She can hardly close the door in my face.'

'Why not?' Anna asked.

Why not indeed? Bridget said goodbye but felt better, reassured by her daughter's cynical expectations of her grandmother. She had a hot bath and washed her hair. On the very large television she got a weather report delivered by a glossy, blond man in a brown suit. 'Looks like it could be the coldest night in the region,' he said cheerfully. 'There's snow across the Cascades and southern Washington Cascades.' When he was replaced on the screen by a snow-laden palm tree she switched channels and found herself face to face with a coquettish Fergie, Duchess of York, lisping about weight control through a wide, soft-focus smile. Everywhere else the news was of Sonny Bono's death on a ski slope at the Heavenly Valley Ski Resort on the Nevada–California state line. He'd skied into a tree.

'Looks like it got you, babe.' Bridget touched the widely grinning screen face of the dead politician-entertainer.

Sonny and Cher had been riding the charts with 'I Got You, Babe' when she'd first met Victor in Vancouver in 1966. They'd danced to it, sung along with the words, laughed at the way it fitted them.

Bridget decided the death wasn't an omen. The TV said Sonny Bono had been skiing at the resort for more than twenty years. He was a victim, she told herself, of the law of averages. She just wished his average hadn't come up that day.

She was suddenly impatient with the room, with Veronica Baldacci's rudeness and lack of contact. From the window she saw a lightening of the sky, and clouds scudding above the tall building opposite. It was looking as if there was going to be a hiatus before the snow, rain, ice and cold promised for later on; if she was to see anything of the city she'd better do it before a blizzard arrived.

She might even come across the ghost of the youthful Victor out there.

She pulled on boots and a jumper and lifted the phone. Nice, healthy buzz. No technical problems then. Just no one trying to get through to her.

In the street she walked quickly, not clear where she was going but keeping a sniping wind to her back. The freshly rained on footpaths were vitreous and the shining skyscrapers like cliff faces after a storm. At an intersection she ignored the 'Don't Walk' sign and continued with fellow pedestrians across the empty road. The small, anarchic act made her feel better, as if she'd bonded with the city. Dubliners, too, notoriously ignored pedestrian lights.

She stopped to take stock. She was standing on 4th Avenue, elegant and wide. To her right a street plunged recklessly down to the waterfront. If she were to keep on going, veering uphill she would come to the International District, home to the city's Asian community. The prospect seemed a cosier one than exposure to the Puget Sound.

This proved to be a mistake. The International District was bleak, full of wide, windswept streets and small, cluttered shops. Not since he'd died had she felt so totally without Victor. She began retracing her steps to the hotel.

'Hey, most beautiful woman in the entire world.' A black man, small and wizened and with shining, perfect teeth, touched her on the arm. Bridget stepped away from him and he looked at her, full of admiring disbelief as he held out a begging hand.

Confused, Bridget shook her head and turned away.

'You're not the world's most beautiful woman?' his voice followed her, sadly. When she turned, relenting, he'd gone.

She wasn't beautiful but she had been, sort of, once. Beautiful enough for a good man to love her for his lifetime – and to use the words said by the black man the first time he met her. 'There isn't a woman as beautiful as you in the entire world,' was in fact what Victor had said, only half joking. She heard him say it again now, the words setting up a lonely echo in her head.

Then the memories she'd been looking for in Canada came crowding in.

Victor hadn't lived for her since the morning he'd died but he did so now, coming alive to her so intensely she cried out and closed her eyes. For a while she leaned against a hoarding, glad to be remembering at last, careless of the cold. 'Where were you until now, Victor?' She wrapped her arms about herself and watched the clouds break and regroup. 'You went from me so completely I had to come to this place to find you. Don't leave me again . . . I'm not used to being without you . . . you were always there, before . . .' The street was so quiet the urge to call aloud to him was huge.

She faced into the wind and it drew tears from her eyes as she walked on, slowly.

The first time ever she'd seen Victor Baldacci he'd been

leaning against a tree on the campus of the University of British Columbia in Vancouver. She'd been lying on the grass and had looked up lazily to catch him watching her. He hadn't looked away. He hadn't smiled either. He had simply stood, immobile and languid against an old maple, and held her gaze. She'd been the first to look away, turning her head to laugh with a companion on the grass. She knew he would come to her.

'Walk with me, please.' His hand touched her shoulder lightly. With the sun behind him she couldn't see his face but knew it anyway from the way the dappled light had picked out its planes and shadows under the tree.

'Where would you like to walk?' she asked and he held out a hand.

'You'll see,' he said and linked her fingers with his and pulled her from the grass to his side.

He was older than she'd thought, taller too and broader. She didn't quite reach his shoulder. He held her hand tightly and led her quickly back toward the wooded area.

'What's the hurry?' she asked but knew, because she wanted it too, that the rush was to get away from her companions, to be on their own. She never once looked back, even when voices called to her. When they were in the middle of the trees he let her hand go and smiled at her and said, 'There isn't a woman as beautiful as you in the entire world.' It didn't seem extravagant at all the way he said it, just a statement of what was for him a fact.

Bridget spent the rest of the day with him, and a lot of the night too. She was a virgin and she didn't sleep with him, just listened while he talked to her about the life he'd lived in Alaska, where he'd gone to university, and about the Indian peoples he'd lived with and studied. He talked, as the night went on, about things they could do together while she was in Vancouver.

30

Bridget knew that one of the things she was going to do was sleep with him.

'I'm supposed to study while I'm here,' she said. She was doing a summer course in Canadian literature.

'Of course.' Victor grinned.

She didn't study. She went to classes and opened books and wrote down words and the only thoughts in her head were of Victor. Waking and sleeping her thoughts were of him. She lived the week in a state of expectation. Expectation was what she felt when she walked with him or when they sat in a cinema or listened to music.

They made love, within a week of meeting, on the narrow bed in the rooms the university had given him to live in while he delivered a summer seminar on the Aleut and Indian peoples of Alaska.

They had been to an open-air concert that day, a fund-raising event with a mixed bag of rock musicians. Bridget had loved it, the spirit as much as the event. Victor had been amused and gently mocking of her enthusiasm.

'Bunch of ego trippers and bad musicians,' he said.

'Not what you'd call brilliant.' Bridget sniffed. 'But they tried and it was fun.' She felt flattened and all at once a lot younger than him.

'I enjoyed it.' He held her against him and spoke into her hair. 'I enjoy everything I do with you.'

They were crossing the campus to his room and she lifted her face to his, smiling, and saw what she had not previously realized: he cared about her happiness more than he cared about his own. She touched the small frown between his eyes, liking the way it made him appear vulnerable.

'That's good,' she said, afraid and too cool to tell him she felt the same.

'Will you stay with me tonight?' he said.

31

'Why not?' Bridget said and held on tight when he kissed her.

He'd done some decorating in his rooms, hanging Eskimo paintings on the walls and covering the floor with rush matting. His rooms told her everything she needed to know about him, that summer. As soon as he had closed the door behind them she turned into his arms.

'You'll have to show me.' Her heart was thumping.

'You're sure this is all right?' He held her away from him.

'Very sure.' She lifted her arms and slipped her T-shirt off over her head. Her white lace bra made the most of a tan built up over days swimming and lying in the sun but she was all at once self-conscious, wanting to bury herself against him.

'Maybe we should wait.' He didn't touch her. 'You have to be sure about this . . .'

'I'm sure,' she said again. 'I've been thinking about it all week. I want the first time to be with you.'

'And what about the second and third and all the other times after?' His voice was hoarse and uncertain.

He didn't want to lose her. She was not too young to understand that, or to know that she was not something casual and summertime to him. But even then, weightless with desire and abandon, she worried that his love might be too intense, too needy.

'All of those times too,' she said to him and put her mouth against his.

Lying on the bed, naked on top of the Eskimo cover because it was too hot to lie under it, she traced the shapes and parts of his body with her fingers. She'd never seen a man like him, could never have imagined the beauty of a mellow gold skin sprinkled with black hairs.

'I meant what I said,' he spoke against her neck, 'there

32

is no woman, anywhere that I've ever been, so beautiful as you are.'

'And where have you been then?'

'Enough places to know.'

He held her tightly against him and she could feel his heart beat as his hands moved to show her about loving and the ways they could give each other pleasure. Beneath him she felt like silk, all fluid movement as she moved with him, lost to the ecstasy of the feelings he brought to life in her. She cried out and laughed softly at the idea that the sounds of her pleasure might be heard through the open window and identified for what they were across the campus. Victor laughed with her and a little later he came and so did she.

Afterwards they wound their hot, sweaty limbs together and lay and talked until a cool, night breeze came through the window and Victor got up to close it lest she get cold.

They spent every minute together after that, most of it lying on his bed, holding each other and making love as if the world was about to end and this was all the time they had.

'Don't go back to Dublin,' he said one night when it began to rain.

'I have to.' She felt like crying. Her life would end if she left him.

'Marry me,' he said, 'stay here and marry me.'

'Just like that?' she said. 'Life is not so simple, you know.'

'We can make it simple,' he said.

And he did. They didn't marry in Vancouver, but by Christmas he had come to Ireland and they had been married in Dublin.

Their love-making had always been good, for all the years they'd been together. If Victor were to come to her today, ask her to make love with him on a narrow bed anywhere, she would go with him.

The night before the morning he'd died they'd made love. She was glad of that.

The Filipino woman on the reception desk at the Hotel Pacific Nights didn't remember her.

'Baldacci, I'm on the fourth floor,' Bridget said and the woman gave her the key with a wide, unknowing smile. I could be anyone, Bridget thought, and didn't bother asking if there were any messages.

She'd turned off the lights before going out so that almost the only thing she saw when she opened the bedroom door was the flashing red light on the telephone.

'Well, Victor,' she murmured, 'it looks like we've got lift off.'

She felt quite calm as she picked up the receiver and pressed the button to hear her mother-in-law's dry, unfriendly voice.

'I am told by the hotel that you have arrived. I have arranged for some of the family to meet you this evening. We dine at seven. My grandson will collect you from the hotel at five thirty.' There was a pause, during which Veronica Baldacci sighed before going on, 'I will presume, unless I hear otherwise, that this arrangement suits you.'

The digital clock beside the bed showed 4.30 p.m.

Bridget changed into a skirt and light-weight green woollen sweater. The Baldaccis were probably expecting an avenging, warrior widow so she wore the long, jade earrings Victor had given her the Christmas before he died and tied her hair back to show them off to best effect.

At two minutes to 5.30 p.m. reception rang to say a Mr Jack Carter had arrived and was waiting for her in the lobby.

Chapter Three

She saw him as she stepped out of the lift. He was tall, with sun-bleached hair and dark eyes. It was the eyes, and a pair of wide shoulders, which helped Bridget identify him as a Baldacci. Victor had had both. Similarities appeared to end there.

The man standing in the middle of the lobby in a long, stone-coloured raincoat looked bored. Victor had been acutely, awkwardly and often painfully alive to everything and everyone. He'd never been bored.

The man in the lobby was young, about thirty, and he was checking his watch as Bridget approached. Women turned to look at him as they passed. Women had noticed Victor too.

'I'm Bridget Baldacci.' Bridget stood in front of him. He was taller than Victor had been. 'I hope I haven't kept you waiting.'

He smiled and gave her an openly assessing look. 'Hi, Aunt Bridget,' he said and held out a hand. 'I'm John-Francis Baldacci-Carter. My mother is your late husband's sister.' His handshake was firm, and brief. He kept his eyes on her face as Bridget stepped back.

'It's good to meet someone from Victor's family at last.' She smiled too, but carefully. John-Francis Baldacci-Carter's stare had begun to verge on the rude.

'You're not like I thought you would be,' he voice had lowered and softened and Bridget realized with astonishment that he was flirting with her.

'It's hard to be right about someone you've never met and know little about.' She was brisk. 'For my own part I'd no idea you existed.' She paused. 'You're about the age of my children, who aren't children any longer, of course, and are your cousins.'

'So I hear.' His teeth were white in the pale-gold tan of his face. 'You've got a boy and a girl. Same set-up as my own family. There's just me and my sister, Lindsay, in the Baldacci-Carter end of things too. Looks like we've got that much in common anyway.'

'Victor didn't know he had a niece and nephew,' Bridget said, 'so let's hope my coming here is a case of better late than never.'

'Let's hope – ' he took her elbow – 'and let's go now too. I'm pulled in around the corner.'

Pulled in meant just that. The black Porsche he helped her into had two wheels on the pavement and lights flashing on four sides.

'Traffic's a bastard in this town.' Victor's nephew nosed the Porsche assertively into a fast-moving lane. 'It's survival of the fittest.'

'I know the feeling,' said Bridget, who did. Dublin gridlocks were constant and paralysing. Not unlike the Seattle traffic, stalled on every side and with a horn belligerently blowing in the near distance. 'Makes me feel quite at home,' Bridget said, which wasn't true. Her stomach had started a nervous tumbling and she was feeling an awfully long way from anything she was familiar with. 'Tell me about your mother,' she said, 'is she older or younger than Victor?'

'He really never talked about us? Didn't ever fill you in on things?'

'Never.' Bridget paused, studying his profile for a minute. It was a good profile, jawline, nose and forehead all well defined. It gave away nothing of the thoughts of the young man behind it. 'I always thought,' she looked ahead, into the traffic as it moved off again, 'that we would grow old together and that Victor would one day tell me about Seattle and growing up here—'

'My mother is the eldest,' he said cutting her short, 'by two years. That makes her sixty years old, though she stopped counting a long time ago. Her name's Magdalena' – he pressed a button and the sound of a jazz combo rippled into the conditioned air – 'and that's what she's always been called. She's not a Mags or a Lena.' He shifted lanes again and they got a clear, fast run for 500 yards or so. Coming close to a bridge they got bogged down again. 'I don't recall her talking much about her brother,' John-Francis Baldacci-Carter said, 'not what you'd call a talkative pair.'

'Maybe your mother will make an exception in my case and open up,' Bridget said.

'Yeah, maybe.'

They turned onto and crossed the bridge, the city ahead and behind them like fields of spangles in the dark. The stretch of water beneath them was a chilling swell of inky blue.

They'd reached the other side, and a more suburban scenario, before John-Francis Baldacci-Carter spoke again.

'Why'd you come here? Why put yourself through this shit now he's dead?'

Bridget didn't answer immediately. When she did she gave him the reply she'd given Anna to the same question months before.

'I'm here because Victor's dead,' she said, 'and because I'm alive and curious.'

'Don't you know what curiosity did to the cat?' He was smiling.

'I've heard.'

They were silent again as he swung the car into a narrow, tree-lined road and began to climb.

'One of the things I'm curious about, John-Francis—' Bridget began.

'Call me Jack. Jack Carter is what my friends call me, though not the family . . .' He stopped, grinning. 'You strike me as the friendly type.'

'Jack it is, then. My question has to do with why you think my coming here is such a bad idea. Is it just that you've got a negative view of your family? Or is there something I wouldn't want to know about why Victor wrote his family out of his life?' She turned to look at him. The excellent profile had become fractionally more chiselled. 'Because that's what he did.'

'Sounds to me like you've answered the question yourself, Aunt Bridget,' his smile didn't waver, 'whatever happened was before my time and no one wants to talk about it anymore. Seems to me that for a man to write his family out of his life he'd need to be pretty fed up with some situation or other. I just dunno why you'd want to rake over all of those dead ashes, that's all.'

He understood all right, Bridget thought, he just didn't want to be involved. Briefly, she wondered if Jack Carter had written the letter which had been waiting for her at the hotel. He didn't seem the type, but you never could tell.

'I get the feeling, Jack, that I'm a not altogether welcome visitor to Seattle,' she said.

'I don't know, Aunt Bridget, why you get that feeling. It's a free world and we're a hospitable lot around here. As far as I'm concerned you're entirely welcome to Seattle.'

'Thank you. And please call me Bid. My friends and family all do.'

The road became more steeply inclined, more heavily lined by a virtual wall of evergreens on either side. Here and there, as they passed, distant lights indicated the presence of secluded houses. The car climbed steadily, smooth and silent.

'Have you always lived in Seattle?' Bridget hated silences.

'Born, bred and now livin' the good life here.'

'I'm told half the city works for Microsoft. Do you?'

'Do I look the nerdy type?' he said irritably. 'Microsoft's a sweatshop for nerds and high-tech workaholics. I don't fit either category.'

'What *do* you work at?'

'I'm part of the family set-up. My father's the vice president and CEO. Grandmother's the president.'

The road straightened and he drove faster, turning too quickly and with a squeal of brakes into a short avenue leading to a pair of high, grey gates. The headlights shone on large, gently falling snowflakes as he pressed a remote control and the gates began to slowly open.

The inner part of the avenue was lined with an erratic growth of old trees, the bald and wintry mingling with heavy evergreens. They rounded a sweeping bend and a large, colonial-style house came into view. The snow, swirling and denser now, made it hard to see clearly.

'Before you, Bid, is the ancestral home,' said Jack Carter, 'the house your husband grew up in. The house my mother grew up in. Their mother, my grandmother Veronica, lives there now. Alone for the most part.' He shrugged. 'I stay with her from time to time, or sometimes my mother does. But basically she's the independent type and prefers to be alone. She has Hugo, of course, her faithful Hugo—'

'Hugo?'

'You'll meet him.' He spun the car in a wide arc on the gravel in front of the house. There were lights on in several rooms. 'My grandmother's father built this place.'

'So she moved back home with her husband, your grandfather, when she married?'

'That's what she did.'

He brought the car to a halt and turned off the engine. Bridget stared at the long, white clapboard building which had been Victor's childhood home. There was no apparent movement behind the lighted windows and the front door remained closed. An elegant portico ran the length of the front, and the black-painted door was framed by two smaller pillars. The palatial effect was spoiled by two rows of giant evergreens. Leaning smotheringly close on either side they gave the place the look of a mausoleum. They were already sprinkled with a covering of snow.

'How old is it?' Bridget asked.

'Turn of the century, colonial revival. I'm told the portico was inspired by Mount Vernon.'

'George Washington's house?'

'Right.' He got out of the car and came round to open Bridget's door. 'My grand-grandfather, John Langan, was Irish and one of the big social climbers of his day. Don't hold that against the house though.'

Victor had never even hinted at Irish blood or ancestry. Bridget climbed out and tilted her face so that snowflakes fell on her closed lids. It was two winters since there had been snow in Dublin.

'Do you know where in Ireland your great-grandfather came from?'

'Nope. Grandmother will fill you in though.'

The front-door bell was shaped in the nose of a bronze lion. Jack Carter had pressed it a couple of times before they heard slow, even footsteps cross the hall on the other side.

'Come on in.' The small man who opened the door had dust-white hair and narrow, foxy features. The hair was caught into a skinny ponytail. 'It's a bad night to be standing outside.'

He ignored Bridget, and spoke directly to Jack Carter. He was wearing a black suit, red waistcoat and black, red-spotted bow tie and his accent was distinctly Irish. Cork unless Bridget was badly mistaken. She stepped into the house ahead of Jack Carter and smiled at the small man.

'They're waiting for you in the sitting room,' he spoke again to Jack Carter and took his raincoat. Underneath the younger man was wearing a dark wool suit, very designer.

'This, Hugo, is Bridget Baldacci.' Jack Carter looked at his watch and ran his fingers through his hair in a quick, continuous movement. 'She's—'

'I know who she is.' The old man turned close-set eyes on Bridget. His expression was one of lively bad humour. 'I'm Hugo Sweeney.'

'You're Irish.' Bridget extended a hand.

'I am.' He ignored the gesture. 'I'll take your outer garments from you.'

Bridget gave him her coat and scarf and with Jack Carter followed him across the high, wood-panelled hallway. Austere and gloomy, it was relieved by a wide, artfully curved staircase which looked to have been designed for grand entrances.

'Nice staircase,' said Bridget.

Hugo Sweeney opened a door and stepped aside while Bridget and Jack Carter went into the biggest sitting room Bridget had ever seen. It ran from the front to the back of the house and was grotesquely overstuffed with furniture. Everywhere Bridget looked there were gilded chairs and chaises, fat, embroidered sofas, fragile tea tables and lacquered card tables, velvet-covered stools, a pink ottoman. Oil paintings of sombre and bewigged colonials hung in clusters on the walls.

Directly opposite the door, round a marble fireplace with a burning, fake log fire, a group of people sat watching Bridget and Jack Carter.

There were four of them, two women and two men. Bridget took a couple of steps further into the room. Her stomach lurched uncomfortably.

'Hello,' she said, 'I'm Bridget—'

'We were pleased you were able to visit at such short

41

notice.' A tall woman, older than Bridget but not old enough to be Veronica Baldacci, unwound herself from a gilded armchair. 'And on such an unpleasant night too, though I'm afraid it's fairly typical of this time of year in Seattle. You would have found the spring a more pleasant time for your visit.' Her voice was low and modulated, the words only slightly slurred. She extended the hand not holding a drink to Bridget. 'I'm Magdalena Baldacci-Carter. I hope my son watched his manners on the ride here.'

Bridget, crossing the expanse of room to take the proffered hand, could see nothing of Victor in his sister's handsome blonde looks, except that she was tall. She was elegant too, a single string of pearls breaking the severe lines of a sheath-like black dress.

'I didn't come to Seattle for sunshine.'

Standing in front of Magdalena Baldacci-Carter, Bridget saw how bone thin she was. That close too it was impossible to ignore the faint alcoholic fumes from her breath. Her hand in Bridget's was limp and warm.

'It's good to meet you at last.' Bridget smiled.

'Likewise,' said Magdalena Baldacci-Carter. 'You'll doubtless want to meet the rest of the family. My mother is busy right now but will be with us momentarily. Allow me to introduce you . . .' She sipped her drink and gestured vaguely towards the others in the room.

Any one of the three people who stood to greet Bridget could have sent the warning note to her hotel. They were all tall, seeming to tower over her. Her mouth dried and they became a blurry triad as she tried to focus. She wished she had a drink in her hand, wished too that she'd never got the damned note.

But she had and it was more than likely that one of these people had sent it – and extremely likely that none of them wanted her here. She managed not to flinch when a slightly stooped man, sixtyish and with a neat white beard, put a hand on her arm and gave a small, nervous cough.

'Hello there, Bridget. I'm Thomas Carter,' he said. 'I married into the family as well. Married Magdalena too many years ago now to keep counting.' He smiled at his wife. 'We're a small enough bunch, as families go, so why don't we get the introductions over with quickly so we can put a good, stiff drink into your hand.' He adjusted a pair of gold-framed glasses and cleared his throat again. 'My wife Magdalena and my son John-Francis you've already met. But not my lovely and intelligent daughter' – a fragile blonde gave Bridget a nod – 'Lindsay—'

'Enough, Dad,' the blonde woman's smile was impatient. 'Good to have you here, Bridget,' she said. Her voice was neutral to cool as she indicated the fourth person in the group. 'This is my husband, Russell Segal.'

Russell Segal was dark-haired, sun-tanned, fit-looking and film-star handsome. There was an unnerving perfection about the sculpted bones of his face.

'Glad to make your acquaintance, ma'am.' He had even, shining teeth.

'Nice to meet an aunt at last.' Lindsay lit a cigarette with a gush of flame from a silver lighter. 'I've been a bit short on them until now. What would you like me to call you?' She watched the smoke as it circled. 'Aunt Bridget? Bridget? Or would it be more to the point to call you Mrs Baldacci?'

'Bid will do fine,' said Bridget, 'it's what most people call me.'

'Cute name.' Russell Segal rested a long arm across Bridget's shoulders. 'Suits you too.'

'I think it a rather sad diminution.' Magdalena, back in her gilded armchair, crossed a pair of very good legs. The honey blonde colour of her shoulder-length hair had probably been natural ten years before. She swung an ankle

43

outward and looked at it critically. 'Shortening names always seems to me rather childish, not something to be carried into adulthood.' She yawned. 'I'll call you Bridget.'

Boredom, Bridget decided, was probably the reason she drank so much.

'We all know why you feel like that, mother.' Jack Carter sauntered to the fireplace and rested an elegant arm on the mantel. 'Magdalena is not a name to mess around with.' He threw a brief, conspiratorial look Bridget's way. 'Too many lousy possibilities. Mags? Lena? Not your style at all.'

'I do like it when you see things my way.' Magdalena Baldacci-Carter's expression, as she looked at her son, became quite animated.

'Don't I always?' said Jack. Magdalena gave a laugh and shrugged.

Bridget's need for a drink was becoming desperate. She wished someone would invite her to sit: the multitude of chairs and sofas was confusing, most of them looked too old and too precious to risk sitting on.

Thomas Carter came to her rescue.

'Dinner could be a while yet, so let's sit back down. John-Francis will get you a drink.' He indicated a spindle-legged chair next to him and Bridget sat. 'Veronica is overseeing the meal. She likes to be involved, doesn't like to keep a lot of help in the house. What would you like to drink?'

'When in Rome,' Bridget said. 'I'll try a Martini Dry. Three olives.' Victor had liked a Martini Dry with three olives.

'One Martini Dry on the way.' Jack Carter disappeared to a long table with drinks at the other side of the room.

'You have two children?' Magdalena stared into the evenly dancing blue-gold flames.

'Two, yes. Though they haven't been children for a long time,' Bridget said. 'They're in their twenties, late twenties.' The room was unbearably warm.

44

'They had no interest in coming to Seattle?'

'None. They live very full lives . . .' Not like me, Bridget thought, unable to live any kind of life since Victor had died. Magdalena raised an eyebrow and waited for her to go on. 'But they're as curious as I am about their father's family,' Bridget said.

'That's nice,' said Magdalena.

'One Martini Dry.' Jack Carter stood between Bridget and his mother. He handed her a white napkin with her drink and raised his own glass. 'Welcome to Seattle,' he said.

'A drink seems like a good idea,' Magdalena spoke loudly, rattling the ice in her empty glass. Her eyes were still half closed. 'See if you can pour me a decent gin Martini, John-Francis.'

'Oh, God, here we go again,' Lindsay groaned, stubbed out her cigarette and fiddled with one of her small, silver earrings. 'If you people will excuse me, there's something I have to do.' She lifted a small shoulder bag from the lacquered card table nearest her. 'I won't be staying to eat.'

Her mother's eyes opened fully and her ankle stopped swinging. 'You have not been given permission to leave,' her voice had become harsh as well as loud, 'and so you will stay. We are going to make the best of this situation. We are all, as a family, going to share a meal with our guest.'

'I've already eaten,' said Lindsay. 'I wasn't told about this . . . dinner until today. There are a couple of work issues I should be—'

'You will stay here, Lindsay,' Magdalena said. 'You are not in the boardroom now. The business will wait. Your obsession with it has, at any rate, become unhealthy.'

'Unhealthy! You have to be joking, Mother!' Lindsay's laugh was genuinely amused. She lit another cigarette.

Magdelena stood a little unsteadily and Bridget saw her knuckles whiten when she gripped the back of the chair. Thomas Carter moved unobtrusively closer to his wife.

'You, Russell,' Magdalena fixed an imperious glare on her son-in-law, 'get your posturing ass into gear and deal with your wife. I want everyone here to sit down to dinner tonight with Bridget . . .' she paused, 'and I am holding you responsible for Lindsay's presence at the table.'

'I'm not my wife's jailer,' Russell replied laconically, 'I can't even stop her smoking so I don't know as I can exactly put her in chains, Magdalena.'

'Californians! You're all the same. Lazy, dumb, useless, retarded . . .' Magdalena took a long, hissing breath. 'Just tie her down, Russell, do whatever it takes. You're a man, aren't you?' Her eyes narrowed. 'Or are you . . .?'

'Why don't we all calm down.' Jack Carter moved closer to his mother and put an arm round her shoulder. 'Seems to me things are getting a bit out of hand around here. Mother, I'll get you that drink now. Lindsay, why don't you take Bridget outside onto the back patio for a couple of minutes, show her the tree? I'll bet it looks good with the snow falling on it.'

'Jack the peacemaker.' Lindsay gave a short laugh and blew a small spiral of smoke into her brother's face. 'I'll bet you haven't looked at that tree once this Christmas. Come to that, I'll bet you didn't know it was there until Grandmother decided not to take it down—'

'Do I have to get my drink myself?' Magdalena, sitting back into the chair, interrupted sharply. Thomas stood behind her massaging her shoulders.

'Want to come with me see Grandmother's Christmas tree?' Lindsay's face, when she turned to Bridget, was smiling and smooth and lovely. 'Having it out there in the yard's been a yearly event since for ever.' She gave a short laugh. 'You're in luck. As you probably picked up just now, Grandmother has decided to let it stand for longer than usual this year.'

'I'll get Hugo to bring your coats—' Thomas began.

'We won't need them.' Lindsay took Bridget's arm and started with her towards the rear of the room. 'We're not going to climb the tree.'

Circumnavigating the furniture they made their way towards a set of closed double curtains. The room behind them was silent, the rattle of ice as Jack Carter mixed his mother's drink the only sound.

'Peace and goodwill to men.' Lindsay opened a set of French windows the other side of the curtains and stepped out onto a patio. 'What you see before you, Bid, is Grandmother's yearly tribute to the season just past. The Baldacci Christmas just wouldn't be complete without it.'

Bridget stood beside her on the patio, sheltered from the falling snow by a porch, and stared at a colossal fir, lit up and shining in the murky dark of the garden. It was all of thirty feet high, uniquely and dazzlingly impressive as it stood with the snow falling softly about its blue and white lights and settling gently on the bright-green pines. A reindeer, at the very top, had a radiant red nose. Tree and reindeer together made for an eerily peaceful, perfect triangle of light in the dark emptiness of the garden.

The arrival of the snow had taken the cold sting from the air and Bridget took in calming gulps as she went down a set of steps and into the garden proper. A light covering of snow lay on the grass.

'It's a wonderful tree,' she said, 'how long does your grandmother intend leaving it there?' It was now the seventh of January.

'Until she decides Christmas is over.' Lindsay came and stood beside her. 'She's decided it should go on longer this year. She's waiting for a friend to call . . .' She let out a long breath. 'She's more than eighty years old, did you know that?'

'Victor was fifty-eight when he died. I knew his mother had to be about that age.' Bridget studied the tree. Now that

47

she was closer it seemed to her that there was something slightly off about it. She couldn't quite decide what, exactly. 'Are you telling me Victor's mother is senile?'

'God no.' Lindsay shook her head. 'Just that she's an old woman, and that old women do strange things, break the rules a little. They're allowed.'

'Rules are for all women to break,' said Bridget, 'only they don't do it half enough.'

'Are you a rule breaker?' Lindsay looked at her thoughtfully.

'Not often enough.' Bridget smiled.

'Women are, by and large, the law-abiding element in the human race,' said Lindsay. 'By and large. Snow's stopping . . .'

Slowly, as the snowfall tailed away, the Christmas tree came into sharp relief against the pitch black of the garden behind it. Only the occasional flickering of a tree light broke the unearthly silence.

And into this Veronica Baldacci walked.

Bridget had imagined Victor's mother as a woman of height and bearing with an imperious air. It was an image built on a combination of Victor's silence and her own telephone conversations.

The woman walking toward them was all of those things. What Bridget hadn't expected was someone who must have once been very beautiful. Even allowing for the dancing lights and distance she was the possessor of a pair of remarkably high cheek bones and wide-spaced eyes. She wore a long, silver fox-fur coat and was using a black, silver-topped walking cane.

'You're about to meet your mother-in-law,' said Lindsay, 'and God knows when we're going to get some food if she's been wandering about out here.'

Veronica Baldacci, walking slowly and seemingly unaware that she had company in the garden, reached the tree and began to adjust a light bulb. When Bridget made a move toward her Lindsay put a staying hand.

'Wait,' she said.

'Why don't you introduce me?' said Bridget.

'She knows we're here. Better to wait until she comes to you.'

'Is that a rule?' Bridget raised an eyebrow.

'Sort of . . .'

'I haven't broken enough rules in my life . . .' Bridget watched as Veronica Baldacci moved back and stood looking up at the tree. '. . . maybe I'll break one now.'

Veronica Baldacci couldn't have failed to hear Bridget crunching across the snow. But she didn't turn, leaning on the cane and staring at the tree even when Bridget stopped a couple of feet behind her.

'Hello,' she said, 'I'm Bridget, Victor's wife.'

'I was aware you'd arrived,' the voice sounded more tremulous than it had on the phone. 'Dinner will be served in a little while. We will talk then.' Veronica Baldacci turned. She was wearing too much make-up and her expression was stern. 'I would have preferred us to meet formally, indoors.'

'I've waited a long time to meet you.' Bridget smiled. Her first and distant impression of Veronica Baldacci had been an accurate one: Victor's mother had been a stunner, once. She'd known it too. The make-up covering her thin, tight skin and outlining her features was a defiant scream at beauty's passing.

'It would have been better manners to wait for me to come to you,' Veronica Baldacci said.

'It would have been mannerly to receive me when I arrived,' said Bridget.

'Touché,' said Victor's mother and smiled. 'Though I'm inclined to think it would have been better by far had we never met.'

'For you, perhaps,' said Bridget.

'For both of us, I think. Why have you come here?' The older woman sighed. 'Why could you not have left things as they were?'

Bridget studied Veronica's face for a moment before answering: it told her nothing. 'I lived for thirty years with your son,' she said at last, 'why wouldn't I want to meet his mother? His family? Don't you think it natural that I would want to see the place where he grew up?'

'Why bother? He's dead.'

'It seems even more important now he's dead.'

'Death comes to us all.' Victor's mother turned back to the tree and Bridget, closer to it now and following her gaze, saw what it was that had struck her as odd. The giant fir was artificial, every branch and pine needle a tribute to the art of plastic imitation.

'Sometimes,' Bridget said, 'death comes too soon.'

'That's a point of view, certainly,' said Veronica Baldacci.

Snow slipped from a plastic branch with a low plop as Bridget waited for the older woman to add something regretful, kind, even enquiring, about her son. Her feet were becoming cold and wet from standing in the snow. Veronica Baldacci remained silent.

'Forgive me if I'm wrong but you don't appear to feel grief at your son's death,' Bridget spoke quietly, 'your falling out must have been very terrible . . .' she paused. 'It could be, of course, that I am altogether wrong.'

'I ceased to grieve for Victor many years ago,' the older woman didn't turn around, 'long before you met him. He was not a grateful son. I reared him, as any mother would, happy to have the son my husband and I had wanted so much. My husband put everything into his boy, believing in him. By the time Victor left, in 1962 when he was just twenty-three years old, his father was dead, and sadly disillusioned.'

'Are you telling me that Victor was responsible for his father's death?'

'Not in any physical sense, no. But it is not too fanciful to say that he broke his father's heart.'

Bridget stomped her feet, testing that her toes still had life in them. 'None of this sounds like the man I knew. He was intensely loyal to me and our children.'

Veronica Baldacci turned then. But her focus was clearly inward and it was doubtful that she saw Bridget.

'He left himself no other choice,' she said, 'he had cast aside everyone else in his life by the time he met you.'

'But why?' Bridget stared, hating the ambiguity, resisting an entirely irrational urge to shake direct answers from the other woman. 'Why did he leave here? What happened that was so terrible it kept him away?' Rubbing her hands together, the better to keep them away from Veronica Baldacci, she didn't hear Lindsay's approach until she stood shivering beside her grandmother.

'I want to get back indoors even if you two don't.' She hugged herself, her blue silk blouse spotted with snow. 'The temperature's dropping again. Let's go get some food.'

'You have a point, my dear, as always.' Veronica gathered the fur around herself. 'I left the inept woman I pay to cook for me to finish preparing the meal. She should have it ready by now.' She tested the ground with the cane and began walking toward the house. 'She brought her daughter in as help with tonight's occasion but she would have been better off leaving her at home. We will have to hope that Hugo has salvaged things.'

As they climbed the steps onto the patio, Victor's mother turned for a final look at the tree.

'I will leave it stand for a further week. Another seven days is as much as I am prepared to wait. Any longer would be ridiculous.'

'Right.' Lindsay sighed. 'Ridiculous is just what all of this is.'

Shivering violently now she went ahead of them to open the French windows. Bridget walked slowly beside Victor's mother.

'I do hope your journey hasn't exhausted you,' the older woman spoke as if they'd just met.

'Not at all,' said Bridget. 'It's given me an appetite though.'

'I don't like to have my plans hijacked,' Veronica Baldacci said, 'and I had planned to make your acquaintance and speak with you before dinner. So we will talk, briefly, in the library before eating.'

'If you like.'

'I do.'

In the sitting room Lindsay eyed Bridget's sodden boots and said, 'Your feet look about as wet as mine are. I'll get Hugo to bring you a pair of slippers.'

'He can bring them along to the library.' Veronica didn't stop. 'We'll be spending a short time there together.'

Chapter Four

The library was small, too warm, and as overstuffed with furniture as the sitting room had been. Bridget sat in one of three wing-backed chairs and within minutes saw steam begin to rise from her wet boots. Veronica Baldacci shed her waterproof boots and her fur coat and rang a bell. A dress in beige cashmere hung loosely on a body as bonily thin as her daughter's.

'I will come to the point straight away.' She sat down so that she was facing Bridget directly. 'It will prevent us wasting one another's time.' She secured a hairpin and patted her hair into place. 'I did not encourage you to come here because I would have preferred the past to lie at rest. My son, your husband, was the cause of great hurt to this family. You will no doubt say that I should forgive, that I am his mother and should also forget. But I cannot and will not do either of those things, ever.'

'I think that very sad, for all concerned.'

'You may think so, but then you are speaking from ignorance. It is my prerogative and privilege to hold onto my anger and to my hurt.' Victor's mother fixed her gaze on the marriage ring on Bridget's left hand. 'Neither you, nor your children, have any right to sit in judgement, to expect anything else from me. I knew my son. I knew him for what he was and knew what he could not change in himself. It is useless for you to come here expecting recon-ciliation, or an understanding of some kind.'

'Reconciliation?' Bridget was curt. 'There is nothing for me to be reconciled to – I was never part of this family. Nor do I want to be. That's not why I've come here.'

She left the armchair and walked to the window, the heat and sense of claustophobia in the small room was getting to her. Outside a wind had come up, lifting the powdery white cover from the ground and sending it, circling, into the air. The Christmas tree was still beautiful, the garden still a dark abyss behind it. She leaned her hands against the cool of the glass and told herself that the sane thing would be to leave now. She'd met Victor's family.

The really sane thing, of course, would have been not to have come in the first place.

But why shouldn't she be helped to understand? What right had Veronica Baldacci to deny her knowledge?

She turned back to the room, her hands behind her back, palms still against the soothing cool of the window.

'Reconciliation's a different thing to understanding,' she said. 'It's important to me that I understand why my husband denied his mother. Why he denied his entire family. I came here because I want to know what it was that he could never tell me.'

'He said nothing of his life here?' Veronica Baldacci's hands moved from her lap to clutch at the chair's arm.

'Nothing. Ever.'

Was there relief in the pale eyes? Or was it shock which made them freeze and glaze over?

'Yes. That would have been his way. He didn't change then.' The older woman shrugged. 'I should have known . . .' For several seconds she massaged her forehead with her fingers, a cluster of rings on her fingers making the action cumbersome. 'He bore grudges, always silently, as a child. Obviously it wasn't in him to change, any more than it was in his . . .' She made an irritable gesture with her hand. 'Please sit down. Since you're here we will talk. Some.

54

We will also have drinks – if that manservant of mine can be got to answer the bell.'

She reached forward and pressed a bell in the wall, long and hard. It could be head, loudly echoing, through the bowels of the house.

'I hope, in spite of what you've told me,' said Veronica Baldacci, 'that you have not come here looking for money. Victor was not entitled to anything from this family.'

Bridget didn't move from the window. She held her breath for a while and counted to five before she said, 'I have not come looking for money.'

'We will not discuss the subject of greed then,' Veronica said. 'Though I must tell you that there are some in the family who cannot conceive of you being here for any other reason.'

'That's understandable, I suppose. But they're wrong.'

'I hope so.' Victor's mother drummed her fingers on the arm of the chair.

Bridget watched her for a minute, wondering if she'd always been so cold, so controlled. She'd half expected that Victor's family, and this woman, would think she'd come for money.

What she hadn't bargained on was the complete absence of regret, of a mourning of any kind for Victor.

'You may not grieve for your son's death,' she left the window and began to circle the room, 'but do you grieve for his life?'

She turned quickly, and caught a flickering disturbance on the older woman's still, made-up face. It could have been pain, a grief denied, it could also have been anger, or simple irritation.

'Victor was too young to die. Of course I regret his death.' Veronica Baldacci shrugged again. 'Victor choosing to live the greater part of his life at a distance naturally affects the nature of my grief. He created another life for himself and I applaud his independence.' She paused. 'However, I deplore his cruelty.'

'Victor wasn't cruel. He simply didn't know—'

'I don't care to know about his emotional problems. I'm an old woman, not a state I enjoy. I have decided to concentrate on certain priorities for the time left me to live. Victor, and the past, are not priorities.'

This time, when Veronica leaned forward impatiently to press the bell again, Bridget took a minute to study the room.

Excess, when it came to furnishing and decor, was definitely the Baldacci way. The room looked to be a perfect cube. Three of its walls were filled, floor to ceiling, with books; beautifully bound, matching leathers many of them, classics and history titles predominating. Green, in different shades, was the main colour. The lighting came from a collection of ornate reading lamps. Touching one of a pair of bronze noblemen on a table beside her Bridget thought how nicely Victor's casket would sit between the two of them.

'Please be careful.' Veronica Baldacci gave an impatient tsk. 'This room has been put together with great care.'

'I can see that,' Bridget said. The reading lamp behind the older woman gave her face the look of a skull with a blonde halo. Bridget decided against mentioning Victor's ashes, yet.

The door opened without warning and Hugo Sweeney, arms laden, stepped into the room.

'I brought you these.' He put a pair of leather moccasins on the floor in front of Veronica. 'By rights you should be in your room resting before dinner.'

'I can't wear those.' Veronica lifted the walking stick from beside her chair and poked at the moccasins. 'Bring me my cream pumps. And why are you talking about a rest before dinner? Is the meal not ready to be served?'

'Just about,' Hugo said in a mollifying tone, 'another twenty minutes or so. I'll take you to your room.'

'I'm entertaining, as you can see.' Veronica glared at him. 'And I would like you to bring us drinks.' She pointed at the moccasins. 'You may give those to our guest. Mrs Baldacci insisted on an uninvited viewing of our tree. She was not dressed for the occasion.'

Hugo, silently and without once lifting his eyes, placed the moccasins close to where Bridget was sitting.

'You can bring us the drinks straight away, Hugo.' Veronica Baldacci lifted the walking stick from beside the armchair and tapped impatiently on the floor. 'I will have my usual bourbon, a double measure. Mrs Baldacci will have . . .?'

'A cup of tea. No sugar, no milk.'

Hugo Sweeney's face took on a stubbornly resentful look and Veronica tapped more sharply with the stick.

'Get her the tea, Hugo. And while you're in the kitchen check with that wretched Amy about dinner.'

Hugo picked up the fox fur. 'I'll be setting an extra place at the table.'

'I did not ask you to do so,' Veronica's voice dropped and became almost inaudible with fury. 'We will be six, no more.'

'You can't ignore her. She arrived back twenty minutes ago. She'll come to the table and make a scene. You'd be better off accommodating her. It'll cause less trouble.' Hugo Sweeney's tone was deferential, wheedling. Its cajoling rhythm seemed to soothe Veronica.

'You'd better make sure then that she doesn't place herself anywhere near me at the table. Go now, and bring me my pumps and the drinks.' She closed her eyes and leaned back into the chair, balancing the stick in front of her across the arms. 'And be quick about it.'

Hugo Sweeney closed the door quietly and gently after him.

'He runs the house for me. He's useful.' Veronica tapped her fingers on the stick, her rings catching the light from the lamp. She kept her eyes closed. 'He's loyal. You have to be my age to appreciate loyalty truly.'

'How long has he worked for you?'

'Long enough. He's seventy-two years old. He was thirty-one when a priest in the parish asked me to give him a job which would keep him out of jail long enough to stop him being deported. I took him on because he was Catholic.' Her eyes snapped open. 'You are Catholic too, I presume? Victor didn't marry a non-Catholic, did he?'

Bridget didn't answer immediately. First she worked out something about Hugo Sweeney. He'd been forty years ministering to Veronica; he would have known Victor. She might, if she worked on him, get an objective view of what had happened.

'I was a Catholic when Victor married me,' she said eventually, and slowly. The faith she'd been reared in hadn't been of much interest to Victor. It was of much less interest to Bridget now than it had been.

'I'm glad to hear it.' Veronica leaned toward Bridget. 'We must hold hard to the faith of our fathers. The old country has always stood by the church.'

'Your grandson Jack mentioned that your father was Irish,' Bridget said.

Veronica straightened. 'My grandson is known as John-Francis within the family.' She began tapping the stick again with her fingers. 'So. You didn't even know that your husband's ancestory was part Irish?'

'No. All of this is news to me. I presumed, because of his looks and his name, that Victor was Italian-American.'

'His father, my husband Frank Baldacci, was of Italian extraction. Catholic too, of course. Victor greatly resembled Frank, in looks.'

'Your father was Irish . . .' Bridget prompted Veronica when she fell silent.

'I am not deaf and I am not senile,' Veronica snapped, 'so do not prompt answers from me. It is simply that the subject does not interest me half as much as it does you. Yes, my father was Irish. He came here in the eighteen fifties. He'd got word of the gold rush when he was in New York, to where he'd made his escape from the potato famine in Ireland. My family name is Langan.' She spoke quickly, offhandedly, as if the story she was telling had nothing to do with her. 'It may be that Victor chose you because of your nationality—'

She stopped as the door opened and Hugo Sweeney reappeared. He placed a small table between the two women and a tray with a single cup of tea, a glass of bourbon and two napkins. Close to Veronica's feet he placed a pair of almost flat-heeled cream pumps.

'Dinner will be served in ten minutes,' he said.

Veronica took a long drink. 'I want you to attend in the kitchen, Hugo, and to make sure that six, good portions of food are delivered to the table. The seventh, uninvited, guest will have to be satisfied with what she gets. Do I make myself clear?'

'As glass,' said Hugo Sweeney.

'We were discussing the likelihood of Victor having chosen an Irish wife because of my family links with the old country.' Veronica watched Hugo Sweeney carefully as she spoke.

'Not likely at all.' Hugo stood stiffly inside the door. 'I never knew him to have any interest in those as went before him.'

'That sounds like Victor,' Bridget agreed and smiled.

Hugo looked at his watch. 'Time's marching on. Eight minutes now and the food will be ready.'

'I'd like you to tell me something before you go.' Bridget stood and took a few steps towards Hugo, who immediately opened the door. 'Please,' Bridget said. 'All I want to know is what sort of young man my husband was. You knew him . . .'

'He was a serious person,' Hugo Sweeney stepped into the doorway, 'not easy, hard enough to get to know.' With a curt nod he turned and pulled the door firmly behind him.

'Not an easy man to get to know himself.' Veronica slipped her feet into the pumps.

Bridget, sipping the lukewarm tea, was willing to bet Veronica Baldacci knew everything there was to know about Hugo Sweeney. It would have been one of the reasons for his loyalty.

'Hugo spoke of time marching on.' Veronica sighed. 'I find it more true to say time flies, as one gets older. It is equally true, of course, that death urges, knells call, heaven invites, hell threatens . . .' Her milky blue eyes stared at Bridget. 'You are a woman who has put thirty years of her time into my son. My advice to you is not to waste any more of it on this family. You won't listen, of course. You are obviously stubborn.' She paused. 'Thirty years . . . and then to come here. If it is true that you do not want money then you must be mad. We will talk again. I am not inclined to reveal family intimacies to a perfect stranger. I know nothing about you.' Veronica Baldacci stood and leaned on the stick. 'I had hoped that our small talk in this room would satisfy you but you are clearly not a woman who is easily . . . satisfied.' She hesitated. 'How long do you intend staying in Seattle?'

'A couple of weeks, at least.'

'We will talk again but right now we will eat.'

She stood tapping the stick impatiently while Bridget removed her boots and slipped her feet into the moccasins. They were much too big, slapping on the wooden floor of

60

the hallway as she followed her mother-in-law from the library and across to where the dining-room door stood open. It was a long room with a long table.

'There's a place laid for you at the far end,' said Hugo Sweeney.

'Thank you.' Bridget took the chair nearest her. 'I'll be fine here.'

Better to be close to the door, she would not feel so hemmed in by Baldaccis that way.

Chapter Five

'Good to have you back,' said Thomas Carter with a smile and a nod.

Bridget looked at him and decided the remark was as innocent as it seemed. She would have to guard against paranoia.

'Sorry if I kept you waiting,' she said.

'Most of us had the wisdom to eat earlier.' Thomas leaned across the table, an attempt at confidentiality made difficult by the table's width. 'Entertaining is not one of Veronica's fortes.'

Bridget, faced with a basket of bread rolls, was suddenly aware of a rumbling hollow in her stomach. 'I haven't eaten all day myself,' she admitted.

'Oh dear, oh dear,' Magdalena, to her right, murmured reprovingly, 'how very optimistic you were. I would advise you to start on the bread rolls. They may be the best thing on the menu.'

Bridget took one. It felt soft and warm.

The dining-room decor reflected the by now familiar taste for sombre Victoriana. It was, if anything, more suffo-cating than either the library or the sitting room with bigger and darker furniture, numbers of landscape oils and heavy, burgundy-coloured curtains on all the windows but one.

Bridget found herself sitting opposite an empty place setting. Magdalena sat next to her, Thomas sat across from his wife and Lindsay and her husband bickered a little further down. At the far end Jack Carter sat close to where his grandmother had taken her seat at the head of the table. The table, of polished oak, was big enough to have seated eighteen people and swallowed up the six who now sat there. The place settings had been laid widely apart, presumably by Hugo Sweeney, so the occasion was not going to be an intimate one.

'We will begin, Hugo.' Veronica Baldacci tapped the floor with her stick. 'You and Amy may start serving.'

Hugo Sweeney, after a brief glance at the empty chair, all but clicked his heels before disappearing through a door.

'Is there someone I haven't met?' Bridget broke the bread roll and looked up as she reached for, and failed to find, the butter. No one seemed about to answer her question. She rephrased it. 'Hugo says there will be a seventh person joining us . . .'

'Veronica has a house guest,' Thomas said. 'She has just returned from a trip downtown and may join us . . .'

'There isn't a chance in hell of her *not* joining us,' Magdalena said. 'This is the occasion she's been waiting for. A captive audience, a God-sent opportunity to let loose with that crazy ego of hers.' She pushed her wine glass across the table to her husband. 'Just thinking about it makes me thirsty. Pour me a glass of the Chablis, Thomas, and fill it up.' She watched while her husband poured the wine, speaking out of the side of her mouth to Bridget. 'She's been waiting to meet you. It's your fault she's here in the first place.'

'Don't pre-empt things, sweetheart.' Thomas carefully eased his wife's drink back across the table. 'Let's try to keep this thing amicable.'

'Amicable! Amicable doesn't make people go away. Amicable doesn't change anything.' Magdalena gulped at the wine, shrugged and sat silently fiddling with an earring. She looked tired.

Bridget helped herself to a glass of the Chablis. It would help the butterless bread roll down and it didn't look as if anyone was going to pour it for her.

Hugo Sweeney arrived through the side door with a serving trolley and a large, square woman. At a finger-clicking command from him the woman began ladling the contents of a soup tureen into bowls which Hugo Sweeney then delivered to the table.

'Fish chowder,' John-Francis announced after a spoonful.

'That's right.' The square woman beamed. 'I knew you'd like it, John-Francis. That's why I made it.'

'God, is there *any* woman you don't turn it on for?' Lindsay looked disgustedly at her brother.

'That is not the question.' Magdalena smiled at her son. 'The real question is – where's the woman can resist him?'

'You're the only one for me, Mom, you know that,' John-Francis grinned.

'We will say grace,' Veronica said loudly and stood. 'Bless us, O Lord,' she began to intone without waiting against the sound of chairs scraping back from the table, 'and these Thy gifts which, of Thy bounty, we are about to receive. Give us patience too, Lord, and return absent friends safely.' Into a small silence she delivered a sharp 'Amen' and sat.

Veronica was facing the door from the hallway, her back to the one window without a curtain. This overlooked a floodlit, formal garden with two rows of classical statuary, a long, columned pergola and high, evergreen hedging. It had expense and self-conscious style written all over it. It was also, Bridget thought, another possible resting place for Victor's casket.

'Thought I'd take a few days skiing next week,' Russell Segal, speaking for the first time, aimed his remark at no one in particular.

'Might come with you,' said John-Francis. 'Where're you headed?'

'Thought I'd try the backcountry—'

'Forget it' – Lindsay abandoned her soup – 'I'm not financing any more of your vacations, Russell. And you can forget it too, John-Francis. You're expected to be around for the reinvestment deal with—'

'Take it easy, Lindsay, I'll deal with the business end of this later,' Thomas was cool. 'In any event, I don't think skiing's going to be an option for a while to come. The weather service is talking avalanche hazards.'

'Sonny Bono won't be taking any more skiing trips.' Russell Segal laughed. 'Pity he had to go like that though, he was one of the good guys. Cher wouldn't have gotten anywhere without him—'

'He wasn't a good guy,' Lindsay snapped. 'He was a vulgar little man who did a good job of self-promotion.'

'He'd become a useful Congressman.' Russell sounded petulant. 'He was a Republican. I voted for him.'

'I rest my case,' said Lindsay.

'Your wife is quite right, Russell, about Congressman Bono,' Veronica Baldacci said impatiently. 'He was nothing but a showman. Married three times.' She paused. 'Marriage is until death.'

'It is in this family at any rate.' Magdalena, fingers in a frenzy, was reducing a bread roll to crumbs on her plate. 'Our guest will agree with that, won't you, Bridget?'

'It was in my case,' Bridget said.

'Your experience is quite typical, believe me,' said Magdalena.

'Sonny Bono voted against same sex marriages,' Thomas spoke quickly, 'very unCalifornian—'

'Was your marriage to my brother a happy one?' Magdalena, cutting him short, gave Bridget a direct look.

'Yes. Very.'

'You surprise me.' Magdalena, ignoring the soup, made a pyramid of the crumbed bread roll. 'He was such a moody youngster. Strange that he should be the one to have an apparently happy marriage.'

'People change. They grow up.'

Veronica tapped the floor with her stick and Magdalena, through tightened lips, muttered, 'I wish she wouldn't do that.' Bridget found herself wishing the same thing.

'We will have the next course,' Veronica Baldacci called.

Hugo Sweeney, who'd been standing just inside the door, moved silently on the soup bowls. He was deft and quick and full of a resentful energy as he wheeled the laden trolley from the room. He took with him the bowl laid for the seventh diner.

'I brought some of Victor's ashes with me,' Bridget said as the door closed behind him. 'I thought you might like to scatter them in the garden.' She gave a half-smile and shrug. 'Or maybe keep the casket somewhere . . . the library perhaps . . .'

Thomas coughed. Someone else sighed. Through the window, in the spotlit garden, Bridget thought she could see the beginnings of another snowfall. She watched and waited, silently, until Victor's sister at last broke the silence.

'I'm sure you meant well,' Magdalena said, 'and maybe things are done differently in Ireland. But since my mother hadn't seen her son for thirty-five years or more, I doubt she would care to have his ashes as a daily reminder of his desertion.'

'Do you feel the same?' Bridget asked.

'Yes,' Magdalena said, 'I feel the same.'

'No one in this family wishes to be reminded of the unhappy past,' Victor's mother's voice was harsh. 'You should not have presumed to bring my son's ashes here.'

'Maybe you could scatter them in the Bay?' Thomas, after an anxious look at his wife, spoke gently to Bridget. 'There are regular, daily boat trips and you might – '

'Thank you. I may just do that.' Bridget gave him a wry smile.

The man was well meaning. He might just be her letter writer. She broadened her smile. Thomas, looking uncomfortable, straightened in his chair.

'Ah, the trolley's back.' John-Francis gave a low whistle and rubbed his hands together. 'What further delights have you got for us tonight, Amy?'

'Chicken.' Amy dimpled and Hugo Sweeney snapped at her, sharklike, across the trolley. She began lifting dishes from the warming plate and giving them to Hugo.

Bridget's mother, herself a bad cook, had habitually told her offspring that hunger was good sauce. Bridget had never before appreciated the wisdom of the old saying. Amy's chicken was sawdust dry and broke apart like a piece of rotted timber at the touch of a fork. The sauce appeared to be a mixture of salt and cream. Bridget, alone at the table, ate with something like relish.

'I'll have to forego the pleasure of your chicken, Amy,' John-Francis, studying the food on his plate, sounded regretful. 'I have to leave.' He stood. 'My apologies, everyone. Night and the city calls.'

'Thank you for your time, John-Francis.' His grandmother was icy as he bent to kiss the top of her head, lightly.

'You get an early night now, Grandma.' His grandmother didn't return his grin. 'Great food,' he called to the watching Amy as he made his way to the door. To Bridget, as he passed, he said, 'Sorry I can't give you a ride back to your hotel. But maybe we'll do the city tour together before you leave.' He gave a small salute. 'You won't get a better guide.'

'You shouldn't have come here, Bridget.' Magdalena flattened the pyramid of bread crumbs as the dining-room door closed behind him. She was crying, fat tears making tracks through her make-up. She sipped her drink, dabbing at the tears with a finger. 'It's like a cage was opened when Victor died . . . you've come out of it to rake up the past, take what's ours—'

'You're tired, sweetheart,' Thomas interrupted her, 'maybe you should lie down.'

'I'm drunk,' Magdalena snarled, 'how else do you expect me to get through an occasion like this? Doesn't mean I'm not right though. You know I am. You all know I'm right.' She shrugged. 'We are looking at the beginning of the end.' She reached for her drink, missed it and knocked the glass over, emptying the contents into her dinner plate. 'Accidents will happen . . .' She shrugged.

'Get her a black coffee, Thomas,' Veronica Baldacci spoke with cold distaste, 'it might put an end to this maudlin nonsense.' Hugo Sweeney, with Amy in attendance, cleared away the dinner plates. Through the window behind her mother-in-law Bridget saw that snow had, indeed, begun to fall again, feathery flakes of it dancing in the lights and the wind. It looked very lovely, another world altogether from this one.

'Tell me something about this part of Seattle.' She looked down the table at Lindsay.

'Well, where to begin . . .' Lindsay raised her remarkable, almond-shaped eyes to the ceiling and thought for a minute before going on. 'We're pretty good on our history in Seattle.' She smiled. 'We're sort of separatists, I suppose, considered hick until we became fashionable and environmentally PC a few years ago. As for this neighbourhood . . . well, it wasn't always the upmarket area you drove through tonight. In its early days Madison Park was known as White Beach, something to do with the huge numbers of hookers populating the place. We're told it was as close as Seattle ever came to having its own Coney Island. There were amusement parks and horse racing and even, at one time, a ferris wheel.' She became thoughtful again. 'I think I would have liked it then.'

'More than you like today's Madison Park?' Bridget asked.

'Who can say? I'd have had a different history, been a different person, if I'd lived then.' She smiled again and shrugged. 'We'd all have been different.'

'True,' said Bridget. 'And is that life gone from here altogether? Have the hookers all gone out of business?'

'Who's to say?' Lindsay gave a short laugh. 'Things aren't always what they seem. You must know that.'

'I know that,' said Bridget.

Dessert had been served, an elaborate concoction of cream, ice-cream and fruit, and the mood in the room had become almost relaxed when the door from the hallway opened.

Bridget stared. The young woman coming through was tall, dark and, differences in style apart, could have been Anna's twin. Not an identical twin, there were too many subtle differences for that, but her double nevertheless in all sorts of ways. Her hair was the same burnt-almond brown, her eyebrows arched as Anna's did and her wide-spaced eyes were the same inky black. There were differences about her nose, which was longer, and her lips, which were painted a shade of mauve Anna would never have used and were thinner. Bridget had never seen Anna wear anything like the black sequinned top and second-skin black jeans this young woman was wearing either.

Her eyes searched the table and stopped at Bridget.

'You have to be the daughter-in-law,' she said. 'I've been waiting to meet you . . .'

'You need not have waited so long,' Lindsay indicated the table setting, 'you were expected to eat with us.'

'How kind. Someone should have told me. Well, I'm

here now.' She dropped into the empty chair. 'And how thoughtful! You've put me right opposite Bridget.' She reached a hand across the table. 'I'm Eleanor Munro. Has anyone explained who I am? Why I'm here?'

'You're obviously family,' Bridget, stretching over the table, found her fingers gripped tightly, 'since you're remarkably like my daughter Anna.'

Eleanor Munro sat back, shook her head, and began to laugh. No one joined in. Hugo, at a nod from Thomas, put a plate of dessert in front of her. Removing her unused cutlery he dropped it with a loud clatter to the floor.

'Sorry,' he said.

Eleanor Munro's hilarity came to a stop. 'Irony is always worth a laugh. Do you find irony funny, Bridget?'

'It depends. Why don't you try me?'

'The irony of this situation, Bridget, is that I come from what could be called bastard stock while your daughter is the progeny of the son who got away, and yet we're the only grandchildren who remotely resemble our grandaddy. Is that an irony or isn't it?

'It seems to fit the criteria,' said Bridget, 'but fill me in a bit more, please.'

Chapter Six

'Can't say I'm surprised nobody told you about me.' Eleanor Munro looked around the table. 'Everyone here's been wanting me to go since I got here, hoping I'd just disappear. Disappearing's a sort of way of life in this family.'

'We thought we'd let you speak for yourself.' Thomas nodded at the plate in front of Eleanor Munro. 'Dessert's good. Best part of the meal, in fact. Try it.'

'Thanks, but no thanks.' She pushed the plate aside impatiently, 'I'd prefer to talk. You got any cigarettes, Lindsay? I left mine in my room.'

'The room you are sleeping in does not belong to you,' Veronica Baldacci said icily, 'and I do not permit cigarette-smoking at the dinner table.'

'You'll have noticed, Bridget, that one of the more lovable things about this family is the hospitality factor.' Eleanor Munro poured herself a glass of wine. 'You might also have spotted a certain honesty about the past, a desire amongst the people gathered here to set the record straight. Lindsay, have you got a cigarette or not?'

'I need a cigarette too, Grandmother, so just try ignoring us.' Lindsay, shaking a couple of cigarettes from a packet, efficiently ignored her grandmother herself. Veronica Baldacci, face expressionless, signalled Hugo, who immediately placed ashtrays in front of the two younger women. He didn't quite bow as, a miniature sentinel, he took a standing position behind Veronica's chair.

'I don't know why you do it, you two, you know how much damage—' Russell Segal's plaintive plea was efficiently cut short by Lindsay.

'Oh, shut up, Russell,' her voice was low and furious. 'You don't understand anything about anything so just keep out of this.'

'Right. I'll do that.' Russell pushed his chair back from the table. No one tried to stop him as he left.

'Well, Thomas, you're the only guy left – you going to leave too?' Eleanor Munro's voice was mocking. 'Letting the women get on with things is the Baldacci way, after all.'

'Think I'll stay and hear what you've got to say.' Thomas was polite. 'I take it you've joined us for a purpose?'

'Too damn right I've joined you for a purpose.' Eleanor Munro grinned. 'I'm here to tell Bridget a few things she needs to be straighened out on. In public. I don't believe in secrets, as you know. A little straight talking's what's wanted around here.' She sighed and stretched her arms above her head. 'I think this little session could be very therapeutic for all of us.'

'An act of compassion on your part.' Magdalena held up and studied the contents of her glass. 'You're here to tear this family apart and for no other reason. You will cause terrible harm before you leave here. I know it.'

'A terrible harm has already been done, Magdalena, so it's a bit late for agonized histrionics. That's why you drink. You know too well what went on in this family—'

'I drink because I like it.' This time, Magdalena reached for the bottle and refilled her glass herself.

'What is it you want to tell me?' Bridget said. She felt lightheaded, expectant.

'Where to begin . . .' Anna's double smiled through a cloud of blue smoke. She seemed to be enjoying herself. 'Let me introduce myself, properly. I am the grandaughter Grandma Veronica didn't want to know about, the cousin my cousins didn't want to know, the niece whose existence Aunt Mags has been able to deny, along with everything else, with the help of her drug of choice. Of course, I'm not the only issue was ignored. Your son and daughter weren't exactly taken to the family bosom either, were they?' She stopped, slowly and deliberately filled her water glass.

'Anna and Fintan weren't ignored exactly.' Bridget smiled encouragingly. 'But I'd really like to hear your story.'

'You're right, of course, since there was a choice involved in their situation.' Eleanor Munro looked around the table and back at Bridget. 'Their father choose to put this family behind him, to keep his children away . . .' She took a drink of the water. Nobody spoke. 'My mother, on the other hand, needed help and support and looked for it all down the years and got none. She's dead now, just like Victor's dead, and I'm here to put a few things right, just like you are.'

'You've come here to destroy what has been a content and functioning family.' Veronica Baldacci, breaking the family's silence, was coldly formal.

'Content! Functioning!' Eleanor Munro shook her head, laughing. 'What we've got here is hardcore dysfunction.'

'I'm leaving. I really don't care to listen to another of this woman's paranoid performances.' Magdalena got awkwardly to her feet. 'She's trouble and you all know it. Someone should shut her up. Bridget doesn't need to hear this.'

She staggered once as she left the room. Her exit, Bridget thought, would have done justice to an ageing movie star.

'And then there were five,' Eleanor Munro said as the door closed. 'Anyone else want to leave before Bridget and me have our heart to heart?' She turned her dark eyes on each of the table's occupants in turn. 'Everyone else is willing to deal with a dismantling of the world of make-believe you've created around yourselves?'

'You're the one in this room who knows most about make-believe.' Lindsay snorted. 'You're the novelist, the one who makes things up for a living. Trouble with you, Eleanor, is that you don't know the difference between make-believe and reality. Sure, things happened in this family. That's the way it goes. Families are made up of people and people do things to one another.' She shrugged. 'Good and bad things.'

'My granddaughter is right but I would add to what she's said,' Veronica Baldacci's voice was low and Bridget had to strain to hear her. 'You've never been a part of a family, Eleanor, you have no awareness of the concept of give and take. Like your mother you prefer to plunder and tear apart.'

'Quite an impressive two-hander you and Lindsay have got going there.' Eleanor examined her nails, long and tapering and painted the same mauve as her lips. 'But a good performance does not a truthful one make.'

Thomas gave his small, throat-clearing cough. 'This is highly inappropriate,' he said.

'Everything about this family's inappropriate.' Eleanor Munro faced Bridget. 'The only way to give it to you is straight, Mrs Victor Baldacci. You'll have to forgive my blunt, New York manners.' She took a deep breath. 'I'm Frank Baldacci's granddaughter. Difference is, I don't, fortunately, have Veronica for a grandmother. Good old Veronica was Grandaddy Frank's wife but she was *not* his first love. Nor was she his last.' She hesitated. 'In some ways, she's to be pitied. She was twenty-two when she married Frank. He was eight years older and it was all arranged for them, a bringing together in the late nineteen thirties of two ambitious Catholic families, one Italian, the other Irish. Veronica may have been virginal, I don't know,' she gave Veronica a languid look which the old woman ignored, 'but Frank Baldacci

74

certainly wasn't. Fact is, Frank was about to become a father when they married though he didn't, of course, tell his bride-to-be about this. Honesty has never been a prime virtue in this family.'

'The baby was your mother?' Bridget asked.

'Right. The mother-to-be was Grace Munro, my grand-mother. She was sixteen years old and she'd already been Frank Baldacci's plaything for two years.'

When Eleanor stopped again Bridget waited for denials. They didn't come. Eleanor waited too, quietly turning her water glass round and round. She looked fragile and unreliable. She sipped at the water before going on.

'Grace was dirt poor, practically illiterate and besotted with Frank Baldacci. Frank was a man who was used to getting what he wanted and he got what he wanted then too. He wanted Grace and he wanted Veronica and he got them both.' She leaned back, unnervingly balancing the chair on its hind legs. 'He was a man who liked to make the most of opportunities and he used the fact that an hysterical Grace was threatening to make their affair public to strike a deal with his new bride.' The chair legs hit the ground with a thud as she sat forward. 'Veronica agreed to Frank's continuing to have my grandmother as his mistress and to an allowance for the child, my mother, Shelley Munro – she never did get her father's name. In return Grace stayed silent and Frank stayed out of jail—'

'Not what you'd call an ideal beginning to a marriage,' Bridget, feeling compelled to say something, interrupted. She needed the reassurance of her own voice, a few seconds to absorb what was being said. She felt sorry for Veronica but didn't dare look at her. Her feelings about Eleanor Munro was more confused.

'On the face of it, no. But Veronica wanted the marriage and she wanted Frank Baldacci and possession, after all, is nine tenths of the law. She probably reckoned that her charms, and the production of a son and heir, would firmly ensnare Frank and see his illiterate mistress off the scene.'

Hugo Sweeney, from his guardian position behind her chair, leaned over and spoke loudly to Veronica.

'Can I get you something?' He touched her arm and she shook him off impatiently. 'A nightcap?' He was persistent.

'Get me a bourbon,' Veronica said.

There was silence while he poured and brought her the drink.

'It's quite touching, the devotion Veronica gets from some men,' said Eleanor Munro. 'She never did get it from her husband, even if she did have him to herself at the end when no one else wanted him. But you didn't want him yourself then, did you Veronica?'

Veronica Baldacci gave no indication that she'd heard the question. She was looking quietly detached, eyes half closed, as she sipped her drink.

Thomas cleared his throat. 'You're talking about things which happened more than forty years ago, Eleanor. You weren't there. You're coming from the standpoint of your mother's hurt and a lot of second-hand information.' He glanced quickly at his mother-in-law. 'The fair thing would be to allow Veronica to take over now. Bridget's come a long way—'

'Bridget wouldn't be hearing a thing if it wasn't for me so don't give me shit about Veronica telling the family story.' Eleanor's face was contorted and paper white. She stopped then, lowering her voice, continued, 'And I wouldn't be here if it wasn't for Ted Morgan, would I, Veronica? Ted Morgan's the only reason I got through the front door.'

'You're quite right,' Veronica said calmly. 'I would never have allowed you into my home if you hadn't arrived with Ted. He's a good man but gullible. He made a terrible

76

mistake bringing you here. He knows it too and that is why he is not with us tonight.'

'Oh, for God's sake, why can't you ever face the truth,' Eleanor Munro was close to shouting. 'Ted's not here because he doesn't want to be!'

'You are an evil and misguided young woman,' Veronica suddenly and violently banged her cane on the floor, 'just as your mother was evil and misguided. You are the inevitable consequence of her delusions. I should never have listened to Ted. I should never have made you welcome in my home.' She took a deep breath and sat back in her chair, hands tightly clenching the top of her stick.

'You didn't make me welcome,' Eleanor spoke softly. 'I insisted and Ted facilitated. Everything that is now happening was inevitable. What goes around comes around. Once your son died and the past came knocking on your door you were going to have to open it, sooner or later.'

'I would like you tell me' – Bridget took a deep breath – 'what Victor's death has to do with all of this – with your being here – '

'Your husband, in dying, created chaos,' Eleanor Munro spread her hands in a hopeless gesture, 'but that comes at the end of my story. What you need to know first is that my grandmother Grace disappeared when my mother was only fourteen years old. A police investigation failed to find her but it did turn up the fact that Frank Baldacci was the father of her child. There were rumours that Veronica had had a hand in her disappearance.'

Thomas tapped the side of his glass with a spoon. The sudden sound was sharp and as effective as a rifle shot. 'You are causing terrible hurt to an old woman.' He was curt. 'If you feel you must do this then stick to the facts.'

'The facts are more than enough.' Eleanor agreed. 'And they show that nothing was proven against Veronica. But, and this *is* a fact, she and Frank managed a pretty good damage limitation job by giving my mother a home in this house, bringing in an older sister for Magdalena and Victor. Kindness itself.' She stubbed out her cigarette. 'Here's another fact; my mother was taken in to live here but never given the Baldacci name. And another: one year after my mother came to live in this house Frank Baldacci raped her. His abuse of her went on for six years until, one day when she was twenty-one years old, she too disappeared.'

Bridget was feeling slightly sick. So, it seemed, was Veronica, swaying slightly in her chair and shaking her head.

'It is NOT a fact that my husband raped her.'

Hugo Sweeney put a steadying hand on her shoulder as she went on.

'Frank was too kind to your mother, to Shelley Munro. She was a manipulative young woman. Just as you are.'

Eleanor Munro, shrugged dismissively.

'There are a few more facts, Veronica, and you know it. You know too that they bear out my version of events. One of them is that Frank Baldacci hired a private detective who found my mother. She was living in New York and in a terrible state. Frank then turned up and tried to persuade her to come back to Seattle. She didn't go with him. She told me herself once, when she was in a bad way, that she was afraid of him, that she'd always been afraid of him and that her fear had made everything that had happened possible.' There was a long pause while Eleanor Munro appeared to gather her thoughts. 'Frank left. He didn't give her as much as a cent out of the Baldacci fortune. She was twenty-one years old, she was his daughter and had been used by him for sex and he left her there, friendless and without money.'

'He was not a well man,' Veronica spoke in a dull, flat voice. 'He had a stroke soon after getting home. He remained paralysed until he died.'

'And you had the debauched, incestuous bastard all to

78

yourself at last,' Eleanor Munro said harshly. 'Only he wasn't much good to you then, was he? But you got round that, Veronica, didn't you?'

She stabbed the air with an accusing finger, two spots of colour flaming high on her cheeks. 'You came into your own then, didn't you? Didn't you?'

Her voice cracked and she dropped her head into her hands. She sat there, her fingers agitatedly crawling at her hairline while she took deep, gasping breaths. Bridget wanted to go to her but couldn't. It was all she could do to sit, mouth dry and limbs leaden, as she tried to take in what she'd heard. She couldn't bring herself to look at any of the others at the table either.

Their silence was shocking, and it was frightening.

Even if only some of this young woman's claims were true then Victor would have known. This awful story was part, or maybe all, of what he'd grown up with. And, appalling as it was, she had to hear it all.

When Eleanor Munro at last lifted her head she spoke directly to Bridget. She was dry eyed and haggard-looking. 'When her husband became paralysed Veronica took over the business. She could have stepped back and let the board run things but she didn't choose to do that. She moved into the boardroom and took over. Nothing wrong with that – except that she took over the lives of everyone in the family too. She's been running them ever since.'

Bridget, afraid suddenly that she might not learn what she needed to know, found her voice.

'Did my husband know about . . . all of this when he was growing up?' She looked from Eleanor Munro to Veronica Baldacci to Thomas Carter. 'Did Magdalena?'

'You have been given a distorted version of how things were.' Veronica Baldacci was cold and in control of herself again. 'My son, as a child and a young man, was part of a caring family. As was Magdalena.'

79

'Bullshit,' said Eleanor Munro. 'They knew, both of them, that they were part of a diseased family. Look at Magdalena, for God's sake – a life devoted to obliterating everything with drink. Victor took his own way out and left it all behind, for good. We're all adults round this table, Veronica. Spare us the fairy tales.'

'You have done what you joined us to do.' Veronica Baldacci rose slowly from her chair. 'You have presented the past to my dead son's wife in a manner which is entirely destructive. I will not dignify it with denials, or explanations. She can believe, or disbelieve, as she sees fit.'

It was clear she expected everyone else to stand too. Thomas did so but Lindsay, her eyes on Eleanor, stayed sitting. Bridget didn't move either.

'If that's the lot, then I'll start clearing away.' Hugo Sweeney moved to the table.

Eleanor Munro spoke through her teeth. 'Why don't you clear yourself out of here and let us finish what is family business, and none of yours?'

'Hugo knows this family in a way you never could,' Veronica Baldacci's voice was low and harsh.

'I'll bet he does.' Eleanor gave a sharp laugh. 'I'll bet old Hugo understands exactly what's good for him. So do I and I'm here to get what my mother didn't get from this family. She asked you people for help, but you ignored her letters, Veronica, you didn't even reply to her. She was blood of this family, half-sister to Magdalena and Victor, and you just didn't want to know.'

'My children had to make their own way in life,' said Veronica, 'they didn't get handouts. They went into the company and earned what they got. Why should she have been any different?'

Eleanor stared. 'You knew she couldn't come back here. You people destroyed her—' She stopped, shaking her head

80

as if clearing it. 'Ted was right. He said the Baldacci's operated on a moral terrain that was all their own.'

'Don't bring Ted Morgan into this,' Veronica's voice had a shrill edge, but her face was as coldly formal as ever. 'What Ted has to say he will say to me himself, when he gets back.'

'He's not coming back, Veronica. Ted's gone. He couldn't take it any more. He didn't want to come in the first place. I made him come, but the fact is I should never have brought him here.'

'You're a liar. Ted Morgan came back to Seattle, and to this house, because he wanted to.' Veronica took a breath. 'He had unfinished business to attend to.'

'Where is he now then? Where is Ted tonight?'

'He is his own man. He will be back when he is ready. He has things to think about.'

'Jesus Christ, Veronica, did you always fool yourself like this? Ted's gone. I wish he wasn't,' Eleanor shrugged, the black sequinned top catching the light across her shoulders, 'but that's how it is.'

For a moment she seemed to Bridget to be frighteningly vulnerable, bereft looking. Then the expression was gone.

Veronica turned her back on the room and walked to the uncurtained window. The snow was falling still in light, gentle swirls. 'We were never in any doubt, Miss Munro, but that money was what you came here for.' She paused. 'An arrangement will be made.'

'You're damn right an arrangement will be made. But not without discussing it with me.'

'An arrangement will be made,' Veronica repeated.

'There are two of us now. Bridget wants to see right done too. We're not afraid of you people. We're together on this—'

'Stop it.' Bridget stood up.

Her heart was uncomfortably close to her mouth but

she'd come here on her own account and wasn't going to be a part of someone else's fight. 'I don't know what you think we're together on, Eleanor. All I want is to know why Victor left home,' she spoke to her mother-in-law's rigid back, 'and why he never came back.'

Eleanor Munro looked disbelieving. 'You want a hell of a lot more than that. You want what's due to Victor Baldacci's children. These people know that's why you're here. We just have to stick together and you'll—'

'You're wrong,' Bridget managed to keep her voice even. 'We're here for different reasons.'

She began counting, slowly, backwards from ten. It was an old trick, used when she felt panic rising. It usually worked. By the time she got to five she was breathing more evenly.

'But I'm here because you're here.' Eleanor Munro, rubbing her eyes, smudged her mascara. 'When I heard you were coming to Seattle it seemed so right to me, as if the day of reckoning had come and the wronged were to be avenged . . .'

'I'm sorry you thought that.' Bridget meant it. 'But our experiences are different. I don't feel aggrieved in the way you do.'

'This is all wrong.' Eleanor Munro was shaking, the streaked mascara ghoulish against the deathly white of her face. 'We were meant to work together on this thing, you and I. I know it. I feel it. When Ted went, I thought I would have you. I can't be alone. There's safety in numbers . . .' She was gabbling, pouring herself another glass of water, spilling it as she poured and again as she lifted it to her mouth.

'You're pathetic.' Lindsay disdainfully folded her napkin. 'I suggest you go to bed, sleep off whatever it is you're on.'

'And you're so fucking superior. Why don't you try living in the real world?' Eleanor Munro's voice rose. 'You live in this nest of vipers, sheltered by them, fed by them, doing their dirty work for them—' She gave a loud, gulping sob and all at once she was weeping, her head in her hands, her thin frame convulsing as she cried great, hacking tears.

'And this is the creature we have been giving credence to.' Veronica left the window and walked slowly down the room, past the weeping Eleanor to the door. 'She is completely unreliable, just as her mother was. Goodnight, Bridget. We will meet again.' She patted her perfect hair, fingers like a set of bleached bones scattered with rings. 'Thomas, Lindsay – I am leaving the foolish Miss Munro in your hands. See that Bridget gets safely back to her hotel too.'

Hugo Sweeney opened the door, then slipped through it after her.

The sobbing went on, Eleanor's head still buried in her hands, black hair veiling her face. Thomas Carter went to her.

'I'll take you to your room. You'll feel better about things in the morning.'

He put an arm round her shoulders and eased her out of the chair. She didn't resist. Standing, she was almost as tall as he was. She took her hands from her face and, sobs subsiding, roughly rubbed at her cheeks with a table napkin.

'I wish Ted were here,' she sounded as forlorn as she looked. 'He shouldn't have left me.' She looked directly at Bridget. 'I'm scared on my own,' she said.

'There's nothing for you to be scared of.' Thomas guided her gently towards the door. 'You just need some rest.'

In the open door she slipped from under his arm and turned, eyes finding Bridget's again. 'It would be better if you stayed here,' she said, 'in this house.'

'I like my hotel.' Bridget gave her a reassuring smile.

'I wasn't thinking about you. I was thinking about me.'

Thomas Carter, with a wry look Bridget's way, took Eleanor's arm and closed the door behind them.

'Looks like the show's over for the night.' Lindsay grimaced at her dessert plate and lit a cigarette. 'I'll give you a ride back to your hotel when you're ready.'

The traffic was a trickle at that time of night. The snow had turned to rain which was blowing sheet-like in the teeth of a growing wind.

'An inauspicious introduction to the family.' Lindsay drove fast. 'But you can't have been expecting to find the Brady Bunch.'

'Victor gave very few clues for me to build on.' Bridget hesitated. 'How true is Eleanor Munro's version of the family story?'

'All depends how you look at it.'

Bridget felt a surge of irritation. Was anybody in this family capable of a straight answer? 'How do you look at it?'

'I wasn't around for any of the stuff she was talking about,' Lindsay said, 'but the outline's true enough. My grandfather died after a stroke. Eleanor's mother was my grandfather's love child and lived with the family for a few years after her mother took off. The rest is a question of perspective. Truth is never simple.'

'Who is Ted Morgan?'

'He was a nurse engaged by my grandmother to care for my grandfather when he was dying. I'm told by my mother, and grandmother, that he was a kind man and a great help to everyone during bad times. He turned up with Eleanor the day before Christmas.' It was raining hard as they crossed the bridge, the windscreen wipers beating frantically. Lindsay didn't slow down. 'He took off at New Year without saying where he was going. Grandmother would like him to come back. I suppose he was someone to talk to about grandfather.'

It was odd, Bridget thought, the way people who became caught up with the Baldacci family disappeared without saying where they were going. Eleanor Munro had been right about that at least.

In her hotel bedroom she crawled under the duvet, burying her head under the pillow for good measure. She decided against phoning home. She told herself it was because she was too tired but knew it was because she didn't know how to tell Anna, or Fintan, what she'd learned about their father's family.

She lay for most of the night without sleeping. In the small hours of the morning, with distant hotel sounds indicating another day beginning, she slept and had a dream in which Eleanor Munro and Anna together scattered Victor's ashes at the feet of broken, classical statues.

A hammering on the bedroom door at 8 a.m. took a while to waken her. It took a while too to separate the sound of Eleanor Munro's voice calling to her from the Eleanor in her dream.

'Open the door, Bridget.' The hammering sounded like a fist. 'I have to talk to you. Please open the door . . .'

Chapter Seven

The Eleanor Munro who pushed her way through the door was urgent and purposeful. She stood in the middle of the room with her hands in the pockets of a long, black coat.

'God, this is small. Didn't you want to stay in your husband's old home?'

'I wasn't invited,' Bridget said crossly, 'and you weren't invited here this morning either. I haven't had a lot of sleep.'

Now that she was fully awake she felt terrible. She'd had too much wine the night before and a heavy, dull hangover wasn't helping her mood. A sudden, miserable loneliness filled with an ache for Victor made her wish she could somehow hold his hand and tell him she was beginning to see and to understand.

But there was only the casket, out of the drawer and sitting on the desk. Seeing it gave her some comfort.

'I don't feel great,' she admitted.

'Sorry,' Eleanor Munro didn't look it, 'but we have to talk.' She picked up the casket with Victor's ashes. 'Cute. What's in it?'

'My husband's ashes.'

'Baldaccis not interested, huh? I could have told you that. They don't want his ashes and they didn't want you to come here either.' She put the casket down again, gently. 'Look, Bridget, I want you to understand that all of that stuff last night was me trying to force the issue, to get Veronica and Magdalena to open up about what happened in the past. I've been staying in that house since a couple of days after Christmas and last night was the first time I'd spent more than a half hour with any of them. You and me have got to team up, get things sorted.'

'We don't have to do anything of the sort. We're coming from different angles at this thing.' Bridget sat at the dressing table and began brushing her hair. Eleanor Munro remained standing, kept her hands in her pockets. 'My situation really is different to yours.' Bridget's face in the mirror looked to her like that of a stranger, belonging to a woman too uncertain to be the person she knew herself to be.

'You're wrong. You couldn't be more wrong.'

Eleanor Munro caught and held Bridget's gaze in the mirror. Everything about her was black: the scarf under the coat was black and so were her boots, her black hair was loose to her shoulders and the likeness to a vulnerable witch was even more pronounced than the night before. 'We're both in the same situation here. They don't want either of us around. Alone we're not safe, but by sticking together we give each other protection, even up the odds—'

'Stop, Eleanor, just please shut up. I want you to understand something.' Bridget turned round in the chair. 'Sit down,' she commanded, 'on the bed will do.'

Eleanor Munro looked mulish for a minute, then shrugged and sat on her hands on the bed. 'So far I've only heard your version of events,' Bridget said. 'I want to hear both sides. I want to know Victor's story.' She paused. 'In fact Victor's story is all I *really* want to know. I understand why your grandmother disappearing is a big thing in your life. But that was more than forty years ago and, apart from Veronica, the people involved are all dead. It's a different—'

'Nothing's different, nothing's changed.' Eleanor Munro

closed her eyes and began to rock back and forth. A deep furrow ran between her eyebrows and her voice rasped edgily. 'The poison was never got rid of, it's still there, infecting everything that happens, a disease in all of them.' She opened her eyes and, before Bridget could say anything, grabbed one of her hands and held it with a neurotic strength. 'You think I'm over the top. Everyone does. You think because I'm a writer then I'm inventing this stuff, seeing bodies where there are none. Well, you're wrong. You're wrong, wrong, wrong.' She dropped Bridget's hand and threw herself back on the bed. With her eyes fixed on the ceiling she said, 'I can't convince you, but you'll see soon enough that I'm right. There's danger here for both of us. These people are not going to give up anything, their money or their secrets, without a fight. It won't be clean.' She sat up. 'And it certainly won't be played by any of the normal rules.'

'You may be right.' Bridget looked at her thoughtfully. 'But as you say yourself, I'll see soon enough. Why don't we leave it at that and go and get some breakfast?'

'If that's what it takes to get you to listen. We don't have for ever, this is not Disneyland you've wandered into. Don't you realize what you're into here?'

'I'm beginning to,' said Bridget.

The Seattle streets, that bright morning, were sharply alive to a new day. The snow clouds had moved on, no doubt to retrench, and the skies above the tall buildings were a cold blue. Walking with Eleanor Munro passing coffee houses in search of the perfect brew, Bridget began to feel better. At intersections, when she looked downhill, she could see the waterfront and further out the waters of Puget Sound, chillingly lovely and pure.

It felt, for that while, like a good place to be.

'He never told me about any of this,' said Bridget.

'Your husband? He didn't talk to you about Seattle?'

Eleanor Munro hunched into her coat. Her face in the daylight was a blanched white. Her morning lipstick was a deep, dark red. 'Can't say I blame him. Hype and a couple of films and an eco-friendly reputation don't make a city out of a hick town. Don't make city people out of backpackers either. All that water scares me. So do the mountains. They're too close, right on top of the place. I'm out of here as soon as I get what I came for . . .' She stopped in front of a set of smoky, curved glass windows, 'I know this place. It's good.'

She was right. Bridget knew as soon as they stepped inside that they were in more than just a coffee house. The air had a spice-filled welcome and there was an open fire, wicker armchairs, a scattering of morning newspapers and a gentle conviviality. She ordered herself a caffè latte and a helping of cinnamon and raisin focaccio. Eleanor Munro went for an espresso Americano.

'Don't you know anything about cholesterol?' Eleanor eyed Bridget curiously as she bit into the focaccio.

'I know about cholesterol all right. It was too much of it killed my husband.'

'What was he like?'

'He was a good man,' said Bridget and thought that, as an epitaph, this was perfect. Victor had been a good man, in every sense.

'He was entitled. His children are entitled—'

Bridget cut her short. 'Entitled to what?' she demanded.

'A share in the Baldacci millions.' Eleanor had taken off her coat and was sitting in a thin, black wool sweater and skirt in one of the wicker chairs. Her knees were jagged points from which she dangled her hands as she leaned forward.

'Inheritance rights aren't as simple as that,' Bridget said. 'Victor, in effect, disinherited himself when he abandoned his family. He did nothing to help accumulate those millions.

89

That's the way the law will see it, though I'm certainly not going to enter into battle about it.'

'Bullshit. Bullshit to him being disinherited and bullshit to you having to go to law about it. Once you establish the truth of why he left home and stayed away, you have them over a barrel. All you have to do—'

'Oh, shut up, Eleanor,' Bridget said tiredly. 'You go ahead and put the Baldaccis over a barrel and get whatever it is you want. And good luck to you. Just leave me out of it.'

'God, you're so fucking self-righteous.' Eleanor Munro ordered a second coffee for herself. She didn't order for Bridget. 'You're making a big mistake if you think just poking into the past and their secrets will let you off the hook. There's something scary and evil about that family. Ted came up against it. That's why he's gone. I know it is.'

'Tell me more about Ted Morgan,' Bridget said.

'Ted knows about the Baldaccis, knows a lot of stuff they'd prefer he didn't know.'

'Like what?' Bridget said.

'Like he knows about my mother, and the raw deal she got, like he knows about your husband and why he left—'

'Why?' Bridget, cutting in, held her breath.

'I don't know. He never told me. He wouldn't.' She paused. 'Just refused to. But he knows all right. Look, here's the story on Ted.' She took out a packet of cigarettes, extracted one, looked around, twirled it unlit between her fingers, sighed and put it away again. 'Don't want any trouble in eco-friendly land. Right. Ted. He nursed Frank Baldacci when he was dying—'

'So you said, last night.' Bridget was impatient.

'He's one of the good guys, which didn't stop him getting to know the family real well. Inevitable, really, given that he was around the family big time. Night and day, in fact. It took Frank Baldacci a couple of years to die. My mother had already left but Frank knew all about her. He *was* around for Victor's departure from hearth and home, so he knows what that was about too. After Frank died Ted went to live in New York.' She pulled a wry face. 'Funny how everyone puts as much distance as they can between themselves and the Baldaccis when they leave, isn't it? Victor, my mother, Ted – none of them exactly went to Oregon or anywhere close, did they?'

'No, they didn't. Go on.'

'Anyhow, in New York, Ted got in touch with my mother. He said what had happened wasn't right. He was a bit of a loner but he looked out for us, my mother and me, all down the years. He encouraged my mother to keep in contact with Veronica Baldacci; it was because of Ted that my mother asked her for help from time to time – help with medical expenses, with my education, she even asked for money for food, once. None of it ever came through.' She lowered her head so that her hair fell forward, covering her face. 'When my mother died Ted was there for me. He's been a sort of father and grandfather.'

'When did your mother die?'

'A little over a year ago. She overdosed. It wasn't the first time but that time it worked.'

Eleanor Munro raised her head and shook her hair back from her face. Her eyes were a hard, shining black, and unblinking.

'I'm sorry. So very sorry . . .' Bridget thought about offering Eleanor the comfort of a hug. But her grief was an enraged, bitter, off-putting thing.

'Ted kept in touch by reading the *Seattle Post-Intelligencer*,' Eleanor Munro went on slowly, as if putting order on events as she spoke them aloud, 'and there was a piece in there about your husband's death. Fluke really. Some journalist picked it up and did a paragraph along the 'prominent family member dies abroad' lines. Ted, being Ted, wrote Veronica a letter of sympathy. She wrote back and told him

91

you were coming out to Seattle. That was when I decided to come too. I persuaded Ted to come with me. He didn't want to and I suppose that's why he's bailed out. I don't blame him. Veronica was all over him – wouldn't leave him alone. I don't know whether she was talking about the past or telling him to forget it. All I know is that he left the house more than a week ago. He phoned me, once, told me where he was, said he didn't want me worrying and that he'd be going back to New York when he'd sorted a few things out. But when I got down there, to the hostel he was staying in, he'd left there too.'

'And Veronica thinks he's coming back?'

'Yup. But he won't. I know Ted.' The anger in Eleanor Munro had wilted and her thin face looked in momentary desolation at Bridget. 'He says the past should be atoned for but not lived in.'

'He's not far wrong,' said Bridget.

Silently, in a mood of brief companionship, they watched through the windows as the glory of the early morning died in fast, low rain clouds.

'Tell me about the Baldacci millions,' said Bridget as the first rain drops fell. 'How'd they make them?'

'Why? You changing your mind about . . .?'

'No, Eleanor. Just curious.'

'I can tell you what's up front, in the public domain so to speak. They've built up a lot of real estate over the years but the front-line business is a financial outfit called Ulti-mate. Its main line of interest is insurance and it operates in property, life, health and business cover. The financial side has investment and property subsidiaries. Veronica's still the president – she took over the lot when Frank had his stroke and is not about to hand over until death makes that decision for her. Thomas Carter is the senior vice-president and Magdalena is on the board. John-Francis is on the board too and looks after some accounts. Lindsay, who's real keen, is president of Ultimate Properties. The revenue last year was sixty-three point one million dollars. Profit was three point nine million. Those are the basic facts and they're a matter of public record, which is how I got hold of them.'

'Impressive. Sounds like a lot of hard work has gone into Ultimate over the years.' Bridget all at once didn't want to hear any more. 'I'm going to buy an umbrella.'

She stood up. She didn't add the word alone, but on her own was what she wanted to be. Information, bitterness, pain, they were all coming at her too fast. She'd lost Victor somewhere in the middle of it all, couldn't visualize or feel the young man he must have been when he was at the centre of all she was hearing.

Eleanor got to her feet eagerly. 'I'll come with you,' she said.

The coffee and cinnamon smells followed them up the street to the drugstore selling umbrellas and on to the hotel. It's the low cloud, Bridget thought, it compresses everything, even smells. Makes everything more intense. She needed to get away from it all, out on to the bay or up a mountain to see and make sense of what she was learning about Victor's family.

'They don't even sell my books in this town,' Eleanor said as they passed a bookshop.

'What sort of books do you write?' said Bridget.

'Novels filled with romance and sex.' Eleanor's sudden smile was wide and wry. 'Camilla Kidman's my writing name and I'm big in the bodice-ripping game. It's a living. Ever heard of me?'

'No. But I'll look out—'

'I'm going to write poetry when I get my inheritance from the Baldaccis. You could buy your son and daughter the freedom to do what they want to if you—'

'Enough, Elenor,' said Bridget.

At the entrance to the hotel, without thinking and

93

because all at once the idea seemed so very plausible, she said to Eleanor 'Did you send a letter to me at the hotel?' She was half smiling and very watchful as she asked.

'I only write when I'm paid to.'

'That's a no?'

'Absolutely. But now I'm curious.' Eleanor pushed through the door and held it open for Bridget. She looked perplexed. 'Someone wrote you here and didn't sign their name?'

'That's right.' Bridget followed her in and together they climbed the flight of steps up to the lobby, Bridget worrying that Eleanor intended sticking with her for the whole day. 'It was delivered by hand.'

She stopped. She was inclined to believe that Eleanor wasn't responsible and was feeling a perverse loyalty to whomever had written the letter. 'It's not important,' she said.

'Mmm,' Eleanor waited, frowning, as Bridget collected her room key. 'Why'd you bring it up then? It must have meant something. What did it say?'

'Not a lot. It welcomed me to Seattle,' Bridget lied, 'told me to enjoy my trip.'

'And that was it?' Eleanor Munro looked sceptical. 'Look,' she spoke with sudden energy, 'you're going to have to regard everything that happens to you in Seattle as important, Bridget. Everything. You've got to remember that.' Her eyes had the staring, manic look of the night before. 'Promise me you'll be careful, keep yourself alert to everything that goes on around you.' She clutched at Bridget's arm. 'Promise me.'

'I'll be careful, but on one condition.' Bridget prised Eleanor Munro's fingers from her arm. 'I want you to promise you'll be careful too.'

She had no idea why she said this, nor why she waited so anxiously for the younger woman's reply. But wait she did, holding her hand until Eleanor nodded impatiently, and said yes, of course she'd be on her guard, she always was. Living in New York did that to you.

Bridget held up the key to her room. 'I'm going back to bed. I really didn't sleep last night.'

'I'll call you later.'

'Make it much later,' Bridget warned.

She was aware of being watched, of a pair of eyes on her back, as she headed for the lift. Convinced it was Eleanor she didn't turn. She pressed the call button and was resolutely facing the lift door when a finger tapped her on the shoulder.

'My, but you're the early bird.'

Magdalena Baldacci was wrapped in creamy-coloured cashmere and wore a fox-fur hat. She ignored Eleanor Munro, who'd followed and was standing just behind her. 'I've been hanging around here for an hour or more waiting for you.'

'If I'd known you were coming . . .' Bridget muttered, visions of bed and sleep disappearing in the face of the woman's determined, and quite sober, expression.

'I'll take you for a ride, show you a bit of the city. Perhaps you'd like to see the Space Needle?'

'Not just now.' Bridget was firm. 'I was planning a few hours rest. Later, perhaps?'

'Later's impossible.' Magdalena was petulant and glacial. 'I need to talk to you.' Her eyes assessed the lobby.

'Can't it wait?' Bridget asked but knew she herself couldn't wait. Magdalena Baldacci was here for a reason and she wanted to know what it was.

'Is there a bar in this place?'

'There's a bar down there.' Eleanor Munro stepped forward, indicating a flight of descending steps to their left. 'I found it earlier. I'll take you.'

'What I have to say concerns Bridget.' Magdalena's curt

tone became icy. 'What a busy early morning person you are today too, Eleanor. Up and gone before my poor mother had even woken for the day. Thank you for telling us where the bar is. We'll find it ourselves.'

'You're not going to get rid of me that easily.' Eleanor shook her head. 'Bridget and me have agreed to stick together, share our experiences while we're in Seattle.' She stood beside Bridget and took her arm. 'The bar's one of those dark, aspiring-to-be-intimate joints.'

Bridget allowed herself to be led by Eleanor Munro while Magdalena, lips compressed and controlled fury drawing the rest of her face into tight lines, fell into step beside them.

The bar was a low, oval-shaped room with no windows and dull roseate lighting giving it an uninviting, under-ground look. Apart from a couple of argumentative men at a table against a wall there were no customers. The barman, tall and languid and blond, looked at them wearily as they took stools at the bar – Magdalena's idea.

'What'll it be?' He managed not to focus on any of them.

'I'll have a gin Martini.' Magdalena's coat fell open as she crossed her legs. Clad in silvery opaque stockings and dark court shoes they, and Magdalena, looked very at home on the bar stool. She kept the hat on her head.

The barman waited with exaggerated patience for Bridget and Eleanor to place their orders.

'Glass of water, please.' Bridget heard the primness of her voice and coughed. 'With ice.'

'I'll have water, no ice.' Eleanor said and the barman stiffened, looking as if he would argue with this. Then he shrugged, turned and walked down the bar.

'Do you think he's actually getting us the drinks?' Bridget asked.

'He'd better be.' Magdalena drummed her fingers on the bar top and tapped a foot against the stool. If she'd made an announcement it couldn't have been more clear that she needed this drink.

'What did you want to see me about?' Bridget was gentler with her than she'd been in the lobby, but not a lot.

'My mother has given some thought about how we might, as a family, acknowledge Victor's death.' Magdalena's smile was for Bridget alone. 'A case of her conscience rearing its head once she'd met you. You weren't a real person to her until then.' She paused and delicately cleared her throat. 'Contrary to appearances, and even to what she may have said to you, Victor's death really knocked her out.'

'She's quite a performer then,' said Bridget.

The barman brought their drinks and Magdalena paid while Eleanor lit a cigarette and dribbled smoke down her nose.

'Mother feels that a memorial Mass is needed. It's been arranged for two days from now, in Our Lady of Lourdes, a parish church she's got a particular affection for—'

'A quiet church, is it? In another part of town? As far from Madison Park as she can get, is it?' Eleanor, between questions, took quick puffs.

'It's a church my mother has always supported, as a matter of fact,' Magdalena spoke to Bridget. 'She knows the priest there and he'll do it at short notice. Mother feels that if we do the Mass as a family you can go back to Ireland feeling better about things.'

'So this is for me?' Bridget looked sceptical.

'It's for all of us.' Magdalena met her gaze over the rim of her glass.

'It's a way of getting Bridget on side, showing her what a decent family this really is.' Eleanor Munro slipped from the stool and stood facing Magdalena. 'It's my guess you've got a story lined up to tell her about why Victor left.' Her voice rose. The men at the table stopped talking and looked up, the barman raised an eyebrow. 'It's all about divide and conquer, isn't it?' She stabbed with her finger at Magdalena. 'All about getting Bridget out of here before she finds out too much, in the way that Ted Morgan was persuaded to go—'

'You really are a crazy woman, Eleanor, you know that?' Magdalena signalled the barman, who came at a trot, his eyes fixed on Eleanor. 'I bet you believe in every conspiracy theory there is, like every other New York whacko.'

She indicated to the barman that he should bring her another drink.

'Crazy is drinking the way you do.' Eleanor became quieter. 'Crazy is convincing yourself lies are the truth. Don't talk to me about crazy, Magadalena.'

Magadalena, head to one side, examined her face in the mirror behind the bar. 'You don't have to come to the Mass, Eleanor. The invitation is for Bridget.' She spoke to her reflection in the mirror. 'To be honest, we'd probably have ignored Victor's death if Bridget hadn't come visiting. But she did and it's good that we're doing this thing. Good for everyone. Mother hopes, we all hope, that the Mass will bring you peace, Bridget.'

'Preferably the day after the Mass?' Eleanor slammed her empty glass onto the counter. It cracked and lay there in three pieces.

'New York manners?' Magdalena raised an eyebrow, 'or simply the way your mother taught you to behave in bars?'

'My mother, compared to you lot, was Mother fucking Theresa.' Eleanor's face was flushed. 'A church ceremony won't change anything. Not a goddamn thing. And Bridget knows that too.' She spoke through barely moving lips. 'The edifice is crumbling, Magdalena, it's all coming apart.'

Magdalena looked around the bar and shivered. 'I really don't know, Bridget, how you can stay in a place like this.'

'I'm not staying in the bar,' Bridget said.

Victor's sister slipped with a practised elegance from the stool. Her eyes were glazed and too steady and Bridget wondered how many drinks she'd had before arriving at the bar.

'A car will collect you at nine fifteen day after tomorrow,' Magdalena said.

Chapter Eight

Bridget went shopping the following day for Victor's memorial Mass.

In Nordstrom – the slogan 'I'd rather be shopping at Nordstrom' was pasted on every other car in town – she bought herself a coat which matched her hair and a chenille jumper in ochre. She decided against a hat. She'd never worn one while Victor was alive and saw little point in covering her head to celebrate his death. Let the Baldaccis do the hat wearing today. She had no doubt that they would.

The Baldaccis wore black, every shade of it, and some of them wore hats. Veronica, when she arrived in a limousine with Hugo Sweeney to take Bridget to the church, was regal and waxwork-like in draped, jet-black lace. Hugo Sweeney sat beside her in grey-black, a pair of ebony leather gloves across his knees. Folded between them on the seat there was an animate-looking sable coat.

Bridget climbed in and sat with her back to the driver, facing them. They seemed very far away.

'Very roomy car.'

She sat back as they moved smoothly into the traffic. She hadn't spoken to a Baldacci in two days. She'd been glad not to. Eleanor Munro hadn't been in touch either and about this she felt more equivocal.

She'd done the tourist thing for a part of the time, from the top of the 605-foot-high Space Needle (inherited from the 1962 World's Fair) to the underground tour of the original Seattle, and found that the city had a relaxed, nicely diffident sense of itself.

But all the time she'd been haunted by the young Victor, by images of him growing up in a family where incest and cruelty and power games were the everyday way of doing things. If all that Eleanor Munro said was true he was a survival miracle.

Generous, kind, dutiful; he'd been a miracle if only half of it was true.

In bed at night the ache for him got worse and she wondered if it was in spite of all that had happened to him, or because of it, that he'd been able to turn the world on its head when he'd loved her, for hours. On one of the nights she had wept for a long time for everything she hadn't been able to share with him, for everything he hadn't been able to tell her.

She had come to understand something else too, or thought she did. She could see now how grief for her mother's life had made Eleanor Munro come as a terrorist among the Baldaccis.

'I hope your hotel room is adequate. Have you been sleeping well?'

Beneath the black lace of her mantilla Veronica's lips barely moved. She seemed tired, to have lost some of the energy of two days before. Hugo Sweeney, staring out the window, said nothing.

'My room is fine and, yes, I sleep well.'

Bridget lied, knowing it was expected of her. Veronica's question was a polite formula, not an expression of interest.

'The sleep of the just.' Veronica's face went through the motions of a smile.

'The exhausted, more like,' said Bridget. 'I've done a lot

of sightseeing in the last couple of days. Places like Pike Market, the Space Needle, Pioneer . . .'

'What energy.' Veronica yawned behind a black, leather-gloved hand. 'I've almost forgotten those places existed. One's life becomes circumscribed as one gets older, one inhabits an ever-decreasing space.'

'That's a choice, surely,' said Bridget.

'Of course it is. I didn't mean to open a debate.' Veronica, courtesies at an end, waved a silencing hand. Hugo Sweeney hadn't moved.

'Good morning, Hugo,' said Bridget.

'Good morning.' He didn't turn from the window. 'Not a bad day for the occasion that's in it.'

It was a bright day with clouds on the horizon. Suitable, as Hugo had said, for a Mass for the dead.

They drove for a silent twenty minutes through a city and outskirts busy with Saturday-morning traffic. When high buildings gave way to tightly packed housing and streets became narrower and crowded Bridget knew they were in the vicinity of Our Lady of Lourdes Church. A continent might have separated it from the climbing, leafy environs of Madison Park but it was from such places that large congregations for small churches were drawn.

She was right. Victor would have liked the small, grey and blue church they drew up to.

'Did Victor know this church?' She looked from the building to Veronica.

While the driver opened the door Veronica studied the trim façade of Our Lady of Lourdes. 'He attended with me a few times as a child.' She was helped down and stood leaning on her cane while Hugo Sweeney clambered out with the sable. 'You will sit next to me,' she said to Bridget as Hugo helped her into the coat. 'I am not an invalid,' she snapped as he proffered an arm, 'I have my stick.'

Bridget followed them slowly. The church was about twenty feet back from the road, at the end of a path which went through a trimmed patch of grass. Its wooden frame was grey, the doors blue. Our Lady of Lourdes was not a rich church, but it was dignified and friendly in its lack of presumption.

A priest came to meet them. He had bulbous eyes of milky blue and round, pink cheeks. His voice, when he spoke, was thin and wavery and a lot older sounding than his appearance.

'It's good to have you here again.' He shook Veronica Baldacci's hand. 'Though the unfortunate circumstances aren't what I'd have wished for.'

'We are the first to arrive, I see.' Veronica walked impatiently past him to the church porch.

'Plenty of time still, plenty of time.' The priest followed her on his short legs. 'I won't start without them.'

'You will if I tell you to.' Veronica sniffed as he fussed round her. She look through the glass doors into the church and announced, a tone of satisfaction in her voice, 'Everything looks the same.'

'You won't find any changes,' the priest was reassuring. 'Things are the way you always liked them.' He bobbed his head to Bridget. 'You'll be Victor Baldacci's widow. We meet in unfortunate circumstances.' He gave a deep sigh. 'It's a sad thing when a man dies so young. A sad thing for a wife to lose her husband and a sad thing,' he turned lachrymose eyes Veronica Baldacci's way, 'for a mother to see her child die before her. But the will of God is not ours to question. I'm Father Bob Matthews.'

Bridget shook his plump, dry hand. 'My name is Bridget. It was good of you to say the Mass at such short notice.'

He bobbed his head again, smiling a little and showing small teeth.

'The poor man's mother is one of our more venerable parishioners. I'm glad I can do this for her. Will we go inside the church?'

Talking in low, confidential tones to Veronica Baldacci he led the way up the aisle to the front pew. The altar was quite spare, starched white linen and a couple of vases of white flowers breaking up its functional look. As they reached the front pew Veronica stepped smartly away from the priest.

'You can get on with things now,' she spoke loudly. 'We are capable of seating ourselves.'

The priest bowed and scurried across the altar to the sacristy, genuflecting with a flourish as he passed the tabernacle.

Architecturally, Our Lady of Lourdes was traditional, but as spartan as the altar was in style. The narrow pews were of the same polished wood as the vaulted beams and behind the altar there were two long, and quite lovely, stained-glass windows. One of these showed the Virgin during an appearance at Lourdes in northern France. The other was of Veronica, the kindly woman of Jerusalem who wiped the face of Jesus when He fell while carrying His cross to Calvary.

'My father attended this church.' Veronica Baldacci followed Bridget's gaze to the stained-glass saint. 'He had those windows put in when his God delivered him from poverty and gave him a daughter.' She squinted against the light spilling from the window. 'Too much blue. I've never really liked the face of Veronica either.'

'She's rather gentle looking,' Bridget said.

'She has my mother's face,' said Veronica, 'or so they say. She died giving birth to me.'

'Your father brought you up then?'

'Yes.'

And arranged for you to marry Frank Baldacci when you were a very young woman, Bridget thought, but didn't say so. She had a sudden rush of sympathy for the young Veronica. The older woman's critical expression, as she gazed at the work of the stained-glass artist, revealed nothing of her feelings about her father.

A blast of cold air preceded the march of footsteps and murmured conversations up the aisle behind them. When the rest of the family shuffled into the pew behind Bridget she didn't turn and neither did Hugo Sweeney – a church etiquette ingrained in Irish childhoods. Veronica Baldacci did a stiff half-turn, surveyed the occupants of the pew and said, loudly,

'Where are Magdalena and Thomas? I had wanted everyone to be on time. We are a small enough congregation as things are.'

'When I rang to coordinate things Dad said we should go on ahead,' John-Francis spoke in an exaggerated whisper. 'I think Mom was having a late breakfast.'

'In that case,' Veronica faced forward and joined her hands in her lap, 'the priest had better get on with the proceedings. They won't be coming.'

'They'll be waiting at the house when we get back,' Lindsay was defensive. 'This whole thing was very short notice, you know. It wasn't easy for people to make time—'

'Tell the priest we're waiting,' Veronica said, cutting her short.

Lindsay, in charcoal coat and beret, crossed the altar to knock smartly on the door of the sacristy.

'We're happy to be here, Mrs Baldacci,' Russell Segal's voice, murmuring close to Veronica's ear, was reassuring, 'we're all behind you on this one.'

'Thank you for coming, Russell,' said Veronica, 'but it does not mean you're getting that loan you've been looking for.'

It was five minutes before Father Matthews, followed by several altar boys, appeared on the altar to the sound of a plaintive organ playing from the back of the church. The priest was sombre and dutiful, saying a short Mass and giving a sermon which was to the point, for which Bridget gave thanks. Anything prolonged or sentimentally insincere and she would have left, or thrown up, or both. His voice, from the altar, had a clarity born of years of sermonizing practice.

'Victor Francis Baldacci,' he intoned, 'chose to live his life in a land far from where he grew up. It was a tribute to his mother's influence that he choose a staunchly Catholic country. In Ireland he lived what we now know was a good life, rearing a fine family of' – he consulted a sheet of paper – 'two children, a boy and a girl, Anna and Fintan, now sadly without a father. Our thoughts are with them today. They are equally with his widow, Bridget.' He opened his arms in prayerful entreaty. 'Let us pray now, together with Bridget, whom we are privileged and happy to have with us here today, for the eternal rest of the soul of Victor Baldacci.'

The Baldaccis bowed their heads and Bridget, doing the same, wondered how fast Victor was spinning in his casket, back at the hotel.

Eleanor Munro, flushed and breathless and wearing a cloche hat with an inky velvet rose on the side, was waiting outside the church. She grabbed Bridget's arm as their small group emerged.

'I wanted to be here,' she said, 'but . . . oh, what the hell. I didn't make it. Was it terrible? Are you OK?'

'Hello, Eleanor. It was fine. Short.' Bridget eased her arm from the other woman's clutch.

'I left you alone,' Eleanor said sotto voce, 'and I haven't called you. I thought it would be good for you to think, get your head round things. Did you?'

'I did some thinking,' Bridget said as Lindsay, stamping

her feet and blowing clouds of vapour into the cold air, moved between them.

'Grandmother's laid on food at the house. Second time in a week – you're certainly getting the treatment, Bridget. You want to ride back with me, Eleanor?'

'I'd have appreciated a ride over here,' Eleanor was surly. 'Veronica called a limo and left before I was out of bed. Anyone would think I wasn't wanted.'

'You've brought her grief and a lot of shit – what do you expect?' Lindsay said. 'Do you want a ride now or what?'

The Baldacci mansion, by day, had a worn, exhausted look. The columns supporting the portico needed painting and the sharp morning light showed the façade closer to grey than white.

The front door was open and there were five cars parked in front. Two of them were police cars.

'Trouble.' Hugo frowned and leaned forward as the limousine crunched onto the gravelled front.

'The police?' Veronica Baldacci narrowed her eyes. She can't see a thing, Bridget thought, and is too vain to wear glasses. The realization made Veronica all at once more human.

'It's the police,' she touched the older woman's hand, 'but that doesn't have to mean trouble, or that something bad's happened.'

'You don't know what you're talking about,' Veronica snapped. 'The police visit only for the worst reasons.'

Helped by Hugo she climbed from the car with the slowness of the very old. She knows something, Bridget thought, she's been expecting bad news and now it's come. She stood close to Victor's mother as Lindsay and John-Francis came together through the front door and walked toward them. Hugo stood on Veronica's other side.

'What are the police doing here?' Veronica asked as her

grandchildren drew near. She still wore the mantilla, its scalloped lace edges like gashes on either side of her face.

'It's not good news,' Lindsay spoke carefully.

'Of course it's not good news.' Her grandmother, moving forward, was harshly impatient. She passed the police cars, and their driver occupants, without a glance. 'Just tell me what it's about.'

'Come inside.' John-Francis put an arm about her shoulder. 'There's no percentage in us freezing to death while we talk about things out here.'

Veronica allowed his arm to stay where it was but stopped absolutely still. For a moment only she closed her eyes. When she opened them she fixed Lindsay with their implacable gaze.

'Tell me,' she commanded.

John-Francis's hand tightened on his grandmother's shoulder.

'They've found Ted Morgan,' Lindsay said.

'Found him . . .' Veronica removed John-Francis's hand from her shoulder and began walking slowly towards the front door. 'I thought that might be why they were here.' The policeman at the door stood aside to allow her enter. 'Is he alive?' Veronica asked.

It was as if, Bridget thought, she couldn't bring herself to say the word dead. When no one said anything she stood in the centre of the hallway and turned again to Lindsay. 'Answer my question,' she demanded.

'He drowned,' Lindsay answered. 'Looks like he fell in the water.' She moved closer but didn't touch her grandmother. 'The cops say it looks like he was in the Sound awhile.'

'Not alive then.' Veronica let go of a long breath.

'Dad's in the sitting room, and so's Mom,' Lindsay said, 'there's a couple of detectives here too. They say they want to talk with you.'

'Yes.' Veronica didn't move until Hugo Sweeney took her arm. Then she allowed herself be led towards the sitting room.

Inside, dwarfed by the great room and in a tableau parodying the group which had greeted Bridget on her first visit to the Baldacci home, five people were gathered by the fire. Magdalena, Thomas, Russell, a middle-aged, balding man in a navy overcoat and a very tall, very broad black woman in grey trousers and anorak all turned as Veronica and Hugo Sweeney came through the door. Eleanor Munro was nowhere in evidence.

Thomas, after a quick word with the man in the overcoat, came to meet them.

'They're saying it was an accident,' he was wearing a sharp navy suit and dark tie, 'that he was out on one of the old piers, alone, late, that he slipped and fell in . . .'

'Most unlikely,' said Veronica, 'he was not one for taking late night walks alone.' She looked past Thomas to the man in the overcoat, now standing behind him. 'I fail to see either how he could have slipped unless he was drunk. He wasn't a drinker.'

'These are the things we want to establish, ma'am.' Rubbing a pale moustache, the overcoated man stepped forward. 'I'm Detective Lessig and this' – he indicated the woman in the anorak – 'is Detective Jacklin. We apologize for disturbing what I understand is a sad occasion . . .' He looked briefly from Hugo to Bridget. He had small, nut-brown eyes in a round face. 'Thing is, we need to find out how Theodore Morgan came to drown in the Sound and we understand he'd been staying here over Christmas.'

'He was an old friend.' Veronica moved past him, Hugo by her side. She said nothing else until she was sitting in an armchair facing her daughter. Hugo, with a look that stonily disapproved of the police presence, stood behind the chair. 'Ted Morgan was an old friend, Veronica again said. 'He worked for this family once, a long time ago, nursing my husband in his final illness. We had exchanged letters over the years, but I had not seen him since after my husband's death until just before Christmas. He stayed here for nine days and then he left, on January the first . . .' she paused '. . . that was also nine days ago. I have no idea where he went and there is nothing more I can tell you.' She closed her eyes and sat back, the mantilla partly hiding her face. 'His death is very distressing to me.'

'It's a distressing death.' Detective Lessig shoved his hands deep into his pockets. 'We—'

'When did you find him?' Veronica didn't open her eyes.

'He was found two days ago, ma'am, discovered by a couple of kids went down one of the old piers to fish. He'd been in the water for the guts of a week—' He stopped, cleared his throat and rephrased the sentence, 'He'd been in there about five days, from the looks of things—'

'Please don't give me the details.' Veronica opened her eyes. 'So,' she sat looking straight ahead, 'he was here, in Seattle, all the time. I thought—' She stopped.

'You thought what, ma'am?' the detective prompted.

'That he'd returned to New York. Where he lived.'

'Far as we've been able to ascertain he was in Seattle all of the time between leaving this house and dying.' Lessig sighed and thoughtfully smoothed the thin moustache drooping from his upper lip. 'Stroke of luck, tracing him. We wouldn't have known any of this, or even who he was, if we hadn't been on the lookout for another guy went missing from the same hostel—'

'Hostel?' Veronica stared. 'Are you telling me Ted Morgan was staying in a refuge? Are you quite sure we're talking about the same person?'

'Absolutely.' Lessig became brisk. 'The details were all there in his personal belongings. Identity's been confirmed with a fingerprint check. He was staying at the Bible Mission

Refuge. Told them he expected to stay on awhile too.' He paused. 'That's why we're looking at an accident as the probable cause of death and not suicide. Either it was an accident or he was pushed in.'

'Pushed? As in murdered?' John-Francis sounded sceptical.

Thomas coughed. 'Ted Morgan was a well-meaning, inoffensive kind of guy. Not the type who made enemies. Why would anyone . . . push him in the water?'

'We don't know that he was pushed,' Detective Jacklin, in sharp, clipped tones, spoke for the first time. 'It's been hard to tell anything, way the fish got to him.'

In the silence Magdalena began to weep. Nobody else moved or spoke except for Detective Jacklin who, after a slow look round the faces in the room, produced a notebook.

'I'll just take the names of everyone here. Then I'd like to know who was in the house at the time of Theodore Morgan's visit and who the last person was to speak with him before he left.'

She took names and information meticulously over what seemed to Bridget an agonizingly long ten minutes. Magdalena sobbed quietly throughout. Thomas perched on the arm of her chair. Lindsay smoked. John-Francis paced. Russell Segal stared at the mock flames. Veronica sat rigidly unmoving with Hugo behind her.

'You've no idea why he left your home, ma'am?' Detective Lessig looked apologetically at Veronica as his colleague closed her notebook.

'None.'

'And he didn't say where he was going?'

'No.'

Lessig looked from Hugo to the others in the room. 'Did anyone here know where he was staying?'

'No one had any idea,' Lindsay said firmly. 'My grandmother had been enjoying his company. They'd been recalling events of way over thirty years ago, before my grandfather died. He knew he was welcome to stay on in this house.' She hesitated, looking at Veronica. 'My grandmother had been expecting him to return.' She turned toward the garden where a radiant, lit-up Christmas tree still shone. 'She'd even been holding out on taking down that thing because he liked it.'

'It seems I am no longer needed here. I will go to my room.' Veronica gave her hand to Hugo Sweeney and he helped her out of the chair.

'Thank you, ma'am, for your help,' Detective Lessig extended a hand which Veronica ignored.

'I want to say something,' Hugo Sweeney looked up at Detective Lessig, 'and it's this: there's nothing Mrs Baldacci can tell you about the dead man. Ted Morgan was his own person. He left here all those years ago when it suited him and he didn't come back again until it suited him. When he went off nine days ago it was for reasons of his own too. You'll not find answers in this house. The man himself was the only one had the answers to what you want to know.'

'Thank you, Mr Sweeney.' Lessig nodded. 'There's nothing you yourself might have to tell us?'

'I've given you my observations,' said Hugo, 'and that's all I have to say on the subject.'

The door hadn't closed behind Veronica and Hugo before Detective Jacklin, as precise as before, said, 'We need to see Miss Munro. Could one of you people bring her back in here, please?'

'I'll get her.' Thomas gave his small cough and stood. 'But as you saw earlier she is very upset. She and Mr Morgan came to Seattle together.' He paused. 'A nostalgic trip.'

'We need to talk to her,' the detective said.

'Won't take long,' Detective Lessig assured him. Thomas coughed again and left the room.

'Christ, I don't think I can take an Eleanor scene right now.' John-Francis faced the detectives. 'Do you need me here for this?'

'We'd prefer if you stayed, yes,' Detective Lessig said. John-Francis, after a look at the man's face, shrugged and sat down.

'Way I see it,' John-Francis stretched his legs in front of him and studied the toes of his shoes, 'Ted Morgan could have done anything, gotten into all kinds of trouble, made all sorts of enemies, in the thirty-five or more years since he was last here. Are you people looking at the rest of his life?'

'We'll be looking at everything,' Detective Lessig assured him.

Bridget decided to sit down too. She chose the seat vacated by Veronica and had a clear view of Magdalena's ravaged face. Tears had ploughed through her make-up, mascara washing into the furrows created on her cheeks. She looked up and lifted her glass to Bridget.

'Happy holidays,' she said.

The Eleanor Munro who came into the room with Thomas was chillingly subdued. She stood a few feet from the door looking in silence from one detective to the other. Her hands hung by her sides and she was still dressed in the long black coat and cloche hat she'd been wearing outside the church.

'We need to ask you an initial couple of questions,' Detective Jacklin's tones were surprisingly gentle. 'Maybe later, when you feel able, you'd come down to the precinct and talk with us some more?'

'Maybe I will,' said Eleanor. 'What do you want to know now?'

'Just if Theodore Morgan said anything to you about why he moved out and into the Bible Mission Refuge?'

'No. He didn't tell me he was going.'

'But you were travelling companions. You'd known him in New York. Had you expected to travel back with him?'

'We'd made no arrangements of any kind.'

'Did he get in touch with you after leaving here?'

'No.'

'Thank you, Miss Munro.' Detective Jacklin look at her colleague. 'I guess that's it, then. Unless you got anything you want to clear up with the people here?'

'Seems to me we've about covered things.' Lessig began to button his overcoat. 'Except to ask if Theodore Morgan made contact with anyone in this house after he left? Or if any of you know who else he might have looked up in Seattle? No?' He finished buttoning his coat. 'We've got information says he took a couple of calls at the Refuge. Since none of you knew where he was staying they can't have come from this house. Still, I'd appreciate it if you would all think things over, see if there's anything you might have forgotten to tell us.' He hunched into his coat. 'We'll be in touch.'

In the garden the lights went out on the Christmas tree.

Chapter Nine

The house closed in around Bridget, smothering and claustophobic.

'I need a walk and some air,' she said.

'I'll come with you,' said John-Francis. She couldn't think of a way to stop him.

For their walk, along the pathway between the classic sculptures, John-Francis favoured a white, Aran-style sweater. He stayed close to Bridget, attentive and kindly.

'You didn't have to come with me,' Bridget said.

'I'm glad to keep you company.'

He took her arm as they came to a step. When they reached level ground and Bridget tugged to free her arm he smiled and held on.

'Don't want you slipping on frosty grass,' he said.

Bridget ground her teeth and walked faster. John-Francis kept pace.

'Shame you getting mixed up in all of this,' he said and, when Bridget didn't reply, he added, 'I liked Ted Morgan.'

'You got to know him well, then?'

'I wouldn't say that, exactly. But he spent a lot of time with Veronica – he'd a way of making her feel good. Eleanor was more relaxed when he was around. More, uh, sane, if you know what I mean.'

'He seems to have been a sort of father to Eleanor,' Bridget said.

'I suppose.' John-Francis shrugged. 'He was the right age, in his sixties. Too young to die, that's for sure.'

'He was a lot younger than your grandmother then?' Bridget asked, surprised.

'Yeah. A good fifteen years or so younger. He saw her through grandfather's death. I reckon that was the bond.'

'She's taken it badly . . .'

'Yeah.' John-Francis was impatient. 'But Veronica's tough, a survivor. Eleanor's more the problem.'

Bridget agreed about Eleanor. After the departure of the police the younger woman had taken herself back to her room. Her subdued air had had an edge of dementia about it. She's got no one now, Bridget thought, her mother and father-figure both gone.

'Will Veronica look after Eleanor?' Bridget asked. 'See she gets some money?'

It was the first chance she'd had to put the question to one of the family directly. John-Francis, still holding her elbow, hesitated only slightly before answering.

'I don't have the complete story because it wasn't something my parents or my grandmother ever discussed with us.' He gave a half smile. 'The past is another country and all that.'

'So what are you saying?'

'That I don't know what Grandmother will do. We never know what she'll do.'

It was cold in the garden, the grass underfoot already crisp with an early afternoon frost as they skirted the phlegmatic Roman senator.

'Did Ted Morgan nurse Veronica's husband for long?'

'I don't know that either.' John-Francis looked rueful. 'I'm not a lot of use to you, Bridget, on these questions. Do you want to go back to the house?'

Bridget didn't but rounded the last statue with him and they began to retrace their steps. She was studying the statuary as they passed, thinking how humourless it was and how it fitted the mood of the house, when John-Francis said, 'You're in luck. My father's coming to join us. You can put your questions to him.'

Thomas, coming towards them along the path, looked harrassed and more than usually stooped. When he reached them Bridget added tired and apologetic to the way he looked. He rubbed a hand across his forehead.

'I want you to take your mother on home, son. I need to stay here awhile, sort some things.'

'Will do.' John-Francis Baldacci elegantly raised and air-kissed Bridget's gloved hand. 'I leave you in the wiser company of my father.'

'He's a charmer,' said Thomas as his son jogged down the pathway and out of the garden, 'but his sister's the worker in this family.' He sighed. 'Eleanor is back downstairs and is looking for you. She's . . . pretty excited.' he hesitated. 'I'm glad we have this chance to talk, even for a few minutes.'

'I am too. I've a few questions I want to ask.'

'Go ahead.' Thomas gave an unconvincing half smile.

'Tell me about Victor, how you remember him.' A spiteful gust of wind made Bridget's eyes water and she dabbed at them while Thomas framed an answer. He took a while.

'I remember your husband as a troubled teenager,' he said at last. 'I wasn't a lot older than him, four or five years I suppose, but, God, how I envied him his good looks. Handsome and brooding was how I saw him.' He pulled a wry face. 'Did he stay that way?'

'He was handsome,' Bridget said, 'and serious. He developed a few other traits too though. People don't change so much as add experience to the skeleton of what they are.'

'Yes . . .' He looked at her doubtfully. 'You know, you could say that I took Victor's place in the family. After his father died and he left' – he pushed his glasses higher up his nose – 'I became the male family figure for Veronica and Magdalena.'

'I can see how that would have happened. About Eleanor's story – is it all true?' Bridget stared at the ground and willed him to tell her no, that Eleanor Munro had exaggerated, some of what she had said was true but not all, not the incest, not the shocking cruelty.

'It's true,' Thomas's tone was neutral, 'but it all happened a long time ago and to another family, you could say. Everything's been rebuilt.'

Rebuilt. The word struck Bridget as bizarre and she wanted to ask him about the foundations for this rebuilding. What about seepage? Did not some of the rot from the family's cankerous bedrock work its way through, even exist still? But she didn't know quite how to put it so she asked him instead about Victor. 'Why did my husband leave?'

Thomas was gentle. 'That's between him and his mother. She'll have to tell you that. I don't know.'

Bridget didn't believe him. He knew. They all knew.

Lindsay was circling the hallway talking into the mobile phone, controlled frenzy in her voice, when they got back to the house. Hers were the only sounds in the echoing quiet. Bridget, listening, for no reason that she could pin down, knew all at once what she was going to do with Victor's ashes.

'I'd like you to call me a cab to take me back to my hotel,' she said to Thomas. With something like relief he produced a phone of his own and made the booking.

'I'll wait outside,' Bridget said, remembering the stranglehold effect of the house. 'Will you tell Eleanor?'

Thomas nodded, mute and pleasant still.

Bridget was leaning against the paint-peeling portico, thinking the day was as bleak and cold as the unfolding facts of Victor's family life, when Eleanor Munro came to her.

'Don't leave, Bridget.' She looked distraught. 'Don't go

back to your hotel. Move in here with me. I'm scared. I don't want to be alone in this place.' Her eyes had a glittering intensity in a face which was blue-white and drawn.

'You're not alone.' Bridget shook her head. 'Veronica and Hugo will be here. Veronica shares your grief for Ted, in spite of everything. But do call me whenever you want—'

'What I want is you here.' Eleanor clutched at Bridget's arms and shook her. 'I've got no one else now. I want you to be with me. Ted won't be coming back. You heard what they said. He's dead.'

'Oh, Eleanor, my poor Eleanor.' Bridget shook herself free and then pulled the younger woman into her arms. 'I'm so sorry about Ted.' It was exactly like holding Anna; same texture to her hair when she stroked it, same fragile, bony body. 'You'll feel better about things tomorrow, not much, but you'll begin to cope.' She held the younger woman at arms' length. 'There's a cab on the way here to take me back to the hotel. There's something I have to do.'

'I'll come with you. I'm not staying here.'

In the taxi Eleanor folded into herself and was silent. She was silent too as she followed Bridget to her room in the hotel and mutely watched while Bridget lifted Victor's casket from its spot on the desk.

'You can come with me,' Bridget held the casket in her arms, 'or you can wait here until I get back. The choice is yours.'

'I'm coming with you,' said Eleanor.

Bridget got directions from the woman on reception, who was more cheerful today for some reason, and made her way to the waterfront via Post Alley, a cavern of endless steps between high buildings. Eleanor Munro walked beside her in silence. Bridget carried Victor's ashes in her arms, the casket in a canvas hold-all.

On Pier 55 Bridget was told the next cruise of the bay and harbour area wouldn't happen for thirty minutes.

'We've got time for a hot drink then,' Bridget said and led the way to a waterfront bar and restaurant.

'Spiced cider,' she said to the overweight, bearded barman, adding, 'two glasses,' when Eleanor, slipping wordlessly into a window seat, refused to make a choice.

'You ain't going to like it.' The barman, looking at them, shook his head.

'Try us,' said Bridget.

It was sweet and overspiced and he was right, Bridget hated the cider. Eleanor didn't even try it. 'Why do you sell it?' Bridget asked.

'Some folks'll drink anything.' The barman grinned. 'You're taking a trip out on the bay, right? I can truly recommend the Northwest Fish Stew we do here. Call in on the way back. Ask for Stanley. That's me. I'll look after you myself.'

It was the last trip of the day and there were four other passengers on the boat. Bridget and Eleanor were the only two people on the open deck as it swayed gently out along the wooden pier. Was it under a pier like this, Bridget wondered, that Ted Morgan had been found?

She turned her face from the city, held the hold-all tighter and faced the wider waters ahead. The captain, over the tannoy, assured them these were a hundred feet deep in parts.

'That's a lot of water, folks, moving in and out on two high tides and two low each day.' He made this sound unusual. 'The whole thing carved out by glaciers.'

Fifteen minutes out the waters were a penetrating, icy blue. Victor would be at peace here, if anywhere.

Bridget balanced the bag with the casket on the ship's rail; not an easy thing to do since the rail was narrow and the bag a lot wider. She unzipped it and looked at the casket, insignificant in its towel padding. All she had to do now was unscrew the top and scatter the contents.

'Is there something I should know about?' Eleanor spoke for the first time since leaving the hotel.

'No. Nothing,' Bridget said. 'You can go below decks and wait for me. Keep warm.'

'Those are your husband's ashes, right?'

'Right.'

'And you're really going to do this? You're really going to dump them here in the bay?'

'I am.'

It was hard to let him go. The boat was moving fast and there was all of the Puget Sound to choose from. One hundred miles or more of it, the captain had said. Such a lot of water, such a great silence. Ted Morgan had died in these waters and they were telling nothing.

Spray stung her face and she blinked it from her eyes. They'd travelled a long way together, she and Victor Baldacci.

The boat began to swing round, sea birds skimming the waves ahead as it headed back for the harbour. It rolled with the tide, then heaved.

Bridget lost her balance. Clutching at the rail for support she could do nothing but watch as the bag slipped and turned, falling in a wide, slow arc before it splash-landed in the water. She went on watching as it sank, lazily, beneath the waves, until hold-all and casket were gone, for ever she hoped, beneath the water of the Puget Sound.

Ted Morgan hadn't stayed in the water. She added a prayer to her hopes that Victor's ashes would.

Letting go of the breath she'd been holding she thought that some things never change. As so often in her life with Victor a decision had been taken out of her hands. She felt rudderless, and very cold.

'Are you OK?' Eleanor touched Bridget's face, timidly.

'I'm fine, really I am,' Bridget said.

Stanley's Northwest Fish Stew was fishy and it was warm

and for the latter, at least, Bridget gave thanks. She and Eleanor sat close together at a small, round wooden table in curved-backed chairs. A fan whirred in the ceiling and Stanley, in a green striped apron, hovered with a two-foot-long pepper mill.

'I made that stew myself. It all right for seasoning?'

'No,' Eleanor pushed her bowl aside, 'I can't eat this stuff.'

Stanley's hold on the pepper mill took on a whole new aspect.

'There's a lot of cold water out there,' Bridget said hurriedly, 'does much fishing go on?'

'Depends what you mean by fishing.' Stanley turned his broad back on Eleanor and placed the pepper mill safely on the table. 'We get a lot of dead bodies fished out of those waters. One pulled out not more than a couple of days ago.'

'At this pier?' The fish stew's appeal diminished and Bridget stopped eating. She avoided looking at Eleanor.

'Further down. A lot lonelier place than here. Sort of place a man might go to end things, or be dumped by someone doing it for him. It's the kind of thing gives the place a bad name, stops people coming to the waterfront to eat.' Stanley folded his arms and looked contemplatively through the window and along the pier. 'Course there are others come because of the murders and suicides. There's always a lot of talk, people are interested in that sort of thing.'

'What are people saying about this latest . . . drowning?'

'See what I mean?' Stanley winked at Bridget and gave a chortle. 'You're interested. Knew you would be. It's human nature to be curious about death, and how it happens.'

'Well? What happened this time?' Bridget put a warning foot on Eleanor's under the table. The younger woman stayed silent.

'Word is he was helped into the water. Way the guys

down here heard it, he was caught in the struts and eaten mostly by rats, torso and head, not fish. Way they figure it was high tide, he was dead going in and was swept immediately onto the struts to become a meal for those rodents—'

'Stoppit! Just shut the fuck up! . . . I don't want to hear any more of this—' Eleanor's chair crashed to the ground as she stood gagging, a napkin to her mouth.

'Sensitive digestive system, have we?' Stanley removed her plate and turned, businesslike, to Bridget. 'That'll be eight dollars twenty, when you're ready.'

Outside, it was getting dark fast. Post Alley lost a lot of its appeal on the long climb upwards but the effort drained Eleanor of much of the explosive anger she'd built up on account of Stanley.

'Fucking jerkoff,' she panted as they emerged from the alley and hit the streets again. 'Fact that he may be right doesn't give him the right to talk like that.'

'We don't even know that he was talking about Ted,' Bridget said.

Eleanor said nothing while they crossed two intersections and headed uphill again towards the hotel.

'I know he was talking about Ted,' she said and then, 'And I know Ted didn't end his own life.'

'The police will—'

'Like hell they will. The cops'll toss it around for a week or two and then forget it. Ted was a nobody, a vagrant, a refuge inhabitant – that's all they want to know about him. No one's going to make a fuss, no one's going to scream to have his murderer brought to justice.'

'We don't know he was murdered—'

'*We* don't,' Eleanor's mimicry was acute, 'but I do. And I'm going to make a lot of noise. I'm going to keep asking questions.' She stopped, looking up and down the street. Her eyes were manic, and frightened. 'Someone has to. They can't be allowed to get away with it.'

Chapter Ten

At some point during a sleepless night Bridget decided she was going home. She would change her flight. Go for an earlier date. Be out of Seattle in twenty-four hours. Hopefully. The idea helped her sleep. But it was a sleep full of nightmare corridors without end, with still, bottomless waters and, everywhere she turned, the same headless figure.

When she woke she knew she wouldn't be leaving. She couldn't run away as Victor had done. She had to stay until she knew all there was to know about Victor's past, about his family's past – and present.

Because the first two were increasingly, and frighteningly, becoming a part of the second.

It was the reason she'd come. It was what had kept her going in the months since she'd become a widow. If she went home now she would never come back to Seattle, any more than Victor had. She would never really know, never be sure what exactly had so damaged the man she'd married.

But it was more than that, now. Something had changed since meeting his family; a dimension had been added to her reason for being here.

She wasn't in Seattle for herself alone anymore: she was now here for Victor too. She now knew that she owed it to him too to get to the bottom of the whole sorry mess. He hadn't been able to, he'd run away and kept running until he'd found a safe haven. He'd never had justice: he'd lost his childhood and young life and any rights he might have had within his family.

She would put things right for him, see him vindicated. It was the least she could do now she was here. It would be a small return for the happy years, a sort of acknowledgement of all he'd meant to her. She would stay until she'd found out everything possible. The circle of his life would be complete then, the past understood and, hopefully, put to peace.

His children would really know him. She would too.

If even half of what she'd heard was true then Victor's young life had to have been a confused and deeply unhappy one. But it was the straw which had broken his back and driven him from home that she wanted to know about.

It was Sunday. A day of peace and rest. She would take this day, at least, for herself. She would walk and puzzle things through and look at the waters everywhere. She would work on detaching herself from the Baldaccis – it was the best way to see things clearly.

She rang Fintan, then Anna, but told them nothing except that she'd been to dinner chez the Baldaccis. She just didn't know where to begin telling them all what she'd discovered. She had breakfast delivered to the room and sat with it on the bed, channel hopping through endless dissections of Sonny Bono's life and death, weather forecasts, further flashes of Fergie. Nowhere was there news or comment about the discovery of the half-eaten body of a man found at the waterfront. Probably, as Stanley the fish stew maker had said, bodies came ashore there all the time.

She was watching a talk show in which obscenely fat people discussed the virtues of flesh in bed when the call came. She'd never considered the pleasures of burying her head in a billowy stomach, or between smothering thighs, and her mind was distracted when she picked up the phone.

Too distracted to be adamant about keeping the day for herself.

'I hope I didn't get you out of bed.' Veronica Baldacci didn't introduce herself.

'Only in a manner of speaking . . .'

'I would like to talk with you. A car will pick you up in about thirty minutes.'

'I have plans for the day.'

'You need to hear what I have to say. I will be as brief as possible.' The line went dead.

Hugo Sweeney opened the door to her, his narrow eyes taking her in without enthusiasm. The house behind him was so silent it could have been empty. If Eleanor Munro was around she was keeping very quiet.

'Mrs Baldacci is waiting for you,' said Hugo, 'and you might as well know that she's a bit under the weather. She's settled on a death wish and there's nothing to be done but wait now and see if she comes out of it.'

He walked ahead of Bridget up the stairs, his small feet laced into black leather shoes, his white hair limp on his collar. She could feel his resentful energy with every step.

The landing walls were covered with heavy landscape oils, most of them of mountains and lakes. Hugo straightened one and spoke without turning around.

'She's been at the drink – though in her day she could drink more than any man I ever knew. It's different now. Doesn't agree with the insulin.'

'Veronica's a diabetic?'

'That she is.' He stepped back from the picture. It was still lopsided.

'Let me. Sometimes a fresh eye . . .' Bridget angled the picture until it came right.

'A fresh eye. So that's what you think you are,' said Hugo.

'That, Hugo, is what is called a loaded comment. What exactly are you saying?'

Hugo frowned at the mountains and lake. 'Maybe I'm saying that people can only tell you how things look to them and they've all got different ways of looking. The eye can be wiser or it can be foolish in the way it sees things.' He began to walk along the landing. 'Whatever you hear there's only the one truth. You'd do well to remember that, while you're here.'

Bridget followed him. 'I don't suppose you'd care to tell me how you see that truth?'

'I would not' – Hugo gestured at the landscapes – 'she thought that was what Ireland was like. That was why she bought the lot of them. But all of those paintings are of England. She never would believe me when I told her.'

'Hugo, is Veronica dying?'

Hugo Sweeney didn't reply immediately. He smoothed a hand over his thin, white hair and crossed the landing to stand by a door.

'She might be,' he said, 'and then again she might not. She's not a woman who goes by the ordinary rules.' He pushed open the door.

Veronica Baldacci sat in a wooden rocking chair by a long window whose partially opened shutters gave the room its only light. She was dressed in black, a wool dress with pearl buttons to the neck and a silk wrap over it. Her stick lay across her knees and her heavily made-up face was clown-like above the elegant black.

'Sit there.'

She indicated a second chair by the window and Bridget sat. In the murky light she could make out a large, lace-covered bed and, along one wall, a wardrobe and chest of drawers. A functional bedroom with a comfortable bed was how it seemed to her.

A low table between herself and Veronica held carafes of whiskey and water and a glass.

'Help yourself,' said Veronica. She already had a drink in her hand.

'It's a bit early for me,' Bridget said. 'What did you want to talk about?'

'To the point. I like that,' said Veronica. 'I was never keen on the superficialities of life.' Her stare, through the blue-black of the eye make-up, was hard to read.

'In that case, Veronica, perhaps you would begin—'

'I prefer Mrs Baldacci.' Veronica was curt. 'But since we both share the name I suppose I must make an exception. You may call me Veronica.' Turning her head slowly she looked round the room, her eyes picking out objects, resting on them, moving on. After a few minutes she said, 'I have found peace in this room, many times.'

She's playing with me, Bridget thought, she demanded I come here and now she plans to amuse herself and tell me what she has to say in her own time. She got up.

'I have plans for the day,' she said, 'but I'll call to see you before I leave Seattle.'

She was almost at the door when Veronica's voice, subdued and almost pleading, made her stop. 'Death is never pleasant,' she said, 'any more than life is, a lot of the time.'

Bridget turned, slowly. 'Life has its moments,' she said, 'though I'm not so sure about death.' She paused and said what she'd already said to Hugo, 'Are you dying, Veronica?'

'We are all dying, all of the time,' Veronica, eyes on the light through the gap in the shutters, didn't turn, 'but I am probably closer to death than you are.' She sighed. 'Please sit down, Bridget.'

It was the Bridget that did it. She went back to the armchair.

'I have come to a decision,' Veronica said, 'and when I tell you what it is I want you to leave here, go home to your

128

children and your life in Ireland. I do not want you to discuss what I am about to tell you with Eleanor Munro, or with anyone. Do I have your word?'

'You cannot seriously expect me to make a promise without knowing—'

'Yes, I can.' Veronica's expression became one of distaste. 'Please don't lecture me. I've no liking for high-toned moral speeches.' She turned her face from the window and looked briefly and coldly at Bridget. 'I will expect you to do as I have asked and not talk to anyone here, especially Miss Munro.'

'I cannot promise,' Bridget said. The older woman said nothing for a minute, then shrugged.

'And I cannot force you. I will simply warn you that Miss Munro is a woman to whom it is neither safe nor prudent to give information. It would be dangerous to talk to her of the things which we are about to discuss in this room.'

'Secrecy is a way of life in this family,' Bridget said slowly. 'You cannot expect me to go along with a way of behaving I fundamentally disagree with.'

'I do. Some things are best left unexamined. You are, after a fashion, a member of this family and it would be best, for everyone, if you—'

'Obeyed the rules?' Bridget cut her short. 'I'm sorry, Veronica. I would prefer to maintain the detached status I've had all these years.'

For a while it seemed to Bridget that Veronica Baldacci either hadn't heard or registered what she'd said. The older woman was silent, sighing a little and playing with the rings on her fingers. But when she spoke again she was businesslike.

'There is no legacy, no share in the family wealth, due to you or to your children. I disowned my son when he left home. However, despite the fact that neither you nor your offspring are entitled to anything from this family, I am making arrangements for shares in the company to be made over to you. Substantial shares. I am not doing this because of any affection for Victor. On the contrary. I am doing this as an expression of my gratitude to you for keeping him away, for ensuring I did not set eyes on him for thirty years. They will give you a degree of power and a role in this family. It is important for a woman to have power. I doubt you had any in your marriage.'

'Our marriage wasn't about power . . .'

'Of course it was. All marriages are.' Veronica leaned forward. Her breath smelled sweet, and whiskey laden. 'I intend making an allowance payable to Eleanor Munro. It is more than she deserves and will get rid of her.'

She really is dying, Bridget thought, and she's squaring her conscience. She's getting rid of me as well as Eleanor. The surprise was that Veronica Baldacci *had* a conscience. A flutter she recognized as panic started up in Bridget's stomach. She didn't want this. She was being sucked into things.

Aloud, she said, 'Why are you doing this now?'

'Because what has happened has made it inevitable. You are here. Eleanor Munro is unfortunately here. The family needs new blood,' she gave a cold smile, 'and I wish to decide what that blood will be while I am still capable. You will do. Eleanor Munro will not.'

'Ted Morgan—'

'Yes. Ted Morgan helped me see things . . . differently. He is . . . was someone whose judgement I respected. He thought it right that I make arrangements such as these. His death is a great sadness.' Her voice dropped. 'I wish to honour him.'

'I did not come here looking for money.'

'You've already pointed that out.' Veronica's face closed again and she waved an impatient hand. 'Consider this a recompense for the years spent with my son.'

'I was happy with your son. We were happy together.'

'I don't believe you,' Veronica said.

'I would like to know why Victor left home.' Bridget poured herself a small amount of whiskey and a lot of water. 'That's what I came here to find out.'

'We have already spoken about Victor's early years,' Veronica's voice rose angrily, 'I do not want to go over it again . . .'

The door opened. 'Everything all right here?' Hugo Sweeney looked from one woman to the other.

'Pour me a drink,' Veronica said. 'No water this time.'

Hugo poured whiskey into a glass. 'You shouldn't be upsetting her,' he said quietly, to Bridget.

'Leave us, Hugo.' Veronica downed half the whiskey in a gulp. 'We have things to discuss.' She was irritable, but calm.

'I won't be far.' Hugo Sweeney closed the door softly after him.

Bridget walked to the window and through the small opening in the shutters looked down at the curve of the avenue and the slow rain beginning to fall there.

'Why don't you tell me the whole truth about this family, Veronica?' She opened the shutters a little, 'or at least give me your version of the whole truth?'

She turned. In the light from the window, and despite the make-up, Veronica's skin had a decaying look to it. The icy, pale blue alertness of her eyes was unchanged.

'As you please.' Her mother-in-law finished her drink. 'Pour me another.' She held out the glass. 'Do it,' she said, raising her voice as Bridget hesitated. 'The truth is that though my marriage to Frank Baldacci was an arranged one it was also a love match.'

Love. Veronica said the word gently, shocking Bridget, making her aware how little she knew of the nature of love, of the nature of hate.

'Frank had indeed been involved in a liaison with a

131

young woman called Grace Munro.' The gentleness disappeared from Veronica's voice. 'He was unaware she was under age. Immediately our engagement was announced she revealed her pregnancy and claimed Frank as the father. She threatened blackmail, and a lot more besides, and Frank came to an arrangement with her about financial support for her and her child.' Veronica sighed. 'He provided diligently for fifteen years until Grace Munro one day disappeared, leaving her daughter behind.'

'Is it true that Grace Munro was never heard of again?'

'It's true,' said Veronica after only the slightest hesitation. 'It is my opinion that she left the state with a man.'

'Her daughter was Shelley, Eleanor Munro's mother?'

Veronice was silent for a moment, as if remembering. 'Yes, yes,' she said eventually and impatiently. 'And we took her into our home and cared for her as one of our own children. She was a strange, demanding child. Her mother's loss affected her badly and she became neurotically possessive of Frank. She couldn't be persuaded to go to school, nor to do anything else. The time came when she refused even to go outside.'

Veronica looked from Bridget to the bed and then the darker corners of the room. She gave an involuntary shiver. 'One day, just as her mother had done, she left. It was a difficult time. Frank was not in good health. There were business problems.'

A nerve began to tick at the corner of her eye and she rubbed at it with the back of her hand. 'We nevertheless hired a private detective because, though Shelley was twenty-one years old, she was an immature young woman and we worried that she might not be able to look after herself.'

She took the hand away from her eye. In rubbing she had smudged the make-up so that the clown look had become lop-sided and slightly tragic. 'She'd been gone several months when she was found in New York. Frank, though unwell, went to bring her home. She was living with a man and wouldn't leave. She was drinking. He thought it likely she was abusing drugs too. From being devoted to Frank she now wanted nothing to do with him and refused all help, financial or otherwise. The man she was with was her new life, she said, she was finished with the old.'

She stopped. When she went on it was after a deep breath and more slowly.

'Frank left her there and came home. But the trip had exhausted his reserves of strength and within weeks he suffered a stroke. He lived, what was left to him of life, paralysed and an invalid. I was obliged to take his place in the business. I found I had a flair for it. I have been involved ever since.' She shrugged. 'I had no choice in the matter.'

Yes, you did, Bridget thought, watching the other woman as she raised her glass and slowly sipped. There were always choices. Veronica Baldacci had run the business because she liked control. Maybe that wasn't all she liked though. The sad, clownishly smudged eye above the rim of the glass gave her an oddly vulnerable look. Maybe there was a neediness there too. Maybe that's what her love for Frank Baldacci had been.

'Thomas took Victor's place in the business,' Bridget said, 'he told me as much himself.' She sat in the armchair again. The room was uncomfortably hot and she longed to open a window but didn't dare. 'Maybe it's time you told me what it was finally decided Victor to leave home.'

Veronica closed her eyes. It was as if she hadn't heard.

'Was it because,' Bridget raised her voice only slightly, 'his father was having a relationship with his half-sister, with Shelley Munro?'

'A relationship?' Veronica's lips barely moved.

'Did he rape her?'

'Of course not. All of that is a fantasy of Eleanor's sick mind.'

133

Veronica opened her eyes and looked directly at Bridget. 'She is exactly like her mother – diseased of mind. Shelley Munro wasn't even a particularly attractive-looking woman. She had a bad complexion.' Veronica gave a slow smile and held up her empty glass. 'I'll have water this time.'

'Bridget took and filled the glass and gathered her thoughts the while. Veronica's version of the family history was plausible and more acceptable than Eleanor Munro's because it was less cruel. But did that make it any more true?

'Why did Victor leave home?' She handed Veronica the glass.

'You are a persistent woman,' Veronica's voice had become slightly slurred. She gave her a cold smile. 'Such persistence must be rewarded. Victor left because he judged and condemned me, his mother. It had to do with Ted Morgan. Ted was a young man when he came to nurse my husband. Just thirty-two years of age. I was a woman of forty-five but I came to rely on him totally in matters relating to Frank and, eventually, the house. He managed things here while I looked after the business. He looked after me too. He was a good man. We became lovers.'

Bridget nodded. It made sense. If Veronica was capable of hatred, which was what she seemed to feel for Victor, why not of love? She'd already shown neediness.

'Victor knew this?' she asked. Veronica ignored the question.

'I was a middle-aged woman. The man I'd married was gone from me in a wasted body which waited for death. Ted and I kept our affair secret. I did not trust my children to understand, though they were young adults. I was right not to.' Her voice became rough. 'Victor discovered us together. From then until the day his father died I lived with his hostility and disapproval, both of them ferocious, malignant forces in this house. He made me suffer—' She stopped abruptly. After a minute she went on. 'Victor had been groomed for the family business. It would be his place, as his father's son, to take over one day. He drove Ted away, forcing me to choose between my son or my lover. I chose my son, as I had to, and Ted left as soon as Frank died. And then, within three months, so did Victor. Once his father died he denied me completely and then he deserted me. He had been given everything, all his life. He took it all and he gave nothing back. He abandoned this family when he was needed. We, in turn, abandoned him to his choice.'

Bridget was glad when Veronica stopped talking. Seen from the older woman's perspective Victor's leaving had indeed been an abandonment. She herself felt that his decision had been that of a young man unable to deal with his mother's betrayal of his dying father. But there was something missing, still. The Victor she'd known would have been able to forgive his mother's need for love.

'Ted Morgan didn't visit over the years?' she asked after a while.

Veronica gave a small shake of her head. 'Too much damage had been done. It was a . . . shock when he arrived before Christmas.' She patted her hair in an oddly self-conscious gesture. 'He didn't say so but I'm sure he was surprised to find me as old as I am. I had lied to him about my age, all those years ago.'

'You're still a fine-looking woman,' Bridget said.

It wasn't a complete lie. Veronica was faded, withered even, but the formal, cold beauty she'd noticed the first day in the garden was as pronounced as ever. The loneliness there Bridget thought she understood too. To have loved and lost Ted Morgan once was bad enough. To have found and lost him again, the second time to the finality of a violent death, was infinitely cruel. This, then, was what Hugo Sweeney had meant when he'd spoken about Veronica having a death wish. Veronica was bereft – and had all the appearances of a woman winding down her affairs.

The room felt smothering, as well as hot. Bridget stood and went back to the window. The evergreens were brooding, the avenue bleak.

'What an awful waste,' she said aloud.

'Yes,' said Veronica in the room behind her. A sense of loss was everywhere between them.

It was several minutes before Veronica, her voice sounding remote, broke the silence. 'I will be taking care of Ted's burial as soon as the police release his body,' she said, 'I would like you to attend at the funeral.' It was a command.

'Of course,' said Bridget.

'You will arrange to go home then, I presume?'

'I would like to go home.'

It was true. She was suddenly lonely, missing her garden, the house, Anna and Fintan, the friends she'd known for a lifetime, the life she'd built with Victor Baldacci over thirty years and which was still there, even if he wasn't. He wasn't here either, she knew that now. Even so, she would leave when she'd done what she came to do, not before.

'Arrangements are being made for your shares. There will be some paperwork—'

'Please hold things for a day or two,' Bridget said. 'I'd like time to think.'

'What's there to think about?' Veronica's voice held a controlled outrage.

'What it will mean,' said Bridget.

It would tie her to the Baldaccis in all sorts of ways. Victor had escaped them. It could be argued that by accepting Veronica's offer she was undoing his life.

'I will give you a day. One day,' said Veronica. 'I intend meeting with my attorney tomorrow morning. You have until then.'

She closed her eyes and, with surprising force, banged three times on the floor with her walking stick. Hugo

Sweeney came instantly through the door, filling Bridget with an uncomfortable image of him hovering on the other side all the time she and Veronica had been talking. He crossed wordlessly to the shutters and closed them so that only the original sliver of light came through. He looked at his watch and then at Bridget.

'Mrs Baldacci needs to sleep now,' he said. 'You'd best be going.'

Bridget went slowly down the stairs. The rest of the house, after Veronica's bedroom, was refreshingly cool. It was silent too, just as it had been when she arrived, not a sound of Eleanor Munro anywhere. She hoped the younger woman was all right and immediately reminded herself that she wasn't her responsibility. Even so, the worry niggled.

In the hallway she stood, uncertain, wanting to be gone, wishing she'd hired a car, hating the trapped, compromised feeling of having no transport. She would walk. To hell with the rain and the distance. A walk, time alone to think, was what she needed. She opened the front door and saw that the rain had stopped.

'It's not a good idea to let the cold, wet air into the house,' Hugo Sweeney came down the stairs and into the hallway. 'I'd be obliged if you would close the door while I get your outdoor garments.'

Bridget closed the door and Hugo, after disappearing off to the end of the hallway for several minutes, reappeared with her coat and scarf.

'Mrs Baldacci's asleep now but I'm not at all pleased with the way things are looking.' His small face was set in tight, disapproving lines.

'She's very upset about Ted Morgan's death.' Bridget tried to read between the tight lines, but got nowhere.

'Indeed she is. Seems to believe she should have known the man was dead. Complete nonsense. She can't be aware of everything that goes on.'

'What did you mean about a death wish?' Bridget took her coat from him and shrugged into it.

'She's sick in herself,' said Hugo.

'The diabetes, you mean?'

'There's that. And there's the loss of heart for the battle. Still, she knows herself what has to be done and she's always been a woman lived by her own lights.' Hugo handed her the scarf. 'You'll be going now then,' he said.

'Is Eleanor Munro around?' Bridget couldn't help herself. She had to know. The niggle had become an irritating nag.

'Miss Munro left early this morning,' said Hugo.

'Left? As in went away? Packed her bags?'

'Any one of those descriptions would fit. She packed her bags, left her room and went away in a cab. I have no idea where. I didn't ask.'

'And you were the only one saw her go?'

'Mrs Baldacci was not abroad at that hour. If Miss Munro hadn't disturbed me in the kitchen, where I was having a bit of breakfast, I wouldn't have been aware of her departure either.'

'What time was this?'

'Not more than a half hour before you arrived yourself.'

Bridget compromised on the walk. She took a cab from the house to the other side of the bridge, then paid off the driver and walked from there. It took her an hour to get to the hotel but she felt invigorated, as if she'd reclaimed something of herself and a freedom.

But she wasn't prepared, at all, to find that Eleanor Munro had moved into the room next to hers at the Hotel Pacific Nights.

Chapter Eleven

There was a note pinned to the door of Bridget's hotel room. She saw the sheet of folded yellow paper as soon as she left the lift and, if the vehicle hadn't already moved on a floor, she would have got back in and moved on herself, gone anywhere it was peaceful, uneventful. She didn't feel like any more news, good, bad or indifferent.

The words on the yellow paper were written in purple ink.

> I'm at the end of the corridor. Come visit me when you get this. You know what they say – if the mountain won't come to Mohammed then Mohammed must come to the mountain.

Eleanor Munro had signed only with a significant E.

The niggle of worry about the younger woman's safety was replaced by a healthy annoyance. This amounted to stalking. But she couldn't be ignored.

Bridget banged loudly with an open palm on the door at the end of the corridor. The act gave her a sense of being in control of things. She knew this was purely illusory but enjoyed the feeling for the minutes she waited for the door to open anyway.

'Well – where have you been? I've been waiting hours.' After a darting, conspiratorial scan of the corridor behind Bridget, Eleanor pulled her into the bedroom. 'I moved in as early as I could, hoping we could have breakfast together but you weren't here and I've been hanging about ever since.'

She dropped Bridget's arm and cleared a chair for her to sit on. It was late afternoon, and still bright outside, but the curtains were tightly closed and the only light came from a reading lamp on the desk. In the shadowy gloom, not unlike the gloom she'd just left in Veronica Baldacci's room, it seemed to Bridget that clothes and towels were strewn everywhere.

Eleanor was wearing a scarlet, kimono-style wrap and her hair was wet. In the air was the dense, muskily herbal smell of cannabis. Bridget would have known it anywhere.

'Tell me where you've been.' Eleanor sat on the bed and watched Bridget's face. She was palely animated in the murky light and puffing on the joint.

'What're you doing here, Eleanor, in this hotel?'

'I told you, in the note. You read it, didn't you?' Eleanor offered the joint to Bridget, who refused. The lie about them being conspirators, a team, had to be nailed somewhere.

'It's a free world,' Bridget stood up, 'and you're free to stay wherever you like. But we are not a team, Eleanor, and I don't want you involving me in everything you do.' She stopped. She'd made the point and hoped it was enough. 'I'm so sorry about Ted Morgan. It's a terrible—'

'You still don't get it, do you?' Eleanor got off the bed and leaned into the mirror, examining her face. What she saw there made her grimace with distaste and sigh.

'Maybe I don't.' Bridget leaned against the wall with her arms folded and watched the other woman in the mirror. 'Or maybe I just can't accept that you and I are in the danger you say we're in from the Baldaccis. I can't accept it because what would be the point?'

'The point,' Eleanor turned to face Bridget, 'is that we

have rights, both of us, and those people do not want to give them to us, to allow anyone in. Ted saw that. Ted was working on Veronica. He was bringing her round to his way of seeing things, which was that the past had to be put right. Ted, for reasons he never did tell me, felt bad about whatever happened when he worked for the Baldaccis. Him feeling like that was one of the reasons he agreed to come to Seattle with me.'

She stopped, pulled on the last of the joint and stubbed it out. 'Now he's dead and you're telling me there's no danger and that we don't need to stick together?'

'I'm just saying that I don't quite see it like that.'

Which was becoming less true every minute. Bridget could see how Ted Morgan could have felt he'd been to blame for Victor's leaving home. Problem was – if Ted hadn't told Eleanor about his affair with Veronica then Bridget didn't feel right about telling her now.

There was a case to be made, however, for telling Eleanor just how successful Ted had been in convincing Veronica to, in some way, atone for wrongs done to Shelley Munro and Victor; even if it had taken Ted's death for Veronica to see things his way.

'What is it?' Eleanor frowned. She'd shifted her position and now, sitting directly in the light from the desk lamp, her face was drawn and distressed and close to tears.

'There's something you should know,' Bridget said, gently. To hell with Veronica's admonitions to secrecy. Bridget hadn't made any promises. 'Ted actually did get through to Veronica. She intends making over an allowance to you.' Bridget paused, wondering briefly about the wisdom of telling all, before plunging ahead. 'I'm to get shares, though I'm not sure I want them.'

'She told you this? Veronica told you this?' Eleanor stood and began to pace.

'Yes. This morning. She said she was doing it for Ted,

that he'd wanted her to do it. To honour him was the phrase she used—'

'But no one else knows, right? And she told you to keep quiet about it?'

'Yes. I'm taking a day to think about it. But look, Eleanor, I think—'

'Don't think, listen.' Eleanor jumped up and began to root convulsively through a black travel bag. 'Veronica's taken unilateral action. It's the way she's always done things but she's not in control anymore and she doesn't even know it. Sure, she has the authority to do it – to do what she wants with her own shares. But the others aren't going to like it and they're going to try to stop it happening, one way or another. Only we're going to be ready for them.'

From the bag she produced a small pistol.

Bridget stared, moved back and told herself the gun wasn't real, that Eleanor was acting out some sort of melo-dramatic joke. Myth and legend and Hollywood all said that every full-blooded American owned a gun but she'd never believed it. She still didn't. Eleanor had no business waving one about. When she felt the door at her back Bridget stopped.

'That's not funny, Eleanor,' she said.

'It's not meant to be,' Eleanor snapped. 'It's going to help me look out for us, for you and me.' She held the gun with dangerous familiarity. 'They're not going to get us the way they got Ted. They're not going to pawn me off with some fucking miserable allowance either. No way.'

'I don't want anything to do with that gun,' Bridget felt for the door handle, 'and I'm getting out of here if you don't put it away – now.'

She was aware she sounded cross and motherly. She couldn't help it; she was terrified. Eleanor heard the motherly tone too and half smiled.

'Relax,' she said. 'It's not loaded. You don't know much about guns, do you?'

'I know nothing at all about them,' said Bridget.

'They're a necessary evil, and we need this pistol. Believe me,' she held and stroked the gun in the palm of her hand, 'I know what I'm doing.'

'It seems to me that all you're doing is looking for trouble.' Bridget was curt. 'I'm not at all convinced we're in danger. Ted Morgan's death was an awful accident, something to do with his reasons for going to stay in that Refuge. It was a truly terrible thing to have happened—'

'But you think I'm going over the top?'

'Yes. No one's going to do anything to harm either you or me. There's no way they'd get away with it. It would draw too much attention to the family and the past and the business. Now, please put the gun away. I don't want to see it and I don't want to know about it.'

'Ok, ok.' Eleanor stuffed the pistol back into the bag. 'It's not a Pershing missile, you know.'

Bridget didn't move from the door. Eleanor straightened up and her voice was harsh when she said, 'You seem to forget, Bridget, that my grandmother disappeared from that house and was never seen again, that my mother had to leave to save her life, that Ted Morgan left and turned up in the Sound, dead.' Her voice shook. 'You may be able to take all of those things on board but I can't overlook them. There's something else you should know. I'll tell you when the time is right. At this moment I get the feeling you're not really ready to trust me.'

'If you know something and you're frightened why don't you go to the police? Why don't you ask them for protection?'

'God, you think everything's so simple and straightforward, don't you? Thing is, I've been in trouble a few times with the cops. Nothing much. A couple of small narcotics offences – caught partying with the wrong people, so to speak. It's better if I do my business here without involving the cops. Ted thought so too . . .' Her frenzied energy fizzled and died as she said the dead man's name and all at once she became forlorn and drab-looking. 'Christ, I'm tired,' she said. 'I'm really tired. I haven't been sleeping in that house. Not since Ted left. I'll be able to sleep here, I know I will. All I need is someone on my side of the divide. That's all I ever needed.'

'Sleep is what you need,' Bridget said. 'Get into bed and give it a try. We'll talk again.'

But not that day, if she could help it. She'd heard enough, didn't want to hear another word. The something Eleanor thought Bridget should know about might be revealed from her bags as a grenade or an automatic rifle, or worse. Eleanor was a mess. Vulnerable, needy, bitter, obsessive and taking God alone knew what by way of drugs. But for all that Bridget couldn't find it in her heart to dismiss or dislike her.

Partly this had to do with her obvious vulnerability, but a larger part, she knew, had to do with how very like Anna she was to look at. There was a lot of Anna too in her single-minded campaign to get what she saw as her Baldacci inheritance. But Anna – confident, bright, achieving Anna – had been surrounded all her life by tender, loving care. Who was to say that Eleanor might not have been the same, or at least more similar than she was, if her life had been different? Eleanor's mother had died just a year ago from an overdose: she must be feeling raw about that too.

In her room Bridget grabbed money and a guidebook before leaving to head for a half decent restaurant she'd spotted several blocks away. Afterwards she went to see the film *Titanic*, which took up several hours and did nothing to raise her spirits. Back in her room she phoned home again and then briefly phoned Eleanor to say goodnight. She slept a full eight hours before the younger woman woke her, at 8 a.m., with a rhythmic knocking on the door and an invitation to breakfast.

Bridget would be glad she had the sleep, and the distancing break from Eleanor Munro.

'Did you tell Veronica you were moving in here?' she asked as they went down in the lift.

'I left a note for her in my room,' said Eleanor. 'She should have got it by now.'

Veronica had got the note all right. They were eating in the small breakfast room, Bridget packing in cereal and muffins and juice, Eleanor managing a couple of strong black coffees, when a po-faced hotel porter arrived at their table.

'There's a cop in the lobby wants to speak to Mrs Baldacci and Miss Munro. That's you two, right?'

'I don't want to talk with any cops.' Eleanor gripped Bridget's arm as they followed the porter. 'It is not a good idea for me to be around the cops. Oh, God, I wish this wasn't happening.'

The cop in the lobby was young and impressively polite.

'I hope you took time to finish your breakfast, ladies.' He was blond and had a wide smile. 'I'm here because Detective Lessig of the West Precinct asked me to call.' He made it sound as if forcing him to intrude on their morning was extreme bad taste on Lessig's part. 'He wants to talk with you, both. I'm to give you a ride to the Precinct.' He paused. 'Right away, he says.' He sighed and shook an apologetic head.

The West Precinct was on the third floor of the Public Safety Building at Third Avenue and James Street. Detective Lessig was waiting for them in a small, bright room filled with files and a couple of desktop computers. There was a Pirelli tyre calendar on the wall, a large photograph of the

Space Needle and Detective Jacklin working on one of the computers. She gave them an indifferent nod.

'Mrs Veronica Baldacci told us you'd moved out of her home,' Detective Lessig said to Eleanor. 'Is there something that discourages guests from staying too long in that house?'

'It's a bit out of town,' Eleanor said cautiously. 'I moved because I wanted to be closer to the centre of things.' She hesitated. 'And to my friend Bridget.'

'You've known each other a while then?'

'Not really. We've got a lot in common though.'

'This won't take long.' Lessig sat on the desk, smiled and stroked his moustache. It was thin but the hairs were impressively long. 'We need to clear up a few points about the late Theodore Morgan. You're both vacationing in Seattle, I understand from Mrs Baldacci senior. In your case, Mrs Baldacci, you've only been here a short while?'

'A little over a week.'

'Which means that you did not, in fact, have contact with Mr Morgan while he was in Seattle?'

'I never at any point in my life met Ted Morgan. I'd never heard of him until about a week ago.'

He nodded and looked away from them through the window. There was a lot of bustling noise from the rest of the building.

'You've been in Seattle a while longer, Miss Munro?'

'Since before Christmas,' Eleanor said.

Detective Lessig turned from the window with a tired smile. 'Our talk here this morning is informal. We won't be requiring statements, yet. That way *we* get everything wrapped up nice and quick and *you* can get back to spending your money in the city.' He picked up and consulted a notebook. 'You are the widow of Victor Baldacci?' he said to Bridget.

'Yes.' Bridget's patience began to wear thin. 'I don't see what my husband's death—'

'Just filling in a picture, Mrs Baldacci, just filling in a picture.' Detective Lessig, interrupting without looking at her, made a note with a black pen. 'You've never been to Seattle before? Never met your late husband's family?' His look was questioning, manner sympathetic.

'No. Victor had severed contact with his family.' She hesitated. 'I came to see for myself what they were like.'

'Understandable.'

He helped himself to a drink, but didn't offer anyone else one.

'Was it your opinion, Mrs Baldacci, that members of the household were upset by Mr Morgan's disappearance?'

'I couldn't really tell . . . Veronica Baldacci was upset . . .' Bridget stopped. 'I don't feel right about this, Detective Lessig. I'd rather not answer questions which involve my giving an opinion.'

Detective Jacklin turned from the keyboard with a loud, resigned groan. 'This could turn into a homicide investigation, ma'am, and we are not taking a statement here, merely looking for your assistance.'

'Homicide? As in murder?' Bridget asked. Beside her Eleanor made an odd, gurgling sound before burying her head in her hands.

'Homicide, as in murder,' Detective Lessig confirmed. 'Further examinations seem to indicate that Theodore Morgan could have been dead before going into the water.' He paused. 'Though a conclusive examination may never be possible—'

'The fact of the head and part of the torso being eaten away,' Detective Jacklin's interruption was crisp, 'is making things difficult, but not impossible.'

Eleanor dropped her hands onto her lap and stared straight ahead. Detective Lessig sighed gently.

'Miss Munro, I'd like you to fill me in on a few points also, if that's possible . . .'

'I'd like a drink of water,' Eleanor said.

Lessig frowned at the water cooler and sighed less gently and looked at the unmoving Detective Jacklin. 'I'll get it myself,' he said.

Detective Jacklin, tapping assiduously on the keyboard, didn't look up as he fiddled with plastic cups. When it looked as if she was also going to ignore Bridget and Eleanor until he'd finished, Bridget asked,

'Does the need for . . . examinations mean you'll be holding onto Mr Morgan's body for a while yet?'

'That's right. Just a little while longer.' Detective Jacklin nodded.

'It's just that I've promised to stay for the funeral,' Bridget said. 'You've no idea when a burial might be possible?'

'Give it a week.' Detective Jacklin turned from the screen to look at Eleanor. 'You came to Seattle with Theodore Morgan?' Her eyes were bored.

'Yes.'

'You were friendly in New York?'

'Yes.'

'What is your connection with the Baldacci family?'

Eleanor, her voice flat and language businesslike, repeated everything she'd already told Bridget. She made no accusations and said nothing about coming to Seattle for her share in the family wealth.

'Why did you and Mr Morgan come to Seattle, Miss Munro?' Detective Jacklin asked when Eleanor had finished, resting her elbows on the desk.

'Ted Morgan read that Victor Baldacci had died. He wanted to come see Veronica Baldacci again. I came with him out of curiosity. I really don't know why he left the Baldacci home and I didn't see him after he did. Why don't you ask Veronica Baldacci about this? She's the one had most contact with him—'

'We tried to this morning,' Detective Lessig, turning with two plastic cups of water, cut across Eleanor. 'She was too unwell to talk with us. We'll be getting to her. And to the rest of the family.'

He handed Eleanor one of the cups and, when Bridget refused the other, drank from it himself.

'We're just about finished here,' said Detective Jacklin.

'Right. Let me ask one more thing.' Detective Lessig turned to Eleanor. 'The last time you saw Theodore Morgan was in the Baldacci home, is that how it was?'

'Yes.'

'We've a small problem needs solving . . .' Detective Jacklin got up. Standing she filled a lot more space than sitting. 'The people at the Bible Mission tell us Mr Morgan took some phone calls. They say he made some too. Did he by any chance call you, Miss Munro, or did you call at any time while he was staying there?'

'No, I didn't. On both counts.'

'Well, that's about it then.' Detective Lessig sighed. 'We're grateful for your help.' He fiddled again with the moustache, making Bridget wonder if it was a new addition to his face. 'Enjoy the rest of your stay in the Emerald City.'

'That's it?' Eleanor said.

'For now,' Detective Lessig opened the door.

Eleanor refused, for both of them, the offer of a police car back to the hotel. Walking along the hectic, early morning streets in the new boots she'd bought for the funeral Mass, Bridget lodged a resigned complaint.

'I would have been glad of that police car to the hotel,' she said.

'I've seen more than enough cops for one morning,' Eleanor was surly.

'You've certainly got a way with the truth when it comes to talking to the police.' Bridget, choosing her words carefully, stopped walking and, catching Eleanor's arm, stopped her too. 'Why did you lie back there? Lie number one: why did you tell that detective you came to Seattle only out of a curiosity to see the family?'

Eleanor turned her head and stared down the street. As she began to speak she walked on. Bridget walked with her, watching her agitated profile as she spoke. It was filled with a rigid, stony anger.

'I told Lessig I came here out of curiosity because once you talk money to the cops they start looking at your life and I don't want them investigating me.' Eleanor hugged herself as she went on, 'They turn up that narcotics violation in New York that's all those Baldaccis need to cut me out for ever. I'm entitled. This is my chance for a new life. All I've got to do is keep my head down.'

'And get what's yours at any cost?' Bridget took Eleanor's arm again as a sudden rush of people threatened to separate them. 'Even denying Ted Morgan?' She stopped and turned the younger woman to face her. When Eleanor tried to free her arm she held on, tight. 'Your second lie back there was when you denied knowing where Ted Morgan went after he left the Baldacci home.'

'They asked if I'd seen him after he left and I didn't, so that was the truth.'

'Stop being so bloody disingenuous.' Bridget shook Eleanor, hard. 'You know what I'm talking about. You spoke to him, you told me so yourself. He phoned you. He told you where he was, gave you the address so as you could go to him if you needed to.'

'I don't have to tell you anything.' Eleanor yanked herself free.

'The fact is, when I phoned to say I was coming to see him he was already gone.' She looked mulish. 'So, I didn't actually *see* him.'

'No, you didn't. But you still lied and you certainly

denied Ted Morgan. If he was . . . dead before going into the water then someone murdered him. You, Eleanor, have information about his last movements which could help the police find the person who did it. Ted Morgan's entitled to have his death accounted for – are you going to help?'

'I can't right now. In a few days I'll tell the police everything, I promise.' Eleanor, anger gone, looked at Bridget from a white, pleading face. 'There's another way of looking at things, you know. Ted wouldn't have wanted me to blow this thing now I'm so close. I just have to hang on, do things my way for another few days. Stick with me, Bridget,' she caught Bridget's hand, 'please, and trust me. Just for a few days more.'

The red, message light was flashing on the phone in Bridget's hotel room. She said a hurried goodbye to Eleanor and closed the door before she could see it. She didn't trust her.

The message was from Thomas. She phoned him back immediately.

'Veronica's not good,' he said, 'and she's been asking to see you. Says there's something she needs to discuss with you.'

Bridget could hear him waiting, wanting to know what possible business she had with Veronica. That Veronica was keeping him in the dark about the shares didn't surprise her. The Baldacci family code, if it had any, was about secrecy and deceit and playing all sides against the middle. On the other hand, maybe Veronica had good reason and maybe it was better not to say anything to Thomas, for now.

'I'll come out to visit her this afternoon,' she said.

'That sounds good,' Thomas said. 'But, uh, I need to ask you to, uh, come alone—'

'Without Eleanor, you mean?'

'Right.' Thomas sounded relieved. 'Veronica doesn't want her around the place.'

Visiting the Baldacci house without Eleanor Munro was a lot easier said than done. She phoned as soon as Bridget finished the call to Thomas and, in spite of Bridget's plea for time alone, arrived at the bedroom door ten minutes later.

'Let's go eat,' she said, 'I never ate at breakfast. I'm starving.'

'I don't want to.' Bridget knew she sounded petulant. Anna sometimes had the same effect on her, usually when she tried to organize Bridget's life, as Eleanor was doing now.

'You going to stay in this room all day?' Eleanor looked disdainfully at the repro desk and unmade bed.

'I thought I'd go to see *Titanic* in the cinema. Alone. I want a break from all that's been happening.'

How easily the lie came, how quickly she was fitting herself to the Baldacci way of doing things, how lucky she'd seen the film already and could give an account of it if necessary.

'I've seen it,' said Eleanor. 'You won't enjoy it. Unrealistic love story between an actor who's still a boy and looks it and an actress who looks like a full-blooded woman. I'd never have written a romantic coupling so fundamentally unsexy myself. Why don't you and me go to—'

'I want to see *Titanic*. Alone.'

'Fine. Waste an afternoon. It's your life. If watery special effects and simpering boys are your thing then go ahead, go—'

'Oh, shut up, Eleanor,' Bridget said.

Eleanor sniffed, tossed her hair back and turned on her heel. 'I'll be in my room,' she said. It was another Anna-like performance.

*

Thomas opened the door to Bridget, his usual benign courtesy blighted by a distracted air.

'Good of you to come, especially in the circumstances.'

He led her to the dining room where he stood looking out a window and talking over his shoulder in quick, short sentences.

'Veronica's clearly not well. Magdalena's – oh, let's not talk about Magdalena. I'm worried about Veronica. I don't like her being on her own. She won't hear of a nurse. There's Hugo . . .' He coughed. 'I dislike being away from business during the day, from the office I mean. I worry things will collapse without me, which they won't, of course.' He coughed again. 'Couldn't get either of my offspring to come over here when their grandmother called. Don't get me wrong. They're good kids,' he sounded defensive, 'especially Lindsay.' He gave Bridget an apologetic look. 'She puts so much damn time into the business.'

He made an imperceptible adjustment to the curtain and gave another throat-clearing cough.

'Veronica's waiting for you,' he said.

'How is she, really?'

'Well . . . she's . . .'

Thomas looked for a minute in silence at the straggling line of conifers along the avenue. He looked very neat in his grey suit and silver-grey tie.

'Her fire seems to have gone out. She's acting like . . . her mind was going. Only thing she seems sure about it that she wants to talk to you.' He turned, leaned forward a little. 'Please remember Bridget, that she is old. And powerless.'

He smiled. It was not a nice smile.

Veronica's bedroom was, if anything, murkier than it had been the day before. She was sitting in the same chair by the window, staring through the same barely opened shutter at the falling darkness outside. Bridget sat again in the chair opposite and looked as closely as the gloom would allow at the older woman. Veronica seemed to her much the same as she had at yesterday's visit, even to the glass of whiskey cradled in her lap. She was pale and freshly made-up and wearing the same high-necked, pearl-buttoned dress. The room was still hot but there was an additional something. Bridget tried without success to pin it down. Thomas's smile had unnerved her.

'Have you thought about what I said?' Veronica demanded after a while.

'I have,' said Bridget.

There was a smell, that was what was different and additional to the day before. It was of nail-varnish remover, or at least of something with a strong acetone base. Veronica, along with making up her face, obviously manicured her nails on a daily basis. The smell was oddly pervasive.

'Well?' Veronica was querulous.

'I don't want the shares, Veronica, though I appreciate the offer.' Bridget hesitated, then leaned forward and touched Veronica's arm briefly. 'Whatever way I say this will sound ungracious and rude. The truth is that I don't want to be involved with this family on an ongoing basis. It would be a denial of Victor, of his decision to make a life apart for himself and his children . . . and me.' She took a breath, let it out. 'I couldn't do that to him. I don't want to.'

Veronica's silence crackled in the room for several minutes.

To break it, Bridget said, 'I will keep in touch, though. I will write.'

By the time she left she would know everything so an occasional letter, on her terms, would not be a betrayal of Victor.

'You are telling me that you will not accept my gift?'

In the gloom, Veronica turned her head toward Bridget. Her face appeared to be still and expressionless.

'I don't want the shares, Veronica. I don't want to be involved in the family business.'

'You are a fool. I might have known that only a fool would have married Victor Baldacci.' Veronica made a harsh sound which came close to being a laugh. 'I have been saddled with a fool and a madwoman, both of them alive and troublesome while a good man like Ted Morgan lies dead and rotting.'

She stopped. Bridget said nothing. Grief needed its outings, however irrational, she knew that. After a few minutes she said, firmly,

'You've put me in an awkward position, Veronica, asking me not to discuss your plans for shares and an allowance for Eleanor with the family, with Thomas and Lindsay, in particular. These things concern them too.'

Maybe Thomas already knew. Maybe that was what he meant when he said Veronica was powerless.

'They do not. They will know about my plans when they need to know. How I choose to distribute my majority shares is my own affair. I hold control until the day I die and I am not dead. Yet.' Veronica stopped, fingering the buttons at the neck of her dress as if too hot. 'I will also decide on the shape the company will take after I am gone.' She stopped again and frowned as if clearing her thoughts. 'You have been hasty. You are confused by all you have found here and you are not, in my opinion, capable of making a clear decision. I want you to give my offer some more thought.' She placed her elbow on the arm of the chair and rested her face in the palm of her hand and it seemed to Bridget that she smiled. Or maybe it was a grimace. The acetone smell was quite strong and her nails looked newly shining. 'It is not so easy to walk away, Bridget. It is not an easy thing to do at all. You will be glad, in time, for what I've done. You will thank me, in time.'

'How are you feeling?' Bridget asked.

'Tired . . .' Veronica sipped her drink.

'Maybe you should get into bed,' Bridget suggested.

'Don't patronize me,' Veronica snapped. 'I will get in bed when the time comes and not before.' She nodded toward the shutters. 'You might close those for me, if you please. The wind forecast by the meteorologists is blowing up the avenue. I've seen enough of it.'

Bridget, after a look at the icy rain whirling in the gathering winds outside, saw the older woman's point and closed the shutters.

'There's snow promised across the Cascades and for the southern Washington Cascades,' Veronica sounded dreamy. 'I haven't been in any of those mountains since I went with my father as a girl.'

'Seems a shame, when they're so close,' said Bridget.

'My son-in-law tells me your hotel is small, noisy. The description,' she held up a hand as Bridget began a protest born of a perverse loyalty to the Pacific Nights, 'is my daughter's but Thomas nevertheless thinks it would be a fine thing if you stayed the night here, with me. He is being pragmatic, of course. He has no desire to spend the night with me himself, my grandchildren are too busy, my daughter, his wife, is drunk. So you, Bridget Baldacci, are being used. They merely want you to act as watchdog for the night.'

'I'll stay if you need me to,' Bridget said, 'but what about Hugo?'

'Hugo is about, somewhere.' Veronica waved vague fingers and her voice developed an unpleasantly wheedling note, 'You can tell me about your children. My grandchildren.'

'I'll stay a while,' said Bridget, 'but first I need to make a phone call.'

Thomas, more obviously anxious than before, was

waiting for her downstairs. Hugo Sweeney hovered within earshot as they spoke.

'I'm glad you're staying,' Thomas said when she told him. He looked it. 'You'll have seen by now how she is. It's a ludicrous situation, you having to . . .' he trailed off. 'I'll get you a drink. Veronica may pull out of this melancholy, or whatever it is. She's gone down before and recovered, Phoenix-like. She's immortal, in her own way. If you could just stay until she sleeps . . .' He hesitated, then said, 'Or even the night?'

'I'll do that. I'll stay the night.'

When she asked for a phone Thomas led her to one in Veronica's small library. Bridget didn't even try to fathom her own reluctance to tell him she wanted to let Eleanor know where she would be spending the night, she put it down to an inability to trust anyone, even Thomas.

'Take all the time you want.' He smiled, closing the door discreetly after him.

There was no reply from Eleanor's room and when Bridget checked with the reception the woman there was adamant.

'Miss Munro is not in her room,' she said. 'She went out a couple of hours ago. I saw her go myself.'

'Did she say when she would be coming back?'

'That is not the sort of thing we ask our guests.'

'Was she alone?'

'She seemed to be, yes.' Frosty didn't describe her tones.

'Put me through to Miss Munro's voicemail, please,' Bridget said.

She left a message asking Eleanor to phone her at the Baldacci house when she got in. That way she would at least know when she was safely back in the hotel.

Chapter Twelve

Thomas was waiting for Bridget when she got back to the hallway. He took her hand for a minute, saying nothing, looking very much like a man wishing he were elsewhere.

'I appreciate all that you're doing for us.' He dropped her hand and rubbed her arm in an awkwardly appreciative gesture. 'Staying here tonight – well, it's a big help in the present situation.'

'I wasn't exactly turning down dinner invitations,' said Bridget and wished she hadn't when Thomas blinked and looked startled.

'You could have been invited somewhere else?' He stared at her. 'You have friends in Seattle?'

'No, I don't. Unfortunately.'

All at once she would have given anything to have someone to phone, to have a link to life outside this house. Even Eleanor had gone missing. No one in the world knew she was here, except the Baldaccis. Thomas's relief that she'd agreed to stay was palpable, she'd wanted to stay herself so why, now, was she feeling manipulated? As if she'd been set up?

Thomas reached for an overcoat lying across a heavy, wood-carved armchair.

'Would it be all right with you if I left right away? I've been out of my office a lot lately and one or two things need attending to.'

He shrugged into the coat. His head, buried in the

collar, looked remarkably small. He looked slightly lost and she warmed to him all over again.

'No need for you to stay.' She smiled. 'I presume Hugo is around if I need anything?'

'Hugo is here, yes.'

Thomas buttoned the coat neatly and carefully. A man used to looking after himself, Bridget thought; not much chance that Magdalena had ever mothered him.

'He'll get you whatever you want.' He stood with his hands by his sides. 'This is not the ideal way to spend your vacation,' he said, 'but it's certainly a way of getting to know your late husband's mother.'

'How ill do you think she really is?' Bridget asked.

'I've seen her like this before.' Thomas took his gloves from his pocket. 'It's as if her spirit just goes right down. Understandable, when you know about the rough times she's had. Ted Morgan dying the way he did . . .' He pulled on the gloves, smoothing the fingers carefully. 'She'll come round. She always does.'

There it was again. The family belief in Veronica's immortality. She's eighty-two, Bridget wanted to say, she mightn't 'come round', she could very well die.

'As long as I've known her,' Thomas went on, 'she's been independent in all things. Like I said earlier, she's refused the doctor, says she won't let him near her. Isn't that right, Hugo?'

'She's quite adamant.' Hugo Sweeney, appearing from the end of the hallway, had clearly been there all the time. 'Her diabetes is controlled and there's no moving her on the matter of seeing a doctor.'

With small, busy steps he walked past them to open the front door. He stood there with his back to them.

Thomas, unexpectedly, leaned forward and kissed Bridget lightly on the cheek. 'As with everything else in her life Veronica will not die until *she* decides,' he spoke close to her ear. 'Believe me, Bridget, I would not leave you here if I thought there was anything seriously the matter. Hugo was wrong to think she has a death wish. He realizes that now. That sort of thinking comes from being too close to her – and Hugo's always been close to Veronica.'

He stepped away and handed Bridget a card. 'My number, our home number too, Magdalena's and mine, in case you need us.' He left then, quickly, Hugo Sweeney stepping aside to let him through the front door.

Outside, where the sky above the trees was unrepentantly sullen, an early frost had settled on the roof of Thomas's waiting car.

'Good night.' Bridget waved the card as he slipped into the driving seat. Thomas, head down, didn't respond. She waited until the car's tail lights disappeared round the bend in the avenue before turning to face Hugo.

'Looks like you're stuck with me for the night.' She gave him a wry grin.

'It's looking that way,' Hugo, not disposed to be humoured, was unsmiling, 'so we'd best put up with one another. I'll get you a drink. Coffee or tea?'

'I'll have a gin Martini,' said Bridget. She needed it.

'I'll bring it to you in the sitting room,' Hugo said. 'Mrs Baldacci's sleeping at the moment so there's no good you going up to her right now.'

He was a long time getting the drink. Bridget studied the paintings and the furniture in the big room and spent a while at the window looking at the darkened Christmas tree. When the silence and the claustrophobia became too much she wandered out and into the hallway. Hugo's voice, low and confidential, came from behind the half-open door of a nearby room. Bridget hesitated, wondering if Veronica had come downstairs, and was about to push open the door when Hugo said goodbye and hung up a telephone.

Deciding on discretion as the better part of valour she slipped back into the sitting room.

When Hugo reappeared minutes later he was carrying a tray on which he'd arranged what amounted to afternoon tea. Along with a silver teapot there was a selection of miniature sandwiches, pastries, milk and sugar.

'Looks good.'

Bridget searched hopefully for her drink as Hugo fussed and laid the contents of the tray out on a table. There was no gin Martini.

'It is always my task to prepare tea in the afternoon for Mrs Baldacci. She wasn't up to taking it today and there's no point in letting good food go to waste.' He poured tea into a delicate pink china cup. 'Milk? Sugar?' He placed a chair beside the table. 'I'll leave you to it then.'

Bridget sat on the chair and eyed the food. She didn't want sandwiches and she certainly didn't feel like pastries. A gin Martini was what she felt like. She sipped the tea.

'Why don't you get another cup and join me?' she said to the still hovering Hugo.

He shook his head. 'I'm too old a dog for new tricks. It's my custom to eat on my own.' He moved the plate of sandwiches closer to her on the table. 'I was talking to Father Bob Matthews on the phone just now. You'll have heard me when you were out in the hallway?'

'I heard you on the phone, yes,' said Bridget, 'though not what you were saying or who you were talking to, obviously.'

The man missed nothing. He was watching her now.

He said, 'You'll remember Bob Matthews from the memorial Mass?'

'Yes, of course.'

'Well, he's on his way over here now.' Hugo consulted a pocket watch. 'Should arrive in about fifteen minutes.'

'An official or social visit?' Bridget tried and failed to catch Hugo's eye. Could Veronica have agreed to the last rites? Or was Hugo organizing a priestly blessing on his own initiative?

'A social visit,' said Hugo. He went on hovering.

'If there's something you want to say, Hugo, then for God's sake say it,' Bridget said briskly, putting down the tea cup.

'You don't want the sandwiches then?' Hugo nodded at the plate. 'Nor the pastries? More tea?'

'No. Thank you.'

'Well, then . . .'

Hugo locked his hands behind his back and began to rock on his heels.

'I'll be brief about what it is I want to say. It's this: for the past while I've been wanting to put a few things in order around here. I was the one sent you the letter you'll have found in your hotel room when you arrived. I thought it would be best if you didn't stay long in Seattle, didn't add to the trouble brewing here.' He paused. 'I was thinking along the lines of maybe bringing about a bit of damage limitation.' He stopped rocking on his heels long enough to align a pair of silver candlesticks on an inlaid table beside him. 'You can always tell when Mrs Baldacci's not around,' he muttered, 'place goes to the dogs.' He looked critically around the room before beginning to rock on his heels again. 'I was sure you'd be the powder which would ignite the situation but I was wrong. I see now that you weren't really the one who was going to do that. Not on your own anyway.'

'What situation? What trouble?'

So Hugo had sent the letter. Bridget was surprised how easily, and with what small degree of shock, she accepted this. Of course he'd sent it. Hugo was one of those insidiously manipulative people who were always trying to control things.

She looked at him steadily while, with obvious care, he put together the words to answer her question.

'I'll tell you something of my story,' he said at last. 'It'll explain a lot of things to you. Bob Matthews has other things to tell you when he gets here. Between the two histories you can make up your own mind about things.'

'Why not?' Bridget was curt and, all at once, feeling bitter. 'I've been given the other versions of family events. Why not yours, why not Father Matthews'? Go ahead.'

Hugo gave a quick, small shrug and sat, with fastidious care, on a spindle-backed Windsor chair.

'You, no doubt, see a controlling old woman when you look at Veronica Baldacci,' he began. 'I see a beautiful woman, in the prime of her early middle years. I always will. That's my cross and that's my salvation. That was the age she was, with the looks of a Grace Kelly, when she rescued me from a life that would have surely ended in jail or the gutter, and that's the simple truth of it.' He stopped and met Bridget's eyes, briefly. 'It's not too fanciful to say that she has been my mother, my wife, my sister, my friend . . . my redemption.' He stopped again, this time to spread his hands. 'And there you have it.'

'There I have what?' Bridget's patience gave out. 'You've got a great turn of phrase, Hugo, and you've got a sad story to tell. But so what if Veronica rescued you from a bad situation and you've lived here, worked for and been beholden to her ever since? That doesn't tell me anything much about what's going on here today. You've given me the bones of your story. Now,' Bridget stabbed a finger at him, 'give me the flesh.'

'I don't at all care for your metaphors,' Hugo said huffily. 'I'm inclined to leave it to yourself to put two and two together—'

'You do that and I'm going up to drag the story out of the priest – out of Veronica if I have to!'

'You don't need to know—'

'I'll decide what I need to know from now on,' Bridget snapped.

Hugo, with a long, raspy sigh, rested his narrow, veined hands on his knees.

'I've never put my story into words before,' he said, 'so

you'll have to bear with me while I tell it my own way now. I was in serious trouble with the law when Veronica Baldacci took me in. I arrived in Boston from Cork and from day one got myself in with the same sort of company I'd left behind me.' He gave a small, irritated shrug of his shoulders. 'I got out of Boston with the cops on my tail about some matters involving thieving and arson and the like. I was staying in a boarding house close to Our Lady of Lourdes when I got myself into another spot of bother. Bob Matthews, who was a young curate there at the time, talked the parishioner I'd robbed into not pressing charges. I gave back the money and I talked to the priest. I hadn't an intention in the world of staying on the straight and narrow but in the church with him that day I met Veronica Baldacci.' His expression was tired and sour. 'I was a young man, still. Bob Matthews was a young man too, about my own age, and he was bent on a mission to save souls. He set about saving mine.' He gave a thin laugh. 'It was a bit late for that, but when he got Veronica Baldacci to give me a job looking after the gardens he at least saved me from jail.'

Bridget nibbled on one of the sandwiches. In the dry heat of the room it had begun to harden and go stale. 'Frank Baldacci was still alive when you first came here then?' she said.

'He was.'

'And my – Victor was still living here too?'

'Victor Baldacci was in his late teens.'

'Was he very unhappy?'

'I wouldn't have called him a happy young man. He didn't confide in me. I didn't think a lot about him.'

'Do you know why he left?'

'I do. And so do you. Mrs Baldacci's already told you the reason why . . .' His voice tailed off and he looked, for a minute, both very old and very sad.

'Tell me,' Bridget said changing the subject, 'what made you give up a life of crime to work as a gardener?'

Hugo Sweeney contemplated the tips of his shoes and spoke with dispassionate fervour.

'Love. You could say it was love turned me around and you wouldn't be far wrong. When Veronica Baldacci stood in front of me and said she was of Irish stock and would I look after her gardens, it never occurred to me to refuse her.'

He folded his arms and leaned back and looked at Bridget. He seemed to her to have grown smaller in the days since she'd met him.

'What I was thinking about was that I would hide out here for a few months and then be on my way. Well, the months stretched on and I got to like the gardening and the day came when I didn't know how to leave either the gardens or the woman.' He paused. 'Of course I was a drinker then and the drink is a great man for dulling the feelings. There was never any shortage of drink around here.

'My health went and things got to a stage where it was easier to stay than to go. It was only as I grew older, and the drinking got less, that I was able to face the reasons I'd stayed and the feelings I had for her. She knows, of course. She's always known, from the first day, and she's used it. She needed someone she could trust in this house and she got someone in me. She had a power over men, in the way that icy women have. I never wanted her the way other men did, and that's the truth. I wanted only to be where she was.' With an air of finality, he said, 'So now you know.'

Bridget could think of nothing to say. Or do. She sat in silence with Hugo Sweeney in the vast room for long minutes, the emotions and loneliness of the story just told resonating about them.

When sounds came of a car coming up the avenue, and its lights shone across the closed curtains, she broke the silence.

'You knew everything that was going on in this house, didn't you, Hugo?'

Hugo Sweeney didn't answer, just shook his head slightly from side to side, the colour of his face almost exactly matching the still, cold grey of his eyes.

'You knew about Shelley and Frank, about Grace Munro.' Bridget made her voice firm. 'What happened to Grace?'

'All history, but not my history,' Hugo said. 'There's no good to be served going back over things that're dead and done with.'

'What about Ted Morgan? He was a part of that history but he came back and—'

Bridget stopped. Dead and done with, about described what had happened to poor Ted Morgan.

'Ted Morgan's part in all of this is something you need to know about.' Hugo stood and moved quickly across the room as the front-door bell chimed. 'The priest will tell you about him. He's the one with the first-hand information.'

While Hugo attended to the priest's arrival, taking his coat and explaining that Veronica was still sleeping, Bridget found a phone and called the Hotel Pacific Nights. There was still no answer from Eleanor Munro's room. The receptionist, when she got her on the phone, was disinterested.

'Miss Munro has not returned,' she said, 'would you care to leave a message on her voicemail?'

Bridget didn't. A message wouldn't adequately explain what she was doing in the Baldacci home. She tried to ignore a nagging unease about Eleanor's whereabouts as she put the phone down and went to greet the priest.

He was waiting for her in the hallway, the rosy skin of his choirboy's face stiff and anxious-looking. A benign, practised smile split his cheeks as she came towards him. Hugo was disappearing quickly up the stairs.

'Keeping well, I hope?' The priest shook Bridget's hand formally. 'It's kind of you to stay. Mrs Baldacci is far too often on her own in this house. I have prayed that she be sent company.' He looked around the hallway as if expecting a legion of angels to appear. 'It would appear that God has listened.' He smiled hopefully.

'I am only staying for one night. You will need to begin praying again tomorrow. Surely Magdalena or Veronica's grandchildren—'

'Busy people, all of them.' The priest, interrupting, waved a gently dismissive hand. 'It must also be said, however, that Veronica can be a difficult woman.' He fell silent, the smile fixed on his face.

'Hugo's been talking to me,' Bridget said carefully. 'You've known each other a long time, it seems. That there are things you might explain to me . . .' Bridget waited.

'Call me Bob,' the priest said.

'Bob. Please tell me what's going on. I need to know.'

The priest clasped his hands in front of him and studied them. 'I understand. Hugo has been talking to me too. He thinks you should know what was happening with Ted Morgan before he died. I guess you should.' He pursed his lips. 'What I am about to tell you is confidential.'

'Of course,' Bridget said. But this was not a confessional and she would not be bound with oaths. There were too many secrets which needed to be outed.

She was aware, as the priest began to talk, of Hugo Sweeney coming back into the hallway.

'Mrs Baldacci wanted to marry Ted Morgan.' Bob Matthews shook his head. 'She wanted, she said, to put right their relationship of years before. Also, she wanted a companion and she trusted Mr Morgan. I was to marry them.'

'What did Ted Morgan want?'

'Primarily, not to offend Mrs Baldacci. He said he wanted to put the past to rights but wasn't sure that marriage was the way to do it. He left this house to have time alone to think things through.'

'Who else knew this?' Bridget said.

'I don't know. Mrs Baldacci didn't intend telling the family until everything had been settled. Things were by no means settled when Mr Morgan disappeared – died.'

Bridget took a deep breath. 'Do you think Ted Morgan's death was in any way connected with Veronica's marriage proposal?' She stopped, thought quickly and went on, 'Could it have had to do with someone not wanting him in the family? Resenting his influence with Veronica?' Possibilities piled up in her head. 'With fears that he would outlive Veronica, have too much control—'

'Mine is not to judge,' said the priest.

'Oh, for Christ's sake,' Bridget exploded, 'yours is to help where you can, surely. And I need help here.' She looked the priest full in the face. 'I need to know because I am spending the night in this house. I need to be sure I'll be safe. Who's to say I'm not resented in the same way? Now tell me.'

'I have thought long and hard,' Father Matthews pressed the palms of his hands together in a pleading gesture, 'and the most I can say, even to myself, is that there's a possibility his death may be connected to family fears such as you describe. I do know,' the choirboy face sagged, 'that Ted Morgan was uneasy about things. He told me so. "This plan of Veronica's is not welcome within the family" was how he put it. I said to him that it would be a strange family which would welcome the matriarch taking a husband at eighty-two years of age. He said . . .' the priest paused, frowning as he tried to remember exactly the words spoken to him, 'that the Baldacci family was stronger than most and that he was trying to talk Veronica out of the idea of the marriage. He left this house the next day. I did not see him again.'

'Did Veronica know how he felt?'

'If she did she said nothing to me about it.'

'Did you talk about any of this to the police?'

The priest cleared his throat and shook his head. A nerve twitched at the side of his eye and he raised a hand to stop it.

'Things are not as simple in this country as—'

'They are not simple in Ireland either. Why didn't you tell all of this to the police?'

'You have to understand,' he moistened his lips, 'that Veronica Baldacci has been good to Our Lady of Lourdes. She has donated generously for many, many years.' His expression pleaded for understanding. There was fear in it too. 'She saw to it too that I was given Our Lady of Lourdes when my time came to be made a parish priest.' He squared his shoulders. 'Her secrets are safe with me.'

Bridget stared at him, putting the pieces of what he'd told her together out loud. 'You're obligated to Veronica . . . you know about things which happened in the past . . . you're afraid they might come out in an investigation . . .' She took a deep breath and let it out again. 'So you didn't go to the police because you're protecting Veronica's secrets.'

'We're both of us, Father Matthews and myself, beholden to Veronica Baldacci,' Hugo said. 'She's saying now that she wants to see the two of you. You first, Father.'

Bridget, waiting for the priest and Hugo to return, paced twitchily between the hallway and dining room. The urge to tear upstairs and be a part of what was going on was a physical thing.

But Veronica was old and not well and the two men in her room with her were old too and, in the priest's case at least, frightened.

Father Matthews didn't stay long. In less than ten minutes by Bridget's watch she heard him on the stairs again with Hugo, his voice low and insistent. Hugo, except for the barest of monosyllables, was silent. Bridget stood at the bottom of the stairs waiting for them.

'I'll be back in the morning,' Father Matthews spoke hurriedly from the bottom step. 'She's asked me to visit again.' He looked panicky as Hugo left them. 'It's a good thing you're staying the night.' He didn't look at Bridget.

Hugo reappeared with the priest's coat and together, pointedly ignoring Bridget, they walked to the front door. When he had closed it Hugo turned to Bridget.

'She'll see you now,' he said. 'You can go on up yourself. I've things to be doing down here.'

Veronica was sitting in bed with a silver-grey shawl around her shoulders. She had loosened her hair so that it lay yellowy gold on the pillow. Her tightly stretched skin seemed held together by the glue of a fresh make-up job and she smelled strongly of a sweet, musky smelling scent. The room itself still smelled of acetone.

'How are you feeling?' Bridget said.

Veronica ignored the question. 'You've been talking to the priest?'

'Yes. And to Hugo.' Bridget stood at the end of the bed. 'You'd planned to marry Ted Morgan.'

'I would most definitely have married Ted, had he been allowed to live. I'm old.' She spread, and looked at, her hands on the white of the bedcover. The rings, grotesquely shining, sat just below the knuckles. 'I am often alone and I don't care for it. Ted and I understood one another.' She folded her hands and the rings, even more grotesquely, bunched together. 'I've asked Hugo to make up a bed in the room across the corridor. It was your husband's room as a boy.'

Bridget held a breath until she was reasonably sure the sudden, shaky feeling had passed.

'Thank you, Veronica,' she said, 'that was thoughtful.'

Victor's mother nodded. 'I wish to sleep now. You should do so too.' She reached toward a bell in the wall by the bed.

'Hugo will show you to your room.' She smiled. The effort at agreeableness seemed to Bridget both sad and cynical. 'Sleep well.'

'Thank you.'

Bridget stood and put a hand over Veronica's where it was poised on the bell.

'There's no need to call Hugo. I'll make my own way to Victor's room.'

It was not a big room. The dull green of the walls were splattered with faded squares and rectangles where, long ago, pictures, or posters, had hung. The wardrobe and drawers were empty and the brown wool cover on the single bed hadn't been turned down. There wasn't an echo of Victor anywhere in his room. Even so, the white lawn nightdress lying across the bed looked out of place. When Bridget lifted it from the pillow to her face it had a sweet, musky smell.

In bed Bridget coaxed and pounded the single pillow until she found a way of lying that was bearable. For a long time she tried to imagine the teenage boy who'd become the man she'd married. It was enough to visualize him; he would have been dark-eyed and bonily thin. Trying to make sense of how he must have felt about the loveless cruelties of the family he'd grown up in was more difficult.

Around her the old house was silent, the wind beyond the shuttered window a small rustle of sound. Had Victor lain in a silence like this and heard Ted Morgan with his mother in his father's bed across the corridor? Had he heard his father too, engaged in incestuous couplings with his half-sister Shelley Munro?

Listening as the house whispered its sad horrors she cried a little, for herself, for the injustice Victor had done her by not trusting her with his secrets.

After a while she slept, but restlessly and for only a short time before the rustling sounds awoke her.

They had become louder and smotheringly close . . .

Chapter Thirteen

Veronica Baldacci's silky grey shawl brushed gently over Bridget's face.

'Wake up, Bridget Baldacci, I want to talk with you.' The old woman's bony fingers were on her shoulder, shaking her. 'Wake up . . .'

Bridget, fully conscious, pulled away from the stifling effect of the silk on her face and sat up. Even then she could smell, rather than see, Veronica; the familiar smell of acetone mingling with the musky perfume.

'What is it? What's wrong?' Bridget pressed herself against the wall. Veronica was too close; she could feel the dryness of her, a sense of her withering.

'I am restless. I cannot sleep,' Veronica's voice was disembodied, somehow apart from the slightly weaving rest of her. 'I cannot talk to Hugo. He is not the kind of person one talks to. But you are here and will have to do.'

Bridget could see her more clearly now, hair floating loose on either side of the pale shape that was her face.

'I'll turn on the light . . .' she began.

'No!' Veronica hissed the command. 'There is enough natural light for our purposes.' She lifted her walking cane and pointed. 'I want you to open the shutters. The worst of the night's dark has passed and there's a moon, of sorts.' Her laugh was like glass splintering. 'We will talk by its light.'

She sat in an armchair not far from the bed and waited while Bridget opened the shutters.

For just a minute after she'd done so, watching the wild sky and fitful moon, Bridget stood and gathered her thoughts. Then the armchair in the room behind her creaked impatiently and she went back to the bed, pulled the covers around her and sat facing her mother-in-law. The moon, suddenly free of the clouds, spilled into the room and by its light Veronica's mouth became a purple slash, her eyes dark sockets in a skull.

Hugo Sweeney knocked sharply on the open door.

'I heard movement,' he said, 'so I thought you might like some sweet tea.' He came into the room with a tray and spoke directly to Bridget. 'You probably need a cup, after being woken up like that.'

He ignored Veronica as he put the tray on the bedside table, poured and handed Bridget a cup.

'You needn't offer me any of that,' Veronica said dismissively.

'I wasn't going to.' Hugo sniffed. 'You've got your drink.'

Bridget took the tea gratefully and smiled at Hugo as he left.

'Tell me about your children,' Veronica said.

'They're children no longer.'

Bridget pulled the bedclothes more tightly about her as a sudden and unexpected flurry of loss went through her for the time when Fintan and Anna had been small and needy and the world had had a focus.

'Fintan is twenty-five, Anna twenty-eight. Fintan is a sculptor and lives in the west of Ireland. Anna is in law and very like her father.' And she missed them, all at once and with an intensity that stopped her breath.

'Go on.' Veronica was impatient.

'Anna looks astonishingly like Eleanor,' Bridget was off-hand, 'even down to some mannerisms. She's got the same hair, same eyes . . .'

'But not, I hope, the same craziness.' Veronica's snappiness lacked energy. 'It would indeed be a tragedy if your daughter were inflicted with a similar insanity. Eleanor Munro is a dangerous woman. Stay away from her.'

'She's a damaged person,' said Bridget, 'of more danger to herself than anyone else.' She paused. 'I feel sorry for her. In a way I even like her.'

'Appalling judgement on your part.' Veronica rapped the floor with her walking cane. 'She's unstable and she's an operator and you,' she lifted and pointed the cane, 'are a fool to be taken in by her. But that,' the cane jabbed, 'is your problem. You chose to come here on your voyage of discovery and you must live with the consequences. I have done what I had to do and my conscience is clear where you are concerned. You have refused my offer of shares but . . .'

Her voice tailed off and she shrugged. When she spoke again her voice was less uneven.

'You meet me at the end of my life. I am grotesque.'

The word, as she said it, had a plaintive edge. It was as if she could see how, with the moonlight on her thin, thin limbs, her cavernous eyes and death-pale skin, she was a parody of faded beauty.

'I was not always so . . . physically feeble.' Her voice became dreamy. 'I want a good death. I'm not sure what happens after I go, in spite of all the church has told me and in spite of the faith of the good Father Matthews. I've always suspected that when we die, we die, and there is nothing else.'

She paused, seeming to lose the thread of what she was saying. After a minute she shook herself, frowning, and went on.

'But I fear I have been a daylight atheist. Now that the light is dying, I want my fears to be wrong. Now I want there to be somewhere else and for Ted to be waiting there for me. Do you hope to meet with Victor again?'

Bridget stared at her. 'I don't know. Maybe,' she said eventually.

'I don't want to live anymore.' Veronica didn't seem to hear her. 'I have given up on nothing in my life. I am not giving up now either. It is simply that there is no longer anything to give up, nothing to live for. My life has run its course. I want to move on to whatever's next.'

'There is your family,' said Bridget, 'they are something to live for—'

'Don't be ridiculous.'

'You make it sound as if death is imminent.' Bridget took a couple of deep breaths, trying to keep the panic in her stomach at bay. The room was beginning to seem like a grey tunnel with Veronica at the end of it. If she had really decided to die, if all of this wasn't simply histrionics and some game she was playing, then Bridget didn't want to be a part of that death.

'Death is always imminent,' said Veronica, 'yours, mine, everyone's.'

She plucked at the shawl around her shoulders and Bridget felt an all-consuming chill. She had seen that same fretful fingering before: her mother had plucked in just such a way as she lay dying in a hospital bed.

'We have lived with a lot of secrets in this family,' Veronica's voice was low but the words were clear enough. 'It was how we functioned. Every family has its way of being. Every family has secrets. The family, by its nature, is a secretive institution. I'm sure our secrets were no more shameful than most.'

'You're overtired,' said Bridget, 'I'll take you back to your room.'

She slipped from the bed and stood beside Veronica's chair. She felt desperately in need of sleep herself. Even her legs felt leaden. She'd probably got out of bed too quickly, been sitting in the same position too long.

'I'm tired myself,' she said.

'I was glad when Frank became ill,' Veronica again seemed not to have heard her, 'glad when he became a dumb, useless thing in the bed, glad to see the end of him as a person.'

She spoke in sighing pauses, hands plucking all the time at the shawl as if it were a great weight against her body.

'I was happy to be loved by Ted Morgan.'

She brushed uncertain fingers across her face, as if there was a cobweb there. Or a tear.

'Leave me,' she said and her voice was stronger. 'Go to my room and ring for Hugo. Tell him I would like to be helped back to my room.'

'You need to see a doctor.'

Bridget's tongue felt thick, her mind foggy as it tried to deal with what she knew was going on.

'Give me a number and I'll call her . . . him . . .'

'I will send for him myself,' Veronica said, 'in the morning.'

'Now . . .' Bridget said.

'I will not see anyone tonight.' Veronica's face closed. 'I want Hugo to help me back to my room. No, you will not do,' she said as Bridget caught her arm. 'I want Hugo.'

From the door of Victor's room Bridget called to Hugo. When she called for a second time and failed to get a response she remembered the bell beside Veronica's bed. She would ring from there.

The other room seemed very far away; tiredness forced her to hold on to the wall as she made her way there. But the movement helped liven her up and she was reasonably awake by the time she found and pushed the button by Veronica's bed. The tiredness came back, waves of it, as she waited for Hugo to answer. Sitting on the bed she had to resist fiercely an urge to sink into the bank of lace pillows.

'Hello,' Hugo's voice was brisk and clear on the intercom.

'Veronica would like you to help her back to bed,' Bridget spoke slowly and carefully.

'I'm on my way.'

'I don't like the look of her, Hugo. I think her doctor should be sent for.'

'You just leave things to me,' said Hugo. 'I'll look after her. Go on back to your room.'

Bridget, making her way along the corridor, stumbled twice. To keep herself awake she squeezed her eyes tight shut and opened them quickly. She squeezed and opened, squeezed and opened . . .

'Victor's coming . . .' She stood in the bedroom doorway at last, propping herself upright with a hand on either side.

'Victor's . . . dead,' Veronica's voice was indistinct and distant, 'and Ted's dead and so is Frank.'

Bridget reached the bed and sat there. Veronica was a wraith in the chair.

'There was something in the tea,' Bridget knew she was forming words but wasn't sure how they were coming out. 'Hugo put something in the tea he gave me. I can't stay awake.'

'Why . . . would . . . he . . . do . . . that . . .' Veronica's response came slowly, long pauses between the words.

Bridget, not sure the other woman had understood, was beginning to explain again when Hugo Sweeney quietly appeared by Veronica's side. He helped her out of her chair and she stood, leaning on him and on the cane.

'I don't forgive anyone.' Standing seemed to have given her a return of strength and her voice was clear again. 'I have forgotten nothing.'

Bridget slept after that, only vaguely aware of Veronica and Hugo slowly leaving the room and of the door closing behind them with a small click.

She slept until the blue light of morning and a bitter wind through the open window brought her groggily awake. The bedroom door was open too and there was something else, a sound . . .

The sound, a phone shrilling unanswered close by, brought her fully awake. The siren-like ringing didn't help a needling headache. She lifted an arm and, as the embroidered cuff of the lawn nightdress fell away from the face of her watch, remembered where she was, how she'd felt before falling asleep, all that had happened the night before.

'God, oh dear God' – her head reeled – 'Hugo's tea . . .'

It was eight o'clock. She'd slept for eight hours or more. It was years since she'd slept more than six. Even the sleeping tablets she'd taken after Victor's death had only knocked her out for that long. Whatever he'd put in the tea Hugo Sweeney had intended it to knock her out until morning. But why?

And where was he now? Why wasn't he answering the damned telephone.

Standing, she didn't feel too bad. Apart from the headache, and a dryness in her mouth, she was reasonably intact. Alert enough to be certain she hadn't opened either the window or door. The room was like an ice-box; someone had meant her to waken.

Closing the window she saw car coming quickly towards the house through the avenue of trees. She watched until it came to a stop in front of the house and the driver got out. Lindsay, in a business-like coat and gloves, didn't look up as he strode toward the front door.

Veronica's grey shawl was on the floor by the chair. Fallen there, most likely, when Hugo had helped her out of it the night before. Bridget picked it up and wrapped it round her shoulders before stepping into the corridor. The telephone was still ringing, coming clearly through Veronica's open bedroom door.

Bridget knew, the instant she stepped into the room, that Veronica Baldacci was dead.

Victor's mother lay against the pillows, her hands gracefully resting on the bed, one either side of her. Her white, lawn nightdress had been buttoned, nun-like, to her neck and her hair, a dusty ochre in the morning light, fell so carefully across its rucked shoulders that it had to have been arranged that way during the wait for death. Under the make-up her parched face had a garish peace, lipsticked mouth gentler than Bridget had ever seen it in life.

The room was thick with the smell of acetone, nothing now to disguise it for what it was; the smell of death and whatever had killed Veronica.

Chapter Fourteen

The ringing phone was on a table beside the bed. Bridget picked it up as Lindsay came into the room behind her and made a small, choking sound.

'Hello.' Bridget kept her eyes on Veronica as she spoke into the phone.

'Mother? Is everything all right? I've been calling and calling . . . Mother?'

'This is Bridget.' It was hard to think what next to say.

'Bridget? Where is my mother? Why . . .'

'Your mother's dead, Magdalena,' Bridget said and listened to the silence on the phone. She turned and saw Lindsay, hunched and hugging herself as she stared at her dead grandmother.

'Are you sure?' Magdalena's voice came at last, precise, in a way Bridget had never heard it before.

'Quite sure,' Bridget said. 'She died in the night. You should call her doctor and . . .' she paused, 'I think she planned to die, Magdalena, so maybe you should call the police too.'

Lindsay pulled up a chair and touched one of Veronica's still, waxen hands. She went on staring at her dead face.

'Where's Hugo?' Magdalena asked.

'I don't know. He doesn't seem to be about . . .' If he was in the house surely he'd have answered the phone?

'Of course he's about. Hugo is always about. Call him. I

must speak to him . . .' Magdalena's voice was losing its precision.

'I think it would be a good idea if you and your husband came over here,' Bridget said. 'Hugo Sweeney's gone.'

She knew, as she said it, that this was true. Hugo had aided and abetted Veronica, his last and most loyal act, and now he was gone. He had put Bridget to sleep, sat with Veronica while she died and then taken himself off.

'Her insulin . . . Oh, Christ, the godamned insulin . . . Can you tell what happened to her?' Magdalena asked.

'No. But she doesn't look to have suffered pain before she died.'

'Thank God for that,' Magdalena said. 'She didn't deserve any more suffering . . .' she stopped to listen to someone in the background, then added, 'We'll be there immediately,' and abruptly hung up.

Arriving ten minutes later with Thomas, Magdalena was surprisingly in control of herself.

'She was alone when it happened?'

She climbed the stairs with Bridget. Thomas followed behind. He was withdrawn and silent. We all deal with shock in our own way Bridget thought. To Magdalena she said, 'I don't think so. I think Hugo may have been with her. I was asleep.'

In her bedroom Magdalena kissed her mother's forehead and touched her lips and left her exactly as she'd arranged herself, or been arranged, for death. Lindsay, visibly pulling herself together, asked if Veronica's doctor had been called.

'He's on his way with the medical backup. I called the priest too.' Magdalena studied her mother's face. 'You were right, Bridget, when you said she didn't seem to have suffered pain. She looks peaceful enough.'

Thomas stood with his back to the window and looked around the room.

'It's hard to take in,' he said.

'I often wondered how it would happen,' Magdalena said, 'but my wondering was always in the nature of a fantasy. Something that would never really happen.' She touched her mother's forehead again, smoothing a furrow there. 'She'd given up. That was another thing I never thought she'd do. Her being strong and in control allowed the rest of us . . . to be what we are . . .'

Lindsay came and stood by her mother and took her hand. After a minute she took Bridget's too and together the three women stood in what would be the only peace surrounding Veronica Baldacci's death.

The house became crowded with death's hectic aftermath. Thomas took efficient charge as ambulance people and Veronica's doctor filled the hallway. Father Matthews, an uncontrollable shake in his hands, set candles and oils about Veronica's bed.

'I can't take this stuff,' Lindsay said.

'Then you'd better go downstairs,' said Magdalena.

Bridget knelt with Magdalena while the priest administered the last rites of the Catholic church.

Hugo's disappearance was complete. The bed in the room in which he'd lived for most of his life hadn't been slept in and everything he'd ever owned had been removed from the rest of the house.

'He was a miserable shit, but he was always here,' Lindsay's anger was diluted by a confused concern. 'You'd have thought he'd have wanted to, well, be around for the funeral and all that. He gave his life to grandmother, after all.'

They were in the kitchen, everyone gathered together in a tight group by a worktop by a wide window. It was as if, Bridget thought, the overpowering size of the other family rooms had driven them to herd together in this relatively small corner of the house.

No one was saying much. John-Francis, looking the worse for wear and unshaven, sat slumped in a chair with his eyes closed. Bridget recognized a bad hangover when she saw one. Russell sat a little apart, cracking his knuckles. Magdalena, Thomas by her side, stood stiff-backed with a drink in her hand and contemplated the view of the garden and plastic Christmas tree from the window.

Only Thomas, grey-suited and shaven, seemed in control of himself and the situation.

Upstairs, in the bedroom, Veronica's doctor was with her. The priest had been put out of the room and was waiting to go back in.

'Hugo may come back,' Thomas's voice was cool. 'Veronica dying spooked him, that's all. When he comes to himself and calms down he'll come right back . . .'

'I don't think he will and I don't think it happened like that,' Bridget spoke loudly, and slowly. Lindsay was the first to turn to her but she waited until she had Thomas's attention too before going on. 'I think Hugo aided and abetted Veronica's suicide.'

'What makes you so certain it was suicide?'

Magdalena didn't turn around and nor did she raise her voice. She sipped her drink and went on staring through the window.

'Things she said to me,' Bridget said. 'She'd been talking fatalistically for days. Ever since Ted Morgan's death. I can't have been the only one to notice, surely?'

'I noticed. I didn't pay a lot of attention. Veronica hated being old. She hated the way she looked and she often spoke like that, as if her life was over.' Lindsay, irritation on her blanched features as she dragged on a cigarette, stopped and frowned at the sound of Russell's cracking knuckles.

'Fact is, it was nowhere near over. She had more instinctive business knowledge in her head than anyone I know. She knew it too . . .'

'We all hate being old,' said Magdalena.

'Bridget's right,' said Thomas, 'it was different this time. I've had the feeling for a while that her mind was going. She'd come up with a few crazy plans for the business and didn't seem able to keep her mind on other things . . .'

'She was upset about Ted Morgan was all,' said Lindsay, 'and Eleanor Munro being here and bringing up all sorts of shit didn't help, nor did Bridget's arrival help much.' She gave Bridget a carelessly apologetic look. 'Sorry, but it's true.'

Thomas cleared his throat, 'I think Bridget's right, that Veronica had decided to end things. I had a sense that things weren't right.' He turned to Bridget. 'I was wrong to ask you to stay last night.'

'I doubt it would have made any difference who was here. Veronica planned what happened and more than likely got Hugo to help her.'

'Why are you so sure?' John-Francis, speaking for the first time, massaged his forehead with two fingers.

'Because he gave me something to make me sleep – put it in the tea he brought up to my room late in the night. Veronica was there too, only she refused to have anything to drink. He made sure I didn't oversleep, that I found Veronica this morning, by leaving my window open so that the cold air would waken me early.'

'You could be right,' Thomas said, 'all she had to do was mess around with her insulin dose – and Hugo could have helped her there. I always thought,' he took Magdalena's free hand in his, 'that she would die when she wanted to die. Looks like I was right in that and that she made the choice.'

Magdalena took her hand from his and smoothed her

hair. 'How simple you make it seem, Thomas. But then you always were a simple man. My mother was not a simple woman.' Her thin body shuddered involuntarily. 'I wish I'd been with her.'

'I wasn't aware of Grandmother making any business plans recently, crazy or otherwise.' Lindsay's expression had sharpened. 'What sort of plans were they?'

'Nothing that had got beyond the ideas stage.' Thomas shrugged. 'Nothing I thought worth bothering you with.'

'You did know she was making shares over to Bridget?' Lindsay's tones were neutral.

Thomas nodded. 'She told me about that plan. It was a good one, and fair. I approved.'

'But?' Lindsay raised an eyebrow.

'No buts.' Thomas shook his head. 'I was completely for it.'

'I know you, Dad,' Lindsay said. 'There's a big, fat *but* written all over you.'

'Not about the principle of Bridget getting shares, there isn't,' said Thomas. 'What you're picking up is a worry about the legal end of all this. She was being secretive about it and so I'm not exactly sure what Veronica had arranged for Bridget but if—' He stopped, took off his glasses and pinched the bridge of his nose.

'You're stalling,' Lindsay said calmly. 'But if *what*?'

'Well, *if*, and this is only an if as yet, Veronica took her own life then we may have a problem. The law's funny about suicide, takes the view that it's the act of someone whose judgement was unsound, mind unhinged. It would have been better if Bridget hadn't had those meetings with Veronica. Bridget being in the house the night she died is going to look bad too. The legal people are going to ask questions about undue influence and that kind of thing. That's all I'm saying . . .'

'If that's all, we'll deal with it.' Lindsay was offhand. 'The legal people don't need to be told anything that's not their business. Things'll be fine, Bridget, no need for you to—'

'I don't want shares in the company,' Bridget said sharply. 'I'd already told Veronica that, yesterday morning. This is all unnecessary and inappropriate.'

'You're right,' said Lindsay, 'we'll talk about it some other time.'

'There won't be any need for us to talk about it, ever,' said Bridget.

'How naïve you are,' said Magdalena. 'I'd have thought living with my brother would have taught you that things are never that simple.'

'Where's the New York flake? Anyone think of telling her the old lady's dead?'

Russell stood and stretched his large frame before bending over to touch his toes. Guilt and panic did a sickening double turn in Bridget's stomach. She'd forgotten to make contact with Eleanor that morning. Learning about Veronica's death, after everyone else, was going to reinforce her neurosis about a conspiracy to get her.

But then Eleanor hadn't returned the message Bridget had left for her. Maybe, like Hugo, she'd gone.

'Eleanor's staying in my hotel,' she said, 'I'll give her a ring.'

'No need. I called her a short while ago. She's on her way.'

So much for conspiracy theories; Lindsay and the family had thought to tell Eleanor when she, Bridget – her supposed ally – had forgotten.

Chapter Fifteen

Veronica Baldacci's doctor confirmed what Bridget had suspected and Hugo had known: Victor's mother had ended her own life. Veronica had ensured this would happen by not taking her insulin for three days. The smell in her room had indeed been of acetone.

More specifically, it had been of the keto-acidosis of the last stages of uncontrolled diabetes.

'No way you could have known this.' Dr Luke Kellerman patted Bridget's hand.

'Not what was causing the smell,' Bridget removed her hand, 'but I knew there was something wrong. She seemed to lose track of what she was saying from time to time, to grow feeble very quickly . . .' She looked away from the doctor's moist, overly understanding eyes. 'I should have been more insistent about calling you—'

She stopped. This, and the sleeping tablet, was a line best not pursued. It would be self-recrimination at its most dishonest since she knew in her heart that Veronica and Hugo had together conspired to prevent her getting the doctor to the old woman's bedside. They would have been altogether more ruthless if she'd gone against them.

Another thought came.

What right had she to judge Veronica if, at eighty-two, she wanted to die for love of Ted Morgan? Given the confusion of truths about the old woman's life she didn't feel at all equipped to join the chorus of righteous and disappointed disapproval.

Dr Kellerman sighed. 'I've been her doctor for many years, and Mrs Baldacci was not a woman who could be diverted from a path of action once she'd made up her mind.' He pursed his lips. 'Please be assured that she did not have a lot of pain.' His sad gaze roved over his small audience. 'Death would have come with a gradual drifting, a loss of sensation and final coma.' He selected John-Francis for a full-frontal focus and condoled with him directly. 'She was a remarkable woman and her death, if you'll forgive my saying so, became her as much as her life. She choose her time. She would have hated the slow decay of extreme old age.'

'That was still some years away,' Magdalena said icily, 'and if you've finished, Dr Kellerman, we would prefer to be alone, as a family.'

'Of course. If there's anything else I can do . . .' murmuring gently the doctor stood up, 'please call.'

A heavy man, he stood dolefully with his bag on the kitchen table. There was about him the air of someone used to attending on the very rich.

'She will need to be taken to the hospital but I will attend to the autopsy and to the legal details. They will be a formality, nothing more. There will be no need for you to concern yourselves.'

No one said anything. As a group, with Eleanor a recent, potentially explosive addition, they had uneasily occupied the kitchen for an hour or more. We're like geese, Bridget thought, scratchily circling one another while we make protesting sounds.

'Thank you, Luke,' Thomas said, when it seemed the doctor would stand indefinitely awaiting acknowledgement.

'No need to prolong the pain and upset of the living.' Dr Kellerman lifted his bag from the table.

'I blame myself,' Thomas said suddenly. 'I will not tolerate any blame being placed on Bridget.'

'I don't think that will arise.' The doctor looked surprised.

'Why should Bridget be blamed?' Lindsay said.

'She was here alone . . . I should not have allowed it to happen . . .' Thomas, who'd moved to sit at the table, beat a tattoo with his fingertips on its marble top. 'I handed over to her and left . . .' He put his head in his hands and leaned his elbows on the table. His short, greying hair stood on end as he massaged his forehead.

'Oh, God, Thomas, this isn't about you.' Magdalena knocked back her drink. 'We all know how caring you were of her. We just don't need to be reminded right now. I presume, Luke, that you will want to take my mother away immediately, or at least pretty soon.'

'It would be best.'

'Veronica dying had nothing to do with Bridget,' Eleanor watched the smoke from a cigarette circle in the air, 'so don't think, Thomas, you can lay that on her.'

'You're poisoning every one of us with that cigarette, you know that?' Russell, clutching his chest, opened a window wide.

'You are such a stupid jerkoff, Russell.' Eleanor dragged on the cigarette and blew more smoke in his direction. 'You're worried about smoke and nicotine inhalation while the fallout from the malignancy in this family is the real poison in the air around here.'

'This is not the time for anger, my child,' Father Matthews touched Eleanor's arm timidly. 'These things can be discussed another day—'

'Damn right they can.' Eleanor cut him short and fixed Bridget with a bayonet stare. 'And they damn well will be discussed too.'

'Death is a terrible business,' the priest murmured, 'it

reveals as much as it conceals. But the least the dead deserve is our blessing for a peaceful passing.'

'Just what the hell are you trying to say?' Eleanor, while the priest moved closer to the door and watched her with cloudy, remorseful eyes, got up and closed the window Russell had opened. 'People die from frostbite too,' she snapped. 'Now you,' she stabbed her cigarette at the priest, 'tell us all what you mean by death concealing as much as it reveals.'

'I was thinking that we take secrets with us to the grave and that that is a good thing,' Father Matthews said. 'I would advise you, Miss Munro, to let the past die with Mrs Baldacci. There is peace in letting go of unhappy events.' He spread his hands and fixed a look of appeal on his face. 'We should all of us see the passing of this good woman as a time for reconciliation and moving on—'

'Cut the crap,' said Eleanor. 'If there's something we should know then cough it up. Now.'

'I've said all I *can* say,' said Father Matthews. 'I am bound by an oath.'

'The confessional cop-out.'

'A man-made promise, which I am going to keep.'

'You hypocritical old druid.'

Eleanor advanced on the priest until she was standing over him.

'You got what you wanted out of her over the years. Your church was funded. It's easy for you to forget the past. It's even easier to deliver a righteous sermon to those of us who haven't got what we want. But why don't we do the hard thing here – why don't you tell us about those old secrets? The ones Veronica's taking with her to the grave? If you really want there to be peace and reconciliation then tell us what it is we're supposed to forget, and forgive.' She poked him in the chest with a long finger. 'The past needs to be sorted, so start talking.'

'Please. I entreat you.'

'No, Father, I'm the one doing the entreating here. Talk.'

'No.'

The priest drew himself to his full height and took a step back. He was suddenly a man with a mission.

'I will not reveal what the dead woman thought it best to conceal. I made the point only because to be forewarned is to be forearmed.' He looked round the assembled faces, his expression righteous. 'This family has had enough sorrow. With God's help we will rise above this situation too.'

'This family has lied and cheated and worse for three generations.' Eleanor stared at him in disbelief. 'You know it too. You took Baldacci money and forgave Baldacci sins and that makes you a fucking hypocrite—'

'That's it.' John-Francis, moving quickly, took Eleanor by the arm. 'This thing has gone far enough.' A muscle twitched in his jaw. 'I suggest you leave now, Eleanor, and cool off somewhere else. We can do without this shit here today. In fact we can do without it any day. So,' he shoved his furious face close to hers, 'are you going to leave or am I going to help you on your way out of here?'

'Mrs Baldacci would not have—' the priest's protest was cut short by a vicious aside from his defender.

'Shut up,' said John-Francis. 'If you'd kept your mouth shut in the first place this would never have happened. Are you leaving, Eleanor?'

'I'm leaving. But it would be a terrible mistake to think that I'm going to forget why I came here.' Eleanor Munro, straight-backed and shaking, looked around the assembled faces as the priest had done a minute before. 'The past hasn't died with Veronica. You could say, in fact, that it's just about to come alive again.'

*

Eleanor was pacing beneath the portico, shoulders hunched and head down as she waited for a taxi, when Veronica's body was carried from the house to the waiting ambulance. She kept her distance, leaning against a column, as Bridget and the rest of the family stood to see the stretcher loaded and the doors closed. Magdalena, the doctor and the priest all travelled with the body.

Bridget went to Eleanor as the vehicle moved off.

'Are you all right?' she asked.

'What's it to you? You abandoned me to play house with the Baldaccis as soon as I let you out of my sight. You—'

'I left a message for you on the voicemail in your room. You know I did: I don't believe you didn't listen to it. Where were you last night?'

'I decided it was time I had a night on the town,' Eleanor said offhandedly. 'Only I could have saved myself the money and energy spent.' She shrugged. 'This is one miserable dump when you get right down to it.'

'I was worried about you,' said Bridget, 'seems I could have saved myself the energy spent on that.' A taxi hove into view on the bend of the avenue. 'I'll get my things and come with you to the hotel. I need to shower and change.' She paused. 'And I really want to get away from here.' She caught Eleanor's hand and turned the younger woman to face her. 'Maybe at the hotel you'll be able to find your way to telling me the truth about last night.'

Eleanor was silent on the journey to the hotel. As they were crossing the bridge they got stuck in traffic. Watching the slow boats in the water below, she said,

'You wouldn't believe me if I told you the truth about last night. Not yet, anyways. I need to get it sorted in my head first.'

'Why don't you try me?' Bridget said.

'Because I need to think what I'm going to do about it.

Also . . .' Eleanor gave a quick, childlike smile and Bridget had a first, brief glimpse of a happier, free-spirited Eleanor.

'Go on.' she prompted.

'I don't want to be influenced by your opinion of what I should do. You're a persuasive lady and I don't care to have common sense decide things here. The situation needs . . . this needs a strategy. I'm good at strategies.'

'I've noticed,' Bridget said drily. 'Please tell me when you come up with one.'

After that Eleanor stayed silent until they got to the hotel. At the door to Bridget's room it seemed she would walk past, wordless to the end. But then she stopped and quickly caught Bridget in her arms and held her smotheringly tight.

'See you in a little while.' She let go and stepped back, her face glowing a little, almost happy-looking. 'We'll talk when you've had time to shower and change.' She pulled a playful grimace. 'And boy, is there a lot to talk about.'

Bridget's room, even to the tassels and repro furniture, had the calming reassurance of a port in a storm. She lay on the bed and contemplated the ceiling for several quiet minutes before ringing home and connecting with the blessed sanity of Anna's response to her grandmother's death by suicide.

'What a sad, sad end to a life. How terrible to have nothing to live for, poor old woman . . .'

Bridget heard her take a breath, then let it out slowly. She knew her daughter would be biting her lip and making her small, frequent frown. She envied the young woman her distance from Seattle and the Baldaccis.

'Are you all right?' Anna asked. 'Isn't it time you were coming home?'

'I'm fine. I'll leave immediately after the funeral. Should be home in a week, maybe less.'

'Great. It's raining here. Pissing cats and dogs, as a matter of fact. I called at the house the other day to check on things. The garden looks a bit lost.'

'I suppose it does.'

It wasn't until after Bridget had hung up, changed into a towelling robe and was on her way to the bathroom that she saw the envelope. Buff coloured and rectangular just like the first one, it was close to the wall and had clearly been shoved under the door. She'd been too preoccupied coming in to notice it.

She knew before opening it that it was from Hugo Sweeney. She read it while running a bath; the sound of the water was soothing. It was longer than the first letter, but then Hugo knew the person he was writing to this time. He'd been painstaking, writing carefully in blue ink with meticulous punctuation.

Dear Bridget Baldacci,

You would be wise to take my advice this second time: go home to your life in Ireland, now. By the time you read this I will be far away myself and Veronica Baldacci will be gone to her eternal rest.

There is no point in your staying in Seattle. You already know more than enough about your dead husband's family. Any more and you will know too much and that would do you no good at all. It would be more likely to bring harm to you. Knowledge will not bring an end to things either. The cycle is unending and will repeat itself. Go home.

Who knows, maybe we'll meet in Dublin one day.

PS: I will be slipping this under your door at the hotel. To leave it at the reception would betray our correspondence to the Munro woman. It would be dangerously unwise for you to discuss my letters with her. Look out for yourself and let Eleanor Munro and others look out for themselves.

He hadn't signed it. He was too careful for that. He hadn't put a date on it either but Bridget felt certain he'd written it in the hours before Veronica had died. Probably while packing to go away.

She wished, all at once and with a sense of foreboding stronger and fiercer than anything she'd felt before, that she had never come to Seattle. Events were building to something, she didn't know what. Victor's death had further destabilized an unravelling family.

Veronica's and Ted Morgan's deaths were not coincidences. They were merely a consequence of the secrets and struggles which controlled the family. Bridget didn't for a minute believe their deaths had resolved things, any more than Victor leaving or Grace and Shelley Munro disappearing had resolved things. The rot at the heart of the Baldaccis had taken over. Veronica knew this, had known since Ted Morgan died, if not before. She'd been unable to keep it at bay any longer and had decided she didn't want to go on.

A chain of events was in motion which could only end badly. There was too much money and power at stake, too much decay and corruption and far, far too many unspoken and unresolved secrets.

She could leave, of course, but knew that she wouldn't. She needed the resolutions she'd come for – justice for Victor, answers for Anna and Fintan, peace of mind for herself. She would wonder, later, whether the cost of those things had been too high.

But that morning she still believed she had a choice.

It was just after midday when she stepped out of the bath and got into bed. She slept for a couple of hours and woke feeling restless to a day which had turned moody and dark.

The ringing telephone, inevitable as the rain and probably Eleanor, dragged her unwilling from the bed.

But it was Lindsay Baldacci on the phone, brisk and almost cheerful sounding.

'I've decided the way to deal with Grandmother's death is to drop out of working for the day,' she said, 'to do the dutiful, family thing.'

'And this somehow involves me?' Bridget wasn't encouraging. She didn't want to see Lindsay, or anyone else just then. What she wanted was time alone to put the events of the previous night, and this morning, into perspective.

'Sure does.' Lindsay sounded upbeat. 'I know John-Francis offered, but none of us have shown you anything of the city—'

'I've done the tour on my own, thanks.'

'Not the same as getting a native's perspective on things. To be honest, my motives are entirely selfish. I want your company. I don't seem able to tolerate my own right now.'

'Where in the city had you in mind?' Bridget tried to keep the resignation out of her voice. She'd never been good at saying no when she felt needed but she made a half-hearted attempt to put Lindsay off. 'The weather's not promising – doesn't look as if it's going to be one of the five days a year it's said not to rain in Seattle.'

'That's the thing about Seattle, it's a real unpredictable place, so you just never know.' Lindsay's voice dropped. 'The autopsy's to be tomorrow morning and Grandmother will be buried at the end of the week. You'll be out of here after that and I may not have another chance to do something like this.'

'You don't have to do anything, Lindsay, I'm quite happy to—'

'But I want to. Please let me. You were with her last night and it seems to me right that I should spend time with you today. I need to talk about her. We'll go walkabout, take in Pioneer Square, maybe even do the sewer tour.'

'Sounds good,' said Bridget, and meant it.

Lindsay needing to talk about her grandmother changed everything. Lindsay was sharp and bright and not noticeably hung up on the past. She might be the one to make sense of things.'

'I'll even go beyond the call of duty and take Eleanor along,' Lindsay said magnanimously. 'I'll be there in thirty minutes. We'll have dinner on me this evening too.'

Funny the things people do when a loved one dies, Bridget thought, remembering her own midnight gardening forays after Victor's death, the long months during which she'd been unable to grieve. In the light of her own behaviour Lindsay's desire to act as a tour guide didn't seem at all unusual.

Eleanor was asleep. So deeply asleep it took three minutes of Bridget's knocking on her door to persuade her out of bed.

'Lindsay wants us to sightsee with her?' She gave Bridget a bleary, confused look. 'You're sure?'

'That's what she said, though needs might be a better word,' Bridget admitted. 'She's restless and upset about Veronica and wants to do something dutiful with the afternoon.'

'She said that?' Eleanor yawned, then frowned. 'Did she say what part of town?'

'Yes. She's talking about looking at Pioneer Square and the underground sewer tour.'

'Pioneer Square?' Eleanor shook her head as if clearing it. She took a deep breath. 'Well, that's a part of town I've already had a look at but maybe I should see it again. I'll meet you downstairs.' She gave another yawn. 'I need to have a quick shower.'

Lindsay arrived in exactly the half hour she'd promised. Dressed in sneakers and a bulky jacket she looked as if a cross-country trek was what she had in mind.

'Very noble of you, acting as a tourist guide like this,' Eleanor said as they went through the doors together into the street.

They walked quickly, three abreast with Lindsay in the middle setting a brisk pace and speaking in sporadic bursts. Bridget sensed a tension between the two yonger women which she hadn't noticed before. If she was lucky the day might yield more than the sightseeing trip.

'We're headed for one of the city's oldest neighbour-hoods,' Lindsay told them. 'It's got real character, it's full of squares, cafés and galleries. Crime's a bit of a problem there, but show me someplace crime isn't a problem and I'll show you a place that's dead to the world.'

'Yeah, right,' Eleanor said caustically. 'Nothing like a daily murder rate to make a neighbourhood interesting. I hear it's where the homeless and citizens like work-release prisoners hang out too.'

'It's a while since I've been to this part of town,' Lindsay admitted. A sharp wind at their backs hurried them along. 'The history of the square goes back to when Seattle was first settled and moves on to when it was destroyed by fire in 1889. When they rebuilt it they raised the sidewalks and streets a storey higher than before so as to avoid tidal flooding from Elliott Bay. The original streets are below-ground passageways now.'

'From what I've seen you could call some of the above-ground streets passageways too,' said Eleanor, 'as well as half the population of the place being derelicts.'

'Some of the area's like that,' Lindsay conceded.

When they came into view Bridget immediately recognized the red-brown nineteenth-century buildings of Pioneer Square. Along with the Space Needle they were pictured on the front of almost every brochure she'd ever picked up about the city. When they came closer and moved into the square she saw that it was both smaller and more homely than she'd imagined.

'What do you two say to starting off with a drink in Merchant's Cafe?'

Lindsay's cheer, as she led the way to an impressively worn and aged building, was unconvincing.

'It's the oldest restaurant we've got here, used to serve five-cent beer to miners during the gold rush while they queued for the upstairs brothel.'

'We've read the guidebooks,' Eleanor said carelessly as they sat at a long table. She drummed her fingers impatiently. 'Any chance of these guys bringing us a beer if we pay them today's rates?'

Lindsay ordered and they sat, the three of them, in a silence filled with unasked questions while they waited for the drinks to arrive. Why do I feel, Bridget wondered, that there is more to this outing than meets the eye? Is it because I've got used to things not being what they seem in this family – or because there is a real and root cause to the undercurrents I can feel between these two women?

'This part of town's seen a lot of misery, I'll hand you that much, Eleanor,' Lindsay broke the silence when their drinks came. 'Yesler Way, just across the square, used to be known as Skid Row, gave the nation a name for areas where the—'

'Down and out congregated. We know all that too,' Eleanor, interrupting, sounded peevish. She encircled her glass with her hands and turned it round and round.

'God, this town is sad. It looks sad and it feels sad and it's full of sad people. Now that we've had the word on Skid Row,' she arched an eyebrow at Lindsay, 'I suppose you think we should take the sewer tour?' She sipped from the glass and grimaced. 'Or maybe,' she spoke softly, 'you think it would be more interesting if we took a walk down by Second and Yesler to see where the homeless and the lonely live?'

'OK, Eleanor, OK – you can stop hitting on me.' Lindsay pulled her jacket round her as if suddenly cold. 'You're right about why I brought us here – but then you must feel the same or you wouldn't have come along. Why don't we go there now? I'll explain to Bridget on the way.'

'Why don't you explain to me before we leave?' Bridget said coldly.

'Because this way we save time,' said Lindsay.

'I'm not in any hurry,' Bridget said, 'and I'm not going anywhere until you explain what this is about.'

Lindsay took a deep breath and, making an obvious effort, spoke slowly. 'I want to see where Ted Morgan stayed when he left my grandmother's home. I need to see for myself where he went to. I sort of feel it might be easier to understand what happened – how it could have happened – if I see the Bible Mission Refuge. I didn't feel I could go there on my own and I thought if I asked you straight you wouldn't want to come with me. So I came up with this plan to' – she gave an apologetic smile – 'lure you two into coming with me. Only Eleanor guessed what I was up to because she knows this part of town and knows it's where Ted Morgan holed up.' Her eyes pleaded to be understood.

'So – now that you know will you walk that way with me?'

'Yes,' Bridget said, 'but you should have been honest with me.'

She should have been, but couldn't. Lindsay, like the others, understood only the devious.

'Veronica died because Ted Morgan died, because she didn't want to go on living with him dead. It's as simple as that and it's important to me to lay Ted's ghost to rest. Taking a look at the refuge will help.'

'Let's go then.' Eleanor Munro stood and pulled gloves from her pocket.

Bridget, crossing the road to Yesler and Second, wished she'd brought gloves too. She wished even more that she knew whether Lindsay had known about Veronica's wedding plans and if she believed that her grandmother's suicide had only to do with Ted Morgan's death. Given the Baldacci attitude to truth, and the fact that Bridget had been told about the proposed marriage in confidence, there didn't seem much point in asking.

But answers would have helped her feel a lot more comfortable about heading into the narrow, downhill streets on the wrong side of the square.

Chapter Sixteen

They walked three abreast again, this time with Bridget between Lindsay and Eleanor. The ground was uneven and when the footpath narrowed Eleanor stepped into the roadway and walked there.

There was no traffic, and there were no people. Rain began to fall lightly. It was very cold.

'Where to now?' Bridget stamped her feet when they came to the end of the street and arrived at a T-junction.

Eleanor raised her eyebrows at Lindsay.

'It's your city,' she said.

'Yes.' Lindsay frowned. 'I checked a map and by my reckoning we go one block along and then take a right. After that we should be close enough to see Ted Morgan's Bible Mission.' She stamped her feet on the ground as Bridget had done. 'It's cold. Best to keep moving.'

The right turn brought them into a narrow, dark street which was no more than an alleyway. The buildings on either side were for the most part unlit and unused and by the time they'd walked five hundred yards had become completely derelict. They looked like warehouses, tired lettering on some windows indicating they might at one time have housed shipping or other offices.

The ground underfoot became even more uneven as the street curved and got darker. The quiet was penetrating, and Pioneer Square and the main thoroughfare they'd just left might have been miles away.

There was nothing resembling hostel accommodation anywhere.

'You're sure we're heading in the right direction?' Bridget said.

'I'm sure.' Lindsay stared ahead, as if expecting a beacon to show the way. 'How in hell did he find this place . . . we must be almost at the waterfront.'

'He looked hard, that's how,' said Eleanor. 'He needed somewhere he could hole up and not be found. He needed it to be cheap too, in case he had to stay on a while. Ted wasn't a rich man.'

'He told you all this?' Bridget said.

'Yep. The other thing he told me was not to come down here. So I didn't, until now.' She looked around and for a moment it seemed as if she was going to turn tail and run. But she hunched her shoulders and kept going. 'I've a feeling I'm going to regret doing what he asked for the rest of my life.'

'Did he tell you precisely why he left the house?' Bridget tried, but failed, to see Eleanor's face. In the murky light and with her hair falling forward it was a whitish blur, nothing more.

'He told me that too,' her voice sounded strained. 'He wanted to get away from Veronica's talk of marriage. He cared for her but he didn't want that. But he did want to stay round for me.' She shook her hair back and looked sideways at Bridget. 'You know about Veronica's plans for them to marry, though, she had to have told you.'

'I know she wanted to marry Ted Morgan, yes.'

Bridget stopped and, a few steps ahead of her, the two younger women stopped too.

'You told someone in the family where Ted was staying, didn't you Eleanor? You think that person might have . . . harmed him, or caused him to be harmed, don't you?' She put the question flatly and waited, without moving, for an answer.

'Yep. I told someone.' Eleanor looked at Lindsay. 'I told two people, as a matter of fact.'

'I was one of them but you only told me last night, a bit late for me to get excited about Grandmother's plans to wed, given that the man involved was already dead. Why don't you tell Bridget who the other person was?'

'Good idea,' the strain had gone and Eleanor's voice had become flat and expressionless. 'I didn't tell Bridget because I didn't believe Thomas had anything to do with Ted's—'

'You told Thomas?' Bridget said.

'Yes – and he probably told someone else. I should never have told anyone where Ted was staying. Once you tell a secret it belongs to the world. God, it's cold. Can't we move on?'

They began walking again, close together, along the empty road. The rain got heavier. Bridget added a couple of things together in her head.

'And you didn't tell the police because you wanted Thomas on your side working on Veronica for your inheritance,' Bridget said. 'That's it, isn't it?'

'That's about right, yes,' Eleanor said.

'You trusted Thomas,' Lindsay said.

'I trusted Thomas,' Eleanor agreed.

What was left of the late afternoon light shone wetly on the road ahead. At a corner they turned right, into a slightly wider street where dull yellow street lighting made for shadows and not a lot more visibility.

'This does not look promising.' Bridget stopped.

Doors on either side were closed and bolted and a building not fifty yards away was propped up by scaffolding. The street curved and sloped downwards, the buildings high and close together, allowing only small amounts of the dying daylight through.

Lindsay was ahead now, looking carefully about her as she went.

'It's OK.' Eleanor's arm on Bridget's shoulder was a surprising comfort. 'The Bible Mission's got to be around here somewhere. It's not as bad as it looks and anyway,' she squeezed Bridget's shoulder, 'you'll be OK with this big city gal.'

'I've got a bad feeling about this,' Bridget confessed. 'Nothing rational, nothing I can put my finger on. I just feel we should get out of here.'

'Let's go then,' said Eleanor. 'This is Lindsay's thing, she can go the rest of the way alone. I don't feel all that comfortable about the set-up either.'

'We can't leave Lindsay here alone,' Bridget protested.

'Do you see her leaving because you want to?' said Eleanor. 'Or because I want to?'

'No . . .'

'Well, let's go then.'

'We can't leave her here,' Bridget repeated. 'Not just because of an irrational feeling of mine. Looks like it's too late now anyway. She's calling to us. Why don't we stick with her until we at least find the Bible Mission?'

Lindsay, when they caught up with her, pointed ahead. 'It's just along there,' she said, 'and there's a coffee shop opposite.'

The Bible Mission Refuge, the name in white letters on a green background, loomed out of the shadows a couple of hundred yards further on. The glass, double doors were at the top of a set of scrubbed granite steps and just inside it they could see a wooden desk and several deep, dark-brown armchairs.

'How far do you want to take this thing, Lindsay?' Eleanor asked. 'Do you want to go inside?'

'I don't know.'

Two of the armchairs were occupied by Bible Mission

residents. As the women stood watching in the street one of them, red-faced and straw-haired, gave them the two-fingered sign.

'Maybe we'll just go across the road, have a coffee and warm up a little before we head back.' Lindsay turned away.

The coffee house was in shades of yellow and black. They sat on black wooden chairs at a yellow table beside a black wall and had coffee from glossy, yellow mugs. They were the only people there.

'Poor Ted.' Eleanor traced a question mark in a coffee spill on the yellow table top. 'He was a good man who got caught in the wrong place a couple of times and tortured himself about it until he died. And that about sums up his life . . .'

When she fell silent Bridget, studying the punctuation mark, prodded her with a question of her own. 'The wrong place was Seattle?'

'One of them was. The other wrong place was New York.' Eleanor drew a circle around the question mark. 'The New York thing happened because my mother wrote to Veronica when she heard her father was ill. She wanted to come back, help nurse him. When Veronica got the letter, she sent Ted to New York with $25,000 to pay her off. Ted was persuasive. My mother took the money and stayed in New York and that was all she ever got. Ted never felt right about it and it was part of the reason he looked out for my mother. Me too, I reckon.'

'And in Seattle?'

Eleanor looked Bridget in the eye. 'Seattle was where Ted had an affair with Veronica and was caught, as the Romans used to say, *in flagrante delicto* by Victor, who was, by Ted's account, an impressionable young man. He left.' She paused. 'You knew this, didn't you?'

Bridget nodded. 'Veronica told me. In her account Ted

Morgan left before Victor.' She looked questioningly at Lindsay.

'That was the version I heard too.' She shifted uncomfortably in her seat. 'It's getting dark,' she said, 'and I've gone as far as I want to with this thing. I want to buy dinner to sort of make up for dragging you two down here. We're real close to the waterfront so why don't you two walk on down there in about,' she looked at her watch, 'say twenty minutes? I'll bring the car around and pick you up. No sense in all three of us going back to the car park and I'm at least dressed for a run. How's that sound?'

'Sounds to me like you can't stop organizing people,' said Eleanor, 'but since you were the one got us here you may as well get us out as painlessly as possible.'

'I'll get going then.' Lindsay stood and zipped up her jacket. 'Wait for me by the first pier you arrive at. I'll find you there.' She took a wallet from her pocket. 'Let me get this. See you in a while.'

Once in the street Lindsay started to run.

'She's got a different way of doing it,' Eleanor said, 'but she's just like her grandmother when you come right down to it. Lindsay Carter gets what she wants, same way Veronica did.'

'I've noticed,' said Bridget.

Eleanor looked thoughtful. 'We're here, where Lindsay wants us to be, while she's gone, running in the trainers she was so conveniently wearing. Right?'

'That's certainly the way it looks.'

'And we are going to walk to the waterfront to wait for her to pick us up by the waters of the Puget Sound. Why are we going to do this?'

'Because Lindsay asked us to.'

'Right.' Eleanor paused and pushed her hair back from her face in one of her Anna-like gestures. 'The trainers were so goddamn convenient.' She narrowed her eyes again. 'Do you think her wearing them was a coincidence?'

'Probably,' said Bridget, 'but only because I don't see why she would want us here.' What possible gain was there for Lindsay in having herself and Eleanor wandering the early evening backstreets and waterfront?

'Two coffees and two of our sticky pecan rolls.' A young man with a tray stood smiling by their table. 'Ordered and paid for by your friend who just left.' He hummed 'Lilli Marlene' as he arranged the food and drink in front of them.

'She's making sure we stay here,' said Eleanor.

Bridget touched the oozing stickiness of the roll and pushed it away. There was only so much her stomach could take.

'I lied to you about going on the town last night,' Eleanor said. 'I spent last night with Lindsay. She came to the hotel . . .' Edgily pushing aside the food she looked around, and said, 'Why don't we get out of here? Head on down toward the waterfront and look for a cab? I'll tell you about it as we go.'

The rain had become a dense, freezing drizzle that stung their faces and fell about them like millions of icy needles. It was dark too, the street lighting failing miserably to illuminate threatening corners and doorways. They stood briefly in the light thrown onto the footpath from the coffee house and the Bible Mission doorway opposite.

'Left?' Bridget asked.

'Left,' Eleanor confirmed.

They'd walked a bare twenty yards when a voice from behind hailed them.

'Bridget! Eleanor! Hold on there . . .'

They turned together, towards a figure hurrying in their direction from the other end of the street. His leather-soled shoes made neat tapping sounds as he called again and then he came close enough for both of them to recognize it was Thomas.

'Thomas,' said Eleanor, 'this is a real surprise.'

Bridget, close beside her, felt her go rigid. Oh God, she thought, this is not good. There's something else here I don't know about.

'Couldn't believe it when I saw you,' Thomas said.

'You didn't expect to find us here?' Eleanor asked.

Thomas, coming out of the shadows into the light from the coffee-house window, stopped a few feet away and smiled. 'I didn't expect to find you with Bridget,' he said.

'It's a surprise all round,' said Bridget. 'We didn't expect to meet you either.'

There was an ending here. She knew it as surely as she knew that the kind and gentle Thomas was no longer either of those things.

If he ever had been.

Chapter Seventeen

'Bad night to be out . . .' Thomas stepped closer.

Bridget tried to meet his eye but all she got was the coffee-house window reflected in his glasses.

'I'm long past believing in coincidences, Thomas,' Eleanor's voice was rough. 'What're you doing here?'

'It's an out of the way part of town for all of us.' Thomas looked around, then up and down the street, then back at Eleanor. His smile didn't waver. 'Maybe we should all explain what we're doing here.'

'We came with—' Bridget got no further. Eleanor, swearing under her breath, turned furiously.

'Keep out of this, Bridget.' She shook her by the arm. 'You haven't a fucking clue about what's going on here. I'll handle this.'

'Handle it? For God's sake, Eleanor . . .'

The fury in Eleanor died. 'Just do what I say. Please. For a little while, that's all.' Her voice was pleading and her eyes, fixed on Bridget's, had a manic desperation Bridget had seen there before.

'Fine. The show's yours,' she said.

If standing back would calm Eleanor down, ease the situation, then she would stand back. For the little while she'd asked for, at least.

'Why don't you let the woman speak?' Thomas, watching them, sounded icily amused. This was another Thomas. 'Tell me, Bridget, who was it you came down here with?'

Bridget shook her head. 'I really don't know what's going on here, Thomas, so I'm going to keep out of it.'

'Too late for that,' Thomas said. 'You're part of the family. You're involved.'

He rubbed his gloved hands together. The movement was strangely threatening, seeming to promise other, more violent movement to come. The benign, kindly air he'd worn as the concerned consort of Magdalena and indulgent paterfamilias to Lindsay and John-Francis had been replaced with a detachedly cold one. But there was a nervousness there too, and a feverish anxiety that no amount of icy detachment could disguise. Dear God, Bridget thought, I wish I knew what was going on, what games these people are playing.

The sane thing would be to walk away but she knew, with an awful certainty, that whatever was to happen would follow her.

Thomas was right. She was involved. She was family. And she couldn't leave Eleanor.

'First things first, Thomas Carter,' Eleanor's voice came so loudly beside her that Bridget jumped. 'You're not going to do a thing to make sure I get my due rights in this family, are you? You never were, were you?'

'Oh, Eleanor, Eleanor . . .' Thomas shook his head resignedly, 'you must learn to stop being so paranoid, to stop thinking about yourself.'

'Answer the questions,' Eleanor snapped.

'You've blown it.' With a sharp, hard laugh Thomas suddenly dropped the pretence of civility. 'I *was* willing to do something, see you got a decent pay-off, but not any longer. Not since you moved to that hotel and got this conspiracy thing going with Bridget.' His voice was as hard now as his laugh had been. 'There was a time when I thought I might take you on board, that you might be useful in the way a dangerous dog can be useful. Not any more. You've become a handicap. Things have changed now Veronica's dead. I've no fallback. I've got to take all the risks myself and you're a risk I'm not willing to take. Anyway, you're even crazier than I thought you were if you think I'm going to keep you around after the stunt you tried to pull here tonight.'

'What're you talking about?' Eleanor's eyes narrowed.

'You know what I'm talking about.' Thomas rubbed his hands together again. 'Let's clear up a couple of things here and now and you can be on your way. We can get out of this rain in the coffee house. But you should know that I'm willing to deal in a one-off payment, nothing more.' He shrugged. 'Once we've sorted things you can both get out of here.'

'You know your way around this area pretty well—' Eleanor began.

Without warning the pool of light around them disappeared and they were standing in murky, near-black shadow. Bridget jumped and gave a short, hysterical laugh as the young man from the coffee shop appeared in the doorway and began to lock up.

'It's pretty dark around here when we turn our lights out,' he said, 'there's a problem with the street lighting. Should be fixed by spring, if you want to wait that long.' He looked at them curiously and jangled the keys in his hand. 'There's not a lot goes on after we close for the day.' He stuffed the keys into his jeans' pocket and zipped up his jacket. 'Unless you're planning on booking in across the road my advice to you is not to hang around.'

'Sounds like good advice.' Bridget moved after him as he jogged away up the street. 'I think we should take it.'

'Not just yet.'

Thomas's hand on her arm stopped her. His grip was tight and for a minute she thought about screaming. But years of self-control, thirty of them as a wife and mother holding fort and family together, stopped her. The young man from the coffee shop had jogged out of sight by the time she turned to Thomas, her arm limp and unresisting.

'Fine,' she said, 'but I think it's time you gave me a reason why we should stand here in the wet and dark and cold.'

'Because, like I said, we've got a few things to sort out,' Thomas let her arm go, slowly. 'Like the implication in what Eleanor's just been saying.'

He took a step closer to Eleanor. Bridget's eyes had got used to the murk now and she could see the tight, hard line of his mouth. Eleanor stood her ground but Bridget could feel an almost convulsive stiffening in her long body. It took all of Bridget's own self-control to stop herself running.

'No implication, more like a statement,' Eleanor's voice rose accusingly. 'I'm saying, straight out, that you had something to do with Ted Morgan's death and that I'm not going to keep quiet about what I think anymore. Don't ask me to believe in coincidences. I told you where he was staying and within days he disappears and the next anyone hears about him he's dead.'

'You told me where he was staying.' Thomas, repeating the phrase, nodded and stared at her. 'Listen to what you're telling me, Eleanor. You're saying that you knew where Ted Morgan holed up and that you told me. That's as far as any real knowledge on your part goes. Who's to say you didn't come down here and have some argument with him that ended badly?'

'That's bullshit and you know it.'

'Do I? What I know, Eleanor, is that you're one freaky lady. What I know too is that just because you told me where Ted Morgan was staying doesn't mean I came down to visit with him. Why would I do that? He was an adult, a fairly senior one at that. He knew his own mind. He wanted to stay over there.' Thomas's sudden jerk of his head toward the Bible Mission startled Bridget into a gasp and made Eleanor flinch. Thomas smiled. 'God knows why he moved lodgings,' he said. 'God knows why he came to Seattle in the first place. I don't know why he did these things and I don't care. I didn't ever care.'

Rain began to fall more heavily, the icy drizzle turning to heavy drops which bounced at their feet. Instinctively they moved closer to the shelter of the coffee house front, all three of them.

'This makes no sense, having this conversation on the sidewalk,' said Thomas. 'I'm parked a bit from here in a side street. Why don't we get into the car and drive out to the house and talk there?'

'I'm not getting into any fucking car with you,' Eleanor's voice rose. 'I'm not going anywhere with you, you murdering bastard.'

Bridget, with the detached part of her which was still rational, thought: murderer . . . is that what he is, this man who was once so pleasant and kind to me? Is the queasy lurching in my gut telling me that yes, this is a man capable of taking life?

She decided she'd been silent long enough.

'We've arranged to meet Lindsay by the waterfront.' She gave Thomas what she hoped was an apologetic look. 'Eleanor and I should really begin making our way there now. She'll be waiting for us.'

Thomas's eyebrows shot above the rims of his glasses but he said nothing, just looked past them, towards where the street sloped and curved down to the Puget Sound. His silence was deliberate and calculating and frightening.

'Christ, Bridget, why didn't you shut up like I told you?' Eleanor's voice was ragged. 'You've really fucked things up now.' She turned to Thomas. 'Lindsay brought us here,' she said, 'she said she needed to see the Bible Mission so as she could deal with Ted's death—'

'Cut the crap.' Thomas's eyes were narrowed and calculating. 'Where is the man you came to meet?'

This is the reason he's here, Bridget felt a glorious relief rush through her, it's all a misunderstanding, he thinks we're here to meet someone.

'We weren't meeting anyone,' she spoke confidently and clearly, 'so it looks as if standing here is a waste of everyone's time.'

She linked her arm through Eleanor's, tugged, took a step. Thomas stood in front of them, blocking the way. He ignored Bridget.

'Where is he, Eleanor? Where's your witness? Is he inside the Refuge? Is that where he is?' He was blinking fast, his hands clenching and unclenching by his side. 'Bring me to him, Eleanor, now.'

Bridget took a deep breath. 'Whatever this is about it can be sorted out—'

'Shut up, Bridget. Just shut up and keep out of this.' Thomas went on looking at Eleanor. 'It's too late to be polite. Way too late. Why don't you explain to her, Eleanor, exactly why it's too late?'

'Because I don't know what the fuck you mean or what you're talking about,' Eleanor yelled.

'Your witness, Eleanor, I'm talking about your witness, the guy you came down here to meet, the bullshit artist you were going to give the money you borrowed from Lindsay to. Where is he?'

'This is crazy stuff. I told you already; I didn't come down here to meet anyone and I certainly didn't borrow money from Lindsay. Coming down here was Lindsay's idea.'

'Eleanor's telling you the truth,' said Bridget, 'Lindsay wanted—'

'For the last time, Bridget, stay out of this,' Eleanor said more calmly. 'I'll handle it.'

She stepped away, separating herself from Bridget and Thomas by a couple of feet. She was breathing quickly and even in the bad light her skin was ashen-looking.

'The person who knows all about this is Lindsay. We'll talk it over with her.'

In her hand she held the small pistol she'd shown Bridget in her hotel room.

'Turn around and start walking towards the waterfront.' Eleanor held the gun steadily, close against her body. 'We'll all go together to meet Lindsay.'

Bridget, disbelieving, shook her head. 'This is crazy, Eleanor, this isn't going to—'

'Shut the fuck up. I really mean that. Don't say another word. I'm getting to the bottom of whatever's going on and I'm not taking any more shit from anyone. I can't trust you not to go AWOL so you'll just have to come along and do as I tell you. Now move, both of you,' she made a tight, small gesture with the pistol, 'and don't think I won't use this thing. I'm crazy, remember, a whacko. Why wouldn't I use it?'

She was close enough for Bridget to make out the small black hole of the muzzle at the end of the gun's barrel. It would be a very simple thing for Eleanor to pull the trigger, would take very little the way her mood was swinging.

Trying not to think about it she began to walk, with Thomas beside her, in the general direction of the waterfront. As they passed the glass doors of the Refuge she looked quickly across the street. One of the men in the brown armchairs had fallen asleep, the other stared blankly and without recognition as they moved on by. He doesn't see us, Bridget thought. Now, when we want him, he doesn't even notice us.

'Eyes front and move it. Faster . . .' Eleanor's voice was close, and hoarse-sounding.

Bridget looked ahead, at the rain on the uneven pavement slabs, at the diminishing light as the street sloped backwards. You were right not to come back to this place, Victor, she thought, right to believe that the evil men do lives after them.

216

Chapter Eighteen

It was all downhill. The rain got heavier and ran in gullies along the sides of the cracked sidewalks.

For a lot of the time they walked on the rough surfaces of empty, vehicular-only streets between high, disused buildings, an occasional rat scuttling out of sight as they approached. Eleanor, prodding them along, spoke only once and her tone was conversational.

'You forced this on me, Thomas, you left me no option.' she said. 'I trusted you. You said you'd look out for me and for that I was willing to go along with not saying anything about you knowing where Ted was staying. But I was wrong, wasn't I?' She was silent for a minute, thinking. 'You shouldn't have come after me and Bridget and you sure as hell shouldn't have come on all threatening like that. There's nothing for it now but to find out everything. When I have the whole picture I'll decide what to do.' She took a shaky breath. 'I want to know why you killed Ted and what the fuck you and Lindsay are up to. I don't know what witness you were talking about back there on the street but Bridget will be my witness when we get to talk with Lindsay.' Her voice lightened. 'You know something else, Thomas? No, don't turn around, just keep right on the way you are. That's it. You too, Bridget. Well, the something else is that I'm enjoying this. It feels good to be in control of things, to know I'm not going to be fucked around any more.'

'You've got this whole thing wrong.' Thomas kicked a

loose stone ahead of him. 'You're crazy if you believe I had anything to do with Ted Morgan's death.'

Eleanor, swearing under her breath, moved quickly to lay the cold, wet length of the pistol's barrel along Thomas's cheek.

'Don't use the word crazy when you talk about me,' she spoke so softly Bridget could barely hear her, 'don't do it ever, ever again. In fact,' she smiled and stepped back, 'don't open your mouth again until I tell you to.'

There was an inevitability about the strip of waterfront when it appeared, shining, ahead.

Encouraged by Eleanor they crossed a wide road onto a disused wharf. They stopped then and Bridget, looking out across the darkly heaving glitter of the water, thought she had never in her life been so wet, or so frightened. Her stomach, acknowledging the fact, had settled into a remorseless lurch.

Thomas, standing beside her, cleared his throat.

'I'd like to clean my glasses,' he said. 'The rain . . .'

'Give them to me,' said Eleanor.

'I'd prefer—'

'Give them to me with one hand,' Eleanor said and Thomas, with infinite care and even greater reluctance, handed over the glasses. 'Thank you.' Eleanor dropped and ground them underfoot. 'Should have thought of that before,' she said, 'not too much you can try on now you're half blind.' She took a deep breath. 'Rain's easing and it's nice and private and sheltered here so we'll talk a little, before we head along to the pier to meet Lindsay.'

She leaned against a low building, resting the elbow of the arm holding the gun on a window ledge. Bridget didn't for a minute think she was as relaxed as she appeared. Nor did she think there was any way on God's earth, or on that piece of Seattle waterfront, that a scream of hers would have been heard, not with the noise of the traffic thundering on what looked like a flyover road behind them and the sound of the water against the wharf. Whether by accident or design Eleanor had chosen well. Bleak, abandoned, noisy, it was the ideal spot to hold two people at gunpoint.

'I want you to listen to me, Thomas,' Eleanor said. 'If I get answers that sound right we'll continue on down the waterfront to meet with Lindsay. If I don't' – she shrugged before straightening up to hold the gun with both hands – 'then it might just happen that I really will go crazy and use this thing. There's no knowing what a crazy woman with too much control will do in a situation like this. Are you willing to risk finding out by fucking me around Thomas?'

Thomas grunted and stared blindly as she poked the gun against his chest. His hands twitched by his sides.

'Tell me,' Eleanor said, 'why you followed me today.'

Thomas looked away from her and the gun, before he began to speak. His voice came in a flat monotone. 'Lindsay said you were meeting a man at the Bible Mission Refuge who was willing to swear he'd seen me with Ted Morgan about the time he died. She said she gave you money to pay him off. I wanted to see the guy for myself.' He turned to Bridget and his face twisted with distaste. 'I don't care to waste company funds.'

'Lindsay was lying,' Eleanor said. 'There was no man. Why do you think she wanted you to think there was?'

'I've no idea. Why do you want me to think there wasn't?'

'There wasn't any man,' Bridget corroborated. 'It was Lindsay's idea that we all go to the Bible Mission.' She pondered the implications. 'She set you both up, for whatever reason. Me too, I suppose.'

'Thank you, Bridget,' Eleanor said, 'for the support—'

'Do you have to keep pointing that thing at us?' Bridget gave way to a sudden surge of anger. 'You've got us here and we're talking. You don't need it any more.'

'I need it,' Eleanor was curt, 'and you're a fool if you

think you can take over control with sweet reason. I need to think about what's happening here and I don't want you to speak again either unless I say so. Got it?'

'Seems fairly clear.' There were a lot of things she could say; none of them would make any difference.

Eleanor became suddenly restless, jerkily looking around her. The gun wavered, but never enough to create a doubt that she would use it if anyone moved. Bridget watched her, carefully. She didn't for a minute believe Eleanor was a killer. What she did believe, with certainty, was that the younger woman was on a knife edge, likely to pull the trigger if pushed and to realize too late what she'd done.

In the circumstances, she might just as well have been a killer.

'What are you and Lindsay up to?' Eleanor spun suddenly on Thomas, the gun in front of her aiming at his stomach. 'Tell me, or by God I'll use this thing. I feel like using it. I feel like causing you pain. You killed Ted. I told you where he was staying when you asked me because I trusted you. Then you went there and you killed him. I didn't believe it before but I do now. I knew it when you appeared in that street tonight. I don't need any witness to tell me. You told me not to tell the police about you knowing where Ted was staying and I didn't tell them. You fucked around with my head, Thomas, you and Lindsay both.' Her voice, which had been rising as she spoke, dropped suddenly to a low snarl, 'Tell me, Thomas, tell me what went on, what's going on here.'

'I'll do a deal.' Thomas lifted his head and looked Eleanor squarely in the face. 'I level with you about the problems we've been having and we all go to meet Lindsay, get in the car and go home. Deal?'

'Depends on what you tell me,' said Eleanor.

She pushed her wet hair from her face with her free hand. The rain had eased back to a drizzle. Bridget was wet enough to have become indifferent to the condition, cold enough to be numb, almost. She supposed it was the same for the other two.

'What I want to know is why you killed Ted,' Eleanor said roughly.

'But there's something you should know before that, Thomas Carter, and it's this.' She took a breath. 'I had a very long talk with Lindsay last night. Your story better be the same as hers.'

'I didn't kill Ted Morgan.' Thomas cut her short and turned his head seaward, searching for words. Bridget was struck by the chilling stillness of his eyes, made unnervingly obvious now he wasn't wearing glasses. He shook himself, as if from a reverie, before going on. 'It is more accurate to say that I didn't kill him intentionally,' he said and Bridget caught her breath. 'Ted Morgan dying was an accident, something I'll spend the rest of my life—'

'I don't want to hear about your problems with your conscience,' Eleanor said. 'Tell me . . .'

'Veronica wanted Ted to marry her. She told me so herself.'

Thomas spoke into the wind, his head still turned away from where Eleanor stood.

'I went to meet with him to talk him out of the marriage. It would have ruined everyone, as well as everything I've worked for all these years. To be honest,' he lifted one shoulder in a shrug, 'I went to buy him off. But he said he was against the marriage himself, that he'd moved out of the house to get away from the pressure from Veronica. He'd had left town altogether, headed back to New York, if it hadn't been that he was worried about you, Eleanor, and wanted to hang around until you'd got things sorted out. That's what he said, but that was only part of it.' Thomas turned and looked again at Eleanor, his eyes squinting with the effort. 'He told you where he'd be staying so you could keep in touch with him, right?'

'He gave me the address, yes. He came here on my account and then he got killed. But you know what?'

With a sudden, violently stabbing movement she brought the gun to within an inch of Thomas's face.

'I'll feel a lot less bad about it when I get what's mine. That's what he wanted and it'll vindicate his death.' She gave an impatient shrug before going on, 'But what I want right now is some more explaining. Talk.'

The rain had eased again and the air had become colder. Behind them Bridget could hear the waters of the Sound give great, heaving sighs, as if it would haul itself up and over the wharf sides. She kept her eyes on the gun and didn't look round.

'You have to take some of the blame for his death,' Thomas spoke in his old familiar voice, soft and kind. 'As you say, he was in Seattle for you and he was staying in the hostel because he didn't want to leave you alone in town. The row which led on to the accident that killed him was about you.'

'Don't you try to lay Ted's death at my door,' Eleanor's voice had become ragged.

Thomas gave a sad smile.

'He said he wasn't going to marry Veronica. I didn't believe him. He'd have done it in the end. Veronica spent a lifetime getting what she wanted; she was going to have this marriage too. I offered him money and he laughed. I upped the price and he told me I was wasting my time. He didn't want to talk in the hostel. We walked down here, to the water. Just walking and talking. We were down the way a bit . . .'

Thomas gestured and Eleanor, with a small scream, shoved the gun in front of him again.

'Keep your hands by your sides,' she yelled.

Thomas shrugged and Bridget closed her eyes against the agonized confusion and misery on Eleanor's face. The other woman's mood had shifted; she wasn't enjoying her power anymore, her fragile control of herself was disintegrating.

'He wouldn't talk to me. Wouldn't listen.' Thomas, his hands by his sides again, went on relentlessly. 'He started to go back to the hostel.' Thomas hesitated. 'I tried to stop him.' He hesitated again, for longer this time. 'I've thought about how things happened then. Over and over. It's the same every time and it never makes sense. I grabbed him and he shook his arm free and I yelled at him and he stepped back and I grabbed him again. I shoved the money at him and he did something, sort of jerked, and I let go and he fell. As he went down his head hit the wall beside us. There was blood everywhere by the time he hit the ground and once he lay there he didn't get up, didn't move again. I looked at him for a long time. But I knew before I touched him that he was dead. It was deserted, like now. I kind of carried and dragged him along until I could tip him into the Sound.'

Bridget broke the long silence, raising her voice above the heaving water, the gulls and the traffic. 'Why did you do that?' She tried to keep the disgust and incredulity out of her voice. 'Why didn't you take him to a hospital, call the police?'

'Couldn't expose the family. Listen,' Thomas, turning short-sightedly her way, spoke with the air of a not-so-patient parent to a recalcitrant child. 'Ted Morgan was an old man with nothing much left in his life. He could've ruined all that this family's built – made of itself. He was not an important man, no one to miss him. He's already forgotten by everyone but us three. The cops don't care. As far as they're concerned he was a drifter, couldn't stay put anywhere. Why stay in a refuge if he was above board? That's the way they think.' He shrugged. 'On the other hand, if the family business was damaged, and it would have been, hundreds of people would be affected: they'd have been out of work and neither they nor their families would have had the luxury of forgetting the consequences. Put simply, the consequences of a collapse in confidence in the business would have been catastrophic for a huge number of people. It's a question of priorities.' He looked from one to the other of the blurred faces in front of him and settled his gaze on Bridget. 'You see what I mean?'

'Yes.'

Bridget saw what he meant all right. Ted had been a problem and Thomas had killed him. She didn't believe him that it had been an accident. She'd seen the other terrifying Thomas outside the Bible Mission Refuge, and he was a man in whom things she didn't understand were at work. Violent urges, evil intentions ... all of them driven by a need to protect what he saw as the Baldacci empire.

Eleanor didn't believe him either.

'I don't believe you,' her voice was high, uneven. 'You're a murdering liar. You came down here to kill him and it had nothing to do with any marriage. Lindsay told me—'

'You told Lindsay I knew where Ted was staying?' Thomas sounded curious.

'I told her,' said Eleanor. 'She called at my room in the hotel yesterday and took me out to eat. We talked, about a lot of things. Family things. All of it while Veronica was dying, though we didn't know that at the time. Want to know what she told me, Thomas? You'll really want to know, Bridget. This is the big one they've been keeping from you.'

When she looked at her Bridget saw that Eleanor's eyes were bright not just from the wind. Eleanor Munro was crying.

'You killed him because you found out that Victor Baldacci wasn't Veronica's son.' She took a deep breath. 'Victor's father was Frank Baldacci all right, but his mother was Grace Munro, my grandmother. Veronica couldn't have any more children after Magdalena and Frank wanted a son and Grace provided one. Money can do anything and it was made to look like he was Veronica's. Even the church took their cut and helped out – Father Matthews kept Veronica's secret until the end. But Veronica was losing it and she told Ted and Ted was going to tell me so you killed him.'

'None of that makes sense.' Thomas was gentle, soothing almost. 'Even if it were true, why would it be a reason to kill Ted Morgan?'

'Because the truth makes Victor my mother's full brother and makes Victor's children my full cousins.'

Eleanor was openly weeping now, her breath catching as she spoke. The gun in her hand had never seemed so dangerous.

'The truth makes the Munro-Baldacci side of the family numerically equal to the Langan-Baldacci side. There's me and my cousins on the one side; Magdalena, Lindsay and Jack on the other. You don't count, Thomas. You're nothing, just the boy brought in to marry Magdalena and take over what should have been Victor's role in the business. You're not a Baldacci and neither is Bridget. But the rest of us have the blood and we've got rights in law under a charter drawn up by Frank Baldacci. You knew I would line up with my cousins, you knew the power we would have once Ted told me—'

'You're a crazy! You can't prove any of this!'

'Don't call me crazy,' Eleanor hissed; hunched into the long coat she looked ominous. 'And you're wrong. I can prove everything. The old priest might want to keep Veronica's secret but there's no way he can hold on once a serious, legal investigation gets under way. If you ask me he'll be glad to get things off his chest.'

Thomas had become very still again. For several minutes the only sound was the pitiless sucking sounds of the water behind them. Bridget's hands, in her pockets, broke into a cold sweat as she looked quickly from Thomas to Eleanor and back again, and wished she hadn't. They both had the cold, hard look of people for whom there was no going back.

Thomas, without warning, began to shout, 'You've said your bit, you crazy bitch – now what're you going to do?'

He's calling her bluff, Bridget thought. She's going to have to use the gun, or walk away – forget this whole thing and admit she was bluffing. Very gently she eased her hands from her pockets, then flattened her cold, sweaty palms against her wet coat. For just a few seconds she closed her eyes against the scene.

She opened them with a squeal of heart-thumping fear as her arm was twisted viciously behind her back. Thomas's voice, behind her and very close, was rough and spitting. 'Shoot now, Eleanor, why don't you?' he said. 'Why don't you shoot the mother of those cousins you're so keen to tie up with?'

He jerked Bridget's arm and she felt a wave of sick pain. She wouldn't have believed a man so slight could have such strength. She doubled over, trying not to vomit. Thomas twisted her arm. She gave a low, agonized scream.

'Keep your head up.' She could feel his breath in her ear. 'You're going to be my protection, Bridget, so stand straight and maybe we'll all make a deal here. Depends on Eleanor.' He gave Bridget's arm a convincingly vicious twist. 'You want to shoot me, Eleanor, you're going to have to shoot Bridget first.'

'I don't need Bridget and I don't need you.' Eleanor took a step closer. 'The difference is, Thomas, that I truly hate you.'

Eleanor's face took on a dreamy look, and Bridget, held tight against Thomas, felt him tense. Then she was pitched forward, clawing the air as he pushed her from him and threw her bodily at Eleanor. She tried to stop herself from bringing the other woman crashing to the concrete with her. But she'd been thrown too hard and too fast, and even as she fought for balance Eleanor screamed, hit the ground beneath her, and lost her hold on the gun.

Bridget rolled free, on to her hands and knees, in time to see Thomas's feet step smartly after the clattering sound of the gun on the stone. There was nothing she could do to stop him when he bent to pick it up.

'On your feet.' Thomas caught Bridget by her hair. 'Up.' He jerked her to stand in front of him and pointed the gun at Eleanor as she struggled upright. 'I will shoot Bridget, dead, if you don't do exactly what I tell you to do. And do not think that my half-blind state will prevent me. At this range any one of the six bullets will most likely kill her. You too, in all probability. Now walk ahead of us, slowly.'

Eleanor began to walk. She was limping.

'Hurt your leg? Good.' Thomas put the gun against the back of Bridget's neck. 'Follow her, Bridget. You're going to be my eyes as well as my protection.'

They made their way to where the wharf narrowed and a disused pier stretched out over the water.

'Start along the pier,' Thomas commanded, 'and keep going.'

He prodded Bridget with the gun, casually cruel, as if the weapon was a part of the everyday paraphernalia of his life.

Wordlessly, Eleanor stepped ahead of them on to the pier and began to walk out over the water. Bridget, a numbness filling her with an unreasonable calm, followed.

'Where are we going?' she asked.

'Just a little further.' Thomas prodded her again.

Rain began to fall once more, carried in from the sea on high, whip-lashing winds. Under their feet the boards moved and sighed with the swelling motion of the sea. As they went it was clear to Bridget that he had been here before. He was too sure of things, too confident about where they were going for a man with limited vision. This had to be the pier along which he'd dragged Ted Morgan's body, off which he'd thrown it into the waters of the Sound.

Chapter Nineteen

'I'm not going out there.' Bridget jammed her hands into her pockets, clenching them until she felt a nail break through the skin of her palm. She turned to face Thomas. 'Whatever you're planning will have to happen here.'

Thomas rapped the side of her head, hard, with the gun. 'Keep going,' he said.

But Bridget, her head throbbing as if with the motions of the sea, couldn't have moved to save her life.

'You're going to have to shoot me here,' she said. 'I'm not going on.'

She didn't feel brave, just strangely calm. Images from her life floating through her mind. She had loved and been loved and she had children on the other side of the world whom she loved more than life. She wasn't ready to die, didn't want to. She just couldn't go on.

Eleanor, ahead of them, stopped and turned, the rain plastering her hair across her pale face.

'What're you going to do now, Thomas Carter?' Her voice was full of a wild triumphalism. 'If you shoot Bridget here there's no way you're going to get me too. And if I escape I'll blab everything, you know I will, and to anyone who'll listen. I'll go to the cops and I'll go to the press and to the law. So what are you going to do, Thomas Carter? What're you going to do? What're you going to do . . . do . . . do . . . do . . .?'

The chant, as she went on, and on, was caught in the wind and carried, whirling and falling, about them.

'It'll be your word against mine,' Thomas shouted, trying to drown her out. 'And the gun is yours, you're the one who brought Ted Morgan to Seattle, you're the one who moved into the hotel to keep an eye on Bridget.'

His voice sounded wrong: twisted and panicky and not his own. Thomas too was losing control.

'It won't be just my word against yours,' Eleanor called across to him. 'There's Lindsay's word too.'

'Lindsay won't speak against her father.' Thomas sounded more confident. 'There are loyalties you could never—'

'Loyalties? Father?' As laughs went Eleanor's was real, full-bellied. She scraped a ribbon of wet hair from her eyes. 'I wouldn't bank on Lindsay's loyalty, Thomas, if I were you.' She laughed again.

'Why don't you tell me about it,' Thomas invited.

He lifted the gun, pointing it in such a way that Bridget was its target, making it impossible for her not to look again into the black hole of the muzzle. Black and small and round, it cut through her growing hysteria, concentrating her mind terrifyingly on the prospect of death.

'I've got a much better idea. Why don't we go find Lindsay and hear what she has to say?' Eleanor was unconvincingly cool.

'Why don't we?' said Thomas.

He lowered the gun a little and Bridget felt the tension give inside her, like the snapping of an elastic band which had been holding her together. She turned slowly towards Eleanor, moving her head with caution. She had almost got the other woman in focus when Thomas, with a primitive, grunting sound, lunged, grabbed her round the neck and pulled her hard against him. Choking, the world darkening to a black-red landscape behind her eyelids, she tore at his arm and screamed. Once.

'You make a noise like that again and I'll kill you.' Thomas's breath was rancid with rage.

Bridget believed him. She kept her eyes shut and prayed wild imprecations that Eleanor would believe him too, wouldn't do anything which would make him carry out his threat.

She didn't plan what happened next. Maybe it was the fact of her eyes being closed to the sights around. Maybe it was a simple and primitive survival instinct. She was never able to say, even a long time afterwards, how it happened that she managed to grind the heel of her boot onto Thomas's shoe so viciously that he loosened his hold of her and dropped the gun, making it possible for her to whirl, bring her hands up to his face and begin a demented tearing at the flesh there, at his eyes and nose and mouth.

She couldn't stop. Not even when she felt hot blood running through her fingers nor even when she felt a jelly-like substance from his eye under her nails and heard his anguished, animal bellow above the sound of the wind. She was free of his hold on her, free of the paralysing fear that she was going to die any minute. And she was going to stay free, fight on, claw until he was abject, defeated, no longer had the power of her life and death in his hands.

'That's enough, Bridget, lay off him now.'

Eleanor's hand was on her shoulder, pulling her away from Thomas, halting the frenzy of the attack. She heard mewing sounds and knew they were coming from her own throat, felt a hot stream on her face and knew it was her own tears. When she stopped, shuddering, she felt Eleanor's arm go around her and she blinked, hard, shaking her head, seeing again the thunderous sky and cold, cold sea.

Hell couldn't have been any bleaker but it was a hell in which she was alive. She gave a sob that was sheer, agonized relief.

'Everything's going to be all right now,' Eleanor said. 'I'll look after you.' She pointed the gun at Thomas and together and silently they looked at him. He was hunched over, a bloodied hand covering one side of his face. As they stood he straightened and stared at them, unblinking, out of the uncovered eye.

'You've destroyed my eye,' he said.

'I'm sorry,' said Bridget.

She looked around. They were a good halfway along the pier, the timbers underfoot uneven and slippery in parts. This far out the water was truly convulsive, tormented in its lashings. Thomas took his hand away from his eye and the rain on his face ran with the pouring blood and diluted it until Bridget could see where her nails had torn and gouged along the side of his eye: it was a red, pulpy thing hung with slivers of flesh. With his good eye he looked past them to the city at their backs.

'Take a good look at me,' he said. His face was set and rigid and Bridget offered a half-hearted prayer that his pain wasn't too great. 'I built the business,' he said thoughtfully, as if speaking to himself, 'and I held it together and she would have destroyed it all, broken things up if she'd married Ted Morgan, given shares to you, Bridget.' He let out a long breath. 'To allow that to happen would have meant I'd lived my life for nothing. All of those years . . . all that I'd done . . . for nothing.'

The damaged eye glittered. With the blood pouring it was hard for Bridget to see exactly how much harm she'd done but at least it was functioning, shining as malevolently as the good eye.

'We killed that man together, Eleanor, you and me.' Thomas didn't even raise his voice. 'I did it because he couldn't be allowed to bring down what I'd built, but you were the one got him to come back to Seattle and that's what got him killed. You were as responsible as I was and you're going to have to live with it too.'

'Move.' Eleanor gestured with the gun towards the city.

'What if I don't? Are you going to kill me? What'll you do when I'm dead? Who'll run the business? Who else knows it? Shoot me, Eleanor, and you shoot yourself in the head. Let's end this thing.' He held out his hand and moved towards them and said, coaxingly, as if to a child, 'Give me the gun, there's a good girl.'

Bridget, instinctively, took a step backwards. This is all wrong, she thought, he's treating Eleanor like a fool and she's going to lose it.

Or maybe that's what he wants her to do.

Eleanor also stepped back. 'Don't come any closer, you mad bastard.' She waved the gun in a way that made Bridget whimper and close her eyes. 'I swear to you I'll use this. I'll decide what's going to happen here.'

Bridget opened her eyes and instantly regretted it. Eleanor was aiming the gun at Thomas's head, holding it very steady with her finger on the trigger.

'Don't!' she cried. 'Jesus Christ, Eleanor, please don't—'

'Keep out of this, Bridget,' Eleanor's tone was frighteningly normal, conversational even. 'If you can't cut it just turn away.' She kept the pistol pointed at Thomas's head as she went on. 'The prospects look more appealing from this side of the gun so why don't we deal, Thomas, like you said? I've been thinking and it seems to me it would be very stupid to bring the cops on to our case again. Looks like they can't prove anything about Ted, not unless I help them out. So why risk blowing the whole thing apart by giving them another body? Much better if the three of us could come to an amicable agreement.' She hesitated and then said, in a clear, slow voice. 'All I've ever wanted was a family to belong to. So, what about it, Thomas?'

'I think you're mad.'

Thomas turned and began walking slowly down the middle of the pier towards the open waters.

'Fuck you,' Eleanor's shriek, as she started after him, was full of an agonized loss. 'Don't make me shoot you in the back!'

Thomas laughed without turning round. 'You're not going to shoot me anywhere, Eleanor. But do you want to know something? I almost wish you would. I'm stuck with you, you and the widow. There would be nothing if it wasn't for me and now . . .' He came to the end of the pier and stood there, looking out to sea with a hand covering the damaged eye. He looked lonely and broken and Eleanor came to a fatal, undecided halt.

'Why can't we deal?' she called.

'Because it's too late.' Thomas leaned forward, over the water.

'No!' Eleanor began to run, her coat flapping about her in the wind. She reached Thomas and put a hand on his shoulder. 'No,' she said again.

Thomas turned and Bridget, ten feet away, saw what followed as if trapped in a dream from which she couldn't look away. In the time it took her to break from the spell of transfixed horror the worst had happened. Thomas's hands had caught Eleanor by the throat and lifted her into the air, a long, flapping rag doll to his frenzied executioner. The gun went off as he shook her, the sound dulled by the clamour all about, the bullet exploding harmlessly in the air. Bridget, shocked into life, screamed,

'No, for God's sake, no . . .'

Then, with the utmost simplicity, the seemingly inevitable happened, Eleanor's arm, as her head jerked forward, curved in the air above Thomas's head and the gun, in a randomly graceful gesture, became directly aimed at his face. Thomas couldn't have known anything as it went off and blew the side of his head away.

Bridget, running towards them, could see in front of her

only the spurting, splattering, volcano of red which, seconds before, had been his face.

When she reached her, Eleanor was standing looking at the collapsed thing at her feet with her face blank and her shoulders slumped. She didn't notice when Bridget stood beside her, made no response when Bridget put an arm about her. Thomas's body jerked a few times, then, apart from a thick, slow ooze of dark blood, there was no further movement.

'We should put him into the sea ... or something...' said Eleanor.

The blood splattered across her coat was already beginning to stream and wash away in the rain.

Bridget looked from the dead man to the woman who'd shot him and shook her head. There would be nightmares later, dreams filled with black figures dancing in grey rain which slowly turned red. For now there were things to be done.

'We can't put him into the sea, Eleanor,' she said, gently. 'We'll have to call the police.'

Eleanor shrugged but was rigid and impossible to move when Bridget tried.

'This isn't doing you any good,' Bridget said. 'It's better if we go at once, get help ...'

'There's no help for him now,' said Eleanor, 'nothing to be done for him anymore. Except to bury him. The sea would do that ...'

She put her head back, closed her eyes and let the rain wash over her tight, white face.

'We need help, you and me,' Bridget pointed out. 'All of this mess has to be put right so that life can go on. We need to deal with it with some sort of decency – '

'Decency! Oh, God, Bridget, you're like something from another planet. Decency is dead; as dead as Thomas is dead . . .' Eleanor covered her eyes with a hand. 'Decency, in this family, died years ago, if it ever existed, if there was ever anything more than a malignant, cancerous growth where decency should have been.' She took her hand away from her eyes and looked around. 'I'm one of them and I'm diseased too and I've killed a man. I'll never be free of that . . . I'll never be . . . decent.'

She stepped from the circle of Bridget's arm and smiled at her, an infinitely sad smile that was full of the loss of hope and a chilling self-knowledge.

Then she lifted the gun to her temple and pulled the trigger.

Bridget sat with her for a long time, cradling her poor, blasted head in her lap, Thomas's body a dark and lonely outline beside them.

'Things are going to be OK,' she said more than once, to herself, to Eleanor's corpse. She didn't believe it, no matter how often she said it.

The rain had stopped and a pale moon had broken through the shifting clouds before a patrolling police car stopped at the end of the pier and two policemen got out and began walking towards them.

The cold was like nothing she'd ever known.

Chapter Twenty

'Living with Thomas did this to me.' Magdalena finished one drink and poured another. 'Had to blur the reality somehow.'

'He's dead,' Bridget said, 'you don't have to live with him any longer.'

'Might as well drink to his memory.' Magdalena shrugged, uncrossed her legs and stood. 'Not a lot else to do around here at the moment.' She paced restlessly before crossing the sitting room to a mirror where she stood teasing her newly platinumed hair. Apart from a rope of amber beads, she was dressed all in black. 'When do you leave?' She plucked critically at her roots.

'Friday,' Bridget said. Magdalena knew when she was leaving. She's asked Bridget once already that morning, twice the day before.

'Couple more days then,' Magdalena said, 'and you'll be gone.'

'That's right,' Bridget agreed.

In less than three days she would be home. Seattle would begin to become a memory. Some of it she could start trying to forget. She'd have gone home immediately after the night on the pier except that she'd had to stay to help with the police enquiries. In between times there had been the burials of Veronica, Ted, Thomas and Eleanor.

She wasn't at all sure Eleanor would have wanted to lie in a grave next to the Baldacci plot in a Seattle cemetery.

But that's where she was, in death as in life close to, but apart from, the family she'd hated and wanted to be a part of. Bridget prayed she would rise to haunt the living Baldaccis who had rejected her, but doubted there was that much justice in their world.

Bridget had told the police everything she knew as well as a lot that she thought they *should* know. They'd been kindly enough, in the way of police forces almost everywhere.

Ted Morgan's murder they attributed to Thomas, and Eleanor's death was proven a suicide. The evidence all pointed to Eleanor having shot Thomas.

What had happened to Grace Munro looked, like the identity of the area's Green River killer, as if it would remain unknown and unsolved. The police inclined to the view that either Frank or Veronica, or perhaps both of them together, had had something to do with it. Everything else, the years of incest, deceit and cruelty, were family matters and, in instances where the law had been broken, unprovable.

Lindsay, by plotting and bringing Bridget, Eleanor and Thomas together where Ted Morgan had last been seen alive had not broken the law. She'd wanted to create a situation, she said, in which the truth of things might emerge. The police, reluctantly, accepted this. Their witnesses were dead.

Eleanor's death haunted Bridget. Not just the last terrible act but the hour which went before it and the torment of all the maybes, the things she might have done to prevent it. She should have seen it coming, known where that last conversation was going. She could have stopped Eleanor using the pistol on herself. It would have taken so little; a different choice of words, a promise of solidarity, a gesture . . .

She *should* have stopped her. That she had not would stay with her for ever, her legacy from the Baldaccis.

Magdalena had moved back into her family home after Thomas's death. Less memories, she said, though Bridget found this hard to understand. Bridget had moved in too. Memories were the same for her wherever she went in Seattle and the Madison Park house was, in the end, given all she had to do with Lindsay and Magdalena, more convenient.

'The men are here to take down the tree,' Lindsay said coming through the door. She was wearing a suit of dark blue, long and lean on her slim frame. Her hair was smooth, skin glowing. Her move into the role of Chief Executive had been seamless.

'Ask them to be quiet, please, and quick.' Magdalena didn't look round. 'This house is so *busy*. I plan to change things.'

'You do that,' said Lindsay, 'and do you think you could lay off the booze while you're at it?'

'Why should I?'

'You tell her.' Lindsay turned to Bridget.

'Why should I?' Bridget countered. 'I doubt anything I say will affect your mother's decision to drink herself to death, one way or the other.' She walked to the French windows and stood there, watching the men who'd arrived to dismantle the Christmas tree. 'I can't, in any event, think of a single reason why Magdalena should stop drinking.'

'We have to talk.' Lindsay, coming up behind her, was curt.

'Do we?' Bridget sighed. 'I can't think of a single reason for doing that either.'

Magdalena laughed. 'How well you've settled in, Bridget. You sound just like one of the family. What a pity you have to tear yourself away from us.'

There were three men at work on the tree. One had set about dismantling the base structure, another was playing spiderman from a hoist and removing the lights. The third man was busy spreading a vast net over the frosty grass.

Suddenly, Bridget was aware of Lindsay moving from behind her and running down the room. She turned.

'Have another drink, why don't you,' the younger woman said frenziedly, and began pouring drinks from bottles on a table. She poured three in a row, great sloshes of vodka and Martini. She worked quickly, intently, messily. 'Have a few drinks, mother, and then a few more. Why the hell not?'

'How thoughtful. Don't mind if I do.' Magdalena drained the glass in her hand and moved languidly toward the table.

'You would too. You'd down the lot, wouldn't you. Bridget's right – you've decided to drink yourself to death.' Lindsay, white and shaking, used the back of her hand to send the glasses splashing and splintering across the room. 'Is that what you've decided? Is it? Tell me?'

'Looks like I'll have to get my own drink,' said Magdalena. Very slowly, with only a very slight stagger, she left the room.

Bridget, at the window, thought how Hugo would have hated the situation, the damage, the disintegration. These two women, alone with the disaffected Jack and the ineffectual Russell, were all that were left to keep the Baldacci dynasty going and the money machines churning. Hugo wouldn't have been able to tolerate Lindsay in charge either. Just as well he was gone.

'I need some air and I need to keep an eye on what those clowns are doing to the tree.' Lindsay, her hand shaking, lit a cigarette and walked back to Bridget. 'We'll talk on the patio.'

'There's not a lot I want to say,' said Bridget, 'or listen to.'

But fresh air sounded like a good idea and when Lindsay opened the French windows she followed her through. The air was sharp. She put her head back and took deep breaths and looked at the limpid, wintery blue of the sky above.

The man on the hoist was having difficulties with the reindeer on the top of the tree.

'Doesn't want to come down from there,' he called cheerfully, 'guess he likes being on top of the world.'

Lindsay, squinting up at him, said sourly, 'Strip the goddamn tree and get out of here. That's what you've been paid to do. I want you out of this place in thirty minutes.' She walked ahead of Bridget to the steps down to the grass. 'Last time there'll be a tree like that in this yard. Grandmother only had it put there to please that runt Hugo anyway, only kept it there for Ted Morgan's sake.' She flicked her cigarette end on to the grass, where it sizzled. 'Men were her weakness. Her only weakness.' She turned her cool, pale look on Bridget and half smiled. 'The old order changeth, yielding place to new.'

'What is it you want to say to me?' Bridget asked.

'There's something you need to know,' Lindsay said.

'There was a lot I needed to know, and for a long time. Now I know more than I ever want to.' Bridget folded her arms across her chest and leaned against the wall of the house. She'd been walking every day since the night on the pier. She walked by the lake, along the roads, even here in the garden. It kept her in touch with the realities of the mercurial weather, of the way days continued, reassuringly, to follow one another. She had a feeling now that Lindsay was about to start dealing in Baldacci realities.

'You need to know a few things about the old order.' Lindsay frowned at the man with the net and with an obvious effort stopped herself from telling him what to do. 'It will help you understand the new order, your place in it.'

'I have no place.'

'The old order was rotten,' Lindsay went on as if Bridget hadn't spoken. 'Take Hugo, your countryman, for instance. It would be better if you had no illusions about him. He double-crossed everyone in the end.' She gave a small laugh.

'Hugo Sweeney is a survivor, that's the most you can say about him. He helped Grandmother to die because he was jealous of her feelings for Ted Morgan and because Thomas paid him to. He came cheap, he was going anyway once Thomas told him of the wedding plans. He couldn't take that, after all the years. Then,' her tone held an element of awe, 'he did the dirt on Thomas by bringing in the priest to tip you off about Grandmother's wedding plans. He always knew how to play all sides against the middle. You do know,' she arched an eyebrow and lit another cigarette, 'that it wasn't an accident of Fate you were the one with Grand-mother the night she died?'

'The thought had occurred to me,' Bridget said.

Nothing that had happened since she'd arrived in Seattle had been an accident, of Fate or otherwise.

'Thomas wanted you with her,' Lindsay said in precise tones, 'because he planned to make it look as if you'd influenced a suicidal and demented old woman into chang-ing her will. A lot of Thomas's little schemes went awry. He really wasn't much good at anything once he stepped out-side the boardroom. I'd no idea how dangerously useless he was until the night Grandmother died. The talk I had with Eleanor that night made a lot of things clear. That was when I discovered, for instance, that my daddy knew where Ted Morgan had been staying. Ted was a worry, both because he might have married Grandmother and because, once Grandmother gave him the news, he would almost certainly have told Eleanor about Victor being Grace Munro's son . . .'

'Please stop.' Bridget, leaving the wall, walked slowly to where Lindsay was standing. She looked the other woman in the face. 'There's something I want to understand and it's this. Why didn't you tell the police you suspected your father had killed Ted? You wanted control, you've made that clear,

242

and loyalty isn't an obvious factor in this family. So – why not?'

'Ah, yes.' Lindsay gave a low laugh. 'That is the question that gets to the core of things.'

She turned her face away to look again at the men at work on the tree.

'Well, the fact of this little matter is that Thomas Carter wasn't my father. Not in the biological sense. When Magdalena was married off to reliable, well-connected Thomas for the business' sake, she took to the consolations offered by adultery and drink. Thomas never knew I was the progeny of one of Magdalena's infidelities.' She paused. 'I didn't know myself until she told me in a confessional mood brought on by Victor's death. I didn't tell the police my suspicions about Thomas because I thought, in the circumstances, it would be better not to involve them any more. I planned to trap Thomas into telling you and Eleanor what he'd done. Afterwards, when I'd told him the truth about my paternity, you, me and Eleanor would have had Thomas where we wanted him. Blackmail is an effective weapon of control. I would have taken charge, as I have now, and you and Eleanor would have—'

'I would have gone to the police,' Bridget said. 'How could you have believed I'd do otherwise?'

'I intended looking after Eleanor and she knew that. It would have been your word against hers and mine.' She sighed. 'Thomas had been in my face for a long time, voting against my plans, screaming caution, restraint.' She paused. 'He wasn't my kind of person; I thought so even before I knew he wasn't my father.'

'Eleanor . . .' Bridget said the name softly.

'I didn't want Eleanor hurt.' Lindsay shook her head. 'I truly didn't. She was a whacko but, Christ, how could she have been anything else in the circumstances? I didn't want you to get hurt either. I'm sorry about what happened.' She sighed and ran a hand through her hair, then she smoothed it again. 'It was all a terrible, terrible mess. Not the way I wanted things to happen at all.'

'Something was bound to happen once you started playing God,' Bridget said harshly. 'Thomas was falling apart and he'd become dangerous. You were setting him up to become a serial murderer.' She closed her eyes, briefly, and had a flash of Thomas, hunched and soaking and manic, before she opened them again.

'Wrong,' Lindsay snapped. 'He'd have been neutered. We'd have done it to him together.'

'If none of this had happened would you and Magdalena have gone on allowing him to believe he was your natural father?'

'Oh, yes.' Lindsay gave Bridget a sideways glance as she lit another cigarette. 'He'd have marginalized me if he'd known before and Jack, as his only issue, would have found power and favour coming his way. Jack!'

The idea silenced her. She sucked on the cigarette, her beautiful face only slightly flawed by a scowl.

Bridget said nothing for a while. Everything, it seemed to her, had already been said.

The tree was coming apart quickly now, the last of the lights coming off.

'I want you to know that I feel an affinity with Victor.' Lindsay, smiling a small smile, became confidential. 'His mother wasn't who he thought she was, my father wasn't my father. Odd, isn't it?' She thought for a minute. 'Strange too how it was Victor, the one who opted out and who had nothing to do with anything, who should have been the one to . . .' She shrugged, pulling on the cigarette and narrowing her eyes at the men and the tree.

'The one to bring about an accounting for the past?' Bridget finished for her.

'That's not the way I see it,' Lindsay said. 'Looks to me like your husband's death was timely. Magdalena's drinking was getting worse, Grandmother was getting older and beginning to lose it. Victor's death brought to a head a crisis waiting to happen.' She gave a light laugh. 'What we've got now is a fined-down instrument in which only the fit and able in this family have a say.'

'You. Magdalena. Jack. Russell. The fit and the able?'

'Oh, God, Bridget, you can be so mind-numbingly coy. I hope to God you're not going to be a problem in the future.' She tapped Bridget lightly on the shoulder. 'We'll have to get your attitude sorted.'

Bridget moved away quickly, closer to where the Christmas tree was at last beginning its descent on to the spread-out net. She brushed at the spot Lindsay's fingers had touched.

'My attitude is quite sorted, but your presumption, Lindsay, is obscene. *Don't*, please, come any nearer.' Bridget held up her hands as Lindsay took a step closer, 'and don't, please, presume to include me in your thoughts or plans for the future. I meant it when I said I didn't want Veronica's shares. When I leave on Friday . . .' she looked up along the high windows of the house, 'I'll be leaving all of this and all of you . . .'

'You're certainly entitled to make that decision for yourself.' Lindsay stayed where she was and went on smiling. 'But you've no right at all to deny Victor Baldacci's children their birthright. Veronica's last, and alternative, arrangements were very clear. Your daughter and son are to have a part and a share in things, independently of you. I've already written them.'

She turned, with a relieved sigh, as the Christmas tree sank finally and gently to the ground and spread its heavy plastic pines across the net.

'It's down. Done at last. Grandmother would have been

pleased to see it happen so smoothly.' The confidential tone came back into her voice. 'I do hope you learn to relax a little, Bridget. Your Anna and Fintan are blood of our blood, when all's said and done. They deserve to be a part of things.' She smiled. 'I want them on board. This family needs them.'

They watched as the men, with expert ease, spun and wrapped the great tree tightly into the net.

ROSE DOYLE

Kimbay

Pan Books £5.99

In racing as well as love, glory always has a price . . .

Flora Carolan is young, in love, carefree – and forging a career for herself in Europe. Then comes the cloud to darken her dreams . . . It takes her father's death to bring her back to Ireland and to Kimbay, the once successful stud farm Ned Carolan had worked all of his life. But the glory days are over. Now only a miracle can keep the beloved farm and stables for a new generation.

To everyone in Ireland, the Carolans belong to history. Could Flora achieve the impossible and restore the stud's fading fortunes? Or would others' jealousy destroy her – along with Ned's dying wish?

ROSE DOYLE

Alva

Pan Books £5.99

*Alva Joyce has always known that she alone
has the key to her happiness . . .*

After a solitary childhood spent waiting for life to begin,
Alva defies her father to become a journalist in Dublin.
Unschooled in the ways of the heart, she is soon abused
and betrayed in both love and friendship. Battered and
humiliated, she finds herself seeking refuge in a small
country-house hotel.

As co-owner, Alva discovers the hard facts of financial
survival when overheads spiral out of control. Turning to
a last minute offer from a film company, a new set of
characters suddenly enters her life – in particular Jack, the
producer. But will Alva recognize the real motive behind
his charm? And at the end of filming, can she find the
courage to face crucial decisions about the house, the
people she has come to rely on and, most importantly,
her own future?

ROSE DOYLE

Perfectly Natural

Pan Books £5.99

*How the lives of two women touch and shape the present; how
they love and desire – in one case not wisely and too well –
makes for a story as suspenful as it is, ultimately, tragic.*

Born in London to a young, unmarried Irishwoman, Sive
Daniels never knew her natural father. On the violent
death of Eileen, her enigmatic, much loved mother, Sive
comes to Gowra, the rural town in Kerry her mother left a
quarter of a century before with only the baby she was
carrying in her womb.

In her search for the truth about her parents, Sive is
unexpectedly helped by Abbie, a retired GP and woman
of independent mind and compassionate nature. Better
than anyone, Abbie knows the dark and unsavoury truths
in that small community – buried but not forgotten . . .